I LOVE HIM LIKE HOME

LOVE IN BIRCH BOROUGH

I LOVE HIM *Like Home*

BY SARA NORTH

of Story Boréale

Library of Congress Control Number: 2025922665
ISBN: 979-8-9892125-4-5 (paperback)
ISBN: 979-8-9892125-5-2 (ebook)

First edition December 2025
Cover Illustration: Karyssa Adair
Cover Design: Taylor Waldron
Editing: Brittany Howard
Proofreading: Jenn Lockwood – Jenn Lockwood Editing
Formatting: Erica Dansereau

Published in the United States by Sara North of Story Boréale
www.authorsaranorth.com
@authorsaranorth

For Hailey

I'll remember you through every book (and story) I write.

And for everyone waiting for the love that gives warmth,
may your heart not grow cold.

I am
The essence
Of a soul
In fragments
Of brilliance
Adhered to moments
Of sheer humanity
And the craving
Of perfection
Became tiresome
The heart crumbled
The mind wandered
And stumbled
To the ocean
Where the waves sing:
"You're enough."

"Enough" by Sara North

Chapter One

Ivy

My ears catch the muted rhythm of pointe shoes caressing the stage, the echo resounding in my ears, each delicate whisper a familiar sound, a perfect sound. It's a sound that keeps my dreams of the ballet alive, though it also keeps me awake at night just as often. I'll feel that sound in my bones for the rest of my life because each beat has meant moving forward rather than going backward . . . until now.

Waiting offstage for my cue, I close my eyes, the reverberation of the live orchestra working its way through my frame, murmuring that soon it will be my turn to move from the wings of this stage and emerge in the spotlights that burn with the heat of what feels like a thousand bonfires. The lights are both blinding and comforting, revealing all of me to the audience and yet hiding me from myself. I'll admit that they've been a good distraction from the voice within my head, echoing that I'm not worth holding. Not worth loving. Maybe I'm worthy as a dance partner, but clearly—if my past relationships have anything to say about it—not in life.

This voice is always accompanied by another—a murmur of perfectionism that tells me that if I can just alter *one* more thing in my life, fix one more flaw, then I'll be more worthy of love. But even as I shift, the end goal keeps shifting too, so achieving the dream version of myself feels impossible.

If I can't find peace within myself, how will anyone find it beside me?

Glancing at Dmitri, who's working through his preperformance ritual like he's never chasséd over my heart in three-quarter time, I'd say he's enough reason to forget why I wanted to dance on this stage in the first place. When you have a run-in with heartache, people have a strange way of tainting what we love and making it a shadow of the wholeness that we knew before the betrayal. This, I feel strongly. Something that should be lovely becomes unfamiliar.

And now, it's been a long three months of rehearsals and performances with my dance partner for this show. I'm tired.

For the last six years, I've been a principal dancer with a world-renowned ballet company in New York City, The SoHo Ballet. After a brief stint in a summer intensive in Boston, I was recruited to the city after they saw a performance that someone recorded, which then went viral—well, viral in the ballet world, at least. It opened a handful of opportunities, one of them being a relocation to NYC.

As a young, optimistic ballerina, I was transported from my small hometown of Birch Borough to the hustle and bustle of the city—a place that inevitably sifts you into either quicksand or rock. The move was exhilarating and felt like the most gorgeous transition, the perfect storyline: small-town girl makes it in the big city and doesn't look back. It's an adventure that's proved to be a dream and yet also a nightmare. Funny how that works.

I haven't looked back, though. While I've missed Grey, my best friend in the whole world, and my family and dear friends back home, such as Sparrow and Lily, I've been driven to make something of myself outside of the tiny New England town that I used to call home. Now, I have connections across the world, know what it is to dance on a stage that legendary dancers have graced, and have learned how to time my steps to a live orchestra. To be fair, I learned that skill when the local band played jazz in the gazebo back in Birch Borough each summer, and I danced under the starlit sky to the nostalgic tunes. My love for music, especially of the classical kind, has carried me through not only my career but my life as well. It has touched on the love, the loss, and the deepest parts of me that process emotion through music.

And soon, I'll return to my hometown for Christmas break. To say I've been counting the beats until I get to leave would be underselling my enthusiasm to go home.

After a grueling performance schedule, in just a few hours, I won't need to have my hair in a bun so tight it gives me a headache or smell the scent of hairspray so strong I know I'm at a higher risk of flammability, especially when I'm near the stage lights. For now, I stay still, doing my best to avoid bumping into the stage crew and the other dancers moving between the wings backstage, my mind preoccupied with wondering which French pastry I'll treat myself to first from Sparrow's Beret when I'm back in Birch Borough.

Dmitri appears beside me, knocking me out of thoughts of warm croissants. My shoulders stiffen at his proximity, his presence a signal I stand at attention, waiting for the performance of a lifetime to unfold at this matinee showing of *The Nutcracker*, also known as the Super Bowl of ballet. While I should be elated, I'm ready to get this over with. I'm ready for this to be the last afternoon that I have to feel the man's hands around my waist. It'll be the last time I'm encouraged to smile toward him and pretend everything is okay.

Though it's been a couple of years, I can't forget the moment I found my current dance partner with Victoria, a soloist aspiring to become a principal, making use of an empty studio in ways that could've gotten them kicked out of the company. Through the tiny window in the door, I saw them holding each other. It was then that I turned myself around and decided that the time I'd spent pining for him, believing him when he looked at me like I was his world, trusting that he reserved a special grin only for me, and accepting when he said we should keep things professional until the season was over or he got a promotion, was real.

But it wasn't.

And yet, the worst part of the whole hurtful situation happened in rehearsals a few weeks ago, when Dmitri and Victoria announced their engagement. Long ago, I stopped wanting to be a part of his life outside of the stage—and even dance has been tainted by his presence. But knowing that people who lead others on can find love while I'm still waiting for it doesn't sit well on my heart.

"Ready, darling?" Dmitri approaches me with a smile, as

if we're not about to pretend to play house in an opera house.

"Oh, we both know that I've never been your darling," I reply, grit entering my voice with unexpected huskiness. "Have I?"

His eyes widen, and he gives his shoulders a quick shake, his demeanor and stance changing just before I feel his arm wrap around my waist. The embrace isn't romantic; it's practical, as this is how we'll enter stage right in about twenty seconds.

As the instruments hum and flow over our frames, I steal another glance at the man in whom I've invested so much of my time and energy. We met when I first arrived in the city, and Dmitri has been a constant in my life since I got here. There was once a time when he helped me learn the culture of the ballet company, showed me how to take the subway, and led me to invest myself in a future that proved never meant to be.

Sadly, Dmitri isn't the first to break my heart. He's not the first lesson I've had to learn in mistaking potential for a lack of integrity. But right now, I have a job to do. So as the music plays, and I remind myself to appear to be the perfect ballerina for the little ones in the audience who are dreaming of being like me one day, I also tell myself that it's the last time I'm going to be an understudy and not the lead when it comes to love.

And later that night, when I'm on a plane to Boston and Birch Borough grows nearer minute by minute, I peek through the window at all of the lights below, their layout the grounded reversal of the night sky, and wish that, someday, instead of home being a place, my heart might find rest in a partner—not in dance but in life.

As I walk toward the pavilion, the rush of the river roaring over the icy rocks and under the bridge sounds like the melody of growing up in my small town. I've been home for only a day, but I'm nearly sprinting to reach the temporary ice-skating rink set up in the middle of town like a beacon of Christmas cheer. The rink is small, one that our town constructs for a few weeks each year around the holidays. While there's a full-sized rink in the next town, it wouldn't be Birch Borough without creating its own unique way to celebrate the season.

My red coat is a blur over cobblestone streets and paved walkways as I speed toward the spot where Grey may already be waiting, doing my best to avoid the families distracted by their adorable little children.

First on tonight's agenda is ice skating. Then I know a warm cup of hot chocolate is calling my name. If I'm lucky, I'll be able to get one with extra whipped cream on top. The chocolate goodness might be enough to distract me from the quiet voice that tells me—now that I'm back home—that I may not have the courage to go back to my life in the city.

But maybe it's finally time for me to come home for good.

When I see the twinkle lights strung around a rectangle of people skating beneath the evening winter sky, I let myself really smile for the second time since I've returned. The first time was hugging my parents at the airport. Something about seeing people I've known throughout the years all around me feels like comfort and joy. As I reach the rink, I look for

Grey, but I don't see her yet. Pulling my skates from around my neck, I remove their guards and sit on a bench to lace up. My legs are humming with energy, and my nose is already tingling from the cold. It's the perfect night.

Once I'm laced up, I stand and move toward one of the doors in the middle of the temporary rink, watching children whip past me. Classical music flows through speakers positioned around the ice. My face looks up to the sky as I glide onto the ice, lost in appreciating the illusion of warmth the twinkling lights above me bring to the frosty terrain. I take a deep breath of the chilly air, my heart reveling in the magic of the season, refusing to contemplate what happens after the new year.

The relief of being home fills my lungs. My skates spin across the ice, my arms outstretched, the smile spreading . . . when I crash into what feels like a moving mountain. My arms flail as the collision knocks me off balance, and I charge toward the ice.

"I've got you," I hear a masculine voice say above me.

A strong arm wraps around my waist. It's a move that is familiar but devastating. Warmth immediately wraps around my midsection. I'm so embarrassed to have almost fallen that I close my eyes, scrunching my face. I don't even want to see the expression of whoever is in front of me.

"Good thing it was Tchaikovsky." A molasses-covered voice pirouettes throughout my limbs.

"You know Tchaikovsky?" I mutter in disbelief, my eyes still tightly closed shut in hopes that this is a dream and I won't ever have to face the one who rescued me from the frozen water beneath my feet.

"Of course. If music by Stravinsky was playing, this may

have been a different situation entirely."

A surprised laugh escapes me. This man knows his classical music. He's probably married or, at the very least, not single, but my heart lifts in unexpected hope. While I used to dream of being with a dancer, my experiences have cemented a need for a man who knows music over choreography any day.

The wool of his coat scrapes against my fingertips, and I finally dare to open my eyes. I feel them widen as I confirm that the moving mountain is, indeed, a living, breathing man. I find that he is protectively shielding me, his arms preventing me from falling to the ice, and I forget to breathe. My head tilts backward as I follow his towering frame up and up and up.

Inky, dark hair curls loosely, falling in perfect ringlets near his face, longer on the top and shorter on the sides. I catalog his chiseled features and his full mouth and finally land on eyes that are the darkest amber in tone. Their color appears almost like a rich maple syrup just before it drips onto pancakes or gingerbread fresh out of the oven. I've never seen such a striking eye color on a man. And as my neck lifts to maintain eye contact, I know I was right to first consider him a mountain. His broad shoulders look constrained within his well-fitted peacoat, hints of muscle evident even through the layers of clothing. He must be four to five inches over six feet, at least.

For a moment, I have a crazed desire to let myself imagine how easily he could catch me in a lift.

"You surprised me," the stranger says in a tone that's laced with intrigue.

"Well, you surprised me too," I counter, lifting my face

to him boldly, unsure of where my sudden comfort with a stranger is coming from. Maybe I'm exhausted from the pain of being repeatedly polite. The man's jaw twitches at my quip, a hint of a grin pulling at the left side of his mouth. A line in his cheek has me wondering what gloriousness would unfold if he managed an actual smile. Would there even be a devastating dimple hiding within?

"No, I'm so sorry. I . . . should've looked where I was going," I begin, my breath following my words in a wisp of white air through the dark night and artificial lighting hanging above us. As often as I've been close to men on stage, I am fully convinced this man is the only one who could've kept me on my feet no matter what, even if we stumbled.

"I was looking at the lights," I continue. The irony is not lost on me that to look at him, I must crane my neck to look up. *Good thing I have a flexible neck*, which also happens to be a thought I've never really had in my entire life.

He lifts a brow and moves a hand to adjust his coat collar. My eyes zero in on the perfect view of the tattoo on his hand, a stunning design of an antique clock trailing over the top of his overtly masculine hand in a way that will be forever etched in my mind. I look to his other hand to see if there's a matching one, but it's tucked away in his pocket.

Following the direction of my eyes, he drops the hand to slide it into his other pocket. I'm unnerved by his gaze. Not because I feel threatened but because I feel as though he's reading me. His eyes pierce mine, seeing me in a way I didn't think was possible.

A chorus of voices around the rink yells, "Welcome back, Ivy!" Everyone keeps skating around us as if we've become part of the terrain. His physique really could be akin to a mountain.

"It's good to look up at the stars every now and again," he reassures me.

My shoulders relax. His response unlocks something in my mind. Inexplicably, I feel the urge to pour out my deepest thoughts to this man and see how he reacts. I want to give him the unfiltered version of my life to see if his strength could hold it up, as I suspect. It's shocking how much his presence reminds me that I can still feel flutters in my stomach and a man can still make new tracks in the fallen snow of my heart.

"I'm glad you're okay, though," he continues kindly, and the tone of his voice is a song I want to dance to. "Especially since you just arrived."

"How do you know I just arrived?"

He grins. I can officially confirm he really does have a devastating dimple, and I want to choreograph ways to see it again and again.

"You're wearing a bright-red coat and look as though you belong on the stage . . . perhaps in front of a camera. There's no way I would've missed you if you were here earlier."

My cheeks heat up but out of delight rather than embarrassment. His attention feels like it's building me up instead of wearing me thin, and I want to see how much of his energy I can absorb before we go our separate ways.

"Well, I—" I begin.

"I hope you—" he begins simultaneously.

We freeze and share a nervous laugh as I will myself to memorize the shade of his gingerbread-colored eyes, because I know I'll soon be trying to find their exact color in everything I see. Snow flurries flutter around us like we're in the middle of a snow globe.

"Have a good night," I say quietly, wishing I could think of something cleverer. Connecting with men has never been my strong suit.

Lightly, the stranger's eyes caress my face. They trace my jaw, fluttering over my lips and studying my cheekbones until they move to meet my gaze, lingering for a moment longer. After a beat, he gives a brief nod and a small smile and then skates away, looking back over his shoulder once before focusing again on the ice. I want to skate after him or call to him. But I don't.

"Here you are!" Grey's voice trills from right next to me, her wide smile a relief to my bones. Turning, I wrap her up in a hug and hold my dearest friend close, but over her shoulder, my eyes catch the mountain of a man as he glides toward us in another pass around the ice.

In a movement so swift I think I must imagine it, he kisses the tips of his fingers and lightly taps my mittened one before skating past us while mouthing, "Merry Christmas." Releasing Grey, I bring my mittened hand to my mouth, the sensation of connection unfamiliar. I stare after him. Already, the back of his inky hair is breezing away as he makes his way off the ice.

Within minutes, I've caught Grey up on the events of running into the stranger and the inexplicable way I wish it hadn't been goodbye before we ever truly met.

Her eyes sparkle with glee. I know what she's thinking. "I think you should find out this man's name. At least find out who he is. It's a small town; you might see each other again," she advises. "Besides, I've never seen you look at anyone like you just looked at him."

I laugh and shake my head, a blush rising on my cheeks. "No, what would be the point? I'm going back to New York soon."

But then my eyes lift again to find the stranger looking at me from across the makeshift rink as he leans against the barrier. Reluctantly, I turn away and pull Grey to glide with me over the ice.

After we've made at least a dozen rotations around the rink, Grey pulls me to a stop. "I should get going," she says over her cat-eye glasses. "I just wanted to see you tonight. I know we usually skate until our legs are worn out and then get hot chocolate, but I need to get back to the bookshop early. Dad's doing inventory, and you know how that can go." She snaps her fingers. "Why don't you come by after I'm done and stay the night?"

I laugh because I do know. Grey's dad, Luke, will have sci-fi mixed with cookbooks if she doesn't get back soon.

"Snow check on the rest of our skating date?" she says, utilizing the phrase instead of "rain check."

"Yes, of course." Subtly, I glance around to find the stranger, but he's already gone. My heart sinks, but I stand a little taller, quieting my mind from wondering again about a man I may never see again.

The cold, fresh air feels good in my lungs as I make my way to Four Leaf Cookies, cutting down a side street to reach the steps that lead down to the bottom of what once was a gallery and is now a cookie shop. It's open later when there are special events in town, and, of course, Christmas rules them all.

Grey isn't with me, but I've decided to still walk to the cookie shop. The shop itself is a novelty. They have cozy chairs and delicious cookies and decadent hot cocoa, and the space is filled with bookshelves that remind me of Grey's bookstore.

Their hot chocolate calls my name. It's a tradition, and I don't think I could go to sleep without it tonight. I open the door, the tiny bell jingling as the golden interior welcomes me, and my heart instantly begins to race. The music-loving mystery man sits at a table directly in front of me. I freeze, taking in the single curl falling over his forehead and the ceramic cup sitting in front of him. Ever so slowly, his eyes lift to meet mine, and my lungs expand with hope.

"You're here." His rich voice cuts through the smell of warm cookies and hot chocolate. Softly, he smiles, and that devastating dimple makes an appearance again. He stands, moving around the table and pulling out the chair across from him. "Would you like to sit with me for a bit?"

The invitation is the last thing I expect, but as a smile forms across my face, I think it may be exactly what I've needed. A pulling feeling in the center of my ribs warns that I'll regret it if I don't accept his invitation. There's no stage to hide behind or opportunities to overthink. I just know I want to spend more time with this man, and time seems to be on our side with this fated meeting. His gaze lingers heavily on mine, a hint of playfulness around the edges.

"Who do you belong to?" My mittened hands wrap together behind my back like a Degas painting, the press of my palms together preparing my heart for however long we're together this evening.

"Belong to?"

"Mm-hmm. Everyone here belongs to someone. They must. Are you a friend, a family member . . . How did you end up here? I've lived here my whole life, and we've never met before . . . Well, I do live in New York City now."

A wide smile spreads across his face, making my breath catch. "I live a few towns over. My sister has been looking for a place to put a storefront. She's a great baker. Just thought I'd come and see what all the charm was about."

"The charm?" I step closer to him.

He nods. "Everyone within a hundred-mile radius surely must know about the town of Birch Borough. Its events and people are legendary. And apparently, it's also home to a woman I'd rescue from an unpleasant encounter with an ice-skating rink. The last part is a new, but welcome, addition."

His eyes scan my face as he says the words, starting at the corner of one of my brows and slowly roving over until they land on my lips. The blush rises to my cheeks as his eyes shift sharply to mine.

"Noted," I say breathlessly.

At this, a full grin pulls at his moody mouth, and my knees nearly give out. This man is saying everything so visually, but it's so effective. Never in my life have I ever been this moved by so few words. I'm getting the intense feeling that he'll never say more than he means, that he *only* says what he means, and a haven of comfort wraps around me at the thought.

"As for sitting with you, I would love to," I admit, circling to his original question.

The way he tilts his chin down farther makes me sway toward him as he extends his hand. "I'm Jace," he says.

Jace. His name creates a pattern of hope in my mind. I pull off my mittens, and when our palms connect, every nerve ending in my palm feels like it's being awakened. I sink into the chair across from him.

"You okay?"

A lilt to his voice catalogs my senses, and I lean back, looking up, up, up into his eyes. I'm not sure what I'll find there, but it feels like there may be an answer for me somewhere within their amber depths. A sudden hesitation grips me.

"I—well, I—how do I know that I can trust you?" I release his hand and cross my arms, willing the throbbing of my heart to quiet enough for me to hear what it wants me to do next. *He won't stay.* The thought creeps in. And then I hear another whisper within. *Maybe he'll keep surprising you.*

His hand moves up, the clock face on his tattooed hand wrapping around his chin. He glances at the menu board. With an air of decision, he pulls out his phone and dials a number. I see the contact's name, M&M, on the screen when he turns it toward me. Jace sets it to speakerphone as we wait for the call to connect.

"Jay, why are you calling me?" a sweet, clear voice rings through the cookie shop, causing Jace to laugh. I can't help but wonder if this man is a player or already married. Or both.

"My sister," he says as if reading my mind.

I nod, waiting for him to continue and doing my best not to find the idea of a grown man calling his sister when he's in trouble or asking out a woman quite literally adorable.

"Mina," he says for my benefit, "I'm in Birch Borough . . ."

"Yes, you texted me ten minutes ago," says the voice on the line. "Are you still looking for that woman you crashed into?"

My eyes widen, but I laugh with delight, the glee bubbling up as this strong man's cheeks turn crimson.

"Funny you should mention her. I just found her again, and I think she might be an angel. Or a shooting star."

My eyebrows lift, the blush creeping along my own skin with fresh heat. I half expect his so-called sister to laugh or ask if he's feeling well.

"Impossible," she says, as if this wasn't an odd thing for him to say.

"No, no, it's true," he says into the phone. "I'm just as surprised as you. Anyway, I need you to vouch for me so I can buy this woman a hot chocolate. Maybe you can convince her I'm worth knowing. Do you think you can do that?"

His concentration is totally focused on his phone, unbothered by the customers moving around us, and a look that I could only describe as nervousness is creased into his brow.

"What's her name?" Mina asks.

His eyes meet mine, a question knocking on the invisible door between us, and it feels like the moment strangers become something more.

"Ivy," I speak into the phone, looking at Jace while I utter the word. But I find that his gaze is too intense, his eye color too rich. Instead, I have to focus on the way his phone looks like a child's toy in the grip of his hand.

"Ivy," the voice on the other end of the line rings out, "my brother is many things, but being smooth is not one of them. He's more likely to be watching a romance movie or reading a book than frequenting a bar."

Another delighted laugh escapes me as I look at Jace again. He simply shrugs.

"Jay, you should've brought your glasses. Did you bring your glasses?"

Jace sighs, his shoulders dropping slightly. "I did not."

"Never mind. I think I painted enough of a picture," Mina quips.

My heart feels light. "So you're saying he's worth trusting with my fate? Or whatever it is that sent me nearly colliding with your brother again?" I grin at him, willing her answer to be *yes*.

"Oh, he's definitely worth trusting—if you're into the whole tall, brooding but goofy type, that is. Also, can I just say . . . your voice sounds like a rock star, Ivy."

I'm used to people commenting on my voice; it's notably smoky and something that seems to stand out about me, which never really helped me in the dance world since my life has been spent in silence on the stage.

"She's the most beautiful woman I've ever seen, Mina," Jace adds, and suddenly, tears sting my eyes. It's not the words; it's the sincerity with which he said them. "Golden hair. Eyes that remind me of hot chocolate. The good kind."

There is a pause, then, "Jay, you'd better not mess this up!" Mina's voice rings clearly between us through the phone as Jace laughs.

"I love you, M&M. Thank you for your vote of confidence."

"M&M?" I ask.

"Her nickname. She loves the candy." Jace sits up a little taller, watching me as if I'm the most fascinating thing in the world. The fact that he hasn't even noticed the Rudolph knockoff dancing outside the window beside us this whole time is a testament to his ability to concentrate. His attention is solely on me, and I get the sense that his focus might be a spotlight where I could be found instead of lost.

"Okay, then, Mina," I say into the phone. "I think he just may be worth the chance."

Jace lifts a fist in the air, a quiet testament to his excitement, and gives me a smile I'll think about whenever I need to remind myself there's still magic in the world.

"Talk later, sis. Thanks again."

"You're welcome. And if she ends up being the one, you know you owe me that new easel I've wanted, right?"

He smiles. "The very best one. See you at home!" Jace sighs in relief, excitement spilling from his frame as he motions to the counter behind us. "Shall we?"

"I think I just might." A feeling of joy settles into my bones as I pull off my mittens, and he reaches over to help me out of my coat, hanging it off the back of my chair. He stands.

"What would you like?"

I nearly stutter as I try to answer. "A candy cane hot chocolate, please."

Jace nods and heads to the counter. I study him while he orders, observing the way he holds his shoulders and the intriguing image of a clock tattooed on his hand as it moves through his hair. He shifts his weight as he waits for the order, glancing back at me once or twice, the first real sign of nervousness I've seen from him.

When he's across from me again, delivering our drinks and a plate of Christmas cocoa cookies—which are as delicious as they sound—I'm struck by how tiny the table looks in light of his big frame.

"You've really never been to Birch Borough before?" I question.

Jace lifts his arm to take a sip of coffee, and I follow the movement of his muscles beneath his shirt. This man could be in a museum as the textbook example of the way muscles should be chiseled beneath fabric.

"I haven't," he says, taking another sip.

"And what were you doing before you made your way to our town this evening?" My question hovers in the holiday-treat-filled air.

"I was at a boxing studio, training some of my students."

I attempt, in vain, not to think of him wrapping those manly hands with tape and the way his muscles must work as he punches a heavy bag. But the thought has already taken residence in my mind and installed a mailbox to celebrate.

"But now you're making me want to buy a ticket to a dance performance, if you're in it." An easy smile brightens his features in fascinating ways.

It's the first moment I've ever considered being able to look at a man's face for the rest of my life and finding something new every time.

"How do you know I'm a dancer?" I ask, delighted he would say such a thing.

"Your feet are turned out."

I look at my feet under the table, my toes angled in opposite directions as a result of training my body to move as a ballerina, and let out a laugh. And as I look back toward him and see the smile on his face as he takes a huge bite of a dreamy dessert from Four Leaf Cookies, I think coming home might have brought me some holiday luck.

Chapter Two

Ivy

"What do you want to be known for?" Jace asks a few cookies later. His eyes are alight with curiosity and a hint of what could only be described as playfulness.

What a question. I grip the diner mug of candy cane hot chocolate and draw it closer, the rings of cocoa on the inside an indication of how long we've been here, enjoying each other's company. I'm down to the dregs, a swirl of cocoa and remnants of whipped cream hanging onto the sides, like I have been to every word Jace has said.

I've discovered he's funny, interesting, and intelligent, asks riveting questions, and is clearly capable of creating with his hands. In addition to being a boxing coach, he's also a woodworker. He's told me that his dream is to own an artisan furniture business, and at that bit of information, I tried not to focus on said hands.

Jace looks at me as if he wants to never forget me.

The longer I sit with him, the safer I feel, despite the fact that he towers over me and could move me across the room in his arms better than any of the dancers I left behind in New York City. The thought of dancing with Jace in any way sends heat climbing my neck. I clear my throat to will away the foreign emotion.

I've felt attraction before. Of course I have. But a sense of *more* accompanying the attraction is new. As much as I love dance, I don't often love being touched. Ironic, considering how many times I get tossed and lifted during any one rehearsal or performance, but it's true. You have to earn my trust to get my affection, but then I give it with everything I have.

Which is why it's shocking that I'm still here with Jace. With other men, even Dmitri, I thought of them holding me, and everything got fuzzy, almost like the rest of the vision would have to play out only after they made a move. But with Jace, I'm seeing our future play out like a movie in my mind. I can picture the way his fingers would wrap around my chin to lift it so I could fully look at him. I can see the warmth of his smile when my eyes widen at his touch. I can feel the softness of his curls against my skin if he buried his face in my neck. For the first time, I can feel it all even before I've lived it, and it makes me want more from a man than I've ever wanted in my life.

When Jace shifts on his side of the table, the movement pulls me out of my thoughts. His eyebrow lifts as he studies me, almost as if he can sense what I was just imagining.

"To be known for?" I barely get the words out, returning to his question. He nods, a grin at play on his face. He's on his third cup of coffee, while I'm holding on to my mug like it's a lifeline. The grip of my fingers around the ceramic says maybe if I don't take the last sip, this evening will never end.

I look about the shop; there's a hint of sugar and butter in the air, along with the scent of melted chocolate.

"Well, I mean, I'm a dancer. It's what I've always been known for," I finally answer with a smile, putting the more surface-level answer out there in case that was all he was after. Recently, I've been on a stage almost every day, so I must be doing what I always wanted to be known for, even though the experience of life as a professional ballerina hasn't been as satisfying as I'd hoped.

He shakes his head, somehow understanding I'm holding back. "The real answer."

I laugh, disbelief lacing my voice. "You know, we still don't know each other very well, and here you are, asking deep, soul-searching questions."

"I'm trying to get to the real heart of your response. As for the questions, I want to really live, to ask the questions that matter. And something tells me you don't want to settle for less than that either."

Humming, my hand swirls the remnants of whipped cream in my mug as I wait for clarity. *What do I want to be known for?* But though I think I don't have an answer, I hear it, the whisper deep within my ribs. Somehow, I will the courage to speak it. Counterintuitively, looking into Jace's eyes helps. His gaze says I'm holding something he's been searching for, and I dare to try to see if it's true.

"It's not so much what I want to be known for; it's just that I want to be known in the first place," I confess, casting my eyes down but glancing back up to find his warm face once more.

His torso leans even closer to me across the tiny wooden table. Well, it isn't so much that the table is small as that he makes it look tiny in comparison to his strong frame.

"You can trust me," he urges. "I'll call my sister back if needed." His wink tells me that he's easing me into the truth, sensing I need the support.

I take a breath, his proximity giving me a hint of spice and something else that is soothing, like a calming forest at Christmastime. And maybe it's wishful thinking to reveal parts of my soul to a near-stranger, or maybe honesty is exactly what I need to get out of the general sense of heartache that's been crushing me for months.

"I want to be *known*," I admit. "Not just the facts or the feelings. I don't want to be driven by the need to be perfect or think that if I could only fix one more flaw, I could be loved more in return. Not only that, but I want to *want* to be held by someone, and I don't want that person to ever let go. If home can be found in a person, I want to find out."

The words rush out of me, stinging my throat and eyes. I focus on the crumbs from the cookies we demolished an hour ago between us on the table, the sound of jazzy Christmas music playing softly through the speakers. The taste of glorified chocolate milk lingers as I finally finish off the mug of what was once hot chocolate. I've laid it all out there, and now I feel exposed.

There's silence at the table, and I calculate how quickly I can grab my bag from between our feet on the floor. How quickly can I make it around the corner and disappear into the streets of Birch Borough? I know that wouldn't play out because we have only one main street. Instead, I play with the handle of the mug and keep my attention on my hands. Suddenly, I see Jace's large hand reach out to cover one of my own. Immediately, the warmth of it releases the tension stuck in my system. My eyes flash up to find his, the amber color arresting and intense, kindness hovering around the edges. In the dim light of the cookie shop, I can almost believe the color is in motion, painting his emotions in real time.

"Like starlight," he says, the richness in his voice like a blanket.

"What?" I don't think I heard correctly.

"Like starlight. Sometimes, even in the noise and the pollution, you have to look for it, search for it. But once you see it above, you realize it's the most beautiful light. It will always be where you are if you only look up."

"Not the moon? Or the sun?" I reply with a smile, my heart jolting at the aftermath of his words.

"Overrated. Give me the gentle, steady light from the stars any night to remind me that the world still holds beauty."

"You're very smooth, you know that?"

He lets out a laugh before his grip, though still gentle, presses on my hand. "Ivy, don't settle for anything less," are the words he lays between us next. I cling to them, the unexpected permission to pursue my own kind of dream etching itself into my heart. "Promise me?"

And while I can't imagine that my promise could mean anything to him this soon, I know I must find a way to hold on to it. "I promise," I whisper.

He nods, his shoulders release, and his swoony smile returns to his face. "Now, tell me, has your voice always been this mesmerizing?" The humor returns to his tone.

There's a sense of affection brewing and infusing my system with more energy than I know how to handle. I don't care that it's growing later and later, and I've ruined my rigid bedtime routine. For tonight, I'm free.

Finally, I can fully breathe after my confessions, and it feels right to order another cup of candy cane hot chocolate, fully intent on being here until the place closes down.

After Jace's fourth cup of coffee and my second hot chocolate, we step into the night once more. The cold air snaps with even more frigid briskness after the warmth of the cookie shop. We wander down the street, neither of us thinking of the time, talking like we've known each other forever. Somehow, we find our way back to the ice-skating rink. It's empty, the lights hanging above the only illumination. It's freezing, and my red coat does little to keep out the chill.

Still, I don't want to leave him. Something pulls at my soul, telling me that this moment is too good, and it will soon be gone, never to return to me.

It's been a beautiful, fulfilling evening, full of surprises and exactly what I've needed. Jace's hand moving to the small of my back grounds me in the moment. I turn toward him, willing this night to become a core memory.

What's happening between us feels like wholesome intimacy. It feels like time standing still, or perhaps I feel like the most gloriously bright version of myself. I don't want this night to end. My heart once again picks up speed like the train in our town moving down the tracks. There's a reason we've found each other tonight, and I pray I'll know the answer to the questions I have for the future—if not tonight, then one day.

As wonderful as this unexpected evening has been, fear creeps into my mind. I can't imagine—even if I wasn't going back to New York—that Jace would want to pursue me. How could anything beyond this night be possible? But something in me wants to find out.

"Jace," I whisper.

He freezes, his captivating attentiveness piercing through my hesitation. "Starlight," he breathes, the new nickname sinking into my bones. His dark, maple-syrup-colored eyes take in my features with an almost reverent hunger.

In a few hours, I've gone from feeling invisible to feeling more seen than I have in the past nearly twenty-six years. In his presence, my fears about my flaws and imperfections have quieted. A tentative feeling unwraps, a wondrous thought emerging that if he were to see the things I try to hide, he'd celebrate them rather than tolerate them.

In the space of an evening, this man has done what no one else has been able to: He's reminded me that I *am* worth someone's time.

I think of my life in New York City and Birch Borough, the quiet ice rink sparking a revelation that allows me to be hyper-focused on Jace's proximity. Lately, I've been so surrounded by bright neon lights, the honking of car horns, the buzz of street vendors and taxis, the echo of pop culture Christmas songs, ride shares, and celebrities that I can't think. I'm continually among a myriad of people, yet somehow, he and I found each other when I traveled home.

Home.

I begin hesitantly. "Jace, I know we just met, and I have

to go back to New York . . ." I trail off.

On his face is a charged grin, full of encouragement, but I see the sadness under it too. It feels like my heart is being set on fire with an ember of affection. In one evening, he's done more for me than I can say. He's rekindled hope. I didn't realize how close I really was to losing it.

In the movies, there's some sort of magic found in a kiss, even more so around Christmastime. If a princess's curse can be broken with a kiss, maybe my loneliness can be broken with one too. And maybe Jace is the one meant to change my future. My gaze returns to him, and my lungs expand with a new dream just from looking at him.

My next words are a surprise even to me. "Please . . . let me kiss you?" I ask, holding my breath as I wait for his answer and hoping he'll meet me in the middle of this moment.

If Jace is surprised by my boldness, he doesn't show it. Any man with an ego like the ones I've been surrounded by in the company would've laughed off my request. They would have given a smug smile or attempted a smolder to seal the deal and push my boundaries. Instead, he blinks rapidly a few times, a hint of moisture pooling near the edges as he gives a quick nod. And the sight of that nod alone is enough for me to lift on my toes, wrap my arms around his neck, and pull him toward me.

Jace doesn't hesitate. Leaning down, he meets me, and the warmth of his full lips on mine reminds me of why I ever held out hope for a love that feels like coming home. It was this moment right here.

The clock in the Town Hall chimes. I haven't heard it ring at this time of night in years. The sound feels like the world is affirming the magic that is unfolding for Jace and me with a sign echoing through the night. After a moment, we break apart, and his breath is warm and sweet against my face as he places a kiss on my nose.

Somehow, that move makes it the greatest kiss of my life. It was over far too quickly. And I know with all certainty that I don't want to fall asleep tonight, still wondering what it would be like for him to initiate affection too. As if reading my mind, Jace leans down again. He pulls me even closer, one hand now on my waist as the other rests between my shoulder blades. In the lights of the ice rink, I study his face, the hint of red on the tips of his ears and the bridge of his nose matching the brightness of his lips. The evening flurries settle on his coat and nestle in his hair, melting when they reach his skin.

"Please, let me kiss you," he declares into the night, repeating my words back to me as our combined breath swirls in the winter wind.

At the reverberation of his voice in my chest, my heart pulses to a changing rhythm. I bite my lip to contain my smile and give a nod as another chime rings through the brisk air.

He bends toward me, his nose nuzzling lightly against my own. Gently, he tips my head to one side. His palms have memorable calluses, and they brush across my skin as his hands cup my face. His fingers extend into my hairline, pulsing at the top of my neck. With a sharp intake, I inhale, poignantly aware of the noisy world getting quieter and the sound of my heart getting louder. I close my eyes to focus on the sensation of his breath fanning my face and nearly gasp when his warm mouth meets mine once more.

The sensation is as perfect as a Christmas light turning on for the first time in the season. It's a candle lighting a dark winter night. His lips press against mine as if he's painting them with brushstrokes of devotion, cataloging the bow of my upper lip, the edges of my mouth that turn up when I really smile, and the dip of my lower lip whenever I want to cry.

Whereas our first kiss was tentative and careful, this kiss is wild and free. It's laughter after a surprise. It's an emotion you want to immortalize. When he pauses, I nearly whimper at the gush of frigid wind that replaces the warmth of his face. Before I dare to look at him, I swallow. Jace pulls back slightly, and I see his eyes are closed. A smile is on his face through his slightly swollen lips. When he opens his eyes, they track every aspect of my countenance.

I'm inordinately proud that I'm the reason he's been affected in this way. Hands still holding my face, his thumbs glide slowly from the curve of my jaw to the soft spot beneath my ear as if he's memorizing the feeling of it. A shiver moves through my spine, but my throat feels warm.

"I don't want you to catch a chill. My body heat can only protect you so much in this New England weather." He gives an adorable smirk, and I want to take a picture and frame it.

I can't wait to tell Grey that I may finally understand why romance books are superior to all other books, because they have male heroes who will forever remind me of Jace.

"When can I see you again?" he says softly.

We must have more time.

"Tomorrow?" I ask as we look out to the ice rink before us. I imagine how it'll look when it's full again, with

Christmas music blaring and families skating.

"Here?" he counters, a smile playing on his lips.

I nod. "Seven o'clock?"

"Okay, tomorrow at seven."

And suddenly, I have a date tomorrow at seven. I'll be counting down the minutes.

I wrap my arms tighter around him and peek up. His face is turned down to me, his arms holding my fragile frame up. I'm the glass ornament on the Christmas tree, and he's the bear in the forest, yet somehow, I know I've never been so safe. I believe that every heartache I've ever felt may have been worth it if it led me here.

"Should we . . . I don't know . . . exchange numbers or something?" I ask, happiness moving through my spine at the thought of being able to text him.

He looks up to the sky for a moment. "Do you believe in fate?"

I follow his gaze and see the stars greeting us one by one, twinkling brighter the longer I focus on them. "I believe there's a magic to the world if we believe in it. Is that enough for you?"

"Hmm," he muses. "I have a feeling that you'll always be enough. But I think tonight was proof that there's some sort of magic at work. Maybe it's the only magic I'll ever need. I'll never forget this night, Ivy," Jace says with all sincerity, the weight of the truth between us.

I'm terrified to dim the light surrounding us. "Jace, I really do have to go back to New York after New Year's."

He hums. "I figured as much. But there's something between us. I know you feel it too. I'm confident we can make it work."

"How are you so sure?"

"Because seeing you for the first time shifted something inside me. I've never met a woman, talked with her for hours, and wanted to kiss her like I've kissed you tonight."

My hands reach to grip the front of his coat, needing to be closer to him while I can. He lets out an appreciative sound.

"I think that nothing could ever feel the same again without you."

His words illuminate me. This moment seems too good to be true but also inevitable. Perhaps if we just keep showing up, our love story will be written for us.

"So what you're saying is," I begin, "you're confident we'll find our way back to each other tomorrow night?"

He peeks down at me, eyes sparkling and alight with affection. "Yes, I think so. It's beyond technology or the elements. I think we can trust it."

The idea is risky but romantic.

"Well, even so . . ." I trail off as I reach into my dance bag, unzipping the secret compartment that's been sewn inside. I pull out a piece of ribbon that was once on a pair of my first pointe shoes. It's been my lucky charm, a sentimental nod to dreams and grit and fighting my way through fear to be on the stage. I'm hoping it will do the same for my love story. It's not much to anyone else, but it means something to me, and I'm counting on it bringing us back together. "For you," I say as he reaches out for it, not even asking for an explanation. "To remember this night by. And it represents a promise, because it's my lucky charm, which means you have to give it back to me."

"Oh, Starlight," he says, his voice rich with what sounds

like hope. "There's nothing on Earth that could keep me from finding a way back to you."

My smile could light every Christmas decoration in the whole town.

"Can I walk you back?" he asks me sweetly.

"Not necessary. I'm going to stay at my best friend's house tonight."

Since I'd planned to arrive at her house earlier in the evening, I let Grey know that I'd be delayed. She texted no less than five times in the past hour to tell me I'd better not go to sleep before sharing my news. Truthfully, I'm not sure how I'm going to sleep at all tonight after meeting Jace, anyway.

He raises a brow and exhales, giving a resolute nod. "Before you go . . . may I hold you once more?" Jace asks, the confidence in his tone steadying my heart.

The fact that he asks my permission at all settles deep in my bones. Already, Jace seems to understand something fundamental about the way I show affection. At my nod, he pulls me close, his strong arms going around me and making me feel like I'm in the safest space I could ever be. If hugs could heal, this would be the one to do it. And even though we're going our separate ways for now, I want to remember him just like this: whimsical, deep, funny, hopeful, strong, confident, and vulnerable.

"To tomorrow," he says quietly, leaning down and kissing my cheek, the warmth of his lips a contrast to the cold all around.

"To tomorrow," I repeat, my eyes stinging with happiness as we finally say good night.

Chapter Three

Jace

The winter moon illuminates the winding road in front of me. I'm driving home in my Jeep, and despite the snap in the frigid air, I'm tempted to roll the windows down just to keep the crisp air in my lungs. Everything in me wants to turn my car around and find Ivy again, just to set eyes on her one more time. But I know I need to be patient. Admittedly, patience isn't one of my strengths.

For years, I've been waiting to meet a woman who would unlock a feeling in me like the feeling my impromptu date unlocked in me tonight. I know I've finally found her. *Ivy.* From the moment I heard her voice, her name wrapped around my soul, intertwining with my lungs. Seeing her for the first time made me feel like a kid on Christmas morning, finding gifts under the tree that I hadn't even known to ask for. I didn't know it was possible to dream someone like her into reality, and yet, she exists.

My drive home takes another ten minutes, the rural parts

of New Hampshire pulling me farther from the quaint town of Birch Borough. When I told Ivy I was looking around to see what all the hype was about, that was true. Turns out, the town holds as much charm as I've heard. And I'm struck that the only thing disappointing about tonight is the fact that it must end.

When I'm still a few minutes away, I pull up my favorites on my phone, hitting the button for M&M, and smile. I know my sister will be waiting for an update. Of all our siblings, we're the closest. When we were younger, she'd follow me around, and something in me could never turn her away. I was never too cool for her. If anything, she was undermining her own popularity by hanging out with me. After all, I was the brother who looked like he should be on the football team but who would rather go to the symphony.

"Jay!" Mina's voice rings loudly throughout my Jeep. I can only laugh, the joy too much to contain. "You're smiling. I know you're smiling."

I am smiling. "You're not wrong," I admit. One hand rests on the steering wheel while the other pats my pocket. It holds a Polaroid of Ivy and me. Since I got in my truck, I've been continually checking to make sure it's there, like it's a passport for my heart to document our meeting.

"I knew it! I knew it!" No doubt, Mina is punching her fists in the air with the phone pressed to her ear. A crash on her end confirms it. I laugh again, knowing she'll be back on the line soon.

"Sorry about that," she mutters a second later. "Dropped my phone. Okay, tell me everything."

"First, thank you for vouching for me."

"I meant everything I said."

I clear my throat to keep back the emotion. "Thanks, Mina. You know you've always been my favorite."

Her laugh is the response I was hoping for. "Yeah, yeah. Okay, now tell me. What's she like?"

Thinking of Ivy and how to describe her has my heart racing like I'm back in the ring. "Ivy is . . . she's . . . she's beautiful. She's so beautiful. But she's also a stunning person on the inside. Quick to laugh, witty, driven, and works in the arts. I feel like I've been caught in a photo flash, and I won't ever get the imprint of her out."

The memory of the kiss we shared distracts me. I can almost feel my fingers threaded through her dark-golden hair, and I nearly swerve off the road. As I pull the wheel back, I say a prayer of thanks that I'm okay and shake my head.

"Wow. Okay, I knew this was going to be good, but this is beyond my expectations."

I settle back into my seat. There's no one on the road except me, and something about the endless path before me feels poetic.

"Mina, she's the most captivating woman I've ever seen in my life. She was so open. Completely adorable. But she's also elegant. She's a dancer in a ballet company."

"So, not a rock star?" she teases. "That's so perfect for you! You love classical music!"

My face hurts from smiling. "Yeah, I do. And her best friend's family does something with books. I was so nervous that the cookie I was holding started shaking, so I can hardly remember what it was, but still!"

"You love books!"

I approach the last traffic light before I turn onto the

street that leads to the house where Angie, Mina, Edgar, and I live. Our parents live a few houses down from us. When we were old enough, the four of us decided to get our own place so we could have some independence and yet still be together. I'm a guy who's grown up in New England and never moved to the city. My family has been enough for me, and I can't imagine being away from any of them, but I wouldn't want to be parted from Mina most of all.

"I'm almost home," I tell her, knowing that she's going to be waiting by the door, ready for more information.

"Excellent. I'll put the tea on."

I hear her moving and then the shuffle of cabinets opening.

"Don't wake Edgar," I whisper, even though there's no way I could disturb him from my truck.

"I wouldn't dare," Mina whispers back, and I hear her filling the kettle. "I thought I would when I yelled earlier, but the coast is clear so far."

We say our goodbyes quietly, even though we'll see each other in a minute, the habit unbroken from sleepovers in the living room growing up. Mina and I are only a year apart, and even as we progress through our mid-twenties, we're nearly inseparable.

As soon as I pull into our driveway, my Jeep taking its place as the last in the line of cars, I flip off the headlights and bolt from the car. Mina is already waiting in the doorway, the lights behind the glass door illuminating her small frame. She hops out onto the front step when I reach the bottom one—in her socked feet and all—and jumps into my arms.

"I'm so proud of you," Mina encourages in my ear, and

I hold her close, her signature smell of peppermint and acrylic paint tickling my nose. "I know it can be hard for you to open up to anyone besides me or the rest of our family. But you did it."

The best part about Mina is that she sees people and accepts them as they are. I pull her closer one more time before releasing her.

"Let's get you inside before you freeze."

I follow her in and quietly take off my shoes. Within minutes, we're huddled together on the enclosed back porch—something I built to keep the warmth in on nights like this. My telescope is in the corner, the one I've been tracking stars and constellations with since I was in high school.

"Before we go any further," Mina says, the steam from her cup of tea trailing toward the wooden ceiling, "Mrs. Lark came over to thank you for shoveling her driveway again."

I shrug like it was nothing.

"And I suspect the firewood at crotchety Mr. Cohen's house was you as well?" she continues.

"He needed it after his hip surgery."

"Hmm." Mina looks at me with squinted eyes. "And the new easel engraved with your signature clock etching that I found outside my door after our phone call?"

Since we were kids, Mina has loved to paint. The easel is an early Christmas gift that I stayed up several nights to make. "You needed a new one."

Mina sets her tea on the coffee table between us and squeezes my arm while her head falls to my shoulder. "Thank you." She studies me in the dim light. "You know, for all the good you do for others, you can also extend that kindness to yourself."

My head shakes from the discomfort her words bring up. She's always telling me to care for myself too.

"You're loyal. You care for others. And I'm just so happy something good is happening for you now." She grabs my cheek and pinches it like only a sister could. "You're a softy, my big brother."

I laugh and move out of her grasp. "Your opinion of me is far too high." I take a sip of tea, the pressure from her now-absent fingers still pulsing on my face.

"Please. You may be the quieter sort, but the day you become crochety or withdrawn from the world is the day I'll know something died in you." Her teasing smile hitches up on one side.

I set my chin on the top of her head, and she leans in for just a moment before she pops up. "I truly can't wait to paint with my new easel!" Her swift movement nearly causes my mug of tea to spill. "Yikes, sorry." She winces and laughs. "Okay, okay. Tell me again. You ran into her, or she ran into you?"

Because we share nearly everything with each other, I tell Mina every detail of meeting Ivy. As I share, the smell of the cookies that lasted five seconds before we devoured them wafts into my memory. I know I'll never forget the way Ivy opened up to me over that tiny table like no woman ever has.

"She said it had something to do with us being strangers. But it was more than that."

"Jay, this is amazing." Mina's eyes are filled with unshed tears, and I have to hold back my own. "It sounds like she really is interested in *you*. And not how much you can bench press." She makes a slight gagging gesture.

"Tell me how you really feel about my muscles," I laugh.

"No, it's true. I'm tired of women who just throw themselves at you for your good looks without bothering to discover that you'd rather drink tea than energy drinks, and your favorite thing in the world is to look at the stars."

The tea is now lukewarm. I take another sip and put it on the coffee table, the clink of the ceramic on the tile coaster like a bell ringing through the night.

"What was the most surprising thing about her?" Mina's eyes are shining.

I can't deny that it feels good to talk to someone about this experience. Edgar and Angie will be supportive, and I can't wait for them to meet Ivy too, but having my favorite little sister to share this moment with makes it that much better.

The answer comes easily. "She trusted me enough to tell me what she wants to be known for."

"You asked her that question?" Mina almost gasps with shock.

"Yes, I did. Because I think it's important. You know Mom and Dad have always told us to be clear with who you are and what you want. I was curious."

"Gutsy to try that with a stranger."

"Yeah, but it didn't feel like the two of us had just met. There's something different about her, Mina. I can't describe it yet."

Her hand comes to rest on my arm, her expression thoughtful. "Jay, you've always been so strong for all of us. You've been my protector more than once. You make everyone who gets the honor of knowing you feel like they're important." She claps softly, her final words coming in a rush. "And you love Christmas more than anyone I've ever seen in my life, which has to be one of your most endearing qualities."

I laugh, picking up the mug of tea—both to drain the last of it and to do something to distract myself from the uncomfortable attention. Talking about Ivy is one thing. But talking about who I am is harder for me, especially because I've so often been misunderstood by anyone other than Mina. Although now, it seems that Ivy might be interested in getting to know the real me as well.

"What's not to love about Christmas?" I say toward the windows. The chill from the frigid air is starting to creep in despite the space heater that looks like a fireplace on blast in front of us. A chill runs down my spine, but I shake it off.

"Did you get her number? When are you going to see her again?" Mina reads my mind and throws me a blanket from the basket beside our seats.

"Tomorrow." Preemptively, I wince. "But I didn't get her number."

"What?" my sister's voice rings loudly throughout the space.

My eyes widen, and I crouch down as her hands fly to her mouth. We are frozen for twenty whole seconds before we realize that no one has woken inside the house. We've escaped getting caught out of our beds like when we were kids.

"What do you mean you didn't get her number?" Mina hisses a few moments later.

"I'm trusting fate with this one."

"I'm sorry, what?"

"Like *Serendipity.*"

"You modeled your love life off a heartbreaking movie?" Mina has always preferred action movies more than the romances I enjoy, but her furrowed brow does not bode well for her opinion of my choice. Her lip is pulled in between her teeth, and an uncomfortable feeling settles in my stomach.

"Was that not a good idea?" I put my head in my hands. "It wasn't, was it?"

"Hey, don't do that." Mina grabs my arm. "You took a chance. That's so . . . unlike you."

I nod. "I know. But in the moment, I just felt like I had to go with it. Like what was happening between us was bigger than me. It felt like something we could tell our kids about one day."

Mina's eyes widen.

"You know, if that ever happens," I say quickly, realizing that I've absolutely shown my hand. I know that meeting Ivy has to mean something for my life. I'm determined not to mess up this gift I've been given.

"Okay, well, if your meeting was as magical as you say it was, and it seems to have been, then we'll have to believe." A wide yawn overtakes her face, and I shove her knee.

"Thanks for staying up with me, but please get some sleep."

"Okay," she relents, standing to go inside. "I do have students to teach and, hopefully, direct them to paint on paper and not their hair."

I chuckle and collect the mugs, rising to follow her. When she reaches the sliding door, she turns back to face me. "Just tell me this. Did you at least get to hug her goodnight? Kiss her on the cheek?"

The memory of Ivy's lips on mine and the feeling of kissing her back sends an immediate flare of heat across my skin. I toss the blanket over my shoulder with one hand.

"We kissed," I say in a quiet tone.

Mina lets out a squeal and rushes back to sit on the coffee table, facing me. "I love this for you! Tell me more."

"Would you like to see her picture?" The Polaroid feels as if it's burning a hole in my pocket.

"Yes!" She waves her hands in the air. "Why didn't you lead with this? You have a picture? Let me see!"

I pull the Polaroid from my pocket. Only a couple of hours ago, the owner of Four Leaf Cookies offered to take it when he realized we were on our first date. Mina pulls out her phone to shine a light on it and inhales sharply. Her eyes fill with tears, a contradiction to the smile on her face.

"She is beautiful." Her eyes move to mine as she holds up the picture. "And you look so happy, Jay. Whenever I've thought of you happy, *this* is what I've hoped for."

I clear my throat and pull her in for a hug, careful not to bend the picture. "Oh, M&M, what would I do without you?"

"Good thing you'll never have to find out." She releases me and sighs. "Now, I'm going to bed. And you need to do the same. You've got your woman to go and see again tomorrow. Or later today, given the time. But who's counting the hours?" She gives me a wink and rises, a blanket trailing behind her like a cape. She slides the door open to step into the house and turns toward me again. Her smile is sweet and hopeful. "I think this could be your Christmas miracle."

With that, she disappears. The door closes, leaving the porch quiet except for the humming of the space heater. I look at the photo of Ivy and me, even though I've already memorized it. The curve of her red lips and the shine in her eyes are imprinted upon me permanently. Reaching into my pocket, I pull out the piece of ribbon. She trusted me with something meaningful to her, and the significance of that isn't lost on me. I rub my thumb over the edge of the fabric. If it is a good luck charm, then I'll hold on to it with everything I have, just like I plan to hold on to the woman who gave it to me.

Chapter Four

(NEARLY) EIGHT YEARS LATER

Loneliness can feel a lot like doing your best to make it through each day while not having someone with whom to plan your future. You pay the bills, try to drink plenty of water, eat something that has a semblance of nutritional value, consume enough protein to fill Santa's sleigh, stay off of devices but also get work done with blue-light glasses, have meaningful connections, try not to self-isolate, and don't get too many parking tickets (not that I've ever had a problem with the law).

Throw in multiple failed attempts at dating apps, ballet slippers, and the quirkiness of my small town, and you'd see the cycle of my life. This is the rhythm to which I've set my days. It's a daily attempt to hold on to gratitude even though I'm frustrated that I don't currently have someone to hold on to. In the meantime, I've transformed from a professional dancer into a woman who owns her own dance studio. I take care of others. I have a strong community. And still, it doesn't seem like I'm able to make progress in a relationship. Not because I don't want one, but because—even all these years later—no one has looked at me like a man named Jace once did.

When I returned to New York after the New Year eight years ago, the most devastating part of it all was being forced to dance with Dmitri again—newly engaged and not *engaged* in his work at all. The result was the end of my career as a dancer. During the spring, as we rehearsed for a new show, Victoria, his new fiancée, passed by the studio, and in his distraction, he nearly dropped me. To brace my fall, my ankle was forced to bend in an unnatural way. The injury ended my professional career. After all my hard work, my career was over before the new show had even begun. While I recovered gradually and can now dance again, the way my body moves will never be quite the same. I've learned to make peace with that, despite how painful that season of loss became.

Now, I watch vintage ballet performances as a way to remind myself why I fell in love with dance again. The credits to *The Nutcracker* with Mikhail Baryshnikov and Gelsey Kirkland roll while tears fall down my face. I have a junky DVD player, and yes, I still have the DVD of one of my favorite ballet performances of all time. This particular classic from 1977 was a gift from my mom, and even though it was filmed before I was born, the ballet was a deep part of my childhood. The whole thing triggers a sense of nostalgia as it meets an ache in my bones. I want to be Clara, finding a nutcracker who happens to come alive as a prince. While other kids were falling asleep to Disney movies at night, I was falling asleep to the brilliance of Tchaikovsky, imagining how I would one day dance the pieces that had already begun to mean so much to me. And while *The Nutcracker* is infamous across the world, this television adaptation of the story has stayed with me throughout my life.

Many people may not realize that there are a few different versions of the beloved ballet. Some versions call the main character *Marie*. Others will call her *Clara* (which is my preference). Most uniquely, while the most popular choreography I've seen is to have a *pas de deux* between the Sugar Plum Fairy and the Cavalier, my favorite way is as performed in the 1977 version—the Nutcracker Prince himself dances with Clara.

What was once nothing more than a wooden toy comes to life, breathing, feeling, and enjoying a dream world with Clara before they realize that, at some point, the dream is over. The dance creates the most gorgeous storyline of a young girl awakening to love and, ultimately, saying goodbye to the one she wanted to hold. No dream can last forever. But the idea that someone can be woken to life and then be forced to revert to the ways things were before because time ran out is one of the most compelling pieces of dance that has stayed with me throughout life. I pause the performance and sigh into the fur of my beloved golden retriever. "C'mon, Resin."

He's named for the type of substance that keeps my pointe shoes together. Resin has done the same for my life. He's a steady companion who's currently curled up on my lap with his head leaning on my chest, and he's been staring me down ever since I started crying during the *grand pas de deux*.

Grabbing my empty pint of peppermint stick ice cream, I push off the couch and walk to the sink, the spoon hanging partially from my mouth as my phone lights up with a notification. Freddie, my brother—also known as my hero—has sent me another reel. No doubt, it's a reel that will either make me cry from laughing or just simply cry. I make a mental note to call him tonight after I haven't just finished bawling over a ballet that I've seen hundreds of times (yes, hundreds).

At least my family tries to keep the loneliness at bay during Christmastime. They are my rock. Freddie is in the military and is currently at a base on the West Coast. Growing up, we were inseparable, but our five-year age difference meant that by the time I started to get interested in boys and was trying to figure out how to navigate my feelings, he had enlisted. The reality of an older brother in the military could only go so far with punk teenage boys when I didn't have him to walk the halls with me at school or his presence at home before a date.

Despite this, the pressure to be perfect weighed on me in Freddie's shadow, threatening on the edges of our relationship to pull us apart if I compared myself to him. Nevertheless, through letters and video calls or voice memos, we've managed to remain as close as two siblings can be.

My parents, John and Mandie, were high school sweethearts. Now, they're the epitome of a gorgeous couple who have loved each other through the joys and heartache, exemplifying a life lived well. They founded the Birch Borough Inn. It's situated in the middle of town on the other side of a small community park, close enough to join in the festivities each season but private enough to be away from the hustle and bustle. They both went to Boston University and represent the most New England-type of New Englanders one could know. My mother makes clam chowder in the summer, and my father owns multiple pieces of sports memorabilia from every Boston and New England team. During their time in Boston, they also picked up the accent. You'll hear them say "pahk" instead of "park" and "cah" instead of "car." They are the type of people who would have been cast in the 2020 "Smaht Pahk" Super Bowl commercial. And I love them for it.

At least they have each other, I comfort myself. *And I have them this Christmas.*

Grabbing my dance bag and shoving a protein bar and an electrolyte packet next to my giant water jug, I kiss Resin on the head before putting on my boots.

"We'll be together soon, my little love bucket," I say to his brown eyes, noticing pieces of fur disrupted in the middle of his head where I kissed him.

I step outside my apartment. I live in the small unit on the second floor, where my friend, Lily, used to live. Gliding downstairs, I emerge in the frigid air and walk toward the rushing river. The swiftly moving water runs through town and seems to give a sense of cadence to the seasons and the events that unfold.

It's exceptionally cold, and I'm thanking my lucky stars that I decided to wear my lined leggings and an extra pair of socks today. Since it was just Thanksgiving, they even have turkeys on them, but they're hidden in my boots. The vibe is festive. Bright-red ribbons are wrapped around the historical lampposts that line my street, a nod to the holiday season that's just beginning.

Lorelai Gilmore from the top-tier TV show *Gilmore Girls*

claimed she could smell snow. I would adamantly say it's the same for me. I can sense the gorgeous sharpness in the air right before the perfect flakes appear from heaven and remind me that even things that fall can create something beautiful. You can't see the intricacies of an individual snowflake unless you have the proper microscope. I can't always appreciate the beauty of my own life until I zoom in.

I think I love Birch Borough most in the winter. We may have an abundance of town events throughout the year, but the ones that take place around Christmastime are my favorite of all. I love more than the lights hung all around town, bathing all the shops and the streets in a warm glow. And it's more than the special pastries at Sparrow's Beret. It's the way that Lorenzo of Lorenzo's Pizza dresses as Santa Claus every year and the way that Grey wraps up books for people in town, writing their names on them like the biggest game of Secret Santa you've ever played, except they're all from her. I love the way the quiet of the fresh snowfall seems to remind my lungs to breathe. The crackling of wood fires in cozy homes and the scent of smoke that laces the night air are deep comforts that settle into my soul.

Grey and I are still the very best of friends, as were our moms. I got to grow up with mine, but Marlee, the one for whom their family bookstore is named, was taken by cancer when Grey was seven. The loss has forever marked her and her father, not to mention our town. While Grey lost her mother at a young age, she inherited her mother's love for books. After the tragedy, our families intertwined even closer, as loss often tends to do with the people who remain. Grey spent many days and nights at my house while her father kept the bookstore afloat and spent time at the hospital during Marlee's last days. Books became a huge part of both of our lives, and while Grey never shared my love for dance, she's always claimed the music at the dance studio was the best background noise for her to read.

As winter whisks its way into our lives, its arrival brings the joy of the season but also the memories of that one night. Sometimes, I wonder if life consists of mirages. Are there moments that aren't real but somehow feel achingly tangible?

Now, I count Christmases instead of years, each return of the holiday season a painful reminder that my prayer to find my partner is still waiting to be answered.

People talk about the pain of heartache during a breakup. It's undeniably a pivot, a moment when you thought someone would fit into your life, and they just don't. But I hardly hear anyone talk about a certain kind of heartache that comes when you open your heart, and nothing ever comes of it. There's no reward, but there's also nothing devastating. There are only splinters left behind, pointing to the idea that something could've been built if given the chance. It's a drowned match, a lone sock, a haunting melody of a song that could've been.

Sometimes, I think about my lucky ribbon, the one I gave Jace, and I wonder if it was at that moment that I lost the part of me that held on to hope. Objectively, I love my life. I have so much for which to be thankful. There's Grey, who's closer than a sister, and I have other dear friends in this town and people who act like my family. I own a dance studio now, and it's the very one that I learned to dance in.

But I'm lonely. Eight years after that fateful day we met and never saw each other again, the state of my heart is altered, at best. Against my determination to block the memories, my heart keeps going back to Jace. The disappointment of never seeing him again after our perfect meet-cute has embedded itself so deeply in my lungs that it's enough to make me gasp in the middle of the night, especially in the winter.

When he never showed up for our date, at first, I was in shock. Then I was worried. Next followed the anger. I searched for him online, only to realize that all I had to go on was him telling me he was one of four siblings, his sister's name was Mina, aka M&M, he taught boxing, and he enjoyed building things. He was from New England, which we had in common, but we had agreed not to give too many details about ourselves so we could live in the moment. That night at Four Leaf Cookies, we shared heart things more than logistical things. That method proved to be about as useful as a burnt Pop-Tart: a waste of a perfectly good thing. It's not even the fact that I was ghosted that's hurt the most over the years. It's the fact that our connection was so effortless that it left an impression on my very soul, an intricately worked stamp whose mold no one else has been able to match.

That was what Jace and I were. We shared a—dare I say?—magical evening of connection and the promise of more. We kissed, and it's the memory of it that grips my mind like a vise. When I'm between sleeping and waking or holding a cup of tea in my hands and willing it to warm me from the inside, I remember. I waited for him. And he never showed.

As I walk toward Marlee's Books—which is the only independent bookstore selling both new and used books within a ten-mile radius—I have to admit there is comfort during this time of year. I can't help but smile as I pass familiar faces all around. Liam is filming content with his cat, A-cat-pella, on a snowy stump across the way, an ushanka hat perched on his furry head. The lights are glowing in the windows of Sparrow's Beret, and I see Gladys' arms waving at me. Down the street, Ollie is guiding shipments of what must be toys into his shop, his cane tapping against the sidewalk as he follows Henry, our weekend UPS delivery man, into the store. No doubt, he's preparing for the increase in holiday sales and visitors—mostly in the form of children who want to fill their wish list with things from Santa.

I continue walking, relishing the sight of so many of my friends going about their evenings. Birch Borough is an old-fashioned town, a nod to the type of days that many don't experience in our modern times, days when people still knew each other and read the local paper. We have town meetings and annual events that bring everyone together, including tourists and people in surrounding towns. Most of us believe we could have our own television show, but I also think we guard this place, treating it like a well-kept secret as much as possible.

As I approach the bookstore, I spot Grey placing a pile of books on a shelf before picking up a strand of garland and heading toward the window. She's wrapped it around her shoulders and pinned one side before she sees me outside the window. Her eyes widen behind her cat-eye glasses, a smile breaking out on her face as she waves me in. The familiar creak of the shop door and the squeal of my best friend, as if she didn't just see me yesterday, bring a smile to my face.

"Decorating already?" I ask, dropping my dance bag unceremoniously on the floor. In an hour, I'm teaching the foundations of ballet to young dancers. I deliberately left my apartment with enough time to grab a cocoa from Sparrow's Beret and visit with my friends scattered about town—the perks of walking everywhere and living in a place where most of my life is lived within half a mile of home.

"Of course!" Grey says happily, a piece of stray garland stuck within her light-brown hair. I pull it from her strands before tossing it in the trash can. My eyes catch on a book that's open with a sticky note poking out of it.

"Found another book, huh?" I ask, knowing perfectly well that she did. When Grey was around ten years old, she discovered that her mom had written notes on the inside covers of many of her favorite books in the bookshop. Since that moment, Grey has collected them. The found books now sit on their own special shelf behind the counter, properly entitled "Marlee's Shelf." Some townspeople bring the books back if they discover they took home one of the treasured notes, but Grey has developed a whole set of rules around them. She doesn't go searching for them; they have to find her. But when a customer brings a book to the counter, it's fair game for her to check. And since first making the discovery, she's pulled the clues left by her mother and created a sort of road map for her life from their goodness.

"What is the wisdom for today?" I lean toward the book. "I could use a sense of direction these days, I think."

Grey turns to me at the question, a soft smile on her face and her eyes slightly red, the tears no doubt triggered by the emotion of finding another book her mother had touched earlier today.

"'Sometimes love feels like it leaves us, only to return to us.' Found in *Sense and Sensibility*," she quotes, already having memorized the sentiment.

The words tug me closer to her, knowing how deeply it affects her whenever she finds a book. Her lingering grief over the loss of her mother reminds me to enjoy the life that I have. Some people don't get everything they want. We don't always get the love we hope for in the time that we hope. We don't always get the dream in the way that we want. And we don't always get the closure we fought for. But there's still love to be found all around us. And that can be enough to make it through another day.

"I love it," I say simply.

"Me too." She wraps an arm around my shoulders as the bell chimes over the door, alerting us to another person's entry.

Gladys, our resident busybody and undeniably wild aunt-like figure to most of us in this town, lets out a whoop before shutting the door tight. "Girlies, hold on to your socks!" she cries. "I've got a Christmas miracle."

I laugh, crossing my arms and relaxing my usual ballerina posture. "Like I would ever go without socks in weather like this." My laugh is enough to reassure Gladys that I'm in for her story, without having to think of the chilly nightmare it would be to have no socks. My feet have been sacred during my life as a dancer, and my quirks with them are unending. "Also, didn't I see you over at Sparrow's Beret not five minutes ago?"

She ignores my question, her eyes lit with glee. "There's a new man in town."

"Here we go," I say under my breath. "Grey, prepare

yourself to be set up for a dinner date within the week."

My friend blushes but shrugs it off.

"I'm not stupid, my dears," Gladys corrects. "Grey has been pining for that Boston fellow—the person, not the city, of course—ever since I can remember. She's not ready for my matchmaking energy quite yet."

I brace myself against the counter behind me, the dread in my gut already building because I know where this is going.

"Yes, it's *you!*" Gladys yells to me with delight. "Now, as I've said before, his brother has a haircut like a Weedwhacker—we've already established this. But the man I'm discussing looks like a Grecian god who stepped down from Mt. Olympus to give us a glimpse of what heaven is like."

"Gladys, since when do you care about Greek mythology?" I say with a laugh. I already knew she was referring to Edgar, who owns In the Ring, a boxing studio in town. The man who now, apparently, has a brother. Edgar doesn't live in Birch Borough. He only works here, but his sister lives in town. Angela—aka Angie—of the famous Angie's Pies is a lovely baker and business owner whom we've known and loved for several years now.

Gladys is quick to protest. "I've cared about it since I first laid eyes on the man! For three hours, I researched marble statues to try to find the one that looked like him to show you, but not one of them quite captured him. Still, I now have quite an education in mythology."

Grey turns back to the window, laughing softly. She continues stringing the garland laced with twinkle lights across the beam above it.

I pinch the bridge between my eyes and take a deep

breath. I'm trying to think of how I can get out of this conversation and hop across the street to get a hot chocolate before my class without Gladys seeing. Sparrow has recently started making a hot chocolate recipe for me that's mostly dark cocoa, part cream, and a hint of vanilla. But Gladys knows my schedule, so leaving now wouldn't go over well. And no one ever would want Gladys' wrath.

No, it's better to get this over with as quickly as possible. The only way out is through and all that. "Okay, Gladys. I'll bite," I sigh. "What does this man do, and what does he look like?"

Picking up a box of ornaments on a nearby bookshelf, I move to help Grey as she beautifies both the garland and the tree made of books set on the deep windowsill.

"I should start by saying that he is a bit of a crotchety one." Gladys wrings her hands together. "Something happened to him a while ago that took his joy, I gather."

Involuntarily, my nose scrunches. I'm not attracted to the uncaring, unfeeling type. No, I much prefer men who will open their hearts to me and tell me I remind them of the stars.

"But don't discount him quite yet," she hurries to add. "Even though he didn't help lovely Marie with her groceries. She nearly fell on the ice, carrying her bags, and he just walked by her . . . not very gentlemanly."

"No, I should say not," Grey quips.

"And there was the time he left a shovel on the ground in front of the toy store instead of helping Ollie pick it up. Poor thing. You know Ollie's hip isn't reliable these days."

"This isn't a resounding endorsement. You think there's redemption for him?" Grey asks what I couldn't.

I glance over my shoulder to see Gladys' eyes brighten. "He's tall!" she positively shrieks as her arms go high and wide.

I'm not quite sure how to picture the man she's trying to portray, except that he must be a mountain. Immediately, my mind goes back to a winter night in the cold and a kiss that I could have built a life on, but I shake my head to act like I'm interested in Gladys' mystery man.

"Dark eyes, enviously curly hair," she continues. Her eyes widen. "And he builds things. Word is that he visited our town a few times, a long time ago, but didn't stay. He just arrived right before Pumpkin Pie Day. Oh, and the best part? He's single! I think he may also have a daughter, but I need to confirm. To be honest, I'm impressed I got this much info on him in less than a day." She puts her hands on her hips in satisfaction. "And, oh, he's also a boxer! He'll punch out every other creep from your mind, I guarantee it."

My heart begins to quicken. Heat rushes up my neck. Gladys' description sounds all too familiar, apart from the Scrooge vibes she mentioned. But my heart rate is replying with force, nonetheless.

"Gladys," I say slowly and quietly so I don't upend the careful life that I've crafted here over the past eight years, "what is this man's name?"

"John, Jack . . .?" Gladys trails off. Her fingers have a trace of arthritis, bent as she taps against her temple for a moment. "I got it!" she shouts, hands coming together with a clap. "Jace!"

The blood in my ears pulses in time with the movement of the ornament I'm holding as it drops from my hand to the floor and shatters into a thousand pieces.

Chapter Five

Ivy

Jace? You said his name is Jace?" I ask, trying to make my voice firm, but I can feel the weakness behind the words. My breath feels caught in my throat. My thoughts race. A slideshow of images passes through my brain: ice skating on a deserted rink, hot chocolate, the warmest of hugs, the ghost of our kiss, the feeling of his hands cupping my jaw.

"Yes, Jace! That's it!" She pauses, her eyes taking in my distressed state. "Are you all right, dearie? You look like you've seen a fake Santa!"

Grey glides alongside me, comforting me as only she can, with a compassionate smile and eyes full of concern. "What do you say we take a walk and get a hot chocolate, huh?"

Numbly, I nod, grateful that my friend has the decency to know I need some frosty air in my lungs before I fall to the floor and shatter like the poor Christmas decoration I just massacred.

"Gladys, will you watch the shop for me? Dad is

upstairs. I'll bring you a croissant!" Grey doesn't wait for a response before she pulls us out the door and onto the sidewalk in front of the bookshop. My dance bag has appeared around her shoulders, and one of her arms is threaded through mine, our bodies moving as a team toward Sparrow's Beret.

"You don't have a coat," I mumble as Grey rushes us onward, no doubt frightened that pausing even for a moment could leave me frozen.

"I'll be just fine. You, on the other hand . . ." She doesn't finish the sentence but uses her free hand to open the door. The smell of butter, caramelized sugar, and rich espresso brings an immediate wave of comfort on a visceral level.

Sparrow looks up from the pastry case, her brown hair tied back in a ribbon. Her fringe bangs fall into her eyes as she straightens to greet us, and she lifts a hand to brush them out of the way. Her smile is wide before it drops, no doubt seeing the numb expression etched across my face.

"Ivy's special version of your French hot chocolate, with extra whipped cream, please. Stat," Grey says for me.

Sparrow gives a knowing nod, her elegant frame moving quickly to whip up the sweet concoction.

Lily appears from behind the swinging door that leads to the kitchen. A wooden spoon in one hand is dripping melted chocolate onto the floor, her other hand carrying a tray of *pains au chocolat*. The co-owner of Sparrow's Beret and Sparrow's ride-or-die friend and defender of all those she loves eyes my stricken face. "Did someone say 'chocolate'?"

If I weren't so stunned by the announcement of Jace's presence in Birch Borough, I'd laugh and grab an iced sugar cookie from the nearby canister. Instead, I grin politely at

Lily as she moves toward us, her apron covered in drizzles of chocolate and stretched tight over her expanding stomach.

"How are you feeling, Lily?" Grey asks beside me, one arm still wrapped around my shoulders and the other leaning on the counter between us and my two other closest friends in town.

"Oh, you know. This baby seems intent on two things: shenanigans and chocolate. He—or she—won't stop moving. The only time Baby stops jumping on my uterus is when Graham reads to us at night. It's not convenient. But I can't blame this little one. They clearly already know their daddy is a good one and recognize his kind voice."

Her hand, still covered in chocolate, gently rubs her stomach. The sight pulls at my heartstrings. Lily and her husband, Graham, have been married for over a year and are now expecting their first child. After a long road back to each other after a breakup, they had a second chance to heal their heartache. Now, they are about to bring a life into the world.

A decadent hot chocolate with chocolate shavings sprinkled across the top of the whipped cream appears before me. The warmth of it radiates through a ceramic cup with a sparrow design painted on it.

Sparrow, too, has her own love story with Rafe, her French husband. He calls her his muse as a musician and songwriter. Currently, he tours across the country throughout the year and works with various artists to make music that plays on the radio or trends on social media. If I remember correctly, he even has some shows coming up in Europe. The two of them are madly in love, and it's their happiness that has kept me believing that true love still exists at all.

I take a sip of the chocolate goodness and let it warm my throat, hoping it warms my soul as well.

"I didn't think I'd ever see him again. Not really," I say quietly to Grey next to me.

My hand is resting on the counter. Grey gives it a gentle press to affirm that I'm not alone.

He's back.

Where has he been for eight years?

Jace and I were never in a relationship. We couldn't have had a second-chance romance like Lily and Graham. We were never fated lovers, refusing to allow anything to keep us apart like Sparrow and Rafe. But something in me believes that Jace and I missed out on a chance for a deeper connection. After nearly thirty-four years of loving Christmas more than anything, maybe my reward this season is to see the hand of fate—or serendipity—ease the tension in my chest from so many unanswered questions.

But the news that he's back in town hurts. And that's a surprise.

I'm not sure how to feel about seeing the guy who never showed up. The guy who left me standing in the cold for hours, watching and waiting, hoping that if I just gave it one minute more, he'd appear. The next day, I stopped by every shop in town to ask if anyone had seen him.

Once, I thought I would have my own love story, but now I'm not so sure. And after all this time, I've realized that I can't imagine that our one date meant as much to him as it did to me.

After quieting my shock by sipping hot chocolate at Sparrow's Beret and eating a gingerbread croissant in lieu of my usual protein bar, I feel ready to find the joy in my life. Joy, for me, looks a lot like my little students who will soon arrive at my studio. Grey went back to the bookstore while I proceeded alone to my dance studio, En Pointe. What would any of my friends do about the situation I'm in, anyway? Only Grey knows the extent to which Jace affected all other attempts at romance over the past eight years. He was the measure by which I compared all other men. A man I met one time has been the standard for first dates. I shake my head at myself. Somehow, Jace became that important in my head, despite the fact that he stood me up and never spoke to me again. It's no wonder that, after all this time and after every effort, nothing has stuck.

I know what it means to be loved fully and yet never feel like you're fully loved. Because there are all different kinds of love—the love of a friend, the love of a parent, the love I have for Resin, and the love within a romantic relationship. That's the one that has only ever felt one-sided. Maybe it was my perfectionism that annihilated any chance at romance before I could fully grasp it. Maybe my individualism has repelled men. I'll admit I'm constantly dreaming, always wanting to be better than I am right now. And I struggle with believing that I'm not a failure.

Unlocking the door to my studio, I flip on the lights and adjust the heater to warm the space, my thoughts distracted by this unexpected situation.

Oh, sure, there were times—years, even—during which I was convinced that I would end up with someone— someone like Dmitri—only to be jolted to reality by the revelation that what I perceived as affection was someone else's version of a placeholder until something better came along. Objectively, I know that I'm worth the effort to hold on to, but experience tells me no one will be capable of it.

It's hard to see other people moving on. I see Sparrow and Lily living their best lives with their husbands, and I hear talk of families starting all around town. Grey isn't tied down, but her heart is also not free. It's clear to us all that she's been in love with her best guy friend, Boston, since they met at literary camp when they were teens. Even she can't understand the depths of the loneliness I sometimes feel. It creeps in at the edges, whispering that while I've wanted to dance with someone throughout the journey of life, it's been pointless to hope for a partner.

From the depths of my dance bag, I pull out my slippers and slide them on, the pointe shoes so worn they are merely an extension of my foot.

The thing about being a dancer is that I understand all too well the power of partnership. With the right person, I can spin faster and literally fly through the air. I can do things I never thought possible when I trust that someone can catch me. It's exhilarating, and it's frightening. Dancing in partnership brings a rush of adrenaline that has, so far, been unmatched. That feeling ends on the dance floor. With my ballet slippers on and my hair pulled up, I adjust my dance sweater and leggings. I move to warm up at the barre. When I think of an anchor for life, the barre is it. The simple wooden contraption adhered to the wall is the thing I return to time and time again, never feeling disappointed. I've had some of my best moments at this very barre.

There are other moments that have seemed to meld

themselves effortlessly into the fabric of my heart. Moments that would never advertise their need for my attention but, somehow, have stitched their way into my memories. Quiet drives on the way home when the bristling leaves on the tree branches overhead arch over my car as I pass by. The feeling of a cool, cloudy day. The eerie stillness of a snowy winter morning. The low hum of the record machine in my studio before it begins to play the classical music I warm up to.

In just moments now, I'll have a whole class of students in the studio, eager for me to help them get one step closer to their dreams. I love my little ballet students and the way they willingly get their energy out and give it their all while practicing every movement. Even the shyest children seem to find the way they are meant to move and own it by the time they're done with my class. I'm proud of the way I've carried on Ms. Phoebe's legacy. She was the woman who taught me how to plié, and now I own her dance studio. Even though I've traveled around the world and have company experience, nothing prepared me to follow my dreams of dance like this studio tucked away in my small New England hometown. It was Ms. Phoebe's trust, extended toward me through the years, that was enough to carry me through and lead me back all these years later.

I shift at the barre, the chatter of little voices in the lobby falling on my ears as I lift my other leg to stretch and warm my tight muscles. My part-time receptionist, Harlow, steps into the studio. I turn my attention to her, and a smile breaks out on my face as a little girl with nearly jet-black hair looks up at me from beside her. I take a second look at the girl and feel myself startle. There's something so achingly familiar about her face that I feel a tug in my chest. I lower my leg and turn to face them fully.

"You have a new student! This is Emmy," Harlow introduces her with a grin.

I step toward Emmy and bend to her level. "Hi, Emmy. My name is Miss Ivy. I'm so happy to meet you."

A shy smile breaks across her face, and I clock the dimple peeking out on one side. My hands start to shake. Nervous energy flows through my system, the feeling that my life is somehow changing settling into my very bones.

"Have you ever danced before?" I manage to get out, emotion creeping into my tone. I've never had a reaction like this to a new student, but I'm trying to move through this conversation and make Emmy comfortable, despite my own discomfort.

Everything that I have, I give to this studio. I try to pass my passion on to my students, believing that dance connects us all, which is why I'm delighted when she shakes her head slowly and then looks down at her slightly too-big ballet slippers and her bunched tights.

"At home," she says. "But Daddy says I need to dance again."

"Oh, so you stopped dancing?" I ask, sensing there's more to this story.

Nodding, Emmy looks shyly at the barre and the mirrors, glancing back to a few of my other students who are already starting to stretch and get out their nervous energy in the lobby.

"Emmy is five years old, Miss Ivy," Harlow says for my benefit. "And this is her first official dance class. But rumor has it that she dreams of being a dancer. Isn't that right, Emmy?"

"I want to dance," Emmy says with bright eyes, and I note an amber color in them that arrests my movements. Involuntarily, my mouth opens and closes, my hand moving toward my chest to remind me to breathe. The color is too familiar. And while the truth echoes in my ribs of the person she reminds me of, I'm wrestling with the struggle to admit it.

"Your daddy . . .?" I choke out.

"Do you know my daddy?" Emmy asks, staring up at me with her brows furrowed.

It's not possible.

Gladys mentioned that Jace might have a daughter. But of all the moments that led us here tonight, this is the moment my heart might truly break. I didn't expect to be faced with the reality of who Jace has become so soon. And now, here I have before me his daughter.

"Daddy tries to dance with me, but he says that now that I'm five"—she holds up her tiny hand to demonstrate the number—"I can learn the steps and maybe dance on a big stage like you."

The thought of her dancing with her dad is so adorable that I have to shake my head. Before I can reply, the studio door opens. Another line of my students pours through, their squeals of excitement radiating off the walls. Emmy laughs, too, delight marking her face. Reluctantly, I push aside all thoughts of a man with piercing eyes and a strong jaw, realizing it's time to focus on this afternoon's class.

"To the barre, my little dancers!" I sing into the space, forcing some energy into my tone.

With a glance at Harlow, I extend my hand gingerly. Emmy takes it without hesitation. The feeling of her little hand in mine, so trusting and sweet, makes me clear my throat once again. Trying to release some of the tension, I stretch my neck from side to side and walk us toward the barre. I catch the moment Emmy looks back with a huge smile and gives a wave.

"Dance with you soon, Daddy!" she yells, confidence now flowing through her small stance in anticipation of the lesson to come.

I can't help but swing my head toward her source of happiness, and my distraction causes me to stumble toward the barre. I grasp it tightly with my free hand, still craning my neck toward the lobby. His presence overwhelms me before I see him. The man I never thought I'd see again is standing just a few feet away from the studio doorway. The other parents are busy scrolling on their phones around him, completely oblivious to his tall, broad shoulders, his messy black hair that curls around the ends in different directions, and those whiskey-colored eyes that once marked me for life.

But it only takes five seconds before I clock all the changes in the man who once captured my attention so strongly. The man in the lobby of my dance studio is familiar and unfamiliar in so many ways.

Immediately, I notice his aloofness. Even from afar, his eyes are stormy. His jaw could cut glass. His posture is tense. There's nothing playful or easy about him. The only break in his somber countenance is when his eyes move to Emmy's as she waves at him. They soften just slightly before lifting to mine once more.

I can't control it. My stomach leaps, and then it sinks. The truth settles as I turn toward my class, forcing myself to smile for them. The man that she calls her dad is the hollow version of the man I spent the most magical evening with, the man who didn't show up for me when I wanted him to the most, and the man who never got another chance.

My heart races before it breathes out one single word: *Jace.*

Chapter Six

Jace

Ivy.

My heart breathes the name. It's the only sense of starlight that has shone through my thoughts over the past few years. Emmy, my daughter, has been my sun. It's she who has driven me to get out of bed in the morning and keep moving. But just the thought of Ivy—her very existence—has been the compass, the ticking clock, that's given my nights a reason not to let the darkness swallow me whole. All those years ago, I choked on the disappointment that I couldn't get to her at the ice-skating rink. It has torn at my heart for years.

But tonight, as if the past eight years didn't happen, she pulled on my heartstrings in a way no woman but Ivy ever has.

Since Emmy and I have moved into town temporarily, I realized running into her was inevitable after I saw her face on the dance studio's promotional flyer at the French bakery. Emmy saw it too. That's why we walked into the dance studio in the first place. I never looked Ivy up once her brother confronted me. So, I'll admit I dreaded the possibility of reuniting with her.   But the sight of Ivy in person tonight did something to me that I didn't expect. Her presence became paddles to the heart after it failed. The sensation was like my nerves having blood flow to them again.

Ivy is everything life doesn't seem to want me to have, and that stings.

I tried to connect with her again. I truly did. And I'll never forget the look on her brother's face when he told me not to bother. He said that she'd gone back to New York City and was getting ready for another show. I was the distraction her dream didn't need.

Having Ivy slip through my hands at that time in my life—losing her along with everything else—was enough to nearly drive me mad. After that night, I didn't feel like I had anything to offer her, so I left without a word. Since then, I've grown up. Everything is more serious. Nothing holds the same joy. I'm a shadow of the man I was, and I'm aware of who I've become.

Now, I walk the charming, idyllic streets of Birch Borough as the evening deepens and I wait for Emmy's dance class to be finished, wishing I'd never returned. My hands clench, the bitter cold whispering against my cheeks, reminding me that we're nearly a month away from Christmas. What was once my favorite season has become a source of my greatest pain. Apart from the brightness that seems to radiate from my daughter Emmy's eyes, I haven't been in the spirit.

Christmas shouldn't make me grumpy. But it does. I've

come to think there's too much fanfare around the idea of things magically changing around this holiday. It's like one winter day, our lives are suddenly going to shift and allow us to embrace our best selves while forgetting the crummy things that happened earlier in the year. It's a nice idea, just not practical.

And while I would love to imagine that my fractured heart will repair itself when Santa makes an appearance, I know it's not possible. Because there's no amount of Christmas magic that can make things right with Ivy again. I let myself believe in the restorative power of the holiday years ago, but after what happened that fateful night, I'm still choking on disappointment. The last glimpse of Ivy's smile as we parted at the skating rink is the memory I've tried to hold on to, starting during that night I waited outside the hospital until my limbs were frozen and the staff reminded me to go home.

The memory of our first date causes me to bristle. I wrap my coat more tightly around me. This town feels like a ghost town now, but I'm drawn to it as a space to revisit and remember the times that broke my heart.

"Hey, buddy! Watch where you're going!" an older man clutching a box of wrapped gifts yells while passing me.

Lost in my thoughts, I almost barreled into him on the sidewalk. I can't bring myself to even apologize. Instead, I ignore him, the sting of grief gripping my throat again.

Eight years ago, I got a call that my sister, Mina, was in a car accident while I was on my way to meet Ivy for our second date. By the time I got to the hospital, Edgar and Angie were inconsolable. We lost her that night. The grief was insurmountable. Mina was my confidante, my cheerleader. Without her, nothing could ever be the same.

It took weeks before I could get through a day without crying, months before I could see a pack of M&Ms without doing the same. In the process of it all, I lost Ivy as well.

Like an idiot, I once believed in fate. I didn't get Ivy's number and didn't make an alternate plan. People miss out on life-changing moments every day. I never wanted to miss out on Ivy.

Since then, I've taken out the grief of it all on the punching bag I've come to call my anchor, the custom furniture I've completed to keep my sanity and make me feel useful, and the hours I've spent reading parenting books.

I walk past another storefront, trying to loop through this entire town while Emmy is in her dance class. If I stop, I might scream.

This winter has been another reminder that the things that used to bring me joy no longer do. I want to be the kid I've seen in pictures, the version of myself that was happy to suspend belief and wait for Santa, the sibling who would laugh with my sisters and brother and spend all night playing board games and drinking hot chocolate before we passed out in front of the television with powdered chocolate crusted to our faces. As easily as I could fall back into craving just the sight of Ivy, I'm choosing to retreat into the grumpy shell that's become my armor.

I'm not the same man she met. I was more innocent before the circumstances that caused me to mishandle the heartache of changing plans. The night of my sister's accident left me reeling. Losing my chance with Ivy put me in a lengthy downward spiral. The result was that I made choices I didn't like for a few years following the accident.

There's no way I could have a chance with her now, I tell myself, steeling my heart against the crackle near my spine that feels like heat and hope connecting.

Ivy.

Just her name is enough to set me on edge. She's as beautiful as I remember, the years only deepening her beauty. Her hair is like antique gold, classic and yet mesmerizing. Her eyes can still arrest my heart and call for it to want love again. They're the exact shade of rich, hot cocoa—the good kind with quality, melted chocolate in warm milk that begs to be topped with whipped cream and chocolate shavings, the kind of sweet treat that is more concentrated around the edges with a warmth that could tempt me to stay longer than I planned.

I can't stay longer than I planned. If it weren't for my siblings, I wouldn't be in Birch Borough at all. Angie invited us here so I could help Edgar at the boxing studio for a short time before Emmy and I head to Florida to be with my parents. I'm still building furniture and growing my business. I've added training boxers to be at their fittest to my resume. I'm good at these things. They've been in my bones since I was a young boy. Now, these pursuits keep my schedule flexible so I am able to be around when Emmy needs me most.

When my ex-girlfriend, Jenna, left us four years ago, Emmy was the only reason I got my act together. My daughter needed me. I quit the self-destructive behaviors I was stuck in and learned to sew. I replaced date nights with daddy-daughter movie nights. I found out that I actually like the color pink and the smell of watermelon toothpaste.

Currently, I need something to settle the angst I feel at

the sight of the woman I could have loved. I step into Sparrow's Beret, and the patrons inside look up at my entrance. The French bakery and café has amazing croissants, I've recently discovered. I can eat five of them in one sitting.

"Bonjour—oh, hello!" the woman behind the counter says kindly. She's elegant, with soft movements and features.

"Hello," I say, trying to take the gruff edge out of my tone before I speak but failing, if her slight flinch is any indication.

"I know just about everyone in town, but I haven't met you yet," she says. "Are you new? My name is Sparrow. My husband, Rafe, is a musician. I'm sure you'll see him out and about around town too."

I give a quick nod. My insides protest when I register the table near me, holding cups of the best-looking cup of hot chocolate I've ever seen. At the sight of the tempting drinks, I try to voice something nice, trying to recall how old Jace might've responded if he had just walked into this bakery during his first visit to Birch Borough.

"My daughter would like it here," I finally manage. "May I get one of those hot chocolates to go?" I nod toward the table, feeling the catch in my throat as the scent of peppermint and chocolate brings back a very specific memory. Clearly, I'm self-inflicting my own discomfort. And yet, here we are.

Sparrow's eyes warm at my effort. "I'll throw in a cookie for your daughter, on the house."

I clear my throat. "Thank you."

"It's perfect in this kind of weather." Her warm smile allows some of my tension to ease, but I can't fully relax.

Suddenly, I hear clanging. Something sounds like it's breaking in the back, but Sparrow holds up a hand.

"That's just Lily, my best friend and the co-owner here. She's fine. This is her process." Sparrow is steaming milk and pouring melted chocolate from tiny pots into a to-go cup. Speaking of chocolate, a spoonful of it hits the window of the door leading to what must be the kitchen.

I wince.

"Son of a nutcracker!" a muffled yell comes from the back. Sparrow just laughs. Everyone else in the café keeps working or talking, apparently immune to the chaos happening in the back of this store.

"Do you know someone in town?" Sparrow asks over the sound of French Christmas music playing on the speakers.

"Yes, my brother, Edgar—" I begin.

"Oh! Edgar! Yes, I know him."

"Angie is also my sister."

Her mouth drops open. "Of Angie's Pies? We love her! She mentioned having another brother, and here you are!" She studies my face. "Yes, of course. I see the resemblance now. I can't believe I didn't notice it right away. Your siblings are wonderful people."

"Yes," is all I can manage to say. Without Edgar and Angie, I could never have gotten through everything that's happened in my life; their strength was a steadying force even while they were grieving themselves.

"Welcome to town! Here you go." Sparrow places the hot drink between us, the whipped cream already starting to melt at the edges.

This looks like it may contain magic. The thought brews

before I break it, and I feel a hint of the version of me I can't seem to restore. But before it can take hold, I feel the frown on my face and register Sparrow's brow dipping in concern.

As I take the to-go cup, I move to pull my wallet from my coat, but Sparrow gives a small shake of her head.

"On the house." A bag of cookies appears in front of me, and she smiles.

"Thanks. I'll bring my daughter, Emmy, next time."

"Please do. Stay warm out there!" She waves and moves to clean up the hot chocolate mess she had made. "Oh, and this is a good place to find some hope if you need it. Stop by anytime."

I hear her pleasant voice call after me as I turn and walk away. I want to go back and ask if she knows Ivy, but I can't seem to bring myself to form the words. Ivy has been an elusive dream. I always pictured her living in New York, never dreaming that she'd return to Birch Borough. But now that I've seen her again, I can't imagine she'd be anywhere else but here. This small town suits her. I saw her for only a few moments, but I know this town brings a strength to her I can't imagine she found in the city.

As I step into the frigid winter air again, I remind myself that one of the greatest regrets of my life is leaving our chances to fate, since fate punched me in the face.

The past eight years have been challenging. When I first lost my chance with Ivy, I would drive from a few towns over and go back to the spot of land that held the makeshift ice-skating rink, the place where we were last together. For four months, I'd appear at the same time I met Ivy, in case she ever visited from New York. *Four months.* When questioned, I told my friends and family that I just liked to be there to think, when, truthfully, I hoped to see a glimpse of her again. In vain, I hoped that seeing her would bring me back to the man I felt slipping away more and more each day.

When she never came to the ice-skating rink, I started to wander through town. Once, I went into the Four Leaf Cookies shop and asked the owner about her. When I said her name, a man sitting at a table in the corner looked up, and the first thing that struck me was that he had the same coloring and the same eye color as Ivy. It turned out that the man was her brother.

He knew she was devastated after I ghosted her. Though I explained it was unintentional, he didn't relent. I couldn't blame him. I was younger. I was naïve then.

All these years later, I've come to realize that it's rarer for people to stay with you than to leave you. People shifting through your life can be a blessing. And when you do find the ones who see you at your worst and care about you through it, you have to fight to keep them.

But I didn't fight for her.

After the incident with Ivy's brother, I never stepped foot in Birch Borough again. I didn't visit for Angie's grand opening at the pie shop. I didn't visit for Edgar's ribbon cutting at the boxing studio. I wiped my hands of this town, but now I think I might have been holding a grudge in the wrong direction. The only person I have to blame for my misery is myself.

I take a sip of the hot drink, nearly groaning from the deliciousness of it. The base is real, melted chocolate. Emmy really would love the charming shop.

I think she's going to love this town too—even if the

decorations throughout town are something I personally want to destroy. Well, *destroy* is probably a strong reaction, but at least tear down. If it weren't for my daughter, I wouldn't be celebrating Christmas. I haven't been able to celebrate it well since Mina passed. My brother now lives in Portsmouth, but my sister and my parents relocated here—well, before my parents decided to move to Florida to stay in the warm weather. For the past few years, Emmy and I have moved from city to city. For a while, we landed in Vermont after Jenna left us. But now I've decided to finally stop running and let my daughter grow up with family. When I haven't been training boxers, I've been building furniture. It has passed the time when I can't sleep and gives me something to hold on to that doesn't fall apart in my hands.

For my whole life, I've been fighting against the stereotype of being a jock. Yes, I'm athletic. I like to move my body. It's how I've kept my sanity for this long and processed the world around me. But I've come to realize that women look at the size of my shoulders and not the state of my heart. They want a good time and can't face the truth that my music playlists consist mostly of musicals and classical music. I wear reading glasses. Because of Emmy, I've learned to cook. I couldn't care less about being an influencer and deleted my social media accounts after too many slides into my DMs. Only one woman in my memory once made me feel seen, not for my appearance but for my heart. Her name was Ivy. And as sappy as that may sound, that's the truth of it.

I believe I have so much love to give that I couldn't bench press it. But after Jenna's betrayal, I've questioned everything. I've questioned myself and questioned whether anyone would welcome my touch ever again. It's hard to be built to carry so much and have no one to trust you to do so.

Jenna was there when I needed someone, her whirlwind energy entering my life two years after meeting Ivy. She swooped in, told me the things I wanted to hear, and I thought I loved her. Things went too far. I attempted to process the pain by trying to get close to someone and mistook physical affection for commitment. Once she had Emmy, I offered to marry her. That was when things started to unravel.

Her words were cruel and cut deep.

I didn't make enough money for her. Ironically, I wasn't fit enough. And as much as she had wanted me to show her affection physically, once she got pregnant, I became the last person she wanted to touch her. Instead, she stopped coming home. It was heartbreaking on many levels. And now my daughter has been the casualty of Jenna's selfishness.

I'm the one who's raised Emmy. I was up with her as soon as she got home from the hospital. I'm the one who fed her and held her, who put her against my chest, skin to skin, to make sure she felt my heartbeat. I read to her and dressed her. Immediately, my daughter became my everything. When Jenna decided to officially sign over custody and move to Santa Monica with her yoga instructor, that chapter of my life was over, except for the scars.

I steel myself to pass by the dance studio up ahead, knowing full well that the woman that I haven't been able to stop thinking about is currently teaching my daughter to follow her dreams. After making eye contact with Ivy as the class began, I couldn't stay. Now that the class is nearly over, my shoes could be in a superhero movie for how fast they carry me back across town. It's agonizing, but how can I stay away? The woman is a direct reminder of all the things I've lost. Because we should've had a chance years ago, and if I hadn't gotten the phone call about Mina, we might have had our moment.

I hold my breath and pass by the frost-covered windows, which radiate warm light, the sound of a piano through a record player calling to me like a siren on this winter night. It looks like the students are still finishing their practice. I decide against going into the lobby. I make it past the doors and breathe a sigh of relief but suck in a breath when I hear a rush behind me.

Somehow, I know who it is before I see her.

"Hey!" Ivy's uniquely smoky voice captures me through the cold air. How I've imagined hearing that voice again over the years.

Clenching my jaw, I turn to face her, trying not to notice how beautiful she is, even after all this time. She's better than I remember, and I hate that I now know this to be true when I can't call her mine.

"Yes?" I say, the saltiness in my tone a little much, even for me.

Ivy's eyes narrow. Her shoulders roll back as she stands to her full height, which is still almost a foot shorter than me.

"You're back?" Somehow, it's both a question and a statement.

The feeling of accusation stiffens my spine. I don't want to answer her, but I will. "For now."

Her involuntary sigh unleashes even more frustration. Once, the gleam of affection swirled in her hot-chocolate eyes. Now, they're distrustful, reflecting a wall between us I want to demolish, but I don't know how. My thoughts go to my daughter, because protecting her is the only thing I can control.

"Is it going to be a problem?" I grit out, crossing my arms to cover my heart and hating myself for it. I stare down at her, allowing the gruffness to enter my expression.

"Is what a problem?" Ivy rears back.

"My daughter, Emmy. Is it going to be an issue to have her dance here?" My head hitches a nod toward her studio.

Immediately, Ivy's eyes ignite. "Of course not. I'm a professional. Your daughter will be treated with the same dedication and care as any other one of my students." Her response is as expected, generous despite the fury I triggered, but it makes me sad to think she will never know Emmy as more than her student.

"Glad to hear it," I reply without emotion.

"If you'll just give us another fifteen minutes or so, I'll have her returned to you." A sudden sheen of emotion glistens in her eyes as we stare at each other for a moment, neither of us backing down from our ledges of lost time and unspoken words.

Finally, she grunts in frustration and turns back to her studio, clearly freezing, but pauses when she reaches the door. Her elegant back expands with a deep breath. I will her to look back at me, to give any sign that she's struggling with this reunion as much as I am, but she simply shoves open the door and walks through it.

Shaking off the frustrating experience, I only inhale

again when my long strides have taken me several storefronts away. I don't want to stand in front of her studio window, watching her teach my daughter. But now that I'm near her, I can't seem to stay away. I turn back toward the studio and get a glimpse of her hands moving through the air in a way that stops my breath. Over the years, I imagined what it would be like to see her dance. I thought of buying a ticket to one of her performances in New York and sitting in the back of the audience just to see her again, but I never could bring myself to do it. Now, I see what I always knew. She's grace mixed with strength. Her body comes into view through the window, pointe shoes wrapped up in leg warmers and a sweater over a leotard, but then it disappears again.

I wonder if she's found someone to hold her the way she deserves to be held. Or is she alone, like me? That thought hurts me even more. Because the truth is, I'm ashamed. I'm angry that I couldn't find her, that life seemed to decide that I wouldn't be enough for her without my consent, and that I've made choices that will prevent me from ever being able to earn her love, even after all this time. Being thrown together again almost feels cruel. She's still the most beautiful woman I've ever seen, and I've become the equivalent of something from the deep ocean washed ashore.

"Well, honey, you look like you could outrun a moose and properly throw something big if you wanted to."

The voice stops me in my tracks. I turn back to find a woman with silvery hair and fire in her eyes standing behind me. A wicked gleam of amusement can be found in her grin.

"Ma'am." I nod my head and turn away to keep moving

in the opposite direction once more, but I'm no match for this woman. I recognize her. I've been warned about her, and though she's confronted me several times in the grocery store, I've somehow avoided being a casualty of her direct antics. Even so, I know her name is Gladys.

She follows behind me. "The love that you're looking for might just be in this town," she states with such authority that I almost believe her.

But then I make the most critical mistake of the day: I look back at the dance studio, where Ivy's form appears in the window again, followed by a whole troop of little ballerinas. Gladys positively beams.

"I thought so," she quips. "You know, if you would stop being a Scrooge for five seconds, you might realize that it won't kill you to celebrate the season."

I don't love being compared to a crotchety old literary character, but I can't deny the resemblance.

Gladys continues without pause. "I know you honked your horn at Delores—after she was waiting for some little creature to cross the road, no less." She dares me to challenge her, a gleam in her eyes.

I . . . did not know that. The driver had stopped in the middle of the road, and I nearly spilled coffee on myself. My irritation had boiled over, resulting in the honk. "I will have to apologize for the outburst," I reply to Gladys somberly.

With Ivy long ago released from my reality and with Jenna's betrayal leaving me vulnerable, it's been my daughter or nothing. My heart feels like stone. Other than my brief interaction with Sparrow today, which wasn't all that great, there's not a chance I've been considered neighborly in this town for the short stint of time we've been here. And I haven't cared one bit about the impression I made. For five years, Emmy has been the sole joy of my existence, and even I'm aware that, one day, she's going to grow up. And the emptiness I feel in my loneliness is going to swallow me whole.

"But I'm not celebrating." My tone is flat and unmoving, but her knowing glare has me confessing the truth. "Christmas is only for my daughter."

"Well, that's no way to live, especially given the fact that your daughter will no doubt be in the upcoming Christmas ballet production. And since Ivy is in desperate need of someone to help build the sets, I'm seeing an incredible opportunity here. I feel it in my bones that you are meant to volunteer."

She gives me a grin, and my mind races through this sudden revelation. Ivy needs help? How the woman before me knows I'm capable of building things is beyond me, but I don't dare question her ways.

I can't help Ivy. Now, she knows I have a daughter, so she either thinks I'm married, or with someone, or that whoever came after our brief meeting must mean more to me than she did. I'll always respect the mother of my child. Yet, in this moment, after seeing Ivy again, it's so clear to me that what I had with Jenna wasn't love, even from the start. But I want Ivy to have the very best in this world, which I suspect confirms there was once something that could have been love between us.

"For the record, I tried with her once," I admit, hitching my head toward the studio.

Gladys hums, a knowing smile on her face. "So *you're* why she can't seem to find someone to hold on to. You must've made quite an impression."

My jaw clenches at the casual way Gladys just told me that Ivy is single. Did she wait for me?

At my reaction, she nods, and I see a hint of compassion overtaking her face, her cheeks reddened from the wind. "I don't know what happened between you two, but you can't protect your heart forever, dearest. At some point, you've gotta find someone worthy of giving love another try."

The words make me grimace again, and I resist the stirring in my heart as music from the studio is sent our way on the wind.

"Perhaps for you, she is the worthiest of them all."

My eyes gravitate back to the dance studio, the warm light pulling me toward it like a beacon. What would it look like for me to put my heart in someone else's hands again? But not just someone—the woman who once gave me reason to believe fairy tales might be possible. Am I even capable of loving again?

I shake the urge to tell Ivy everything from my mind. "I'm not sure . . ." I begin, looking over my shoulder toward Gladys. But I find that I'm talking to myself, and Gladys has disappeared, taking my courage with her into the darkness.

Chapter Seven

Jace

Isn't the Christmas Village magical?" The question from a townsperson I don't know rings clear throughout the space. I'm surprised I can hear her since the noise level at the village is next level. Birch Borough has transformed into a makeshift North Pole to make Santa feel at home.

"I don't think what you're feeling is magic," I retort gruffly toward the voice, not caring that my tone is one step away from feral. I want to rip the advertisement poster for the Christmas parade from the brick wall that leads to the entrance of this Christmas fest. I glance at the woman next to me, sadly realizing that this is going to be the most awkward moment with Ivy I've encountered yet. "I'm not sure I'm going to survive this," I mutter, and she glances up at me but doesn't speak.

I have no idea why I'm still here.

Her hair is tucked up into the bun I've seen her wear more often than not. Wisps of hair frame her face, and I have to admit how much I want to feel their softness between my fingers. She's wearing a long red coat, and the sight of it brings me back to eight years ago. Leggings hug her strong, defined legs, and a turtleneck sweater and scarf keep her elegant, slender neck warm. Mittens also cover her hands. She's bundled up against the winter chill, and she looks like a Christmas miracle. How it's possible that she's even more beautiful than when we first met, I don't know.

The biggest difference between now and our first meeting is that Ivy is not smiling at me tonight. In fact, she looks like I'm the last person she wants to see. And it's killing me.

With all the festive people milling around us, there's nowhere to get out of the way. This afternoon, I received a note at my brother's boxing studio that I thought was from Ivy, asking me to meet up with her tonight.

My heart changed tempo as I read the words over and over. But when I arrived at this outrageously festive Christmas Village, and following our awkward greeting, it turned out that Gladys tricked us into meeting each other. Neither of us initiated the notes delivered today. In the space of a few hours, my hopes soared to the sky and crashed to the depths, making both of us miserable.

Moments ago, Ivy took one look at me and spun on her heels to get away from me as fast as her legs could carry her. She turned toward the entrance to the village, and suddenly, Ollie from the toy shop appeared at her side. I had no idea he could move that fast. Ollie threaded Ivy's arm through his. I felt a sharp smack against my legs. I jumped forward, but the series of painful taps continued. Ollie herded us, tapping my legs with his cane until we passed through the gate.

"What in the world?" I mutter as I find myself trapped in a wave of people just past the entrance to the village. It seems everyone in town is here tonight, and they are all crowding to enter the attraction at once. The hand-painted sign that reads "Welcome to the North Pole" only confirms my earlier suspicions. Now, there's only one way out, and it requires going forward through this maze of holiday cheer. The road is shut down near the pavilion, and one side of the river is paved with endless rows of booths and outdoor heaters. On the way in, I spotted homemade ornaments and crafting tables, photo booths, and fudge stations, plus chances to win prizes, purchase gifts, and enjoy local businesses. The scene is community at its finest, with people from all around supporting each other. It's perfectly festive and cheerful, except I'm trying to avoid people and not be caught up in an actual multitude of them. I'm especially not interested in the carolers. I've heard quite enough from them each night as they move throughout the town, singing songs that remind me of Mina and better days.

Ivy moves ahead, the crowd behind us pushing us through the village. I don't have any choice but to follow her. I'm right on her heels, trying not to crowd her. She has barely managed to look at me, and this feels like my nightmare, despite the smell of cookies all around us (I'm convinced there must be some sort of air fresheners affixed to the buildings, pumping out the scent of holiday baked goods).

Emmy is with Angie tonight, learning to make gingerbread cream pie. I thought I was meeting Ivy because she wanted to see me. That alone was enough to make me more prone to endure this holiday cheer. Now, the sight of cheerful people decked out for the upcoming homemade ugly sweater contest feels like a snowball to the face.

My younger self would've loved this environment—an entire Christmas Village to explore—but today, the discomfort I feel is shadowing any potential for joy. The feeling is absolutely weird. I'm questioning everything, the anxiety working through my frame. I've been avoiding all of this . . . happiness and engaging in any festive event in Birch Borough.

Because you don't deserve it.

Jenna's words echo through my mind, and I shake my head to try to get the poison of them out. Suddenly, a soft voice speaks just ahead of me, her head turning slightly back over her shoulder.

"I'm uncomfortable too, okay?" Ivy's arms are wrapped around her waist, her posture rigid and tentative.

I stride up beside her, not wanting to miss a word if she chooses to keep speaking to me. It strikes me that she can sense my thoughts, despite the time and distance that have kept us far away from each other for years. I just want a semblance of what we once had, but it doesn't exist anymore. The man I once was—carefree and full of hope— disappeared the night Mina passed away . . .

"You're not the same," Ivy speaks quietly, but I hear her clearly. Of course I do. I'd recognize her smoky voice if it came from across the ocean. The buzz of this Christmas Village can't erase my awareness of her.

Her gaze settles over me, as if appraising what else could be different about me now. I don't like to think of what she'll find.

"Were you with someone when we met?"

Her unexpected question shocks me. It freezes my feet to the frosty ground. A few people behind us push around me, but I don't budge. Moving ahead, Ivy's pace doesn't slow. When she realizes she's left me behind, she turns and walks back to stand before me. She's so delicate that my frame completely protects her from the crowd.

"When we met"—her breath hitches audibly—"were you with someone? Please tell me the truth. Were you married already?"

She believes I could deceive her like that. I can understand how, from her perspective, her low opinion of me is valid. But the questions send ice running through my veins.

"No." My teeth are clenched so tightly I think they might break. I stare down at her, feeling the heat blazing out from my eyes. "I was not married or dating anyone when we met."

Right now, I register that Ivy is standing in the same position she stood when she kissed me that night years ago, except she's looking at me with disdain instead of affection. Despite my frustration, I want to wrap my arms around her, but I hold myself back. My grip isn't strong enough when it comes to my heart. Instead, I push a hand through my hair and watch her trace the movement.

She isn't done. "Why do you have a clock tattooed on your hand?" Her eyes focus on the antique design I had etched into my skin a few years before I met Ivy. Back then, I was newly graduated, young, and haunted by the idea of life changing suddenly. Even before Mina's accident, our uncle had recently passed away, and the loss changed how I looked at time.

Now, my jaw clenches, but this time, I can't stop the

words from rushing out. Not with Ivy. "It's a reminder that I won't be here for long. None of us will be, really." I pause, the weight of what I just said settling around us. "And it reminds me to be grateful for every moment, even when they're hard to move through."

"The vines are new." It's a statement, not a question.

I search her face, the idea that she spotted the more recently inked difference messing with my mind. "Yes, they are."

But she's not looking at me now, her gaze pulled away to focus on the catalyst for our current embarrassment. Ollie, now dressed as a certain famous snowman, marches up the walkways with flyers for his toy shop, complete with his cane tapping the frozen ground. A flash of guilt overtakes me. I really shouldn't have left the shovel on the sidewalk where it had fallen. Had I known he had a bad hip, I wouldn't have let my irritation with the world stop me from helping him.

Accidentally, Ivy's arm bumps into mine. When she inhales sharply, I know the contact was frustratingly accidental. "The vines," she says, her eyes lifting to mine.

I watch as her hand rises, and her fingers hover over my hand, but she doesn't touch me. There may as well be an ocean between us, even though there's really only a few inches. My voice comes out sharper than I'd like, but I'm going to tell her the truth, even if I'm not happy about having to do it. "Well, a certain woman inspired it. It's not quite ivy, but the idea is the same. It's wrapped around my thoughts on time." My lungs are heavy, and I wonder if I'm going to pass out near the peppermint bark booth.

"How long?" Ivy stares at my chest instead of my face.

"How long, what?"

Her eyes are glassy as she swallows. "How long after we met did you get those vines?"

This festive environment doesn't feel like the time to tell her about Mina, so I settle for the general timeframe. "Two months later."

Ivy wraps her scarf more tightly around her neck and resumes walking forward. I exhale, wanting to express every word I've ever longed to say to her, hoping it's enough to right these wrongs. All I can think of is how much I want to wrap her in my arms.

Instead, I trail along beside her. Ivy pauses near a station where you can create your own ornament. Her slender fingers wrap around an ice skate, and I swallow against the memory.

"You don't look happy," she observes.

She's right.

The last time I was truly happy—besides the joy Emmy has brought to my life—was the night we met. That was the last night I hugged my little sister, my best friend. I take in Ivy's profile, willing the years to reverse, to give us a do-over. She makes me want to return to who I was before the happiness turned into heartache.

"I want to be happy again." My voice halts, the confession shocking me. I shouldn't have admitted that. Ivy releases the ornament, placing it on the table as laughter echoes around us. Shopping bags from unsuspecting shoppers bump us absentmindedly, and someone with a coffee cart near the gazebo is yelling, "Get your eggnog!"

"So what happened to your happiness?"

Her concern is tangible, but it confuses the part of me

that has convinced myself I'll never be worth that level of care and attention. I open my mouth to tell her just how unsure I am that I could ever be fully happy again when a child dressed as a reindeer with a red nose crashes into my legs. He nearly bounces off me from the impact while I barely move. I reach down to steady him to make sure he doesn't get thrown to the pavement.

As he rushes off with a group of other children, someone's mother trailing behind and advising them that reindeer need to fly straight and not bump into people, I make a mental note to order one of the costumes online for Emmy tonight. I think she'll love it since Rudolph is her favorite Christmas character.

"More pressing question: When do you leave?" Ivy's body language is attempting to be nonchalant, but her voice is strained.

Seeing her tension punches me in the gut harder than any match I've ever been in. "Emmy and I are planning to move to Florida by Christmas," I manage to get out. "My parents moved there recently, and it feels like a chance to be near them. To start over."

She bobs her head up and down a little too vigorously. "But Edgar and Angie are staying around here?"

"Yes."

"Interesting." Her shoulders rise nearly to her ears before I see her take a breath and close her eyes.

When she opens them again, the fierceness in their hot-chocolate depths almost knocks me out once more. At this rate, I'm going to be involved in a technical knockout where a figurative referee will call this before I'm able to get up. Nothing about this situation is what I expected it to be. I thought I'd see Ivy in town and then get back to my life. She would have moved on; I wouldn't have. But I'm struck with the feeling that if I leave this town now, I might as well stay down for the count on the mat of my love life.

After seeing her again, I can't deny how I feel. I want Ivy to know me again.

Despite the truth that I want to ignore, I dare to step a bit closer, close enough to smell her warm scent of vanilla and some musky, spicy note that I've associated only with her since the night we first met.

Slowly, we continue walking through the booths, Ivy stopping next at a homemade candlemaker. I open the tops of a few jars, half-listening to the world around me and half-trying to figure out how I can find out more about her life. I'm surprised she isn't doing everything she can to escape me now that the crowd has cleared some, but maybe she is as stuck as I feel. I shouldn't ask questions about her life, but something in me knows I will. Because as disciplined and strategic as I am and have been—in my business and the boxing ring—I let my guard down on love and have never won a round.

After Ivy purchases a vanilla-candy-cane candle, I grab the bag for her, careful not to make contact with her hands. Touching Ivy only to have her reject me is something I know I wouldn't be able to recover from right now.

"Oh, what a gentleman," the older man behind the counter croons, wrapping his arm around the woman I assume is his wife. "It's nice to see young people who have some chivalry in them still."

Now that I'm in my mid-thirties, I'm not that young, and I'm not dating Ivy. The thought is depressing. I give some sort of nod and a grunt, not having the heart to correct them, and turn to move to the next booth.

"Oh, we're not together," Ivy hastens to correct him.

The words cause my insides to churn. I picture her here in this life. One day, she'll be with someone else who will hold her bags and wrap his arm around her. And I'm furious at just the thought. Her future hasn't even happened yet, and the sickness in my stomach is enough for me to grimace.

A few feet away stands a man dressed as an elf. He's holding a basket of candy canes that says *Take One* in what can only be described as a font from the North Pole. The candy calls to me. I take one and rip some of the plastic off with my teeth, shoving the end of it into my mouth while holding the hook. The sweet, cool peppermint immediately takes effect, and I sigh.

It's only then that I register Ivy looking at me, her eyes so wide it's almost comical. Repositioning the candy cane, I draw it out slowly. Her eyes grow even wider. We stare at each other for a few seconds, or perhaps it's minutes. I don't know what to say or do, so I casually put the candy back into my mouth and clock how her eyes linger on my lips.

Wait. Does she find this attractive? A candy cane?

Testing my theory, I pull the candy cane out of my mouth once again and flash a grin, not because I'm trying to be cool, but because I feel so totally *uncool* at this moment. Yet, her composure is clearly affected by what I'm doing. Is this my newfound way to get Ivy to think of me as she used to? Do I need to start hoarding candy canes?

"You all right, Starlight?" The once-upon-a-time nickname slips out with a hint of disbelief.

Her breath hitches. She focuses on the edges of my

mouth as, for a third time, with a little influx of confidence, I let the candy hang from my mouth. I raise my chin slightly, not able to help the widening smile that breaks across my face as I hold it with my teeth.

Her eyes drop from mine, and it's my turn to focus on her full lips, painted a holiday red. I want to know if she still tastes like candy cane hot chocolate and wishes. I could never taste peppermint again without thinking of her, so I banned it from my life years ago. But not anymore. Peppermint is back in my life. The thought of it has me grinning even wider.

"I . . . yes . . . okay."

She can barely get the words out, and my crotchety mood dissipates as I beam. A candy cane can fluster the ballerina. Who knew? I rotate back toward the elf with the basket. Reading my mind, he points me toward a booth a few rows down with homemade boxes of the candies. I pull out a bill from my wallet and toss it on the table while taking a box. I pay way too much for it, but I don't care if Ivy is going to look at me like this.

Her expression is both familiar and foreign. Something seems to have shifted between us in the last few minutes. I have no idea how to be anything more to this woman; I have no idea if I even should try. But my heart whispers its plans when she looks at me. I can't see straight—clearly, because I've paid twenty dollars for one box of the peppermint hooks.

Just as I realize I'm holding candy canes tucked under my arm, the elf laughs and hands me his basket. "Here. I think you need this more than I do." He pats me on the shoulder, shaking his head and walking to the table I just threw money on in the name of unhinged attraction for the woman beside me.

"So this way?" I say with the end of the candy cane still in my mouth. From this moment forward, candy canes, along with hot chocolate, now only belong to Ivy in my mind.

Tensely, she nods, and we keep moving through the booths, passing Christmas cookies and festive housewares, artisan ceramics, jewelry, art prints, and a bright-blue-and-gold tent featuring menorahs. We walk in silence. The end of the row approaches, and I feel Ivy's coat sleeve brush my own. I flinch at the minimal contact, my hand whipping behind my back as I pull my arm away.

Her eyes widen. "I'm so sorry. I didn't mean to . . ." Her cheeks redden.

I swallow. "It's not you." The words are forced but true.

Ivy's eyebrows lift. "Oh, okay. Well, I'm sorry. We just . . ." Her eyes swim with unshed tears, and so help me, if she starts crying here, I'll be joining her.

"Don't worry about it," I say sharply, the discomfort from seeing her emotion tightening my chest. "I'll be gone soon anyway, and you can go back to life as usual."

At that, a tear falls down Ivy's cheek, and my heart cracks. I yank the candy cane out of my mouth and hold it by my side as I move out of the way with the hope that she'll follow me. To my shock, she does, and we find refuge from the crowd in an alcove between booths, next to a Christmas tree that is decorated with what looks like a few hundred nutcrackers tucked among the branches.

"Why is this . . . seeing you . . . talking to you so hard?" She says the words to my chest, her eyes still not rising to mine.

I know that it's better this way—if she thinks I'm disingenuous and angry—but the question feels like another punch to the gut. I sigh, and her gaze hooks on my mouth. Finally, she meets my gaze. *There she is.* My breathing accelerates; my hands clench into fists. "You don't owe me anything, Ivy."

I don't want to bring up her brother or Mina yet. I think if I told Ivy what really happened that Christmas now, I'd collapse on the sidewalk from the pain of it.

She sniffs slightly and turns her head to look across the sea of people celebrating the holidays surrounding us. "Haven't ice skated since." With this confession, she turns back to me and shrugs, knocking the heels of her boots together.

I will myself not to make any sudden movements that would steal from me the sudden revelation that, perhaps like me, Ivy has never fully moved on. I was a hollow version of myself when Jenna came along, trying to forget instead of heal. I'd given in to the idea that I was only my appearance and only my profession. I hid my reading glasses and stopped enjoying fiction books, replacing my favorites with leadership titles. I only listened to classical music and musicals in my car. I stopped eating carbs. In short, I was miserable. And it was never enough.

"Let's get this over with," she says dejectedly as she steps into the crowd once more.

We round a corner, the exit finally in sight. A man with a great voice is on a stage, singing Christmas carols, a band behind him. Ivy stills. I freeze behind her, my frame covering her, protecting her from the chilly wind whipping through and the crowd's prying eyes.

She repositions herself to face me, lifting her chin to look into my eyes. I tilt my head down to get closer. It hits me with full force that she has no idea I tried to find her or that her brother knows about my search. He's the one who told me to stay away. I don't want to start any conflict with her family. Jenna tried to start rumors within my family when we were together, and it was a nightmare.

But I owe her more of the truth. She deserves that much from me. I decide to start with the night I wasn't there for her. "I tried to get to you that night, but my sister, Mina . . ." I begin, and the emotion chokes me.

Ivy's brows lift. "The one I met over the phone?"

I'm shocked that she remembers the conversation, but it's also a beautiful realization that Mina talked to her at all. "Yeah." I swallow and gather my courage. "Edgar called me when I was on my way to meet you again. Mina had been in a car accident. She didn't have much time left. I was told to get to the hospital as soon as possible."

Ivy's sharp inhale loosens some of the grief I've buried.

"By the time I got there, she was gone. And after that, things just sort of . . . fell apart."

Her mittened hands covering her mouth, a tear falls down Ivy's cheek. Instinctively, I catch it with my thumb before dropping my hand back to my side.

"That's terrible. Jace, I'm so sorry."

"Yeah, it was. *It is.* I miss her every day."

Ivy's eyes drift to the carolers passing nearby. "Angie has a picture of Mina in her shop, doesn't she?"

I nod, knowing she's thinking of the picture of Angie and Mina when they were teenagers, taken out near the ocean, a lighthouse behind them as they wear bibs on a picnic bench and hold up bright-red lobsters.

"That's Mina." I grin sadly, the memory enough to remind me that not everything in the world used to feel so heavy.

"She's beautiful." The way Ivy doesn't use the past tense to refer to my sister endears me even more to her.

"So, that's why I wasn't there." My voice is quiet, sounding almost like it's coming from outside of myself.

"Losing her must've been—must *be*—really hard. It sounds like you've lost so much, Jace. And I'm really sorry for that."

She's giving me a look of empathy mixed with uncertainty. Now, she knows why I wasn't there for her. She doesn't yet know the lengths I went to find her. But I don't feel like I can rat out her brother for something I probably would've done too if someone hadn't shown up for Angie. After all, I hadn't even had the chance to tell him about Mina's passing that day at the cookie shop. To him, I was just the loser who'd disappointed his sister. And I was too tired at the time to fight his opinion of me.

"Jace, I . . ." Ivy's voice breaks the silence, something softer within her tone. "I know you're not here for very long, but . . . would you . . . I mean, would you want to try to get to know each other again—or rather, for the first time— while you're here?"

Incredulously, I stare at her. Is it possible that she just said what I heard her say? Her question adds a weighted vest to my chest. I want to give in to her hot-chocolate eyes, her voice laced with compassion, her expression—tentative but hopeful. The emotion builds toward the backs of my eyes, and I scrunch my nose. The idea of starting over and leaving everything behind is more appealing by the second. Because facing my past and this woman is already proving to be agony. I want to be near her. But the truth of what that would mean for me feels like my heart is about to enter a twelve-round championship match in a ring.

She lifts her chin a little higher, giving me a perfect glimpse of her cheekbones, the curve of her mouth, and the slope of her neck under the turtleneck. I have a lot of love to give, but it's trapped beneath my hands. I'm scared to touch her again, never mind to love her. I may have grown over the years, but for this battle, I'm not yet strong enough.

I've come a long way since Jenna. I've developed as a dad, as a trainer, and as a woodworker. But I'm stuck. My love life is on the floor of the ring, with one count remaining before I tap out. The last thing I want to do is disappoint her again.

Her eyes search my face, trailing deliciously over every feature. I would be self-conscious, but the heat in her gaze has burned it away. Even if I shouldn't allow her in, I want her to see me. I want her to know me. If I had one Christmas wish, it would be that she would have the chance to know me like no one else ever has. But I'm just not strong enough to risk my heart yet.

"I'm sorry, Ivy. But you shouldn't hope for anything."

Ivy steps away from me, a fiery determination replacing the softness in her eyes. "You know, Jace, all those years ago, I thought I might have found someone special. I should've known better than to expect a Christmas miracle."

With that, she spins around, and her red coat disappears through the exit. I'm left behind, the noise of the village adding to the loneliness that I've gifted to myself.

Even with the added clarity of Ivy's opinion of me, her presence at this unexpected meeting and unexpected confession was enough to crack something in my ribs like a glow stick.

I realize that I've never before had to prove myself to her. When we flirted, shared, and hoped in those few hours we experienced together, it came as naturally to me as anything else. As I walk back to Angie's with tinsel somehow stuck to my coat, the urge to begin reading a new fantasy series that's still in its plastic wrap on my bookshelf at home consumes me. It may not be much, but it's a stirring of the version of me I used to like. It's a line of piped frosting on a plain gingerbread man, indicating it's nowhere near finished but more complete than when I arrived.

Chapter Eight

Ivy

In an unexpected turn of events, Jace and I spent time with each other at the Christmas Village a few days ago, and somehow, I survived. When I showed up and discovered that I'd been tricked, I tried to leave, but the crowd (and Ollie and Gladys) forced us together. It turns out that it was an opportunity to talk to the man I once knew, but the experience might as well have been walking through a metaphorical graveyard that refused to revive the man I once knew.

It's not like we waited for each other. We had one impromptu date that I've thought about for the past eight years, but now he's all rough edges where once he seemed so smooth. The shock that he was and is still single rattles my heart.

I've thought of him. I pictured him married and raising kids. It turns out that at least part of what I imagined is true. His daughter is the most adorable little girl I've ever taught. When she joined my class, I felt that same sense of knowing each other before we even met that I felt with Jace. My heart wishes I knew the reason.

And now, tonight is Birch Borough's Christmas Parade. As the end of November merges into December, our town enters a season of event after event to celebrate the holiday spirit. I love it; I really do. But I'm just not sure I'm in the mood to see Liam dressed as Buddy the Elf and his social-media famous cat, A-cat-pella, on a float, followed by Mayor Brooks in a Santa suit riding on top of a Wicked Good Farms pickup truck. If we're lucky, some of the local high school kids will launch snowflake confetti into the air out of miniature cannons to mark the official start of the season. I'm not sure I'm ready for any of it.

I tap my boot on the sidewalk, focusing on the unlit LED snowflakes that have been strung across the street. Their clear structure sticks out against the milky grey sky. With a shiver, I wrap my coat more tightly around my waist, waiting for Grey as I wrestle with my thoughts.

This year, not only has Jace been on my mind ever since he showed up at my dance studio, but all I can think about is how much I still need someone to help me with my Christmas ballet production. The start of this season of spirited events just means that we're that much closer to our performances, and I still don't have a set or a backdrop for our condensed version of *The Nutcracker* and a holiday special. When I took over the studio, instead of putting on a whole big production of the famous ballet, I decided to take a few of the famous numbers, make them my own, and then add in a few festive pieces to round it out. That way, I ensured every one of my students could get involved and feel like they matter to our success without the pressure of competing with every other nearby studio and company who also perform the celebrated ballet.

In addition, I also knew I could never achieve the level of performance I've done in cities across the world on my own. And besides the few people who have volunteered to help with setup, I've pretty much been on my own as the town's resident dance teacher.

But since Andy from Fixin's Hardware Store fell off a ladder a few weeks ago (thankfully, he only sprained his ankle and his pride), my go-to set designer is out of commission. I don't know how to do the production this year without him, and everyone else in town has been signed up since last year with their own respective holiday duties. I could seek out help from someone in a surrounding town, but that feels like sacrilege, considering this is a Birch Borough event. For town events, we don't bring in outside assistance. Our general sentiment is *Why would we?*

"Ivy!"

I hear a masculine voice behind me, the single word cutting through the wind. When I turn, Edgar is walking toward me. He's nearly running to catch up with me even though I am standing still. I'm guessing he always moves as if he's approaching a finish line. We've never become close friends since he moved to town, but we've been friendly. Edgar is a nice guy. We don't see him as often as his sister. But as he approaches, I feel the flush creeping up my neck because I can't believe I didn't see the similarities between him and Jace before.

In the past, when Edgar mentioned a brother, it was always an abstract reference. Now that I know his brother is Jace, all the times he talked of a brother feel like I've been living in a dream, a whole series of unknown events orchestrating me back to that one night. One night that ended up being a dream turned nightmare that I can't seem to escape from.

"Do you need me for something, Edgar?" I ask, finding my voice. I want to try to end this conversation before it has even started.

"Yeah," he says. "I just wanted to say that I found someone who could help you with your production. I was going to volunteer, but I think I'd do more harm than good . . ."

At the look of possibility on his face, I will him not to say what I think is coming.

"But Jace can build anything," he continues.

My heart sinks. And there it is. I look at the bunches of snow hovering near our feet. There's no chance I will recruit Jace to help me, no matter how desperate I am for my sets to be built before our production. "That's very kind of you to try to help me," I begin.

Edgar's brow furrows at my hesitation, a line between his eyes appearing. "He really is good. I can have him send some samples or photos or something?"

I cringe, partially because I do need the help, and I'd do anything for my students. The other part of the cringe is because, for once, I don't know how to gracefully get out of this one. He's clearly not aware of the tension between Jace and me. And if Edgar doesn't know that Jace and I connected years ago, that doesn't bode well for having a lasting impact on his life. After all, I couldn't wait to tell Grey and my family after I had the best date of my life.

"I appreciate the thought, Edgar. I do. But . . ." My words trail off as I see Jace leave Angie's pie shop, a box of one of her delectable pies in hand. His other hand is holding Emmy's tiny mittened one. She catches sight of me with her uncle across the street.

"Miss Ivy!" Emmy's voice rings out through the night, causing a few people to chuckle nearby. If only I could fuel this night with her energy. "Miss Ivy!" she yells again, her little frame pulling Jace toward us, even though I know that's impossible, given his strength.

The fact that he follows her means he's either in shock at seeing me again so soon or is content to follow Emmy's will. I fold over to get to eye level with Emmy as they cross the street, willing my gaze not to sneak its way toward Jace.

"Are you ready for the parade tonight, Emmy?" I'm proud of the way I was able to get the words out. *Focus, Ivy.* It's not Emmy's fault that her dad doesn't want to be around me. The little girl practically squeals and turns toward the line of townspeople gathering along the streets, all of us waiting for the mayor to announce the parade's start.

"Bro," Edgar announces while patting Jace's back in that semi-affectionate hug that only men seem to get away with.

"Eddie," resounds the gritty voice that I've been dreaming about for only the past eight years and eighteen hours. Over the course of my life, I've received hundreds of comments on my own voice—its smokiness and tone—but if I could choose one male voice to narrate the story of my life or just the directions on my phone, I'd choose his. Hearing it now, even after all these years, even after all that's transpired, it makes me want to dance and stand still simultaneously. I'm restless and calm all at once.

"Dude, you know you can't call me that."

"I can and I will," Jace retorts.

I hold back a silent laugh at the look of indignation that flashes across Edgar's face. Sneaking a look at Jace, I catch a grin hitching up one side of his still-moody mouth. The sight of it nearly makes me dizzy.

"Listen, Ivy needs some help . . ." Edgar starts, and my mind goes blank.

Oh no. Oh no. Oh no. "Really, it's fine. I'm fine." The lie feels salty on my tongue.

"You have someone else?" Edgar asks quickly.

"Well, not exactly, but there are some . . . prospects." The last word causes me to wince. It's what my parents call the men they try to set me up with when a new guest stays at the inn and recommends their son or grandson. If I had a fish bowl of all the business cards that I've gotten from my parents with the numbers of strange men on them, it would be overflowing. I'm convinced they have a picture of me hidden near their front desk that they whip out to show anyone eligible visiting Birch Borough. It's the stuff of romance, their matchmaking skills.

Jace's eyebrow lifts in my peripheral vision. Suddenly, we're in a battle of wills. I'm determined not to look at him again, but I can feel that his gaze doesn't leave my face, the fire from his eyes like a laser beam burning up my cheeks and bringing a flush of heat to my bones.

"What exactly does she need?" Jace asks, the question clearly directed to his brother as I become a third person in this sentence structure. I don't know what metaverse we've entered, but it's clear we're trying to draw lines in the sand while the tide is coming in. It's impossible and messy.

"Sets. For her Christmas show. Her contractor was in an accident."

I focus on Edgar, hoping he doesn't wonder why I'm only staring at him and Emmy and not looking at his brother. But I just can't give in to the desire.

"Miss Ivy, my daddy builds things! Don't you, Daddy?"

My heart is racing so fast I should be on a spinning ride and not standing on the street of the town I've known my whole life.

"Yes, I do. I build things," he replies smoothly. He adjusts his sherpa-lined bomber jacket. I'm sure the warmth trapped inside is enough to last me the whole winter. As if sensing my thoughts, he nods gravely. "In fact, you could say it's something I'm *known* for."

My face heats again at the reminder of our date ages ago.

"But I don't think I can help this time, Emmy," he continues.

At this, I give myself permission to search his face, while a car horn beeps with delight. It sounds throughout the night, signaling the start of the parade. In the few minutes we've been standing on the sidewalk, people have crowded around us, doing their best to view what will soon be the annual Birch Borough Christmas Parade. Music from the season starts to play across the air, the speakers no doubt installed by Liam and his music store. Michael Bublé's voice rings through the night, and I dare to look at Jace once more.

He's already looking straight at me.

And then we're frozen, staring at each other like it's the first time and the last. I hate it. Because how can you share moments with someone, even from years ago, and they live on in your memory in such a way that you've been permanently marked? It's as if your heart was split like a river by the encounter, and no matter how hard you try, affection will flow into its stream, never ending, always wanting to find its way back to you.

"Daddy, do it," Emmy insists, her little arms crossed in front of her. "'Help others where you can.' That's what you tell me."

Jace winces and clears his throat.

"Don't you want my first show to look *amazinggggg*?" The emphasis on the end of the word makes Edgar and me laugh. Jace remains a statue.

"Ivy!" Grey's voice carries over the crowd before she arrives to stand beside me, her cheeks flushed and her cat-eye glasses reflecting the lights around us. Her mittened hands are full of to-go cups of what I know is hot chocolate. Emmy's eyes sparkle at the sight. There's no way I can drink this in front of her without sharing. Something pulls toward her, and I know that I won't enjoy it unless she's enjoying some too.

"Oh, hello," Grey says sweetly, her eyes tracking the semi-circle of people we've constructed, widening slightly when they move up to Jace. She clears her throat lightly and reveals a genuine smile. This is why she's my best friend in the whole world. She knows me enough to understand that I'm slowly dying inside and need a sense of normalcy tonight. Hot chocolate and Grey being her friendly self is normal—comforting, even.

Edgar and Jace give her a nod, the similarity of their gestures uncanny. "Ja—is it okay?" I motion to Jace, unable to say his name out loud again quite yet. I motion to my hot chocolate and down to Emmy. Grey has also bent lower to introduce herself, their conversation moving quickly between books and dance. Our favorite things. Jace glances at the cup and then at his daughter. His gaze meets mine again, its intensity pulsing through my fingers.

"Thank you," he says preemptively.

I will myself to keep moving. "Emmy?" I ask. "Would you like some hot chocolate?"

Her face turns toward me so quickly that her little ponytail whips across her face. She laughs. "Yes!" Her fist lifts into the air, her smile turned to the stars.

There's such a sense of joy mixed with abandon in her demeanor that it hits me in my core. When was the last time I did anything with that much excitement? I kneel on the ground, my knees registering the chill on the cobblestone street beneath us with zero regrets. Excitedly, Emmy stamps her feet, reaching for the cup. Her hands wrap around the middle while I support the bottom with my own as she sips. She hums when she tastes it, the sound bringing a smile to my face. This is who the hot chocolate was meant for all along, and I'm okay with tradition changing if it means more moments of absorbing her joy like this. She leans back, a line of chocolate on her top lip, then lunges at me and throws her arms around my neck.

"Thanks, Miss Ivy," she says in the way only children can do when they're trying to be quiet, but the whole town can still hear them.

"You're welcome, sweets," I say with a sad smile. I realize that I've been waiting for a little one to hold like this for a long time. And while Emmy isn't my own, a feeling of protectiveness stirs within me. I want to say it's because I care for my students, but catching Jace's tilted brow as he stares at us tells me there's more to all of this than being a good dance teacher. And in another life, maybe someone like

Emmy could've been mine. But such has not been my life. The thought of all that I haven't obtained from life sobers me.

I stand, holding back the emotion and the phantom feeling of Emmy's embrace still lingering around my neck like a scarf. "So Grey and I should get going. My parents saved a spot for us near the inn." I'm inordinately proud of stringing a full sentence together after another awkward encounter with the mountain of a man in front of me.

"Right, well, thanks for making Emmy so happy," Edgar says as I hand him the cup of hot chocolate that now belongs to his niece.

"Of course. Any—" I look up to meet Jace's gaze. "Time."

Time. Something I wish we had and know we don't. As if in response, his left hand rises to run through his hair, the tattoo of that clock face now facing the night sky. The vines wrapping around it pull at my hesitation.

"Oh, Ivy, it's the strangest thing . . ." Edgar continues, suddenly looking between Jace and me. "Doesn't she look just like the Polaroid you had on your shelf all those years ago, Jace? The one in that little frame . . ."

His jaw clenches so hard I can almost hear it. He had our photo on a shelf? We took a photo at Four Leaf Cookies. The owner kept a camera handy for couples, featuring their photos on a wall in the shop. I don't know how Jace got his hands on it.

He leans down to pick up Emmy; the only indication he's heard his brother talking about a photo of us is the faint blush on his cheeks.

It seems Edgar isn't done. "What did you call her . . .

something with a star . . .?"

"Starlight!" Emmy yells.

I cough, the shock of inhaling the bitterly cold air so quickly impossible to keep down.

"We really should be going," Grey intercepts, sliding her arm through mine and pulling us back toward the inn. The floats are starting to move on the street behind us, the local marching band playing through the air.

"Remember, if you need help," Edgar calls after me, "Jace is your guy."

I used to wish for that very thing to be true. I allow Grey to guide our steps toward the inn, staring at Ted on a float with some of his rescue pets and the ugliest Christmas sweater I've ever seen, my mind racing. The reality of the time Jace and I have been apart runs me over like the person in the middle of the line at a Black Friday sale. Little does anyone know just how much I used to wish for Jace with all of my heart.

Chapter Nine

Jace

Jace is your guy.

But am I?

My brother's words to Ivy a few days ago simultaneously thrill and haunt me. There was a time when I wanted to consider myself a contender for Ivy's heart. The fact that Mina knew about her isn't lost on me. It makes me want to both fight for her heart and insist she leave me alone. When Ivy asked if I wanted to get reacquainted with each other, I refused. And I know refusing to be friends with Ivy isn't solving anything. Not immediately agreeing to help her with her production isn't looking good for me either.

I enrolled Emmy in kindergarten at Birch Borough Elementary until the holidays, and I take a walk around town while she is in school. It wasn't easy to get her enrolled so quickly, but her principal took one look at Emmy and caved (thankfully). Moving to Florida seems more ominous the longer I'm here, though I did promise my parents I'd be there for Christmas morning. I walk to keep myself away from Ivy's studio, needing to keep myself moving during breaks from the boxing classes I teach. Since I walked with Ivy around the Christmas Village, I've been trying to figure out how to keep my heart from hoping for more with her.

Friends, indeed. As if I could ever just be friends with her. I nearly roll my eyes at the thought.

My phone rings. I reach to answer just as I spot a man outside the music store across the street, a guitar case at his feet. His hands move expressively in a manner that seems distinctively French. I wonder if he's Sparrow's husband, Rafe. I recognize him from the stage at the Christmas Village.

I clear my throat but let it go to voicemail. If we talk, my mom will absolutely know that something is changing in my life. She'll also comment on how I'm not sleeping well—which, I'm not. How can I when I'm this close to Ivy and still so far away? I never told Edgar or Angie much about Ivy. It felt like a secret that Mina and I had shared. But I finally told my mom one night when Emmy wouldn't stop crying, and she had made me a hot chocolate. A man can only take so much.

I shove my phone back in my pocket as the man in vintage sneakers and a bomber jacket similar to the one I'm wearing approaches.

"What's up, man? You're Jace, right? I'm Rafe!"

His smile is best described as genuine. It seems like he's actually happy to be here, introducing himself to me. He glances toward Sparrow's Beret, and his smile gets even bigger. Ah, so I was right.

"My wife is Sparrow. Have you tried her croissants?" With a head tilt, he indicates the bakery's direction.

I decide to be polite, especially because I know now that Ivy loves these people. "Yes, I have. Your wife gave me hot chocolate and cookies for my daughter on the house. She was kind."

Rafe positively beams. "Yes, that sounds like her. She's the best person I know. Now, tell me, how are you liking our town so far?"

I look about, the darkened mood I've been carrying lately shifting slightly. "It's a good town." So good that it has me questioning all my life choices.

He sighs with contentment. "It really is. We're all pretty close-knit around here. And word on the partially cobblestoned streets is that you have a history with someone we all care about a lot." His knowing grin is laced with both compassion and amusement.

"Yes," is the only word I can get out. Something in me doesn't want to lie to this man who radiates with the sense of just being a good human.

He reaches up and puts a hand on my shoulder, giving it a press. Our height difference clearly doesn't bother him in the least. Usually, guys try to puff out their chest or do some sort of weird sizing up around me. Immediately, I notice there's none of that with Rafe.

"Then fight for her," he says simply. "Because there's nothing better than being able to hold the one who already holds your heart."

He grins, and I find that I envy him. Here is this man who seems to know exactly who he wants, and he's vocal about it. And I've been . . . avoiding. That's the best word for how I've behaved the past week. But I'm not sure how to fight for her when the rules of the ring have changed. Emmy is certainly a fan of her new dance teacher. My daughter's passionate endorsement makes my mind spin. If Ivy needs sets to be built, I *am* her guy. It may be too late for me to have what Rafe and Sparrow seem to have cultivated, but can I give Ivy whatever I can, even if it feels like all I have to offer are the ransacked leftovers from the last eight years?

"Thank you for that," I reply, clearing my throat and putting an arm around his shoulders. I underestimate my strength, and Rafe tips toward me with a laugh.

"*Attention!*" he exclaims, his accent pronounced. "I need my arms to play music!"

I grin and release him. If first impressions are everything, I already like this guy and have a weird feeling of hoping to see him again. It's a change from the hermit I've been of late. I clear my throat. Running a hand through my hair, I turn my attention back to him.

"You were good. At the Christmas Village."

Rafe seems surprised by my compliment, and I think that I really need to be nicer to the people in this town. Have I really become such a Scrooge?

"Thanks, Jace. I appreciate that." He grins again. "*D'accord*, I'm going to go get a croissant. And kiss my wife. Do you want to walk with me?"

Across the way, I catch sight of Ivy across the street with a golden retriever that is wearing padded snowshoes and reindeer antlers. My throat goes dry. Immediately, I shake my head at Rafe's offer. "Thanks, but I think I'll have to catch you next time."

Rafe follows my gaze and gives a knowing nod. "Got it. Yes, *c'est parti!* See you around. And *bonne chance!*"

Dipping my chin, I step into the crosswalk, waving at the cars that stop for long enough to allow me to get to her.

Her face lifts to mine as I approach. "Hello," she says,

the smokiness in her voice sending a shot of energy to my heart.

"Starlight." The name is a test, an experiment, a prayer.

She scrunches her nose in protest. I want to say it again and have her welcome it.

"You know," she begins, "you probably shouldn't use your nickname for me. I thought we called it after our walk through the Christmas Village."

My stomach tenses. I don't want to think about my behavior with Ivy the other day. The truth is that I want to be near her more than apart from her, so I focus on the individual I haven't met yet. "And who's this?"

Her eyebrow lifts, my attempt at distraction not lost on her, but she allows it. I exhale.

"This is Resin," she says.

Hearing his name, the dog's tail thumps against the sidewalk. While some sections of the sidewalk have been set with cobblestones, we're in a smooth part now. I wonder if it's a sign of my relationship with Ivy. Maybe it can be smoother from this point forward, after we keep moving through the awkward.

"Hi, Resin." I bend a knee to the ground, the cold seeping through my pants. I'm rewarded with the retriever's affection and find my shoulders losing their tension. "He looks festive," I observe with a touch of amusement.

"Yes, well, he just finished walking in the pet parade."

I raise my eyes to hers to see if she's kidding. "The what, now?"

"It's a Christmas parade for pets." The tiny lift of her chin dares me to make fun of it, even though her grin carries a hint of timid playfulness.

"Did he win?" I'm not sure how else to ask about this event.

"It's not a winning or a losing event; it's just about participating."

Resin leans against me and nuzzles into my neck. The cold press of his nose against my skin causes me to release a surprised laugh.

Ivy stares at him. "Wow, he's friendly but not usually this affectionate," she states.

"Well, he knows that I—" I stop myself before blurting out how much Resin's owner means to me. Has *meant* to me. How can I say how much her dog and I both want to follow her anywhere without coming on too strong? How can I explain that, besides Emmy, the woman before me might be the person I want to protect the most in the world? Instead, I clear my throat. "He knows that he's got the best mom," I conclude.

To my alarm, Ivy's eyes fill a bit at my words.

"Did I say something wrong?" I rise swiftly. "Clearly, I did, if it's affecting you like this. I'm sorry. I meant well."

She sniffles lightly, reaching up to wipe her eye with one of her mittens. "No, I'm good. We're okay—about that, at least." She pauses. "I just . . . sometimes, I realize he may be the only one to give me that title, even for a pet." I watch her ballerina posture slump a little. "But that's more than you need to know, right? Since we're not friends and will never be."

I open my mouth and close it again. Ivy wants to have a family? My pent-up affection draws me toward her like the moon to the tide. Inconveniently, it also reminds me that one of the stupidest things I could've believed is that I would be able to stay away from her when I first discovered that we now share the same zip code.

"I shouldn't have said that," she hastens to admit softly. "Can't seem to stop saying things when it comes to you."

Her somber grin nearly sends me to my knees. I decide to help ease her anxiousness by changing the topic.

"I should've said this earlier, but you're not in New York," I add quickly, knowing I'm stating the obvious like a fool who has clearly lost his game once more. Note to self: Carry a candy cane in my pocket for the rest of the season.

Ivy laughs incredulously. "No, I'm not."

Her eyes drift to the inn behind me. When I turn to look over my shoulder, a couple is staring out of one of the windows. They are waving, and a grandmotherly woman beside them is giving a thumbs-up.

"Do you know those people?"

"Yes," Ivy says with a laugh and a half-wave in their direction. "That's my family. Well, some of them. My parents and grandmother. They own the inn."

"Ah, I see. I didn't know that."

"Well, we've never had a chance to talk much about each other's lives." Her words could sound harsh, but instead, they're laced with sadness.

I stare at her as Resin leans against my leg. "No, we didn't." My voice is equally sad.

"So, Emmy is a trip." Ivy's eyes brighten when she mentions my daughter.

I hum. "Yes, she is. Big heart. Lots of dreams." I force myself to say something nice to the unique woman in front of me, something that will test the tension between us. "Thank you for teaching her to dance."

"It's my job."

"Yes, but I know it could be challenging since she's my kid. I don't mean that arrogantly. I just don't want to make you uncomfortable—"

"Please, don't say that." Quickly, her face whips toward me, eyes more fiery than I've ever seen them.

"I don't want my presence in Birch Borough to bother you—"

"It doesn't. At least, not in the way you're implying." Ivy's sigh cracks a part of my heart open. "So, Emmy? Dancing is important to her?"

I clear my throat. "Yes, she—she stopped dancing about a year ago. She asked about her mother one day, and she just . . . stopped."

Her eyes widen.

I continue, "And I—I just wanted to see her dance again. Needed to, I think. And yours is the only dance studio in town."

"Not to mention the best one in the county." Ivy's voice is quiet. "I'm sorry Emmy has experienced so much loss."

Blinking rapidly, I bite the inside of my cheek to keep myself from pouring out the truth of every other part of our lives that has tanked since I last saw Ivy. There have been good things too, but it's the loss that stands out.

Ivy leans in slightly, and I'm pulled to her like a magnetic energy still lives between us. "So, you need help building your sets. Why?"

She looks alarmed at first. Ivy's shoulders lift in a delicate shrug, but then she straightens her spine in a way that makes me proud. She's a fighter, this one. And I respect her for her bravery.

"The guy who always helps me accidentally injured himself, and everyone else is pretty much booked. It's an unspoken rule around here that we don't get people outside of town to help, but we're only weeks away from the performance."

"When is it?"

"It runs right after Christmas, before New Year's," she replies. "We've found a greater turnout when all the families are in town. If I don't have the sets ready in time . . ." She pauses abruptly, softly clearing her throat.

"Makes sense." I pause, watching as Ivy focuses on a distant tree dusted with snow. "What else?"

"What do you mean, 'what else'?" The narrowing of her eyes assures me I'm right to pull at this thread.

"There's more to this. I can tell it's important to you. Before we freeze out here, I'd like to know why."

Ivy shakes her head, and there's a hint of a chatter in her jaw. It's the New England marvel where you see and feel the sun but still can't get warm with the temperature this frigid. "Scholarships are at stake with this performance. Birch Borough is pretty well off as far as towns go. Still, I have so many students who may have what they need to survive daily, but the extra income for dance just isn't there. And I know it's helped me tremendously to move through life. The end-of-year performance is when most of our donations for the whole year come in. I can't let my students down."

Resin tugs her in the direction of the smell of caramelized popcorn near the gift shop on the corner. I can literally see it popping through the window, as fresh as fresh gets. The thought that the scene could be on a greeting card feels typical of how this town operates, and it's wild.

"Not now, love bucket," Ivy says affectionately, redirecting Resin to go the other way.

"Love bucket?" I hold back a rusty chuckle as Ivy's cheeks warm.

"He's been the steadiest man in my life." She smiles, looking down at him, but I watch it fade when her eyes lift to me again.

An ache resurges deep in my chest. I wish I could've had the chance to hold that title.

Even bundled in her red winter coat, I sense how fragile she is next to me. I want to reach out and hold her, to remember just once what she felt like in my arms, and to show her how much affection I'm capable of giving. Instead, I give her another reason to push me away, clearing my throat and letting my learned abruptness slip through.

"I don't think helping you with sets would actually be helpful. Ivy, I'm sure it's clear to you that I'm not the same man that I was when we first met. And I wish I could change it, but you should hear the truth from me."

I think it's going to push her away, but Ivy simply shifts closer, her head tilting up until her hot-chocolate eyes look into mine.

"Yes, I see that. But just so you know, I'm not the same woman." With a small nod, she turns toward the bridge, Resin stepping into place beside her. She takes a few steps away then pauses. Her profile is etched against the winter white sky as she continues, "I still may not fully know what you've been fighting inside, but I can see that you've lost your hope, Jace." Her rose-colored lips quirk to the side. "And I think you should allow yourself to hope for everything."

Chapter Ten

Ivy

We're at Town Hall, gathered to look at the Christmas trees decorated by a few of our most creative townspeople. The fine residents of Birch Borough get to vote on which design is their favorite every year.

It gets quite competitive because the winner earns a gift certificate to the General Store and Sparrow's Beret. We also have an anonymous donor each year who matches the number of votes with dollars that go into a fund for whatever is most needed for various town projects. Last year, the donation went to the library. A few years ago, it was used to invest in a new dance floor for my studio. This year, it's going into the budget to repair a damaged part of the bridge.

It's generosity like this that reminds me of how lovely it is to be a part of a community that cares about each other. Often, I reflect on the fact that we all have within us exactly what we need to make our town better as a collective whole, and the holiday season simply reinforces that belief.

But while I usually enjoy this event (I mean, it's Christmas, and Christmas is my favorite, so, of course I do), tonight, I'm distracted. I haven't even removed my jacket to hang it on the coatrack near the door. It feels like I need the extra warmth to insulate myself tonight—an extra coat of armor, so to speak. For the past thirty minutes, Jace and I have been stealing glances at each other. Or at least, I think he's looking at me. I know I've been sneaking glances at him since he walked in, brushing snow off his jacket. His strong hands were absent of gloves when he arrived. It may have been years since I was last held by him (except in my dreams), but I know the man is a furnace.

I can't help but wonder if I handled our last conversation well. Distancing myself from him after he's returned to my world feels impossible, considering the disappointment I felt in thinking I'd never see him again. Now, knowing what happened the night he didn't show up for our second date has me questioning everything I thought I knew.

Though Jace arrived sans gloves, since he stepped into Town Hall tonight, he's kept his coat on as if he's ready to bolt any second. I've been focused on him the way I focus on learning new choreography. His eyes are slightly wider than usual, his jaw is set like marble, and his hands are clenched in soft fists. For some reason, he seems uncomfortable as he glances about the room, studying the decorated trees. Yet, if I'm correct in my observations, his eyes keep seeking me out. And I notice how those amber eyes that look like rare gems keep catching and reflecting the Christmas lights hanging overhead.

Edgar lingers near him but keeps getting distracted by Gladys, who's clearly made it her mission to introduce him to every available woman in town. I don't know what she's playing at, because I don't think anyone could ever really know what motivates Gladys. Rumor has it that she wants to start a new initiative next summer, a livestream from the pavilion, during which Birch Borough's eligible bachelors (not that there are many) will be voted on like a version of *Survivor* meets a reality-dating show. To the surprise of no one, her tree submission for this contest is covered in random pictures of all the men in this town, including Rafe and Graham. The pictures are labeled with months of the year at the bottom. Her tree is topped with a star painted with the words *Admiring God's Handiwork*.

Beside me, Grey shifts and gently clears her throat. "You know, you could just go talk to him."

"Who?" I feign innocence when we both know I've been attuned to Jace so much tonight it physically hurts. It's like every time he moves or reacts in any way, I feel it too. I'm not sure what science is behind it, but I'd bet we could be analyzed by the experts.

"You know who," she replies.

"I don't know how to simply say 'hi' to him," I mutter, feeling done with pretending to everyone else besides Grey that meeting Jace wasn't the tectonic plate slide in my heart that it was. "Do any of your books have anything to say about this?"

She knows which books I mean, and the sincerity in my voice isn't lost on my friend. She gives me a warm smile. "We both know that even if they did—which I'm sure they do, because I'm convinced that books have everything we need . . ." she trails off. "But the point is that this situation is beyond a book, and we know it. Because this is your life.

And you feel for him—real feelings that need to be addressed."

I nod, the anxiety of it all creeping up my spine. I do have real feelings. But I'm not sure what label to put on them or what to do about them.

Jace and I have a purely professional relationship now. We aren't anything to each other beyond my status as Emmy's teacher, but why does it feel like we could have been everything? He seems so unsure, so lost. He told me he's not the same man that he was eight years ago, and while I recognize that to be true, why don't I want to stay away? Yet, I must, mustn't I? If my experiences with looking for love have taught me anything, it's that I can't convince someone to love me if they aren't all in. I can't control others, no matter how much I want their affection.

"You're right," I admit to Grey, my gaze drifting to the man in question again.

Jace is wandering about the hall, his head turning every so often to look at the door like it could hold all the answers he wrestles with if he only walks through it back into the cold, and it hits me that he hasn't seen the tree. *The tree!*

"I'll be right back. Distract Gladys," I say in a rush, suddenly realizing that somewhere on the older woman's tree must be a picture of Jace. And he's going to hate it. Millions of tiny pitter-patters that mimic pointe shoes on a stage float through my stomach. Nerves escalating, I channel all my years of moving effortlessly across the floor to reach the tree. I'm a woman on a secret mission to protect Jace from any more embarrassment. He doesn't deserve it.

When I reach the tree, I take in the absurdity of it all, my eyes trailing over all the pictures hanging from it that were clearly taken from an iPhone. There are pictures of Rafe unloading musical instruments near the theater, Graham eating chocolate cake in Sparrow's Beret, Liam walking A-cat-pella near Aesop's Tavern, and even some of Clark pouring drinks at the pub.

"Gladys, you cheeky mastermind," I whisper, unsure whether to be impressed or thoroughly disturbed by her visual methods of showing support to the men in town. While we all know she's truly harmless, her audacity is impressive. "Where are you, Jace?" I whisper.

"I think I'm right here."

At the sound of his rich voice behind me, I jump and squeeze my eyes shut. Taking a deep breath, I turn and find that my eyes are level with his very broad chest. Warmth creeps up my neck as I let my eyes trail slowly and cautiously up to the notch between his collarbones. I take in his strong, cleanly shaven jaw, and his full mouth and finally look into his amber eyes. My face heats, my heart beating furiously against my ribs. And it's in this moment that I realize my body doesn't know the difference between dancing a two-hour ballet performance and standing in front of this man.

"Hi," Jace says with an unexpected grin that makes my bones feel weak.

"Hi," I whisper in a little more breathless tone than I'd like.

He opens his mouth to say something else, but I'll never know what it was going to be, because his eyes shift to the tree behind me. His jaw goes slack. "What is that?" he demands, the words spoken more to the air than to me.

"Well, you see, Gladys—"

"Enough said." He releases a resigned sigh. "My face is

somewhere on there, isn't it?"

"Yes, I would think so. Although I haven't confirmed it yet."

He nods. His eyes cut to mine. "Were you looking for me?" I bite my lip, and Jace's eyes flare as he clears his throat.

"Well, yeah, I was," I admit. "I walked over to search for your picture because I knew it would make you uncomfortable to see it. I was trying to spare you the shock." I force out an awkward chuckle to try to keep the exchange professional.

I should feel embarrassed; investing energy toward a man's feelings when he doesn't seem to care for mine feels wasteful. Still, all I want is to feel the pressure of his arms wrapped around me again. It's challenging being near him, because I've found I don't know how to move forward when our past meets the present.

"You knew it would make me uncomfortable?" he says.

The man should win an award for prolonged eye contact. Everything in me wants to burn alive from his stare, its intensity excruciating. Because he's beautiful, and he's dangerous for my heart. I have no doubts that, deep within his frame, he feels so much more than most men. I've seen his gentle demeanor with his daughter, and I've seen how much his family loves him.

"I mean, wouldn't it?" I question, suddenly unsure if my assumption was right. But the way his eyes soften confirms it.

"Thank you."

I nod and turn back to the tree, doing my best to focus while I know his eyes are on me. But the emotions I feel pulsating off him are not helping me concentrate in the least. It feels like I'm reading a book of *Where's Waldo?* in which the stakes are the highest they've ever been because the most gorgeous man I've ever seen is beside me, distracting me with his presence.

I can't help but notice how he's changed over the years. He has more age lines, and there's a hint of silver coming in on the sides of his hair. His nose is slightly crooked, but it somehow makes him more endearing. I wonder if his full smile would still make me smile too . . .

Lifting my eyes toward the star at the top of the tree, I finally catch sight of the picture in question and stop in my tracks. Gladys captured Jace all right, but this photo was taken in the boxing studio, and his arms look like they were chiseled from stone. His physique is on full display due to the loose tank top he's wearing in the image. And there are tattoos that I didn't know existed lining the edges of his shoulders and trailing over part of his collarbone.

Given our brief acquaintance, I've never seen him like this. In fact, I've never seen him outside of a winter setting. I've never had the privilege of appreciating the work of art that Jace is. In the photo, his boxing gloves are mid-flight toward a punching bag. The ends of his hair hover over his head, their tips caught in the motion and force of his movement.

I grab the frame quickly, trying to make sure he doesn't notice how I just attempted to memorize each detail. If I were granted one wish in this moment, a photographic memory would've been it. Still, I retained enough of it to add weight to the feelings that were already aimed at him.

Holding out my hand, I offer the frame to him, and I

hold back a shiver when he brushes his palm against the back of my hand before he takes the photo from me. The contact was so quick, but the phantom feeling of his touch lingers. We stare at each other, and to my surprise, he hitches his head to the left, and I take it as an indicator for us to move toward the main space together. I find myself nodding back, a small smile escaping my lips.

His knowing smile matches mine, and we fall into step with each other. As we emerge from around the Christmas tree, Grey catches sight of us first, and her eyes fill with a warm and encouraging light. Sparrow and Lily have arrived at Town Hall, and their eyes widen slightly. They are standing next to Rafe and Graham, who are laughing as they talk. Ever the vocal one, Lily lets out a little "Whoop!" Her shoulders do a little shimmy as her ponytail whips about, and I want to laugh at her antics. I'm leading Jace toward the corner, trying to avoid making eye contact with anyone else, when suddenly, Gladys appears beside me.

"Wait, darlin'!" she yells, and I'm not sure if she's referring to me or Jace.

He catches my gaze. We stare at each other for some unknown reason, and I swallow, my mouth suddenly drier than Aunt Sophie's Christmas fruitcake.

Gladys is wearing a positively conniving grin. Slowly, she moves one of her hands up near her face and points to the ceiling above us. And that's when my life freezes. Instantly, I believe in the ability to stop time, and it turns out that Gladys is the mastermind behind it.

As slow as the molasses used for gingerbread cookies, I look up, up, up until my eyes catch on the wooden beam above us. To my horror, a sprig of mistletoe hangs from it.

We walked right into this trap; we're now standing directly under it, and we're about to have to answer to the whole town.

Gladys focuses all her attention on Jace. "C'mon, you tattooed giant. A good kiss could make sure that frown doesn't permanently mark your face." She waves her hands toward us. "Well, kids, get to it." She's positively beaming.

I take it back. If I had one wish, I'd ask to melt into the floor and disappear. I spot my parents in the corner. My best friends are frozen nearby, waiting for my distress signal. I'm pretty sure the elementary school teacher I had for two years in a row after she got transferred to the next grade at the same time I did is also present. This can't be happening.

Of all the times I've heard it said that mistletoe is romantic, no one was referring to this scenario. I'm sure of it. Because it's not romantic at all to wonder if the man next to you is going to combust from frustration or embarrassment. Maybe it'll be from both simultaneously.

A growl escapes from Jace's mouth. An actual growl. I think I misheard it, but then . . . nope, there it is again. Softer but still as attractive as the first growl, perhaps because it's so intentionally controlled. The picture clutched in his hands is bent beyond recognition. A corner of it has fallen to the floor.

I pull my lips inward to hide my smile as the face-off between him and Gladys heats up. She leans in, kindly lowering her voice so it's for our ears only.

"C'mon, you've both been *dancing*"—she gives me a wink—"around it. I've known Ivy her whole life; she doesn't want to mess this up. And you, sir, have been pushing people away ever since you got to town. Not sure why. But here's another chance to make a move." She looks at Jace.

Desperately, I lean closer to Gladys, not daring to look at Jace. She's right about me, at least. After Jace's explanation of what happened to his sister, it feels like the theater curtain is lifting between us. But what if I let him in and only end up as the understudy for his next partner? Yet, I'm also terrified not to try. "You've gotta take hold of love, dears." Gladys gives me a wink and then directs her gaze to Jace again. He rolls his shoulders beside me. "Well," she taunts loudly enough for the whole room to hear, "are you going to kiss her? Or do I have to label you a coward?"

The silence screams to be heard.

My mouth hangs open. There have been moments when I've wished to kiss the mountain of a man beside me again, but I never imagined it would end (or start) like this. My brain whirls with a thousand conflicting thoughts. I almost *don't* want it to happen in this way, because if he doesn't want it, that would be more haunting to me than if he did and still walked away.

Slowly, Jace looks at me. "May I touch you?" He grits out the words, the low timbre of his voice causing a chill to run down my spine.

I nod, unable to say a word. And then one of Jace's arms wraps around my waist, roughly yet somehow politely, pulling me closer. Willingly, I lean in, and in my peripheral vision, I see the moment Lily's and Sparrow's mouths drop open. Grey pumps the air in a silent cheer. I know she reads way too many romance books for her to miss the allure of his possessive touch. And yet, I feel completely safe. There's no part of me that thinks Jace would intentionally hurt me. Somehow, that makes tears hover at the edges of my eyes.

In a surprising contradiction to his standoffishness, he's suddenly holding me like I matter to him. It's so different from anyone who's tried to hold me in the past.

I dare a glance up at him, my heart picking up speed when it catches on the part of his neck peeking out from his peacoat, the inky tattoo on the tan skin of his hand moving through his hair, and his curls bouncing slightly around his head as he lifts his chin toward the sprig of mistletoe above us.

Staring at Gladys, he reaches with his free hand and snaps the whole piece of mistletoe off the wooden beam. I wince at the sound, though Jace hasn't ruined the clipped plant at all. The nail that was once in the ceiling, however, now hangs limply on the ribbon. Because, of course, he removed the entire thing with one hand and a single try. I'm hit with a sudden empty feeling as he releases my waist to yank out the nail. Jace motions toward Edgar, who takes the ribbon with a look that is both confused and slightly elated.

I think he's going to step away, but not five seconds later, Jace's hand grips mine. Its pressure is gentle and warm, wrapping around my smaller palm like a scene in *Beauty and the Beast* when Belle's hand is in Beast's paw.

It's unexpected.

It's shocking.

And I love it.

"Listen closely," Jace says, his tone lethally stern, as he leans toward Gladys and ignores the stares of the crowd around us. "No one will force Ivy to do anything she doesn't want to do. Understood?"

My eyes widen, and my immediate instinct is to defend her good intentions. "Jace, she means well. It's just—"

"I know she does," he says softly. There's reverence in the way his eyes land on my face. "But no one gets to push you to do anything other than what you're comfortable with."

I swallow and nod, both relieved and stuck on the idea that he would think I wouldn't want to kiss him again. Without another word, Jace nods to my friends before turning toward the door. He pulls me along with him. Lily's slow clap hits my ears, but I avoid eye contact with anyone as we race down the hallway and out the front door of Town Hall.

Jace leads us across the lawn toward a large tree covered in Christmas lights. We've reached it before he spins us around, the branches brushing my winter coat. My ears sting as my body registers the temperature difference, but my heart seems to disagree with the chill as it pumps wildly without my permission. Jace pulls a knit headband from his coat pocket, and a miniature candy cane drops to the earth as he extends the headband toward me. Could Jace have anticipated this moment, when we'd somehow be huddled together in the winter wind as I eagerly wonder what he'll say next?

"In there. Us. This," he says quietly. "I don't know how this will affect things. No matter what, I'm going to help you, and you're going to get those scholarships for the dancers . . ."

My eyes trail to his hand, which holds up the mistletoe, the frailty of the stem bristling from the breeze. My nose stings from the cold, but I refuse to let this moment pass. I nod for him to continue, not daring to interrupt his train of thought with words. We lean toward each other. His hand lifts as if he wants to touch me again. When he hesitates, I try to convey what I want with my eyes. Tentatively, he cradles my face, his other arm wrapping around my waist, pulling me closer. I look up to his whiskey-colored eyes, bright and intense in the cold night. They grow glassier the longer he looks at me. His breath hitches, and he leans forward. I feel the brush of his warm exhale on my face, the hint of the scent I've come to associate with him filling my lungs.

My eyes fall on his lips, recalling how they moved twice over mine on the best night of my life. My mouth tingles in expectation. It feels as if we're impossibly close, and just as I believe he'll close the distance, Jace shifts his face slightly away. I feel the brush of his skin against mine before I register the pressure of his arms wrapping around me in the warmest hug I've ever had. I count to five before he rises to his full height, and his beautiful face leans away.

"I can't kiss you, not tonight." His expression is pained, his breathing rapid. Disappointment creeps over me, but of course, we shouldn't kiss. We're not there yet. Maybe we'll never be again. I can't hold it against him, not after all this time.

"It's okay," I whisper. "Though I used to dream about moments like this with you, it's true."

"When did those dreams stop?" The tone of his voice is empty. Resigned.

"What?" The question catches me so off guard that I step back. For a moment, we're back at Four Leaf Cookies, and he's asking me questions that reach my soul and not just my mind. The truth tumbles out. "They didn't."

Tightly, his eyes close, a long exhale filling the air between us. When they reopen, his gaze is molten. "Ivy, you've been more than a dream to me. Never doubt it."

And with that, he wraps his strong arms around me again and pulls me close. My head rests on his chest, one of my ears near the slight opening in his coat. I feel the warmth of his body and the faint sound of his heart beating rapidly. The truth that we're both still affected by each other in this way makes me grin.

"Why are you smiling?" he asks, feeling the expression move my face.

I tilt my chin so I can examine his face, and he raises his head at the same time to meet my gaze. "Because . . . your heartbeat matches mine. I could choreograph something great from this rhythm."

He lets out a chuckle. "Starlight," he says tenderly, "I don't know how to stay grounded anymore; I've been an emotional nomad for so long. We still don't know so much about each other."

My legs sway at the instant effect of the nickname only he has ever given me. My head sinks forward, and I nod into his coat, willing him to let me in a little more.

Jace continues, "I've been a broken man for a long time. And you don't know the half of it."

Wrapping my arms around him, I close my eyes, the truth hitting me with full force. Love is an investment, and it's going to require risking my heart. Somehow, that gives me hope. "Yeah, well, maybe I can help you with that. We'll let Birch Borough work its magic."

Gripping the lapels of his jacket, I wish again that I could kiss him. But Jace needs more than my affection. He needs community and to be reminded that Christmas isn't ruined, even when it holds both pain and joy.

It feels as if a light has flickered on between us, embers of rekindled fire warming our skin. Maybe the thing that cracked between us long ago is beginning to heal.

"I never thought I'd hear your voice again. Never thought I'd feel you in my arms."

"Neither did I," I confess.

"I leave before Christmas," Jace says into my hair. "But after tonight, I know there's still something here. And I'm going to help you build your sets, not just for Emmy but for you. I've just been stuck in my head and don't know how to get out."

I peek up at him, his amber eyes my lighthouse. "I won't pressure you with expectations. Just knowing the truth is enough." He doesn't need to know. Truthfully, I'll be dreaming of kissing him for the rest of the season, but his wholeness is most important to me. If it's only as friends or only in hope, I'll hold on to Jace however I can.

His gaze becomes distant, like he's slipping away while still standing in front of me. I want to hold him with everything I can. He runs a hand through my hair, and I could cry at how good it feels. Leaning my head against his chest, the pulsing rhythm of his heartbeat radiates from it, a sound I won't forget.

"I promise you this, Starlight," Jace says with certainty. "No matter what happens in this life, you will always change my heartbeat."

Chapter Eleven

Jace

My hands sting, but I ignore the pain.

Edgar's boxing studio is empty. The last student headed out a while ago to get ahead of the snowstorm that's due to hit later tonight. I've been punching a heavy bag in the corner for over an hour, the energy fizzing within me intense enough to keep me from stopping. I'm scared of what will happen if I let myself stop. Because I don't know where to go from here or where to turn after the moment under the mistletoe.

I almost kissed her.

But it's Ivy, the woman with a hold on me that has fully gripped my soul. And while I could never regret my little girl and everything that brought her to me, I can't help but wonder what would've happened if I had never stopped coming back to Birch Borough after losing Mina. What would my life look like today if I hadn't talked myself out of finding the only woman who's come close to pulling me toward a greater sense of life?

I should have kissed her at the tree last weekend. But I couldn't bring myself to do it.

That almost-kiss.

For a few minutes, being that close to Ivy made me feel like myself again for the first time in a long time. And a part of me doesn't want to let that go. The fact that she tried to protect me from embarrassment over the picture lowered my defenses. But hearing Gladys tell her what to do made me primal. I don't know what the way forward with Ivy looks like, but there's still an undeniable chemistry between us. Even after all these years, that much is instantly clear. I'm drawn to her like the tides responding to a lunar pull.

Birch Borough could be a great place for Emmy to grow up, but I'm not happy at the moment. There are too many nostalgic nuances around every corner, reminding me of what could've been. While I've never even lived here, the feeling of this town stuck to me like spiderwebs. There's a stillness here, a sense of community. I could've been happy here, before everything in my life shattered.

Classical music blares through the boxing studio, a cello rendition that I turn to when I'm feeling extra stressed. Today, I'm a clock with broken hands, pieces rattling around within the confines of its system, the alternate version of my hand tattoo. I should be working on new furniture designs, but I'm not because all I can think about is that the very idea of kissing Ivy feels like a fever dream. Something that could've been if only I hadn't let the grief of losing my sister carry me away. Years later, I still feel the hum of her warm lips over my own, the taste of peppermint hot chocolate, and the brush of her exhale across my skin. Today, my heart reminds me of what I desperately tried to forget but . . . *can't.*

In my peripheral vision, I register Edgar stepping onto the main floor from the back, ending a call on his cell phone. I don't have to look at my brother to feel his shock before he jumps into action.

"Whoa, whoa, whoa!" he yells, running to my side. He takes hold of the top of the heavy bag and crouches behind it, attempting to make eye contact with me. "You're going to hurt yourself."

He's right. Already, the burn in my arms and the sharp pain in my shoulders indicate that I've done more damage than I intended.

"Jay!" He uses his serious trainer voice.

I stop moving. Sweat drops from the ends of my hair onto my forearms. I want to keep punching, feeling crazed, my sharp inhales proof that I'm pushing myself too hard. Chaotically, my imagination swirls with all the things that could have been, but each one slipped through my fingers.

Frustrated, I stare at my hands. They are capable and strong. But overall, I'm not a whole man. Perhaps I don't know how to be one anymore. I had Ivy in my arms; I could have held onto her, but I let her go, and that feels like torment. Truth be told, I've had the chance at so much, but besides my daughter, I've never seemed to be able to hold on to what was best for me. And lately, all I seem to be able to do is punch goodness away from me.

"Okay, okay." I nod, my breath ragged and the taste of sweat on my tongue. I try to swallow, but my mouth is so dry from the exertion that it sticks in my throat.

Edgar hurries to grab a bottle of water from the nearby bench and opens it to pour a stream into my mouth since my hands are still encased in my gloves. "Dude," he chides with more concern than I've heard from him in a long time. The single word is both an admonition and an open door for conversation.

Suddenly, the wrist straps feel too tight, the lights shine too brightly, and I'm tired. I extend my arms, too spent to even work to get the gloves off. Edgar helps me remove them, and I wince at the sting of fresh air meeting my throbbing hands. When I see how red my knuckles are, it's a confirmation that I took it too far.

His arms cross over his chest. I know he's waiting for me to convince him that I don't need to be removed from the premises before I hurt myself further.

"I'm fine." It's all I can manage to say before I grab the water bottle and down nearly all its contents before collapsing at the edge of the room, my head leaning against the wall and my legs stretched out in front of me. I let my exhausted arms hang limply at my sides on the floor, palms facing up.

Edgar stands before me, his stern demeanor refusing to waver. "First of all, you are *not* fine," he begins.

I scrunch my eyes shut, expecting him to berate me for being weak, even though he's never given me a reason to believe that he would think so poorly of me.

"And it's understandable," he concludes.

My eyes flash open. I see my brother looking at me like he both gets what I've gone through and doesn't know how to help.

"It's her," I grit out. Discovering Ivy living here is throwing off my plans, and I don't know what to do about it."

He nods and collapses beside me with a fluidity I won't

possess again until my arm muscles aren't destroyed anymore. "Well, if that near-kiss under the mistletoe the other night was any indication, that makes sense. I would imagine a kiss from years ago would be hard to forget. Couple that with an almost-kiss now. That has to mess with you."

I sigh and give a slight nod. This morning, I took my brother to breakfast and told him about the night I met Ivy all those years ago. He's now caught up on the entire combustion that has been my love life.

"Why is it messing with you, though? Do you not want to be with her?"

My disbelieving scoff is my answer. "The other night, I wanted to kiss her so much it nearly brought me to tears. If I were a poet, I'd write a sonnet, and the world would take notice." The words are staggered since I'm still breathing too heavily to get it all out at once. I take a few heaving breaths before continuing with, "Seeing Gladys push her to do something I wasn't sure she wanted to do messed with my head. Rekindling what we had a glimpse of years ago in such a public place just felt . . . sacrilegious." I flush at my own word choice, but it's true. "If I kiss her again, I'm going to do it right and without an entire town watching. The first time we kissed marked me for life. And this time, I know that kiss is going to bring me back to life. Ivy brings something out in me, I guess. I haven't felt this much in a long time."

He hums, his foot tapping lightly on the floor mat. "Good."

I glare at him.

Edgar laughs. "And why isn't her effect on you a good

thing? I'd say you've been a dead man walking these past few years, except for taking care of Emmy. I don't mind someone reminding you that there's more to life than work or being a dad. You have to keep allowing yourself to feel, Jace. That's life: pain and joy. And Ivy isn't . . ."

He pauses, and I know he was about to say *Jenna.* He doesn't need to say her name when the effect of her presence on my life is tangible without words. Emotion creeps up my spine, tingling at the outer corners of my eyes. It's not that I won't cry in front of my brother. I'm secure enough to cry whenever I'm moved. But admittedly, the only time I've shed any tears over the past five years has been in the context of my daughter. When Jenna finally left us, I didn't cry. I was too empty by that point.

"What do you want?" Edgar continues quietly. "Not in the past, not in the future, but right now."

I search my brain, my jaw clenching. Tears start to form, but I suppress them. I don't want to show this emotion here, not when I've got this raw sense of all that should have been pounding in the center of my chest. It would feel good to get the words out, though—the ones I've swallowed down since I started to believe that losing my sister was the start of my world unraveling.

"I want to belong to someone," I finally hear myself admit, and Edgar's eyes widen, the rest of his face remaining neutral. The tiny sign of acknowledgement pushes me to speak honestly. "I know that could seem old-fashioned. Potentially, it's even weak for a man to express the idea of 'belonging' to someone who has the power to break your heart, especially after the Jenna debacle." I pause as my heart races with the truth. "I'm hyperaware of the mistakes I've made. They feel like a weighted vest around my ribs. But as I've been near Ivy again, I'd be lying if I said I don't want it."

Taking a deep breath, the effort pulls at my lungs, and I realize my hands really are on fire. I'm feeling too many emotions to look him in the eye; instead, I focus on the Christmas lights strung on the front windows. They seem to project warmth into the darkness outside, hovering only a glass pane and a few thoughts away. If not for the streetlamps glowing with warmth along the sidewalk, the windows would be an impenetrable wall of night.

"What are you going to do about the job offer?" Edgar broaches a new subject.

He's referring to the call I got this morning from a well-known furniture company in Lakeland, Florida. They've seen the pieces I've sold online and are interested in having me add artisan pieces to their collection. If my designs are accepted, the deal could reach national distribution. It's the recognition a woodworker like me could only dream of. But the offer requires that I relocate to design in-house, as the company hopes to utilize my skills for other ongoing projects.

"I don't know."

"Well, you'd better find out. The woman who got away is just around the corner. She's single. You're single. Maybe this is your chance at happiness."

"I have Emmy."

"Yes, you do. And she's the best thing that ever happened to you. But she's going to grow up. And you . . ." Edgar clears his throat.

Reaching up, I clasp my brother's shoulder, gripping it

tightly through the swelling that's beginning to rise near my knuckles. Edgar and Angie have been my support since we arrived in Birch Borough. There have been times recently when they've stepped in with Emmy when I needed the help, yet they've also given me space as we move through the holidays. I'll always be grateful to them.

"You deserve to be loved," Edgar says with factual emphasis. "Stop being scared to lose again."

What would happen if I believed him? I hum, my eyes drifting to the snow that's begun to fall outside. It's only visible because of the lights on the street. It's been snowing on and off for days, each fresh, untouched blanket of snow a sign that the world can keep being made new.

"Thanks, man," I mutter.

He rises, the emotional weight of what he's passed to me easing away from his features with a grin. "Let's go before we're snowed in."

I grunt as I put weight on my arms to stand. The pummeling I gave the punching bag is going to hurt tomorrow, especially since I'm due to put together sets for the upcoming show. Ripping off my sweat-soaked shirt, I throw on a clean hoodie and struggle with my jacket, preparing for the layer of ice that will feel as if it's made a home against my skin in the next thirty seconds.

"Aren't you going to see her tomorrow since you agreed to help her with Emmy's performance?" Edgar flips off the light switch, the overcast sky and the dim glow of the Christmas lights outside our only guide to the exit.

"Yep, she'll be there."

He laughs, knowing I'll also be surrounded by a dozen or so kids as I work. "And what are you going to say to her?

That is, assuming you can even lift a hammer tomorrow after what it seems you put your arms through tonight. Are you going to tell her about potentially taking a job in Florida?"

I grin, not because of his brotherly banter but at the thought of seeing Ivy again. My heart picks up speed. Even if being near her is temporary, I'll take it. "I'll tell her about the job," I reassure him. "You know I'll always tell her the truth."

"Hey! Or maybe you could just tell her now," Edgar suggests with a smile.

I tense as I look toward the front door. It's just flung open, and Ivy rushes in, her cheeks reddened by the frigid air. The sky is dark with the snowstorm, but the blush on her face is enticing, the glow of the streetlamps and the Christmas lights reflecting on her face. A scarf is wrapped haphazardly around her neck, its color mixing with her golden hair, and her hands are covered by mittens, per usual. She's adorable. The sight of her gives me an irresistible urge to pick her up and hold her close. Or perhaps, I'd rather kiss her again. The aftermath of the winter chill through the open door wakes me up from my thoughts and adds some temporary relief to the heat radiating from my hands.

I clear my throat as Ivy approaches.

"Hi, Edgar," Ivy says with a tentative smile. Her eyes drift to me.

Before this month, I hadn't seen her in ages. Even after all that time, I know in my bones that looking at Ivy is never going to get old for me. "Jace." My name on her tongue sends my heart racing, even though she is standing far away.

When she takes a tentative step forward, I move across from her in three strides and then stop short. I'm still not close enough to her, but my body is frozen. My nerves are ridiculous. I've been around women before. I have a daughter, for crying out loud. But Ivy causes something in me to malfunction . . . or reignite.

"I'm sorry to just stop in," she says quickly. "But I was in the area—well, of course I was in the area; I live here." The words come out in a muttered rush, a nervous laugh accompanying them. "I realized I needed to ask if you still planned to come by tomorrow. You know . . . to help with the sets. Because we need to get them started. But I don't have your number. That's so weird, right? But it's true. I don't. I don't even have your email. So, I decided to just, you know, stop by."

I tighten my lips to hold back a smile. She's nervous. I find myself enjoying the sight way too much.

"Stop by anytime, Ivy," Edgar says kindly, and I give him a nod of thanks while I take a deep breath. He's giving me an out from overthinking.

"Star—Of course you can, Ivy." I shake my head. "Always feel free to stop by."

"Good, that's good." Her mittened hands lift, attempting to take off the scarf, but somehow, it gets stuck around her neck even more. "If you guys are leaving, I can just walk out with you, Jace."

She's adorable. Did I say that already? Once again, I have to clench my jaw to hold myself back from blurting aloud how attractive she is, even when she's trapped by yarn.

Stepping up next to her, I zip up my jacket as Ivy swings back toward the door. Our hands brush. The feeling is electric, even through her gloves. She gasps, going perfectly still, and I growl faintly. Thankfully, if she catches my instinctive sound, she doesn't mention it. But Edgar chuckles just as his watch chimes, signaling a new hour.

My brother turns away. "I forgot I needed to take care of something before I lock up. I'll give the two of you a couple of minutes to chat." He walks toward the back of the gym.

I lift my hand to indicate that I've heard him, and Ivy's eyes narrow in on my knuckles. Within seconds, she's clumsily pulled off her mittens and thrown them in a pile on the ground. Her warm hands wrap around my own. My fears urge me to pull back, but I force myself to be still and leave them to be held by the woman before me.

"What happened to you?" Ivy says softly, her touch gentle as the edges of her fingers hover around my still-reddened knuckles. The concern in her eyes and her willingness to touch me without hesitation nearly knock me over. I use the last bit of my strength to fight to keep my hand still. Forget sparring in the ring (the irony is real since we're at In the Ring); all Ivy would need to do to wipe me out is, apparently . . . question me about this.

"Training," I grit out.

Her brow furrows, her eyes searching mine. For the first time in years—maybe since we first met—I try not to hide. I let her gaze scan my soul. I don't answer her questions but just let her observe. Maybe I'm simply too tired, or the exertion wiped out all my defenses, or maybe it's because she's helping me forget the throbbing in my hands, but I don't put up my guard.

Edgar, God bless him, has busied himself with reorganizing the equipment on the other side of the room to make it less awkward. I owe him a drink.

Ivy's eyes shift noticeably from amusement to attraction, her pupils dilating and then returning to their usual state, and my heart is following along for the ride. I let myself look at her, really taking her in for the first time after all these years. Even though we almost kissed the other day, I didn't get the chance to fully enjoy her without my brain on overdrive. I study the little creases around her mouth as she concentrates on massaging my hands. Her eyes still remind me of hot chocolate, the slope of her nose is still charming, and the wisps of hair around her face are still alluring. But when her expression turns to sadness, I catch tears brimming at the edges. Suddenly, they're swimming, but the tears don't spill over when she gives my hand a light, final squeeze and releases it.

"You're okay," she says quietly.

Not a "you'll be okay." Just a simple "you're okay." Present tense.

The words fill me with relief, and I realize I didn't know how much I needed them until now. She swallows. My hands want to reach out to pull her close. Instead, she gathers herself. "So, tomorrow, when you drop off Emmy at the studio, I thought I could show you a few more mockups for the sets?"

"Of course."

Relief relaxes her taut posture. "That's perfect. I'm hoping we can get these backdrops done before Christmas. The performance is right after, you know. Birch Borough may be generous, but a good turnout and an excellent-looking production really make a difference with those donations. I just want these scholarships for my students so badly."

"I'll be there. We'll crush it," I repeat, admiration lacing my tone. She's so selfless with her talent, pouring it into others faithfully. "Emmy will be thrilled to spend some extra time at the studio anyway. She'll show you the "Waltz of the Snowflakes" dance," I add in case she needed another reminder that my presence is a package deal.

A bright smile breaks across her face. "Can't wait. I mean, I love all my students, but Emmy really does have something . . ." she says with a laugh.

Her assessment of my daughter makes my posture rise a little higher in pride. "She does, doesn't she? And she already loves dancing with you, so thank you again, for taking her in and letting her be a part of the Christmas production."

Seeing that our conversation has turned to less personal things, Edgar wanders over. It's getting late, and the snowflakes have increased outside the window. We need to head out if we don't want to drive on icy roads.

Ivy gives us both a smile and shrugs. "Of course. She deserves to dance if she wants to. Everyone does." She walks toward the door.

I bend to pick up her mittens, then hurry after her, hand outstretched. She turns back to me at the door, her head tilted. "Thank you." She takes the mittens. "And get some ice," she says with a sudden emergence of sass. "I need your hands." Her eyes widen in instant horror. "For the *show*! I meant—mean—for the show. Okay, bye!" With that, she's through the door onto the street, and I can't help but smile freely into the brisk air, my heart warming like mulled cider on a stove.

Edgar's laugh is enough to ground me back to reality, because there's something about the way Ivy gets flustered around me that sends hope pounding into my heart.

"You still didn't get her number," he reminds annoyingly.

We exit after Ivy, and I watch her retreating red coat walk down the street through the snow. Edgar locks the door and waves to a family walking past with to-go cups of warm beverages in their hands. I look at my brother, in too good a mood to give in to his teasing. I inhale the frozen air and pull out my own keys.

"Yeah, well, I'll get that tomorrow."

A genuine smile is his only reply as we walk to our cars. Determination settles into my tendons and bones. It's a struggle these days to trust, especially when it comes to a one-of-a-kind woman like Ivy. But I think being torn out of her life again right now would feel like breathing stale air after finally having a hit of real oxygen. I've been living for my daughter, but I forgot that I'm also a man. One who is desperately trying to believe that if Ivy's kindness toward me is any indication, maybe I'll be able to reframe my perspective and find my worth again.

I walk down the street, something nagging at my subconscious. And then it hits me just as I reach my Jeep. *The clock.* The moment we met and just before we kissed, a clock signaled the time. And tonight, Edgar's watch chimed soon after Ivy walked in the door.

"Christmas magic?" I whisper to myself as I look up to the sky. The lights and decorations strung around town make it feel like a movie set. "It can't be magic. I know it can't be." I close my eyes and clench my hands, which welcome the cold air with relief. Opening the door and sliding into my car, I take a moment to lean back against the headrest and close my eyes. "God, if it's possible to make it happen within the time I have left here, please help me find my home again this Christmas."

The quiet and isolation in my vehicle is the balm my soul has needed. I'm ready to see Emmy, eat dinner with her, and tuck her into bed. But sometimes, we just need a moment of quiet to remind us how loud things in our lives have really been. As I start the Jeep and head to Angie's, the thought of her famous lasagna already giving me something to look forward to, an idea hits me. It's an idea that could put my heart in more danger than it's ever been. Yet, I'm not doing so well working this problem out on my own if my burning knuckles are any indication.

The idea works its way into my brain. Could this year mark a change I've needed for years? Perhaps instead of believing the negative words Jenna spoke over me in the past or focusing on what I currently can't give Ivy, I can dare to believe there's a better version of myself out there, and if I look hard enough, I can find him once more.

Chapter Twelve

Ivy

Why did I find a sign on my studio door this morning saying that rehearsals are postponed to this afternoon?" Moving my hands over my head, I sigh and pin Grey with what I hope is a pseudo-firm stare. "And why did a large, infuriatingly attractive man arrive at the farm today to tell me—even though we've only gone over the blueprints once—that he has already finished one of the sets and just has to paint it? How did he know I'd be out there?"

When I found Jace at the farm where we always build the sets—since there's no room at the high school when students need the theater every day—I was so shocked that I could barely give him feedback on the set he built. He's that attractive and that talented. It's. Too. Much.

"I merely redirected your students to a later timeframe," Grey says, her doe-like eyes shining behind her cat-eye glasses with only a hint of remorse alongside a fair amount of pride. "And I may have talked with Resin to keep you in bed this morning."

It would be a shock if my dog were able to obey such

abstract commands, but he was extra cuddly this morning, and I did have a harder time than usual getting out the door. "Grey, you didn't," I say quietly.

"Oh, I did," she replies, grinning as she picks up a stack of new books from the front counter and heads to the romance section to file them away. The layout of Marlee's Books hasn't changed in years, but Grey and her father have added a sense of wonder to it that somehow makes it feel as if it's always changing, even while maintaining the comfort of its familiar structure. "I figured you and your boy could use the time together and the sleep. Besides, Resin gives the best hugs. Don't tell me you're actually complaining about Jace doing exactly what you've been wanting him to do. Aren't you happy he made the effort?"

I shrug but try to feign being salty, turning the conversation back to Jace rather than her management of my business schedule. "I showed him basic drawings the other day, but he came all alone this morning to show me a finished set, looking better than a Hallmark Christmas movie actor in flannel and with hair that must've been mussed that perfectly just to mess with me."

Grey laughs. "Wow, you have quite a way with words this morning. I think Jace may finally make you see the appeal of the romance novels we stock more than any other genre in here. It's the perfect setup: single dad, missed connection, boxer, craftsman, broody with a broken heart. I mean, even you must admit he's got all the elements for a leading character."

I sigh because she's right. And even though I know we've both changed, and Jace may be too far gone to even want a committed relationship with anyone again, I still can't imagine not being the one beside him. It's wild. It's unfounded. But he's irresistible.

"Do I hear our Ivy girl?" Luke calls from the back room of the shop before he appears with his glasses perched on the end of his nose in a permanent fashion that makes me question how he could ever see out of them. Grey's dad has salt-and-pepper hair that is always slightly disheveled. In short, he looks like a lover of books. Every time I see him, I wonder if he got lost in a chapter or another world, and I want to ask how it feels to come back to the real one. Luke has been like a second father to me. Even though I love my family, his love has been a grounding factor in my life. I'm just as much his daughter as if he were my real family.

I meet him near the book counter, wrapping him in a hug and nodding toward the bag of pastries from Sparrow's Beret that I brought with me. He nods in appreciation and opens it, ripping off a piece of croissant and waving it in the air.

"Now, what's this I overheard about an 'infuriatingly attractive man'?" The bite of flaky pastry gets shoved into his mouth like a chipmunk storing up goods for the winter. He makes an adorable dad figure. You can't help but want to wrap him up in a blanket or, in my case, feed him pastries. Still, his question makes a blush paint my cheeks.

"It's just a guy I might be interested in," I mumble.

"Might be?" Luke stares at me through the reading glasses on the end of his nose.

"Could be . . . probably shouldn't be, but I met him once before . . . and now he's back." I stutter through the words.

"Dad, you know Ivy doesn't talk about her love life openly." Grey attempts to diffuse my embarrassment, but is her statement true?

After Jace, I was so disappointed that I didn't dare speak about what I wanted or felt when it came to romance. Instead, I'd lament as I told stories of my horrible and sometimes hilarious experiences on the dating apps since then.

"I know she doesn't," he says, finishing off the last of his first croissant. I brought him two since I'm not an amateur, and he pulls it from the bag. "But this one's different. Her voice is brighter when she speaks of him."

His observation surprises me. Luke has never pushed us to tell him things. He's the best kind of fatherly confidant in that way.

"My voice is different?" I squeak.

"Mm-hmm," he hums, chewing an oversized bite of a *pain au chocolat.*

I don't know if the noise is in appreciation of the pastry, which is admittedly the best thing Lily makes besides her chocolate cake, or if he's thinking about my love interest.

Luke doesn't keep me wondering for long. "Well, that too. But Gladys also has the 'Gen your business' text thread blowing up this morning. She hasn't seen you in a couple of days and wanted all hands on deck to make sure you're okay after you and Jace kissed near the town Christmas tree last weekend."

I gasp and stare at him as Grey releases a strangled laugh. Her dad's eyes dance with amusement. Something I've been suspicious of for years has just been confirmed. I've always known Birch Borough ran an insider information line. A modern-day phone tree, if you will. It just never occurred to me that Gladys would've launched a text thread with the so-called 'older ones' of this town to watch out for my friends and me.

"'Gen your business'?" I repeat, skeptical despite the grin hovering around my mouth. I've got to give it to her. As shocked as I am to find out that my love life was already talked about this morning, Gladys' shenanigans have no boundaries.

"Yeah, like generations," Luke confirms. "Instead of boomers or Gen X, we're going with a generation known for knowing your business. She even sent a fuzzy picture of the back of your heads. Though I suppose it was more like you two were in motion. I think whoever took it was running."

At this, Grey bends over with laughter, tears running from her eyes from laughing so intensely.

"This isn't funny!" I yell half-heartedly as my own laughter bubbles over. *This town.* "Also, to clarify, we almost kissed. There was no actual kiss."

"Gladys won't believe you. But still, Ivy girl," Luke says as he wipes a dollop of chocolate from the side of his face with one of the crinkled napkins from the to-go bag, "this town loves you. And we're just looking out for you."

"I know." I sink against the counter, already exhausted from the mental hoops I've had to jump through this morning after seeing Jace show up at the farm on his own with a tool belt, dressed in jeans and flannel. Now, hearing from some of my favorite people in the world that nothing is sacred or private in my life. Well, nothing externally, that is. No one will ever know, except Jace and me, the effect his presence has on me and the warmth that passed between us the other night when he held me. The feeling was like remembering a dream, only to realize that the real-life experience was so much better. I clear my throat.

"We'll come back to that later. Or maybe not." I shrug. "I don't think I want to know what our fellow townspeople think about Jace. He's not as grumpy as he first appears, let me just say that. And you—" I turn to Grey, who's back to stocking books, the lens of her glasses smudged from fidgeting with them, no doubt. "Why would you send Jace out there on his own?"

Grey gives me a look, and I understand it perfectly, proving our extensive history and lack of need to articulate our feelings out of anything but courtesy.

"Ok, okay," I mutter, sinking onto a step stool that's been in her family for generations. Her mother and father carved their initials into it, and so did her grandparents before her. Maybe one day, Grey will have hers and Boston's engraved. She's not ready to hear that right now, though.

The phone behind the counter rings, reverberating off pages and bookshelves. Because it's the adorable shop that it is, they still have a landline with a version of the telephone that most people wouldn't have seen since the nineties. Luke answers and begins to discuss a book on the history of Birch Borough with a potential customer. Grabbing a stack of books to help her restock, I move closer to Grey, needing her steadiness and courage.

"Grey," I say quietly, "does your mom have anything to say on a situation like this?" It's hard to ask, but I need more wisdom than I've found to date. I need motherly wisdom like "Find yourself a Mr. Rochester" for *Jane Eyre*. Or "There's always a cost to creativity" for *Frankenstein*. My favorite quote that Grey has found so far is the one she discovered in *Pride and Prejudice*, which reads, "Never trust a man named George." It's especially funny, given the inside joke between Graham and Lily. When we were younger, we'd walk to Dove's Donuts every time we found a new note from Marlee. We'd sit at the countertop and try to think of all the ways the wisdom could apply to our lives.

While we stopped going to get donuts after I left for the ballet company, some things have remained the same. There's a certain belief we've held toward the books. It's like they've each been sent at the right time to guide Grey through her life because her mother can't. Each note is a glimpse of something that was sent back in time to help move her forward.

"Hmm," Grey hums as she sets a few books on their proper shelves and in their proper order. She turns to face me, contemplating, deeply thinking it through. During the pause, I think of how lucky I am to have a friend like her. Grey feels like my family.

She breaks the silence. "Normally, I would say let's go on a hunt to find out what my lovely mother would've written about this situation, and I would be right."

Luke hangs up the phone and disappears to the back office, humming. Grey resumes her regular place at the familiar spot behind the counter, the lift of her posture and the tilt of her head as memorable to me as any other moment I could picture my best friend. If she were a painting, this would be the pose the artist chose, the scene complete with a book in her hand, a Post-it peeking out from the pages with a note inscribed by her mother.

"But," she continues, "I think that this bit of advice is going to come from me. Ivy, you're my best friend, and I love you like a sister. But a part of you has been hollow since Jace didn't show."

I want to retort, but she gives me a knowing grin to let me know she's not finished. She knows the reasons he couldn't make it. I told her as soon as I found out.

"It's like you met him, and he made such an imprint that no one has ever been able to fill it. The idea of his love was so strong that it woke a part of you that you didn't even know you had. You've been missing that warmth ever since."

I nod, wanting her to continue.

"And now he's here." She lifts the book she's holding to cradle it near her heart, letting the courage of a relic from her mother seep into her bones. "Is he the same as he was? Not quite. A lot of life has happened for both of you. But I wouldn't be a good friend if I didn't tell you that I think you should set the past aside and try again with this guy."

My eyes widen with surprise that my bookish friend, who typically errs on the side of caution with her heart, is encouraging me to trust it with Jace.

"Now, whether he lets you try is another question. But he's got a little girl. Another person to give yourself and your love to. And I think you have more love in you to give than you even realize. What are you so afraid of?"

I twitch my nose to hold back the emotion. It doesn't work, but it's worth a shot. Everything she's just said rings true, and her confidence is the reminder I need to find my own again.

"I just want to be held, Grey. For good." I speak to the air that smells like books and memories. "I'm so tired of feeling like I'm falling through people's hands." Finally, I sniffle, using the heel of my hand to catch a stray tear.

Grey leans over the counter toward me, her vintage dress

softening the movement.

And because Grey has the dearest heart I've ever known, she doesn't question my reasoning or my thoughts; she just lets me speak. I know she feels lonely too. It goes beyond friendship or family in the quiet moments; it's the feeling after night creeps in, a call in your heart, a wish to have a partner. We both long to have someone to check on us during the fears and the joys of life, someone who will speak life over our tired hearts at the end of a long day, someone who chooses to make us an important part of his life.

Grey grabs my hand, and I force a grin to reassure her that I'm okay. "You know, this just solidifies it," she says. "Enjoy the time you have with the man who's haunted your heart from the start. Even if it's hard." She sighs. "Oh, my friend, don't give up on him. Sometimes, people just need time to find the healing they need. And needing time doesn't mean they don't love you or want you less. Sometimes, it means they want you so much they don't know how to handle their feelings yet."

My eyes widen when she gives a knowing smile, continuing with, "For the record, I don't think he's as grumpy as people say he is. I just think he's afraid, like Beast."

I let her words soak through my frame. I'm reminded of snow days long past, spent at each other's homes with cookies and books surrounding us while *Beauty and the Beast* played in the background.

"And you're afraid too. But maybe just this once, forget the fear?"

Despite the validity of Grey's advice, I'm not sure I can forget the fear. Not when there's so much at stake. But I can choose to enjoy the moment. My eyes drift to the clock, and I startle at the late hour. Grey may have finagled my morning to give me extra time to rest, but it's time for me to get to my studio to move my body. I'll rehearse there as I can only do when I'm completely on my own. Then it'll be time for afternoon rehearsal, and I'll teach for the rest of the evening. I'm not sure I'm ready to leave this cozy bookshop, though. Wistfully, I look out the window toward Main Street, my eyes drifting past the Christmas tree made of books and the garland on display. Snow falls lightly outside.

I need to leave, but suddenly, I'm distracted by the maple wood table the book tree is sitting on. I don't remember seeing it a few days ago, but it adds height and a warmth to the display in a way that seems intentional. There is a clock etched into the side. When I bend to peek at it, the clock on the wall chimes. And as if by Christmas magic, Jace walks into view, his steps heading in the direction of the boxing studio. He sees me in the window a second after I see him. He stops and makes eye contact as a soft grin takes over his face. Arm lifting, he taps the watch on his wrist. I see an athletic bag draped over his shoulder; no doubt he is headed to In the Ring for a training session. Understanding, I nod, feeling a sense of disappointment that there isn't time to run out to say hello. But his apologetic shrug and the way he resumes walking only to take a step backward just to look into my eyes again give me the boost I need for the rest of this day. I'm not sure what's unfolding between us this time around, but I want to find out.

Motioning with my hand, I indicate that he should keep moving. At my smile, he nods and waves. I think he's going to keep walking, but suddenly, he spins on his heel and walks toward the bookshop, his expression startlingly open and light. He draws a piece of paper from the pocket of his coat and motions to the door. Leaving Grey staring after me at the counter, I rush to it. The cold air hits my face and almost makes me screech as I yank it open. I step outside and draw the door shut behind me, the bell on it jingling.

"Jace," I say breathlessly at his tentative smile. I feel a piece of my fear break off just at the warmth of seeing him so casually. "Fancy seeing you twice in a day."

"Starlight," he murmurs in a low tone, a hint of smokiness and promise within his voice. It causes me to shiver from more than the outside temperature. "I can't stay long; Emmy was having trouble getting out the door so I could go to work. And I just remembered . . ."

At his remorseful expression, I reach for his forearm beneath his black coat. "It's okay. I just wanted to say hi."

"And I just thought I'd take the opportunity to give you this." In his large, callused hand is clutched a piece of antique-looking paper. He extends it to me, and at his encouraging nod, I take and open it. I'm met with what must be Jace's handwriting. It's precise, the words on the paper clear: *Twelve days. Twelve hours.*

"I'm not sure I understand."

"Have you been hearing the clock that seems to chime whenever we are around each other—that one time we kissed years ago, and again at the tree outside Town Hall, and again at In the Ring when you stopped by?"

I think back and nod my head in agreement. It's odd, but he's right. And every time I've heard a clock chime since the first time we met, I've thought of him. It's not common to hear sounds coming from actual watches or clocks these days, unless it's text notifications or alarms. Musing on the coincidence, my eyes trail a path to his hand, studying the clock tattoo that etched itself in my mind long ago, the newly added vine work imprinting itself in my memory as well.

"I might have gotten a job," Jace says, the words coming out in a rush.

I smile for him, a flash of hope bursting in my chest.

"In Florida," he adds. His Adam's apple bobs as he swallows. "There's a company out there that wants me to design a collection of furniture pieces for them. My designs could end up in stores across the country. We're still working out the contract, and I've been planning to go no matter what, but lately . . ."

"Jace, that's wonderful!" What else am I supposed to say? My heart cracks, but my voice remains steady.

"Yeah. It should be what I've wanted for years."

The words hit home. His amber eyes search mine, and I remember sitting across from each other in Four Leaf Cookies with crumbs between us. That night, I felt like dancing should have been everything I wanted. But it wasn't. Everything changed when I saw Jace.

"Are you going to accept?" I ask.

The silence in the air reminds me of the frigid wind swirling between us. There have been moments since we reconnected when I've seen Jace slowly opening up to me. It's made me nearly overwhelmed with the hope of it all. And now his decision to leave Birch Borough or make his home here just got an added layer of difficulty.

"I don't . . . I'm not sure." Jace looks at his watch again and sighs with frustration. "I really have to go. I'm late for a class." His eyes lift to mine. "But you should know that I'm tired of fighting this, Starlight."

"This?" I question, unsure if he means what I think he does.

"Yes, this. There's something about the way we are with each other . . . The fact that you're in my life again in and of itself feels like a miracle." He nods slightly, as if bracing himself for what's next. "There are twelve days left before Christmas Eve. That's the day of our departure. We may not return. I want to make the best decision for Emmy, and growing up with her grandparents in Florida might be it. But for the next twelve days, I want to spend time with you, however much you have available. I know it isn't fair to ask you to sacrifice your time for a guy who might be moving permanently to another state . . . And honestly, I'm terrified. But I still want to know you . . . as more than friends."

In my frozen silence, Jace takes a deep breath, gathering strength. "I'm asking . . . if you can find twelve hours—or more; I'll take every minute—over the next twelve days, I'd be grateful. I'm not sure I trust time to be on our side yet, but I want to believe there's something magical in this reunion. Even if we're only meant to be for this Christmas."

His words sink deep as I take them in. Is Jace actually saying he wants to spend time with me? That he wants to linger with me in this strange time warp in which we've found ourselves? As my mind tries to comprehend what I'm hearing, I think of all the stories affected by time. *The Nutcracker* itself is influenced by the movement of the clock. At some point, Clara had to wake up. And maybe I will have to wake up from this daydream, too, and return to my regular life. But I'm willing to risk it because I need a Christmas miracle this year, not only for my studio but also for my heart.

"What do you think, Ivy?" Jace prompts me. His eyes are gleaming, a playfulness in them I haven't seen since he returned to town.

I make up my mind in that instant. "You've got it." I extend my hand for him to shake. "You've got the twelve days of Christmas—or in this case, the day before Christmas Eve—but in hours."

Jace's expression warms. Reaching out, his large hand wraps around my own. He bends closer, bringing his face toward mine. For a moment, I think he's going to kiss me. He's close enough that if I just lifted onto my toes, my lips would collide with his. For a moment, we linger in each other's space. But then Jace straightens, a curl bouncing in front of his forehead.

"I need to go. Don't want to be late."

"Right, of course, time and all that," I say with a smile, still reeling at how just the touch of his hand seems to change my perspective on how it feels to be close to him.

With a final gentle press of his hand over mine, he turns and walks away, heading in the direction of In the Ring. With his note clutched in my other hand, I hop-dance back into Marlee's Books. I realize how cold I am as I spot Grey, her expression making it evident that she was a witness to my exchange with Jace. Her arms are crossed, and her grin is sweet, despite the hint of smugness in it.

"Let the record show that I believe this go-around is different." She grabs one of the books on the counter next to her with a Post-it sticking out from the pages and holds it close to her chest. "We never know how much time we have, Ivy. Don't waste it."

Walking around the counter, I wrap her in a hug, despite

her protests that I'm freezing, before grabbing my coat and dance bag and heading to the door. It jingles again.

"Bye, Ivy girl!" Luke yells from the back just as the door shuts. I wonder if he was listening the whole time and was waiting for his moment to speak up. I laugh and look toward In the Ring, viewing the building without apprehension for the first time in weeks. As I walk toward my own studio, I treasure the knowledge that the man I met ages ago is still in the present version of Jace somewhere. It feels like he's been buried within a shadow of what he once was, but I see a hint of him returning.

Perhaps I'm only one woman, but there's a magic that flows through this town, following the same path as the river that runs through it. If Jace is willing to try, and if we can get the support of all the townspeople who thrive at making everyone feel like they matter, I just might be able to remind Jace of who he is and what we could be, and maybe it'll happen just in time for Christmas.

Chapter Thirteen

Jace

The clock strikes noon.

"What exactly is it that you need again, Sparkles?" The day after Ivy and I set up our twelve-date arrangement, I'm standing in the middle of a dance shop that looks like its sole purpose is to populate the space with what I now know to be a fabric concoction called tulle.

"Sparkles? Really, Dad?" Emmy says with some sass, her grin matching my own. Her tiny frame moves through the round clothing racks nestled together tighter than tables at a wedding. I know what that looks like because when Jenna and I talked about getting married, she tried to figure out how to cram two hundred people in a space for one hundred because she liked the specific lighting of the venue for photos. I shudder at the memory of what might've been if we'd gone through with it.

"Hey, I'm trying out some new nicknames for you. Seems like the right thing to do since you're growing up so fast." Starlight is already taken as a nickname, of course, but Emmy thrives on words of affirmation and affection, so I know that she enjoys this little game of finding ways to show how much I love her as much as I do.

"I need slippers. My other ones are too big." She scrunches her nose, and I wince. The oversized dance slippers would be my fault. I guessed at her size when I ordered online before I'd had a chance to get her into a proper dance shop. And the slippers are written in different sizes that don't equate with the sizes I'm used to for regular shoes. To be fair, I'm still getting used to this world of dance in the first place.

"Right. Okay, well . . ." I look around the space and spot stacks of thin cardboard boxes that are shoved together to form a sort of bookshelf. You couldn't fit another box on the stack if you tried, and I spot a few rebel slippers with their strings poking out of the ends of the boxes.

"This is probably what we're looking for." I direct Emmy toward the box pile.

I'm aware that a smart man would've asked Ivy for help. I'm way out of my element. For crying out loud, I'm trying to woo the woman, to finally show her how much she meant—still means—to me while I can. The thought of a younger version of Ivy finding happiness in this store loosens something in my chest as my daughter and I assess the stack.

"Can I help you?" a kind voice says from the stairs that lead to an upper level. An older woman is standing on them, looking at me skeptically. Her silver hair is pulled back into a sleek bun, and she's wearing clothing that looks as if she could teach a dance class right here in this store. Seeing boxes stacked near the edge of the landing, I'm guessing she just descended from a stockroom up there.

"Oh, ah, yes," I say with relief. "My daughter needs new slippers. Please."

The woman's eyes soften as Emmy steps into sight around me. Instantly, I realize that she probably thought I got lost and wandered into the shop. Now, the woman's shoulders relax, and she smiles genuinely.

"Of course!" she exclaims. "As you can see, we have plenty!"

She steps onto the mini dance floor that I now notice beneath the stacks of slippers. The boxes remind me of Cracker Jack boxes. Maybe there's a special fit for each person. The numbers and names on the sides of the boxes are still throwing me. It's another language I haven't yet mastered, but I have a feeling I need to, given how much Emmy loves to dance. We're in this world now, and I might as well excel at it.

"I'm Ms. Phoebe," she introduces herself, directing her attention to Emmy. "Are you in Miss Ivy's classes?"

"Yes!" Emmy starts to bounce about, clearly happy at the fact that this woman also knows Ivy. "I love her."

Of course, I recognize that she means this in a way similar to how people mean "I love cake" or "I love snow," but the words still hit my heart.

"I love her too . . ." Ms. Phoebe's brow furrows. Her eyes glance toward the stockroom briefly before turning back to Emmy. "What's your name, darling?"

"I'm Emmy. This is my daddy." Her little thumb hitched in my direction is adorable. "He got shoes that were too big because he bought them online."

Okay, that part was more embarrassing than adorable.

"Well, I'm sure your daddy is doing his best. Right, Dad?"

I nod my appreciation and try to move the attention away from me by pulling a pair of slippers from the shelf, pretending like I have a clue as to how to analyze their quality.

"Don't worry. I'll get you fitted in no time." Phoebe moves gingerly among the boxes, her hands doing what they've probably done for decades.

I decide to start looking around. "Emmy, what else do you need?" I call as I roam five feet away to a rack of children's items.

"A new leotard, pink. And tights."

Ahh, yes. The tights. Those were also my fault. Just once, I threw them in the dryer with my jeans. Let's just say they're now more lavender than pink. And when I threw her other set in the dryer, they shrank to a size that could probably fit Emmy's dolls. I'm now known as the "tights giant" in Angie's apartment. I'm hoping the nickname doesn't catch on. Thankfully, I have confirmed Emmy's sizes, so I feel confident that I can pick them out easily. Well, relatively easily, since the mountains of tulle all around the shop seem like an intentional obstacle for dance parents. "All right, Peanut. I'll get them."

As I move to another rack, the smell of leather and a scent I've never smelled before permeate the air. I reach for a pair of new pointe shoes hanging on the wall and unashamedly give them a sniff. *Huh.* I can now definitively say I know what pointe shoes smell like. Not terrible.

"Are you planning to try those on?" The smoky voice that inhabits my dreams drifts throughout the small space, and I turn so quickly that the hand by my side knocks into another makeshift bookshelf of pointe shoes. Several pairs wrapped in plastic bags fall to the floor.

"I'm so sorry," I say toward Phoebe, still reeling that Ivy is in the shop. *She's here.* Ivy is moving down the steps that lead upstairs, and Emmy squeals with delight.

"Hi, Emmy girl," Ivy says with a smile. "Let me help your dad really quick, and then I'll be back to check on how those shoes are treating you."

Emmy claps then refocuses on her shoe fitting with Ms. Phoebe. As I hastily attempt to restack the shoes I knocked down, I realize that the numbers and codes on the bags of pointe shoes also must be sorted in a special way that I'm destroying as well.

Ivy's voice swirls around me. "Well, I would say the phrase 'bull in a china shop' fits this situation, but I'm not much of a fan of idioms. I blame Grey. Instead, I think you're more of a mountain in a dance shop . . . or a bear. You can take your pick."

She winks, and my heart rate accelerates. I straighten to my full height and freeze as Ivy reaches for me. Correction: She reaches for a ribbon that's somehow landed on my shoulder. I'm not even sure where it came from, but instantly, it makes me think of the one she gave me years ago. I bet she thinks I don't have it anymore. When I open my mouth to ask, Emmy beats me to it by calling Ivy.

"Excuse me, but I'm being summoned." The soft smile she flashes is enough for me to want to sink to the floor. Forcing myself to redirect my attention to the mission at hand, I hustle to find the items Emmy needs as fast as possible so I can move back toward the little group and pretend I'm just casually standing near the action and not thinking of how my heart may explode at the focused attention Emmy is now getting from her dance teacher. Ivy is lifting her arms over her head and directing my daughter in the proper technique of some ballet moves I've seen her practicing at home.

Admittedly, the shoes now on my daughter's feet look much better than the ones I purchased, which were a bit . . . what's the word? Floppy. I grip the packages of tights and pink leotards as Emmy looks at me.

"Daddy, they fit!"

My cheeks flush, embarrassed that I didn't know how to do *this* better. If she'd needed boxing gloves, she would've had the best ones and been fitted like a champion the next day. I'm out of my element with these delicate fabrics and specially fitted items. Instead, I'm a single dad trying to make sure that she grows up to know that she's fully loved and won't ever be in need of anything. I feel like a failure. But I don't voice that out loud.

"That's awesome, sweetheart." I clear my throat; the sting of not only my own inadequacy but also that fact being so clearly displaced in front of Ivy burns my chest. "I'm just going to . . ." I trail off, bringing the items to the counter to take a breath. I hear murmurs of conversation, and then Ivy appears beside me.

"You really are the quietest walker I've ever seen," I observe. "You're stealth on steroids—not that I believe in those."

"Oh, believe me. I don't think anyone could accuse you of using anything synthetic." She scrunches her nose, a habit I recognize from my daughter and am now delighted to see on her.

"Starlight, are you flirting with me?"

"What? No." Her shoulders drop. "Yes. I guess that was flirting, actually."

I laugh.

"I'm not very good at it, I guess. But I was trying?" Her eyes scan from my hair to my shoes, and I stand a little taller.

"Well, you're doing much better at it than my attempts to give Emmy what she needs." My fear—that I'm not a good enough dad for my daughter—hovers between us. Its uncertainty is laced in my words, filling the air around us. I expect her to agree or, at the very least, to look at me with pity for not knowing how to navigate all the unknown firsts of having a daughter that seem to be piling up around me at an alarming rate or even question my ability to provide for Emmy.

But her reply is so full of compassion that it sends an antsy tingle up my spine. "Hey, no, don't do that, Jace. You're giving her everything you can. It's clear how much you love her. And the dance world isn't easy for anyone, not even the ones who grew up in it."

I'm not sure I'm worthy of her kindness, but she grins, and my knees buckle. With relief, I take the reprieve she's offering. "I mean, the numbers on all the shoes. That's confusing."

Ivy laughs and picks up a keychain with a miniature pointe shoe on it, spinning it and fidgeting. Her eyes lift to mine again, and her hands go still. She opens her mouth as if to say something, but nothing comes out.

"We have the shoes!" Ms. Phoebe interrupts with a flourish as she holds Emmy's hand and walks her toward us.

"Right, yes. The shoes!" Ivy smiles at Emmy, replacing the keychain on the checkout display. She turns to me.

"Okay, well, I should . . ." She gestures upstairs.

I find myself not wanting to let her go. It feels like the most inopportune moment for Ivy to walk away. I'm not even sure why I feel that way, except that her presence has a way of reminding me of the parts of myself I used to really like but have since long forgotten.

"When does your shift end?" I find myself asking as Emmy raises her hands for me to lift her up, which I do. Just yesterday, I proposed a twelve-days-of-Christmas-get-to-know-each-other experiment to Ivy. We haven't yet set up our plans for today.

"Oh, I don't work here," she replies, glancing around. "I used to, as a teenager, with Ms. Phoebe over here. But I was just checking her stock for some items we'll need for the show. I get insider privileges in this town."

I nod, an idea forming. "Would you like to get lunch with us?"

A weird-looking cuckoo clock behind the counter chimes just as I say the words. A miniature nutcracker pops out at the last chime. Ivy's eyes widen, her lips parting in a knowing grin.

"Please! Please! Please!" Emmy holds her hands under her chin in the way she does when she wants me to cave. While I make sure to keep discipline and boundaries gently established in our parent-and-child dynamic, this is the move that usually derails my plans. And Emmy knows it. Ivy's smile tells me she's not immune to Emmy's charms either.

"Go on, dearie," Ms. Phoebe coaxes. "It's not every day you get asked out by the most adorable pair I've seen in a long time. I can text you the numbers later tonight. I think I know by now what you need." She looks at me with a wink.

"Besides, if this one stays here any longer, I think he might break everything in my shop."

As if on cue, I overestimate the space I have available to reach into my coat pocket for my wallet and knock over a display of wooden Mouse King ornaments. "I'm so sorry. I'll clean that up."

Ms. Phoebe waves me off. "Please don't touch another thing. I know a good story when I see it. Besides, I really do think you're just too big for my place."

Ivy laughs. At the sound, I decide my embarrassment is worth it as I one-handedly give Ms. Phoebe my credit card, still holding Emmy with the other hand.

Offering us a smile, Ivy turns toward the stairs. "Let me just grab my things."

And my heart soars, because I'm having lunch with Ivy for the first time ever.

We walk about Birch Borough, having just finished lunch at the juice bar and café that recently opened. People keep nodding at us like we're the king and queen of the region, with Emmy as the princess. Too bad it isn't true. *Though maybe it could be if you'd just give in to what you really want*, my love-starved mind interjects unhelpfully.

"So, 'The Battle' scene in *The Nutcracker*," Ivy cuts through my thoughts with her striking voice.

Though it still sends a smoky shiver through my frame, I'm getting increasingly used to hearing it again. Just like the classical music I love, I have a feeling that just her voice alone has been rewiring my brain. I feel happier every time

I hear it.

"I have all the little mice and soldiers ready," she continues. "And, of course, my nutcracker prince. We just need to figure out a way to get the tree to grow from the start. That's really what sets off the scene."

Little does she know that I've already studied the entire ballet. She gave me a list of the numbers the students will be performing, and I searched for them on YouTube. I even found one by the dance legend, Mikhail Baryshnikov. One doesn't need to even know ballet to have heard of him. I studied each recording late into the night with my reading glasses and a cup of peppermint tea in hand. After familiarizing myself with each scene, I'm even more fascinated with what Ivy's world consists of.

I hurry to answer her question. "I think I can figure out a way to make it happen. If we get some scrim or even some other great fabric, we should be able to create the illusion of the tree growing. I just need more lights and a better sense of the space for the height I'm building to."

Ivy pauses on the sidewalk, her eyes bright. "You've researched this."

"Of course I've researched. This is important to you."

She brushes the wisps of hair around her face that I've long appreciated out of her eyes. "Yeah, it is."

"Well, then it's worth researching."

We resume walking again. Emmy's face is cuddled into the side of my neck. I think the grilled cheese she ordered for lunch was truly a comfort food because her chest rises slower and slower as the minutes tick by. She's close to sleep, and it's these moments that I want to bottle and never forget as she gets older.

Ivy looks up at me and then tips her head forward toward Emmy. "She's out," she whispers.

I sigh and reply with a bit of a smile.

"Do you need to head back?"

"Yeah, I probably should. She's usually wound up until naptime, but I think the excitement of the season has been wiping her out."

"Makes sense."

I want to capture Ivy's grin in a bottle too. I'd gladly become a scientist or a historian if it meant the ability to research and catalog all the things that make Ivy as wonderful as she is.

"Jace, I know you need to go, but can I ask you something?"

"Of course."

She sighs, leading us under the awning of a nearby store. There's a view of the river across the bridge in front of us. A brass band plays jazzy Christmas music on the next corner, a space heater and an extension cord powering their holiday spirit.

"Ask me anything," I encourage, just to make sure she knows I mean it.

"You once asked me what I wanted to be known for. Do you remember that?"

I hate the hesitancy in her tone, but it's appropriate given all the other things that transpired that night and after. "Yes." The single word is all I can grit out, even though I want to tell her I memorized every word of our conversation back then. What we shared has been a soundtrack for me during the hardest seasons of my life.

She captures my gaze with her own. "I'd like to ask you

the same question now. What do *you* want to be known for?"

The question pushes the air out of my lungs. I readjust my grip on Emmy, and she shifts. I think of Ivy's brother, the one who would most likely come after me if he knew I'm not only talking to her again, but I'm also helping her with the show and trying to spend as much time with her as possible before I leave yet again. But he's not here. And I am. "That's a big question," I breathe.

"It is. But you used to seem so sure of what you wanted. I'm wondering if those hopes and dreams have changed as well."

I want to tell her that I feel like I've been through the blender of life and have come out as a completely different mixture of a man. But the one thing that hasn't changed is that I'm drawn to her now just as much as I was when we first met. The first time I saw her again, I knew. Despite all the factors keeping us apart, my feelings for her have remained untouched by time and space. Emmy's delicate weight in my arms reminds me of the time lapse. There's another life for which I'm now responsible. A precious life that I've vowed to prioritize above all else. My daughter needs me just as I need her, and putting her first is the driving force in my mind. But that doesn't mean I don't long for the gentle woman in front of me.

"That's a complicated question for me now, Ivy." The faint gruffness in my voice startles both of us. "Things have shifted since I first asked you that question."

Ivy nods.

"I want to be known for being a good father to Emmy. Anything beyond that, I need to think about to answer honestly. Is that okay?"

Truthfully, I do need to think about it. Because there's so much emotion wrapped up within both my memory of Ivy and her literal presence. I still need to sort through everything that I feel. There's so much in my life that is yet unknown. We're walking through the archetype for all enchanted forests. Here, magic abounds, and life isn't complicated and confusing. Birch Borough is a place where life once seemed to suspend itself to bring us together. But then it also tore us apart. In the stage of friendship that Ivy and I find ourselves at the present, I'm not sure how much of the deepest parts of my heart to share with her quite yet. But I'll learn.

"Of course, Jace." Ivy's voice is warm, her tone assured, with no hint of hesitation. "But just so you know, I'm here when you have your answer. I have a feeling I'll really want to know what it is."

"Same, Ivy," I mutter as she walks with me until we have to go our separate ways. "Same."

Chapter Fourteen

Ivy

The clock strikes one.

If I thought a room full of tiny, pre-K dancers with bunched-up tights and cap-sleeve leotards was the most adorable sight I'd ever seen, I was wrong. Very wrong. No, the most adorable sight I've ever seen is those tiny dancers surrounding a strong, rugged, and heartbreakingly gorgeous man wearing a tool belt as he works.

One might think Jace would feel uncomfortable amid all of these little ones, but again, they'd be wrong. He's the picture of ease, working with a confidence that tugs at my feminine heart. Ever in his orbit, Emmy lingers nearby to assist the dancers younger than her. She teaches them how to hold their hands so they look more like arches than claws. Her dad is building a set in the corner of the room while they dance. He's careful not to get in their way and has even joined in on singing for them when Emmy has asked him to. He wasn't kidding when he said he'd do anything for her. He's been all rough edges and a stilted personality that fits like a scratchy new outfit since we first met, but with his daughter, he's fully present, caring, and attentive. Nothing is too silly. Nothing is too outlandish. I think he'd wear one of our costumes if Emmy asked him. The love of a father is stunning.

Today, we're holed up in the performance hall at the local high school for the first time, getting my students used to the stage. It doubled as an opportunity for some of the sets to be built or delivered here instead of having to stage all of it at Wicked Good Farms. It's also a weekend, so it's easier to get into the theater and not get in the staff's way until their show later this evening.

I've had to refrain from squealing at least six times this afternoon at the joy of it all, and that's nothing compared to how often I've dreamed about pulling Jace into my makeshift office (also known as the left wing of the stage) and claiming his mouth with mine. I'm not proud of the rogue thoughts, but my attraction to him is humming through my body and winding through my muscles. Not even stretching could ease this tension.

"Where do you want me next, boss?" Jace's smooth voice speaks behind me.

I shiver. A woman can only take so much of his manliness before she internally combusts. I turn slightly, pretending that I'm focusing solely on my students, but in my peripheral vision, I see Jace leaning closer. The momentum of the movement causes him to shuffle forward a few inches. It's enough to draw me straight into the radius of the heat and tension radiating off his frame. He clears his throat as I make him wait, the gravelly sound of it like tiny rocks kicked along a stretch of pavement.

"Well, um . . . if you could just . . . the sets . . ." My train of thought fades, at risk of being completely lost the longer I look at him.

"You're doing great with these kids, Ivy."

The abrupt change in subject startles me, but his words both instantly comfort and frustrate me. I've met men who thought what I do for a living is admirable but childish, and the few who have seen it as a worthwhile pursuit have been unbalanced. That is probably localized to the men I've personally met and doesn't represent all men as a whole (I would hope), but it's been a long journey. Moving from a world-class company back to my small hometown was hard. It took everything in me not to quit, especially since I've counted on donations for years, not just to keep the studio open but to support these kids that I love to the best of my abilities.

"Thank you," I reply to Jace quietly. "And thank you for helping my students." I turn my attention to the little ones dancing about, the piano music on a track reverberating throughout the space.

"Starlight," he mumbles, and then I'm toast. The kind of toast that's golden and just waiting for butter. Now, I'm hungry. Jace continues, "It's okay if you needed this too. Everyone needs help sometimes. I know my family has been there for me countless times."

I hum, turning toward him. I know there's more to the story with his ex, but seeing Emmy without a mother is heartbreaking. I can't imagine anyone being okay with leaving her. I'm so glad his family stepped in.

"Daddy!" Emmy rushes over, her dark hair curling at the end of her bun. It's starting to unravel. "Hi."

Jace leans down to pick her up as if she weighs nothing.

Within seconds, she's nestled in his arms and kissing him on the cheek. As if they've practiced it a thousand times before, she turns to push her cheek against his and gives the *scrunchiest* (I made that word up) smile. It's adorable. In turn, Jace scrunches his nose and pulls her closer, his arms a big nest for his tiny bird, full of safety and warmth.

When she squirms, he puts her down while I try to will my brain to never forget that image for as long as I live.

"Catch ya later!" she yells, running back to the rest of the students and dancing with all her might, as if that little hint of affection gave her another boost of energy.

"Well, it's clear that your family—those of them that I've met—really loves you."

"They do," he agrees with a nod. "But so does your family."

"You haven't met my family," I say with a laugh.

"Oh, but I have."

"What? When?"

"Yesterday, as I was walking by the inn. Your parents and grandmother popped out of the inn like a jack-in-the-box when I walked by. Blocked my way on the sidewalk."

Mortified, I hang my head. I can only imagine what my grandmother probably said to him. My parents . . . I'm not as worried about them embarrassing me. Sure, they were likely to be incredibly enthusiastic, but I know they wouldn't intentionally say anything that I wouldn't want them to say. My grandmother, however, would have used any and every chance to rattle Jace just for the fun of it. She's similar to Gladys in that way.

"And exactly how much did my Gram comment on your . . ." I wave my hand in the direction of his general frame, not wanting to say the words, namely, his notable attractiveness, his physique, or even—objectively—his top-tier level of hotness. I'm a dancer. I've seen the male figure quite a bit in my life—in tights, at that. So, I can convincingly say that while Jace's frame is bulkier than the dancers I've been around most of my life, he's all muscle, clean lines, and strength. Yes, he's huge. But his frame wasn't formed by bodybuilding. He's not a gym bro. He's a punching-the-lights-out-of-punching-bags-and-building-furniture-by-hand kind of guy. And it's clearly a workout regimen that works.

I come to, realizing that I've gotten lost in listing Jace's excellent physical attributes while standing right next to him. I've officially been thinking way too long about how much I like looking at him.

When my vision clears, his expression is stoic. The only indication that he's enjoying this conversation is in the slight lift of his posture, the flex of his biceps as he crosses his arms, and the amusement flickering like a lit candle in his gaze.

"Your grandmother might've mentioned my height. I believe the words 'gun show' were utilized more than once."

I laugh and cover my mouth in embarrassment at the volume as the kids stop their motions for a minute before resuming their squeals and play. "Oh no, she didn't!" I draw out the words in horror.

At this, a grin tugs up one side of his mouth, that infamous dimple I remember on his cheek making its first appearance since the days of old. I feel a silent gasp overtake me. There really should be a warning that comes with that dimple. Everyone within a five-foot radius: Look out!

"I mean, she's not wrong."

"Jace!" I push his arm, but he doesn't budge in the least. A microscope would be needed to detect any hint of movement. Goodness, the man really is a mountain. "Did you just admit to your attractiveness?"

"No, I stated a fact." He shrugs, pulling a hammer from his tool belt. He turns to face me and slowly walks backward. Pointing the hammer at me playfully, his shoulders lift again. "But you just did."

Heat floods my face, and I can't help but smile so widely that my mouth hurts. The moment is a glimpse of our easy banter all those years ago. Every day, it seems I see a little more of the man I first met. And I love it.

"Miss Jones." I hear a flustered voice behind me.

When I turn, Arthur of the Music and Arts Committee is walking my way. "Merry Christmas, Mr. Collins," I call out. As unfortunate as it is, that really is his last name.

Arthur takes one look at my students dancing and moving freely. He huffs. While our townspeople are known for their kindness, there are a few who feel the need to keep things incredibly orderly and have certain *expectations* as to what art can be. "I don't understand what's happening here," he says with a frown. "I thought you would be rehearsing for the performance."

I paste on a smile and trust it looks genuine. "Oh, but we are. Unrestricted movement and encouragement to move through play ensure that children feel empowered to continue to move their bodies in a way that would benefit them. We're about to begin our number, but until then, they're exploring self-expression and the freedom found in dance." Hoping that sounded important enough, I laugh as one of my students does the chicken dance. It's not ballet in the least, but it's entertaining.

"I'm sure you know what you're doing," Arthur says with a notable degree of skepticism.

"Yes, thank you. Can I help you with something, though?"

"Ahh, yes, I just wanted to be sure that you saw my memo that the Hoffermans are going to be out of town during the performance. Shame, really."

I . . . did not know that. The Hoffermans are the second top donor each year. My stomach sinks. Something about this year has felt extra challenging. Dance isn't a priority for everyone, and sometimes, it feels like an uphill battle convincing the town to ensure our dance studio survives. First, we lost the sets I used to use for the holiday production to water damage after they were accidentally left outside during a snowstorm, then we lost our original set designer, and now, we're losing the influence and generosity of one of our best financial supporters. I don't know how to make it the best show ever this year, not when so many things seem to be falling out of place, but I still have to try. The Hoffermans are the type to want people to know about their support. So, if they're not concerned with being here, I have even more reason to be concerned about the survival of my livelihood.

But I can't say any of that out loud. "I appreciate the update, Mr. Collins," I begin. "It was kind of you to travel all the way here just to tell me."

His feet shift at the compliment, but he doesn't smile. I know he means well, and I'm confident my appreciation was genuine.

"Well, I just hope there are enough scholarships after the holidays to keep you going, is all," he says ruefully.

We both know the importance of this performance is about more than the scholarships. It's about Piper, whose father was laid off. She dreams of being a principal dancer like I was. It's also about Bennett, who is being raised by a single mom. She works two jobs and believes he should pursue dance if that's what makes him happy.

When I was coming up, my parents always provided. For the most part, I never had to worry, but I remember slow seasons during which my parents' inn struggled and stress over the cost of my dance costumes was high. As soon as I could, I scooped cones at Bette's Ice Cream in the summer to make sure I had the money to pay for all my shoes and uniforms throughout the year. And Mom once admitted that she wanted to dance as a child, but her parents couldn't afford it. That broke my heart, and that's why I am passionate about making sure everyone has the opportunity to pursue their dreams.

Because dance shouldn't be optional for people.

As much as it's hard to hear, I know Arthur is trying to look out for me. He wants me to manage my expectations and plan ahead. But right now, I need a little less realism and a lot more hope. Looking at Jace hammering away at something that I think is going to be a box for one of the dancing dolls in *The Nutcracker*, something that feels a little like potential nestles into the center of my chest.

"I think we're going to be okay, sir," I say firmly. "I love dance, but my students mean the most to me. I will do everything I can to ensure that everyone who wants to dance in this town continues to be able to do so."

Arthur's eyebrows lift. He seems uncertain as to whether I just denied his doom-and-gloom outlook. "Right. Just wanted you to know." He turns to my students, who have now transitioned into hopping while meowing like cats. I stifle a laugh. They're adorable. "I'll leave you to whatever *this* is." With that, he turns and heads to the door backstage.

"Okay, thank you so much!" I call with an overly dramatic wave, even though he doesn't see it.

"Tough crowd," Jace says.

He's beside me again, towering over me like before. I'm surrounded by his presence, and I don't hate it.

"He means well, even if he didn't bring . . . the best news."

My watch beeps, alerting me that it's time to begin our actual rehearsal. I'm focused on our time together today. It may be work to corral a whole herd of littles, but it's the most enjoyable environment I've ever encountered.

"What can I do?" the manly voice beside me speaks again.

My heart warms at the fact that he'd even want to do something. Yet, this isn't his fight. Although, I guess he does have Emmy, who happens to remind me of myself when I was her age; her love for dance is as enthusiastic as my own. Jace's arms hang loosely beside him, my own also extended at my sides. Casually, I reach my hand ever so slightly and nearly gasp when I feel the tips of his fingers brush against mine. My skin flashes with heat. He's meeting me in the middle. And that quiet sign of connection expands my lungs.

"Build things?" I wish my question held a little more confidence, but it's all I've got right now. With his help, we have more of a chance at a successful production, no matter how many tickets we sell."

"And that I can do." With that, Jace strides the length of the stage in four steps and is back to working on his box situation.

I shake my head. The weirdness of how . . . not domestic, exactly, but how normal it feels for him to be here is not lost on me. While I'm surrounded by people during my classes, I'm rarely with other adults at my studio besides Harlow.

"Okay, my darlings! *Allons-y!*"

Immediately, my class laughs, familiar with my random terms of endearment or greetings in French. In addition to universal ballet terms, Sparrow taught me a few useful phrases.

"Let's practice for our Christmas performance!"

Later that night, when I'm lying in bed, reading, Resin tucked under the covers beside me and his head lying across my stomach, I hear the familiar *ting* of an incoming message on my phone. I forgot to turn off my notifications before settling in for the night. Picking it up from the bedside table, my screen lights up with a message from an unfamiliar number. My heart changes rhythm.

Unknown Number: Hi, Starlight.

The simple greeting is enough for me to smile and settle deeper into my pillows, my phone hovering over my face while Resin nestles in closer. Of all the messages I've received on my phone—factoring in apps and various dating attempts—this, by far, is my favorite one. I take a screenshot and then decide to have a little fun.

Me: Who is this?

I know it's Jace by the nickname, no question. I've already added his contact info into my phone. But I'm curious to see his reaction. The dots on the screen appear and disappear.

Jace: I'd better be the only one who calls you Starlight.

His slightly possessive tone, while brand new to me, I don't hate. I find I don't even want to tease him anymore.

Me: You are.

Jace: Good. Your gram gave me your number. Hope that's okay.

Instantly, I have so many questions. My grandmother is notoriously bad at technology, so the fact that she not only gave him my number but also figured out *how* to provide it is enough of a Christmas miracle for the season.

Me: You saw her again?

Jace: I think she's a fan.

Me: Wow, an endorsement from Gram is worth a thousand others.

Jace: I'm honored.

Me: So, what are you going to do now that you have the power to write to me at any time?

The little dots once again appear and disappear, and I've never been so riveted by my phone in my life.

Jace: First, I'm inviting you to go sledding.

Jace: Tomorrow.

Jace: With Emmy.

Jace: Emmy and me.

Jace: Both of us.

Jace: And you.

Jace: It's my Christmas wish.

Jace: Well, one of them. *wink-wink*

I laugh. Turns out that the man has zero chill tonight.

Jace: Sorry. I'm nervous, and my thumbs are clearly unhinged. Don't hold it against me.

Jace: Please.

I squeal. Resin groans.

"I'm disrupting your slumber, I know." I pet his head before typing as fast as my fingers allow.

Me: It turns out I'm free for a sledding adventure. Can't wait.

Jace: Me too. I'll text you the time tomorrow. Goodnight, Starlight.

Me: Night, Jace.

I switch my phone to silent, turn off my bedside lamp, and nestle into the covers, wrapping Resin up in my arms and enjoying the weight of him and the sound of his even breaths.

"I feel so light, buddy. I think this might be what happiness feels like." I confess the words into the darkness of my room, the silkiness of Resin's ears a comfort between my fingers. And, for the first time in a long time, I dream.

The clock strikes two.

Today should prove to be interesting. I'm trying to work through the fact that the woman who inspired me to resume watching rom-coms again, the woman I've always had a spark with, has agreed to go sledding with me today. Ivy has been the woman who got away for so long. But doesn't everyone deserve a try at the thing that seems too good to be true?

I'm not sure why I felt the nerve to finally text her. It could've been the shock of Ivy's grandmother giving me her number so freely, or it could've been the way my chest was still burning—not from the effects of punching a bag at the studio but from her proximity at the dance rehearsal. It seems that the more often I'm in Ivy's orbit, the more I want to experience it again.

Emmy rushes out of our bedroom—the one we've been sharing like we're in summer camp at my sister's house. She has a duvet-covered daybed filled with stuffed animals, and I sleep on a twin bed that creaks underneath my weight every time I shift. It's like *Goldilocks and the Three Bears* over here, with my sister probably having the only bed that's just right.

"Daddy, we get to go sledding!" Her bright eyes are the color of my own, and they settle some of my nerves until I remember that Emmy is going to see Ivy again as well. Is it problematic that I want them to love each other? We're leaving in two weeks, after all. To be honest, I feel a primal hope for my child to be accepted by her dance teacher. Maybe it's because Jenna gave up her rights to her daughter so freely a long time ago. I can't imagine anyone not wanting to watch their daughter grow up, but from the moment of her birth, I've been driven and determined for Emmy to always know that her worth is not found in rejection but in her acceptance of herself, as well as from me and our family.

"We do, Emmy Bear," I say, reaching for her. She leaps into my arms without hesitation, nestling her face within my neck before leaning back to look me in the eyes.

"Are you excited?"

She nearly squeals, and I hold back a laugh. Her energy and zest for life are unparalleled. My daughter is the sunshine that wakes me every morning. But now the idea of having a sense of "Starlight" to make the nights magical makes me shake my head to clear my thoughts. A man can hope.

"I'm very happy to go sledding with you." She's still in my arms, lifted above the ground, her laugh at the change in height a reward. "Here's the thing, though: I was wondering if you would be okay if we met a friend to go sledding with us."

"A friend? What friend?" Her eyes are curious, her head tilted, looking directly into my eyes.

I turn to face her and try to maintain my calm. "A good

friend. And you know her too. She's also known as your teacher, Miss Ivy." I hold my breath after the admission.

Emmy shrieks. "Miss Ivy! My dance teacher, Miss Ivy?" She's bouncing in my arms. I set her down, and she proceeds to hop and flail her arms about, her ponytail lifting and falling with a second's delay behind her movements.

Finally, I exhale a laugh. "Yes, it's Miss Ivy. She's going to join us sledding."

"Yes! Yes! Yes!" Emmy punches her fists into the air like she's boxing the ceiling, if she could reach it.

As much as I want her to be fond of the unforgettable woman, I still have to rub a hand over my sternum to press against the anxiety. My hopes are used to being crushed, but Emmy is still young. Already, she's missed out on so much. While I don't think Ivy would ever act unfeelingly with Emmy, I'm not yet sure that our story is a future Ivy would want. Besides, getting to know each other was only supposed to be for Christmas, right?

Emmy runs to peek out the window at the grey sky above that's quickly becoming darker with an impending snowstorm. It's afternoon, and we're going to the pavilion, but even if it gets dark, the paths for sledding are illuminated by the lights overhead. Birch Borough sponsors a makeshift sledding station every year. It begins at the top of the hill, and you slide down until you reach the edge of the ice rink at the bottom.

"Okay, miss, let's get you ready for sledding." I kneel to her level—at least closer to her level—and help her put on her mittens, a hat, and a new pale-blue snowsuit that I ordered for her as soon as I felt the fall weather in the air. Even before we moved to the small New England town, I hoped for moments of adventure outside with her this winter. I'm committed to giving her memories to hold on to for the rest of her life. I decided to provide Emmy with the best childhood possible. That means sledding is essential.

"Ready!" Emmy yells, bouncing to the door and onto the front walk. She looks like an adorable version of a man walking on the moon in her new suit. She waddles into the snow, but at least it will keep her warm.

"Yes, but am *I* ready?" I ask myself before locking the door behind us and heading toward Ivy.

I'm pacing in the snow at the base of the sledding hill, the shouts of overzealous sledders as they fly down the slope hitting my ears from across the way, when I spot Ivy walking toward us. Her dark-golden braid is wrapped over the side of her shoulder, a smile wide enough to power the lights around us on her face. Emmy has been making snow angels for the last ten minutes, since we got here a bit too early. Call it excitement or nerves, but when I see Ivy arrive looking like an actual angel, I know I made the right choice in asking her to join us.

Suddenly, I'm hit with a wave of shyness, my feet planted in the snow and my hands in my pockets. I'm trying to remember all the ways that I've proven to possess even an ounce of charm in the past. Have I ever been suave? What is game? Will I be able to wrestle it from the depths of my younger self? So many questions and life choices unexpectedly swirl through my mind as Ivy reaches us. Without a word, she plops down beside Emmy in the snow and begins making snow angels herself.

My daughter's contagious laughter is enough to snap me back into the present. Instantly, I'm not worried about whether I have swag. Rather, I'm far more concerned with how to make this feeling of pure joy stretch beyond this experience. Because the image of Ivy and my daughter making snow angels will be one that I'll remember when I drift into sleep tonight.

"Are you gonna join us, Bear?" There's a hint of amusement in Ivy's tone. She alluded to me being like a bear in the dance shop. Now, she's apparently turned it into a nickname.

"C'mon, Daddy!" Emmy yells. At her prompting, I plop myself beside my daughter and move my arms and legs like a jumping jack in frozen powder. When Emmy is satisfied that we've made angels pretty enough to satisfy her, she hops up and points to the top of the hill.

"Now, can we go sledding?"

I push myself up to sit on the snow, my back cold but my insides warming as Ivy lifts herself from the snow as well. I finally gather the courage to take a good look at her. Her bright-red lipstick stands out like a cardinal surrounded by winter white. I clear my throat.

"Yeah—yes," I stutter. What is wrong with me? "It's time, Emmy Bear." I wink and watch Ivy's mouth drop open.

"I didn't know you called her that. How long has that been her nickname?" Her slight frown as she analyzes how she managed such a coincidence is . . . adorable.

"Forever," Emmy answers. "He calls me other things too. Wait . . . Miss Ivy, you called Daddy "Bear" when you got here," she adds then dismisses it with a shrug of her tiny shoulders. "I guess he is my daddy, so he'd have to be a bear too."

Ivy laughs. "Yes, he'd have to be." The slight tint to her cheeks, visible even in the soft glow of the afternoon, tells me that she's pleased to have given me a nickname that suits me so well. Rising, Ivy waits for me to do the same before she turns toward the hill.

Emmy's hand reaches for hers. Watching closely, I register the surprise on Ivy's face when she looks down at their now-joined fingers. Emmy is watching a group of sledders who have just taken off from the top of the hill. Of course, she doesn't understand the monumental action of reaching for her dance teacher instead of me. But the sight aligns something in me that I didn't know was out of place.

And when Ivy looks at me over her shoulder, a disbelieving smile on her face as tears brim in her eyes, I give her an encouraging nod. *Those are my girls. My girls.* The thought hits me out of nowhere. Could that be possible? When we first met, I could give her only myself, but now I have a daughter. Could Emmy's presence actually be a welcome bonus to our package deal and not less than what Ivy hoped her life would contain?

As we climb to the top of the hill, we arrive at a tiny makeshift shack with a couple of teenagers handing out sleds near a glass mason jar stuffed with cash, *Tips* written in big letters across the front, along with the high school's logo.

"Whoa!" one of the young men exclaims, looking up at me. "Are you in sports or something?"

"He's a boxer," Ivy interjects, her eyes shining. "He's huge, right?"

"Hey, now," I protest.

Ivy purses her lips together, no doubt to keep from laughing.

"You could play in the NFL or something," a boy with the same haircut I had in high school says. It must show my age if the style is cool again. "Ryan! Get over here. You've gotta see this guy!"

A third teenage boy—I'm assuming Ryan—appears with rosy cheeks and ears, his coat hanging open as only an audacious youngster could pull off while standing on a snowy mountain slope. "Whoa," is all he says.

Ivy's laughter rings through the brisk air. "Maybe he'll sign something for you if you ask nicely."

"I'm not famous," I retort.

Ivy only shrugs, those red lips of hers still tugged up in a grin. I want to kiss her just to see if the color is a stain or if it would transfer to me. But of course, I wouldn't—*shouldn't*—do that in front of my daughter. At least, not yet.

Emmy is now giggling uncontrollably, picking up on the playfulness between Ivy and these *High School Musical*-looking teenagers.

"So, you two are together?" a kid with the most annoying haircut of them all asks us.

"Well, I . . ." Ivy stumbles.

"That's not your business," I answer sharply, the Grinch in me immediately agitated by the question.

"You're right, sir."

Sighing as Ivy gently touches my arm, an idea of how to wrangle these hooligans comes to me. I've dealt with plenty of their type as a boxing instructor over the years, but I think I know how to break the ice with them. "Boys, I could use help building some sets for an upcoming dance performance." One of the teenagers snickers as the other elbows him in the ribs. I continue, "Miss Ivy, here, is the dance studio owner."

Immediately, the boys straighten up.

"Are you dancers?" Emmy asks them, one of her eyebrows lifted in skepticism.

"Uh . . . no, but we can build things." One of the boys steps up, joining the conversation and looking at Ivy like she hung the moon. I know the feeling. "Right, guys? We. Can. Build. Things."

"Yeah."

"Yep."

"Sure."

I chuckle and try to cover it with a cough. Oh, to be young again and trying to impress a pretty woman. Who am I kidding? I'm doing that. Except that I remember I'm now a man—a very tall man whose arms and limbs are proportionate to the rest of my body. And Ivy is here with me, with us. Lifting Emmy into my arms, I gather my boldness and wrap an arm around the woman next to me. To my shock and delight, she nestles in. The fact that she responds to my touch and doesn't pull away thrills me. Even though we've got layers of winter coats between us, the side of me that is touching her is instantly on fire.

The teenagers shove sleds toward us, the three of them standing at attention. "Sir, sleds are on the house," the one called Ryan informs me quickly.

"Good choice," I say, allowing a level of faux intimidation in my voice. "Meet me at Wicked Good Farms, at the red barn, tomorrow night at five o'clock sharp. Wear clothes you don't mind getting ruined." They won't be doing anything to ruin their clothes, but I can't help but throw the command out there. I am rewarded with their wide-eyed stares and shaky nods.

"Thanks, guys. I really appreciate your help," Ivy adds sweetly, the honey to my vinegar.

Their nods make their heads resemble tiny bobblehead toys. I'm sure that's why Emmy giggles. Ivy pulls at my coat, and I follow her a few steps away, noticing how her shoulders are shaking with laughter as well.

"Well, that's one way to get the help we need," she quips.

"Eh." I shrug. "I remember being that age. They need a job. They're helping the community. They're getting experience. And conveniently, they're starting their lifelong journey of trying to impress a woman way out of their league."

"And you get to babysit them," Ivy says with a grin.

We shuffle through the snow toward the line to sled downhill, and Emmy exclaims, "Daddy can show them how to make a box! He built me a box with stars."

At this, Ivy slows her pace. "A box with stars?"

"Uh-huh." Emmy shifts in my arms to look more fully at Ivy. "Last Christmas. It's to hold my dreams."

Under Ivy's knowing gaze, my throat feels tight. I will my feet to move forward until we reach the top of the hill, where Emmy and I nestle together on one sled. Ivy settles on the other. An image of the three of us floats through my mind, and I think of what it would feel like to wrap my arms around Ivy on our own sled while Emmy laughs all the way down the hill, snow flying in our faces. I shake my head to dissolve the image and let Emmy call out our countdown.

"Three, two, go!" she yells, and I push off. With a rush, the wind in our face is so strong that I feel snow fly up my nose, pummeling my teeth. Emmy's happiness is worth it as we shoot down the hill until I put my boots down and pull us to a stop. Ivy slides to a stop only a few seconds behind us. I'm surprised she caught up so fast, given that there's all my weight on one sled and only her tiny frame in the other.

"Ahh!" Ivy yells happily, her arms raised in the air. Eyes bright, she looks at us, and a smile lights her face, snow clinging to the top of her beanie and the end of her braid. She looks beautiful. "Again! Again!" she cries.

I shake my head in affirmation, trying to hold back how overwhelmingly good it feels to just have fun. When was the last time I had fun with someone who wasn't family? *Not family . . . yet.* My mind inserts the thought sneakily, and I once again shake it away. It keeps doing that.

Ivy leaps up, dragging the sled behind her and running back up the snowy hill. Emmy takes off after Ivy, and after watching them for a few seconds, I rise and follow. The two of them decide to go down the hill together a few more times, screaming when they can't seem to beat me. I end up sitting out a few rounds, letting them go again and again, waiting off to the side at the top of the slope. I'm shocked they aren't exhausted after another few excursions down the hill. I'm still watching them when Edgar appears, climbing slowly up the slope.

"Hey, man." He walks over to me and clasps my shoulder, his arm stretching up slightly. I am the taller one, after all.

"Uh, hi." My neck and shoulders feel tight under his fingers. I wasn't expecting to see him here tonight. Now, he'll know I invited Ivy to sled with us. I'm not nervous that he'll do anything intentionally to sabotage me, but integrating Ivy into more of my world feels like it's still too good to be true, so I'll admit I'm nervous.

"Eddie!" Emmy yells, she and Ivy cresting the top of the hill again. I laugh as Edgar shoots me a glare. I encourage her to call him that, sans "uncle" on top of it, and he hates it.

"This isn't over," he says quietly. I think the words are meant to be threatening, but he's too soft for my daughter to care as she runs toward him.

"Eddie! Eddie!"

"Fine," he says, shoulders sagging as he runs to pick her up. He grabs my neglected sled and walks with her to the launching point.

Ivy lingers at the top of the hill with me, tentatively stepping forward until she's standing beside me. She peeks up and sighs contentedly, the sound of it a warm compress on my muscles. There's a height difference between us—a great one—but everyone tends to be shorter than me, so I've been training my whole life to dip my chin for her to make eye contact now. She could be six feet tall, and I'd be drawn to her no matter what. Ivy's soul shines through everything she does, and she just happens to also come in the most stunning form I've ever seen.

"You've been keeping your distance," she breaks our silence as we watch Edgar and Emmy join the line of people waiting to take their turn. Her gaze is full of nothing but a question and a hint of playfulness.

"Well, there have been children present in every circumstance tonight," I reply dryly.

Ivy laughs and swings her arms slightly as if she's either choreographing another ballet or warming up for the next run on the sled. "True, but I meant with your thoughts. Remember that one time you poured out your heart to me over cookies and hot chocolate . . . Oh, wait, you were drinking coffee like a madman into the late evening." Her grin fades, her eyes softening as they roam over my face. "I'd like to get back to that place again."

I nod. She's right. When I first came back to Birch Borough, I let the gruffness I've cultivated for years—that protective armor—slip through in my interactions around town. I've felt my defenses cracking, warmth entering my chilled heart again. But admittedly, I'm afraid to let Ivy, of all people, see all of me at this stage in my life. I want to tell her the whole truth about Jenna. Tell her of all the ways I've thought about her over the past eight years. Because I never forgot that she was the dream that got away.

I clear my throat. "Yeah, well, I have a lot of fires in my head that I need to put out at the moment."

Ivy shrugs. "Sounds like a lonely job. Maybe you don't have to be alone to do it, though?" Her voice hums, the words settling between us, and the effects of her smoky tones pierce my heart.

I struggle to respond, but instead of pushing me, Ivy tilts her head and pretends to look for something near my feet. An alarm clock blares from the makeshift sledding shed with the teenage boys we met earlier, signaling another hour. The afternoon has progressed with ease.

"We'd better get going soon," I say, allowing regret to enter my voice so she knows I'm not running away from our conversation.

"Hmm, looks like you're without a sled, though," she says with a wink.

"I am."

"How are you going to get down the hill? It's a long walk." The corner of her mouth, still wrapped in red lipstick, twitches, and I suddenly think that the expression is a nervous tell, if I had to guess.

"Oh, well, I could just roll. Stop, drop, and all that." I want to punch myself in the face at the evidence of how much game I don't have with that statement.

Ivy giggles. "Or you could go by sled . . ." she trails off.

"But I don't have—" I stop when I see her push the edge of her sled forward slightly. Oh . . . *Oh.* Is she asking us to go together?

"There is one way we could get down there at the same time, I guess." I point toward the bottom of the slope, where Edgar and Emmy are already waiting at the hot chocolate stand by the rink.

"I thought there might be."

I rub the back of my neck with my snow-wet gloves and wince. Ivy reaches out a mittened hand, snow stacked on the knitwear in clumps. I take her small fingers in my own gloved hand, the feeling of how easily they are swallowed by my palm something I want to both protect and remember.

Ivy tosses the sled onto the snow, her tongue peeking out between her teeth in concentration, and waits.

"I'll, uh—I'll just get in first," I finally stutter. And even though I've done this dozens of times with Emmy, I'm self-conscious. I feel too big for the sled. What do I do with my arms and legs? I settle on the sled and decide to just wait, my arms extending slightly off the edges and my heels tucked into the curve at the front of the sled.

Above me, Ivy inhales and then slowly turns to settle in

front of me. She crosses her legs in front of her, the tops of her knees peeking over the edges of the sled. Several inches of space remain between us, but I'm still frozen at the light scent of vanilla hovering just under my nose from her hair. *Ivy.* My heart thumps in my chest, and I remember again how to be myself. It's her, the woman I've wanted to return to me for ages. The awkwardness and tension leave my body at the feeling of her being this close to me.

Drawing my shoulders back, I wrap an arm around her waist. I pull her toward me slightly until her back is resting against my chest. Immediately sinking into me, she leans her head back against my collarbone and hums. My smile would be enough to power us down the hill, but I make sure she's okay with this arrangement, just in case. I can't afford to miss any cues.

"Is this okay?" I whisper into her ear, and she shivers.

"Yes, Jace," she says with a deep breath between the words. "Because I know I'm safe with you."

The trust she's placed in me nearly wipes me out. But she's right to believe that I'd do anything to cover and protect her. Anything in my power.

"You are." I pull her against me even tighter and allow myself to breathe deeply, attempting to convince myself that I have what it takes not to let her down. "Count us off, Starlight."

She laughs. "One, two, go!"

And it's Ivy's laughter mixed with my own as we fly through the air off the slope that brings me closer than ever to believing that brokenness and loss might not be the end of our story after all.

Chapter Sixteen

Ivy

*T*he *clock strikes three.*

"Ivy, dear friend," Sparrow greets me with a smile from behind the register. She moves toward the high-top area of the counter and, leaning forward on her elbows, rests there with her hands casually looped together. A green satin ribbon holds her hair back today, a nod to the Christmas season, no doubt. Her eyes shine in a way that I believe only happens when one is in love. My eyes catch on the simple wedding band on her left hand, the one she wears when she's at the bakery so that she doesn't get her diamond engagement ring ruined with croissant dough. Though, she often declares that croissants hold a bit of magic for her and Rafe. Seeing as how they're both of French heritage within their family trees, I wouldn't doubt it.

"Hi, Rory." I grin back, using her nickname, grateful to be in her calming presence and let the smell of ground coffee and toasted sugar ease my soul for a bit. The sight of my friend and the sound of jazz music in the form of current

Christmas songs bring the first real, full smile to my face all day. Today, Jace was at rehearsal again, assembling things—always assembling things. He was getting organized to help the teenagers he'll be working with later. I've almost lost track of what I asked him to create due to how distracting he is. And my head is now pounding.

The thrill of being near him so often lately has gotten to be a bit much. There's something Jace is still not telling me, and I can't even begin to imagine what it could be. Maybe he has reservations because of his ex. Maybe he has reservations about how he really feels about me. Maybe he's changed his mind about getting to know me, though he was the one who proposed the Christmas countdown. He didn't seem to have any regrets yesterday when we went sledding, finishing off the afternoon with the wind brushing against my face and his warm breath near my ear. When we landed at the bottom of the hill, he pressed his cheek gently against my own and then helped me rise.

Later, when I slid into bed, I found a message from him on my phone. We texted for a bit, but it was only about what time to meet for today's assembly projects and our goal for the timeline. And then, at rehearsal earlier, he was reserved. I'm not sure what to make of it. I've explored relationships before where the man is emotionally unavailable, and this doesn't feel like those. His eyes betray his inner turmoil. There's something holding him back from allowing himself to connect fully, and I just hope he has the strength to push through to the other side and give us a solid chance.

"Your special hot chocolate today?" Sparrow's voice cuts through my thoughts as I approach the counter. Her voice is a bit melodic, not nearly as raspy as mine, but I hear the emotion through it. I've barely visited Sparrow and Lily the past couple of weeks. My mind feels preoccupied, my heart too full to prioritize socializing. And now, she's worried about me. I'm worried about myself. And when I settle myself on the stool across from her and look up, the line between her furrowed brow proves it.

Nodding slightly, I expect Sparrow to walk away and make it herself. But one of her hands covers mine, and she politely asks Anna, one of the bakery assistants here, to make it instead, quietly giving instructions. Sparrow's eyes return to mine as she scans my face, clearly looking for any and every clue of what's really going on in my life. With the rush of the season upon us, the bakery will be open later than usual, and I took advantage of the opportunity to see my longtime friends this afternoon.

"I'm okay," I mutter in response to her unspoken question.

She squints, and a myriad of emotions cross her face, a frown meeting eyes that hold both worry and amusement.

"Hmm," she hums, pointing toward the door. "If I marched myself over to Marlee's Books and asked Grey how she finds your present state, you're telling me she would also say you're doing okay?"

My head drops slightly. She's got me, and she knows it. While Sparrow, Lily, Grey, and I have always been close, circumstances have made it so that Grey is closest to me, just as Lily is closest to Sparrow. The four of us will always love each other and be there for each other, but sometimes, life has a way of forcing a proximity of friendship that ingrains itself into your very being.

"She might?" I reply to her.

I wince as Anna saves me from more blatant questioning by presenting the most delectable-looking hot chocolate. She picks up a sanitizing rag and moves onto the floor to begin clearing tables. Sparrow's and Lily's use of real melted chocolate as the base, with no powder allowed, shows in the quality and taste. The sparrow painted on the edge of the ceramic cup and plate feels like a warm, familiar hug.

I take my first sip as Sparrow gives me the proper moment of silence this treat has earned. Releasing a relieved sigh and allowing the warm chocolate to align my thoughts, I wrap my hands around the cup and look at my friend. "I don't know why I wandered in here," I admit.

"You can always wander in here."

I nod, emotion starting to build behind my eyes.

"Oh, for the love of croissants!" A yell from the back of the kitchen causes both of us to jump, even though we know the cause of the disturbance.

"And there she is . . ." Sparrow mutters.

The door to the kitchen swings open, revealing Lily. She's covered in chocolate up to her forearms, her baby bump rounding out the front of her apron. From the line of chocolate across it, I'd say she's been leaning against the counter while tempering chocolate again.

"Problem?" Sparrow grins. She doesn't leave my side, amusement etched across her face.

"This little cruffin," she starts, pointing to her stomach in case we aren't aware that she is referring to her unborn child (we are), as a drop of chocolate drips to the floor, "he or she—because we all know Graham is so old-fashioned that he wants to be surprised, and Lord knows I love him too much to fight him on it—will not stop kicking when I make chocolate cake!" Her eyes are a bit wild, her blonde ponytail extra high on her head today.

I cover my mouth with my hand to keep from laughing. It's still hard for me to process that Lily is five months pregnant with her and Graham's first child. It still feels like we should be planning our next group sleepover and avoiding gym class. As feisty as she can be, Lily being the first one of us to get pregnant suits her. And as much as she's vocal about everything relating to this new development in her life, she's the biggest softie. Her eyes hold a sheen every time Graham puts his hand on her stomach or talks about their baby.

"Lils, since a great part of your love story has revolved around chocolate cake, I would think that your baby's reaction makes perfect sense," Sparrow says reasonably.

Lily huffs, wiping her arm across her forehead. It leaves a streak of chocolate. I open my mouth to say something when I catch the slight shake of Sparrow's head. Our friend makes her way around the counter and sits beside me, after making a great effort to get onto the stool. When most of her weight is supported, she grins at me like she's proud of herself.

"Okay, Ives, give me the scoop," Lily says. "I need news. Fill my head with some sort of intel that isn't about the terrifying process of giving birth or the fear that my child may hate chocolate."

I laugh. "Impossible."

Lily shrugs, Sparrow giggles, and I'm faced with the power of these two friends giving me all their attention.

"It's about . . . Jace."

Sparrow clasps her hands together with excitement,

leaning her chin on them with a smile. Lily squeals.

"Yes, girl! That man is so fine he could melt sugar without a flame. A proper crème brûlée, I'm sure of it." Lily stares dreamily at the ceiling before turning back to me.

I chuckle. "That makes no sense."

"Look, he's in no way for me. I'm a happily married woman who goes home to a generous lawyer who is the most handsome man I've ever seen in my life, but I can still call it like it is. Jace could lift you with one arm. He could probably—and most lovingly—toss you across the room without breaking a sweat."

"Lily!" Sparrow scoffs.

"I'm talking about dance things, dance-related things," Lily defends, shooting me a wink.

My embarrassment is swallowed up in amusement. "He is quite tall, isn't he?" I say it just to provoke Lily further.

"Girl, Gladys was in here with your gram the other day, and she had herself a party with the number of photos she's gotten of him around town! She claims she's trying to calculate if he's too tall for her annual calendar of the men of Birch Borough. She said she needed to make sure she could fit a lot of him on the page. She also asked if he liked puppies. Is he allergic to anything that you know of?"

Sparrow's mouth hangs open while I snort and cover my mouth. We're all laughing when the door opens. Rafe and Graham walk in together.

"Speaking of handsome men," Sparrow nearly sings as Rafe ignores us to hop and slide over the counter, wrapping Sparrow up in his arms. They hold each other like they haven't seen each other in years and didn't just eat lunch together a few hours ago. I know they saw each other today because Rafe was holding a pizza box when he walked by my studio earlier, and, as expected, he was moving in the direction of Sparrow's Beret.

After an exchange of whispers in French and a soft kiss on her cheek, he turns to us, Sparrow tucking herself under his arm with a content look on her face. Meanwhile, Graham has perched himself on the stool beside Lily, his hand already resting on her stomach and his eyes misty. The love in the air is palpable. I swallow back the emotion it triggers. As sweet as the scene is, I feel like my own thoughts and life are currently in pieces.

It's like everything has descended upon me all at once this season. The list goes on and on. I need the sets to look extra amazing this year. I'm actually not afraid of accomplishing that now that Jace is working on them. But I also need the performance to go well, I need scholarships to be donated for my students, and perhaps most of all, I need to feel a reprieve from the loneliness that seems to haunt me when I'm in the middle of a room full of people. When he returned to Birch Borough, I had a wild moment of hope that Jace could fill that void. Perhaps he was sent to me to be my Christmas miracle. But if he's not able to go all in or unable to tell me the whole truth about what we are or could be to each other, I'm not sure I can risk my heart either.

As I watch my friends, I realize I don't want their lives. I just want a love of my own. And since that fateful night eight years ago, only Jace fits my vision of an ideal man. Even if he does act like a grumpy Beast in the castle sometimes.

"Where's your guy, Ivy?" Rafe asks kindly, with no hint of teasing in his tone.

"Oh, we're not. Well, kind of . . . or at least, I had hoped, but I don't know if it's meant to be."

Graham's brows furrow. "If that's true, I'm not certain Jace knows it."

"What do you mean?" My voice emerges far breathier than I'd like, but it's honest.

All four of my friends look at me with a mix of amusement and genuine concern.

"I'm pretty sure the man would walk through fire for you," Lily adds.

"I thought he was the one making fires?" I retort with a grin.

"What's this about fires?" Graham says. Lily hooks an arm around him to nestle his face near her neck. She pats his beard.

"Don't worry, darling. I'm only encouraging young love."

He grins and nestles into her neck with a smile, not moving, as if he could stay in her embrace for a long time and never complain. The sight makes something in me ache.

"Ivy, do you like him?" Rafe questions again, his curiosity and the hint of his French accent making him an unassuming confidant.

"Of course I do. And the truth is, we actually met years ago, before he had Emmy." My friends focus their whole attention on me and wait for me to continue. I love them for it. "He's . . . different now." What I don't tell them is that I've felt a certain kind of hollow ever since we missed our chance all those years ago.

Lily reaches for my hand and holds it tight, while Sparrow puts a gingerbread croissant on a plate and slides it toward me. I nod my thanks and start to pick at it.

"He did tell me he wants to see me leading up to Christmas, but that's where it's probably going to end if he follows through on his plans to move away. And I know he's holding back. There's this sense of relearning each other while learning about each other for the first time." I'm trying to believe that, because of Jace's genuineness and goodness, there's a chance for us. But I'm also having to push myself to believe in possibilities again at all.

Sparrow's eyes widen as Rafe tilts his head. "Poetic, that," he says with an appreciative nod.

Graham speaks for the first time. "I can tell you from experience that a broken heart changes us—or, at the very least, makes us feel like we can't be the best version of ourselves." He's sitting, shoulders back, with his arm around Lily's waist. His wife leans into him, putting her forehead against his face.

"I love you," she says with conviction. When she pulls back to look at him, a smile passes between the two of them.

"Ivy, you must know Jace is still interested in you." Rafe is now eating a maple croissant, waving it in the air in between bites. "He kept looking at you at the parade."

"And during the town meeting last week," Sparrow adds.

"And near the studio. The other day, I saw him hovering just outside the door, looking as if he was debating going in or not," Graham interjects, his law skills and deductive reasoning rising to the surface.

"Well, his daughter is my student." The words are true, but I'm hoping there's more to it all.

"Oh, please, his daughter may be your student, but that man looks like he'd punch through walls for a real shot with you." Lily smirks, rubbing a hand over her round stomach. Laughter fills the bakery. "Did you ever think that maybe you're so worried about being enough to convince Jace to stay that you're not seeing he's worried that he's not enough for you at all?"

"She's not wrong. And, believe me, I know what it's like to feel like your skin is stretched too tight because of how much you want to hold someone and won't let yourself have what you most desire for reasons you don't even understand." This comes from Rafe, who is ever the songwriter. I can imagine his words will work their way into a lyric someday soon, if not for himself, then for the artists he works with these days.

"I'm not saying no to him, believe me," I protest. "When we first met, it felt like time and space . . . stopped. But then he left my life, through no fault of his own—though I didn't know that! So, I was mad and hurt, of course." I take a deep breath, trying to steady myself. "He's different these days. Life has altered him. I know it's not realistic to hold someone to a past version of themselves, and maybe we just need time to learn the current versions of ourselves. But Jace is supposed to leave . . . before Christmas! Selfishly, I want him to choose to be here. Still, I can honestly say that no matter what happens, I just want him to be happy."

My rant ends breathlessly, and my friends murmur words of comfort and advice. As I finish speaking, the clock on the wall with a sparrow hovering over one of the hands strikes three o'clock. As if on cue, the door to the café swings open.

Jace enters with Emmy by his side, her nose pink and her cheeks flushed.

"Miss Ivy!" Emmy exclaims.

Instantly, I have the urge to wrap her in my arms, but when my gaze moves up to Jace, my thoughts halt. He's looking at me with such intensity and appreciation that I have to grab onto the edge of the counter to keep my balance. We were going to see each other at my studio during rehearsals tomorrow, so this is a welcome bonus.

When Graham is the first to stand and extend a hand, Jace breaks eye contact with me and shakes his hand. Rafe is the next to move around the counter, and Sparrow springs into action, putting macarons and madeleines on a plate.

Lily looks at me with a smirk. "Take it from me, Ives," she whispers, rubbing her stomach as she watches the scene unfold.

Already, Emmy has crumbs across her face as she reaches up to the counter again, Sparrow's hands extending toward her with another madeleine.

Lily continues in a low tone. "Don't believe the lie that love is too good for you or for Jace. We're all worthy of true love, and the right one will stay. He'll hold you and won't let you go." A tear slips across her cheek, and she wipes it away with the back of her hand. "I blame this little cruffin for these hormones." She points to her stomach.

I hug her from the side, drawing her as close as possible. "Thank you for that."

Lily rolls her eyes, wiping another tear as she watches Graham with Emmy. The little girl is now in his arms as she feeds him a macaron.

I laugh and stand. "Such a softie," I whisper in her ear before walking to Jace. He's watching my friends with a look of curious hesitation.

"Are you okay?" I ask, his demeanor not boding well for my heart.

"I don't know if I'm ready, Ivy."

The wariness in his gaze lands like a weight in my gut. He used my first name, which is not a good sign. "You don't know if you're ready for what?" I lower my voice. "For us?"

He sighs. "I promise I'm not being double-minded. I want to try with you. That hasn't changed. It's actually never changed." Jace looks from one happy couple to the other. "But as much as I like what I know of your friends, I'm not like them. It's evident how freely they give of their love, and . . ." His sigh makes me ache. "I just keep thinking of what I've lost instead of what I can give you."

"Jace, I don't want you to be like them," I whisper.

He swallows, tracking Emmy. His daughter is now perched on the counter, held in place by Sparrow. They're both clapping as Rafe sings a Christmas carol in front of them. He's holding his guitar that just somehow mysteriously appeared in his hands.

"What happened, Jace?" I turn back to him. "What's the lie you can't let go of?"

His eyes darken at the truth I've uncovered. "It's a simple story . . . and still so hard to say."

I shake my shoulders and weigh my options. "You owe me two answers, then," I say into the space between us, and his brow furrows. "In addition to your question of 'What do you want to be known for?' I'm adding the one I just asked. But you have to answer them in your own time. I won't force you."

I decide to leave it at that and give him space. Partially because I sense he needs it. And partially because I need clarity too.

He nods. "Thank you, Ivy."

I'm grateful for the opportunity to chat with my friends before he walked in here this afternoon. Some people are worth the glimmer of what's beneath, not because it represents their potential but because that glimmer is indicative of who they really are. I've seen that spark in Jace. And I have to believe that he'll find his way to the words he needs to say.

"Have you tried a maple croissant yet?" I ask him, changing my tone to a happier one.

"I haven't yet. I'm more of a cinnamon roll kind of guy." He grins, and something lifts between us.

I settle in once again to the happiness around us. "Hmm, well, they have those too. They'll only be here for the week before New Year's."

"Maybe you'll save one for me, Starlight?" The question is spoken with a gritty edge. I want to pull him closer.

"Will you be here?" The words slip out before I can rein them in or think them through. I know he already told me that he and Emmy are supposed to be in Florida before then.

Jace's hand brushes against my own in reply. I wrap my fingers around his, the warmth of his hand pulsing through my system. "I want to be," he says softly.

And his honesty is what wills my heart to let go, to imagine what could be possible. "Then I'll make sure they save us some, just in case."

Chapter Seventeen

Ivy

The clock strikes four.

After our unexpected run-in at Sparrow's Beret yesterday, to my shock, Jace texted and asked me to go ice skating with him. _Just_ him. We're going back to a remnant of where it all began, I suppose. Different rink and location, the same us. Theoretically, this rink would give us more privacy and a chance to create new memories since it's indoors and also located in the next town over. I accepted his invitation because I know the importance of moving through something that's gotten stuck in your soul, changing the narrative by the sheer power of being in each other's presence. But agreeing may have been one of the worst ideas I've had in a long time.

Because when I arrived outside of the year-round ice rink, Jace was waiting with a hot chocolate for me and a black, cold brew coffee for himself, even in the frigid temperatures. It took all my effort not to obsess over how good coffee and chocolate would be together, but I pulled myself away from the distracting thoughts long enough to notice that Jace seemed lighter than at the bakery.

Just the sensation of walking into a building together that wasn't my studio or his brother's boxing gym felt like its own sort of miracle. Now, here we are. I'm quietly lacing up my skates. He's putting on hockey skates, making himself stand even taller than usual. He leans against the barrier boards, staring down at me with a look I can't interpret.

Suddenly, I'm self-conscious. I push back the screaming need inside my head to be perfect on every level, to impress him with *who* and *what* I am. The lie that's crept in over the years—maybe from my time in professional ballet or maybe from my own personality and experiences—that I need to be perfect to have a chance at being fully loved wanders through my brain.

"C'mon, Starlight," Jace breathes between us as he holds out his hand. I take it, following him onto the rink, the tension in my legs from pushing against the ice a reminder that the future may be uncertain, but I'm alive. It's a reminder that every sensation I have with him is not only otherworldly but also somehow real. Though the skates are restrictive, it's a surprisingly nice sensation, like a comfortable grip on my muscles to keep me in line as I make tracks across the frozen water.

The rink is quiet, despite the group of children in the corner, taking off their skates after their recent class. Jace takes us gliding onto the ice as soon as the last little one hops off with a squeak. I'm beside him, the air whooshing past me and blowing my hair in a way I only allow while skating. Usually, my hair is pulled back, not a hair out of place unless I'm alone in my studio or, ironically, when I met Jace. It's a habit I've never lost from dancing for most of my life. But today, at the rink, I allow myself to be a little freer, even though it's been so long. For some reason, it feels right to be a little less polished and a lot more reckless on the ice. A fact that is evident by the huge man skating just a few cross steps behind me. His six-foot-five-inch height is now nearly six-eight, and that alone is enough to make a woman swoon. And by the looks of the moms wrangling their kids and the college-aged woman we paid for our rink time, they've noticed and are already figuring out how to accidentally run into him.

I round the corner and spin toward Jace, catching a dangerous grin when we make eye contact. A smile breaks across my own face, the momentum pushing my hair forward like it's reaching toward him, the sound of our blades coasting over the ice. We're moving faster and faster, in an unspoken race to . . . something. All I know is that I'm lost in the way we connect, even in silence. I've only ever felt this way with him. With each moment that passes, I sense the connection tightening like a ribbon being wrapped around my heart instead of my ankles. Then his eyes widen, and I register that I'm falling.

Too distracted by Jace's intensity, my skate hits a groove in the ice, and I lose my balance. Desperate to focus on something, my brain tracks the LED lights on the ceiling above. They center themselves in my vision as I fall backward. I have time to grimace and tense my frame, expecting to hit the cold ice, when a warm hand grasps the back of my neck and curls me forward. I collide with a body instead of the ice and gasp when we both fall. Jace lands beneath me, the two of us falling face-to-face. Jace's breathing snaps me back to attention, his rib cage pressing against my own with deep inhales.

"Are you okay?" he asks, his head lifted, scanning me for any signs of injury. His hands move over my arms, swiping across my spine, touching my shoulders gently. Even though he's the one pressed against the uncomfortable ice, he's treating me like I mean something to him—like I'm valuable—and the unfiltered action has tears stinging my eyes without being summoned.

This is the Jace I've always believed him to be.

Instead of moving, my body weight sinks a little more onto his, a knee coming to rest on the ice, the cold a contrast to my other knee draped over his waist. He takes a breath, most likely realizing that I'm okay. Leaning his head back on the ice, his exhales follow a staccato rhythm.

In no hurry to move, I study him and his smooth-shaven face, the fall heightening my senses. While people expect me to be elegant and full of grace—and I can be—falls are often a part of the equation within my profession. It's true in dance and true in life. You can't expect to execute anything flawlessly without failure. Even though, intellectually, I understand that the idea of perfection is a myth, it's been my lifelong struggle to accept it. I'm strong on welcoming failure with my students, encouraging them to be themselves instead of who or what they believe they should be.

But staring at Jace, I'm not so sure if my theory is true anymore. Magnificence radiates off him, even through the sadness that he seems to carry with him like a mantle, even when I know he makes mistakes. Maybe perfection isn't being free of flaws. Maybe perfection is knowing that someone gives you the feeling that there never would or never could be another person who affects you like they do. Jace is perfect because he's Jace, not because of anything he's done or hasn't done.

Without overthinking it, I extend my gloved hand. "Pull, please."

Jace obeys without questioning, his cool fingers still causing a shiver as he gently pulls the glove from my hand, and they brush my wrist. Subtly, he's checking if I'm okay. Always checking if I'm okay. I give his hand a press and release him, moving my now free hand to slide it slowly up from his jawline until the tips of my fingers find the hairline above his ear. He studies me. His jaw clenches slightly, but he doesn't move, doesn't retreat. We haven't touched each other like this since our almost kiss at the town lighting, and it's taking everything in me to remember why.

I've waited years, chasing the idea of the Jace who lived in my head. And now he's here in real life, not perfectly the same but still the standard. He's told me he's not sure if he's ready to pursue us, and I need to respect that. But for now, I need him to know that he's seen.

"Thank you for catching me," I say softly, so quietly I wonder if he'll even hear me, but he does. Something flashes across his face, another hint of the man I first met, the man he was before he claimed that he was broken, when his heart was more clearly visible.

He nods, a softening around his eyes I haven't noticed before. In one swift motion, he sits up, my hand falling to wrap securely around his warm neck, his arm wrapped tightly around my waist. I shift my legs until I'm almost straddling him, embarrassment creeping over my face, but I don't care. Jace grins, a rare gleam in his eyes.

"I thought you said you were a pro at this," he challenges, a teasing tone in his deep voice. I let out a laugh, the realization that he cracked a joke warming my heart.

"Even the best fall down sometimes," I reply with a shrug.

"Okay, Howie Day, let's get you back on your feet."

Mortification courses through me as I use all my remaining energy to push myself off him, kneeling on the ice, in need of help to pull myself to standing again. He saved me from a gnarly fall, and I've been resting on him like I'm a creature finding a place to hibernate for the winter.

"Whoa, whoa," Jace coaxes. "A real person here." He chuckles, and the sound is as satisfying as slippers sliding across a dance floor. "Steady, Starlight." Casually, he moves to his knees, his hands on either side of my arms. He lifts one knee. One not privy to the cause of this clumsy experience (on my part) could think he was proposing, and while this is in no way a romantic gesture, I know this is the image that will stick to my thoughts when I'm fighting sleep later tonight.

Only seconds pass, but when he stands to his full height and looks down at me, a shiver runs up my spine.

"Are you cold?" Jace asks.

I can honestly say that I'm not. A shake of my head, a wringing of my hands, and I stand to my full height, assisted by his outstretched hand, my chin lifted high to meet his gaze.

He nods, eyes roving over my face like he's studying me. I want to move, but I feel like I might ruin the picture. His gaze takes me in like he's an artist painting this very moment in time, and it would be a shame to mess it up now. When his eyes linger on my mouth, my face heats. I swallow, a reaction to his intensity, wondering if he's also thinking about how much I remember the chemistry in our kiss. There was an absolute magnetism in our connection that long ago altered any chance of truly fitting with another person. I'm a book whose spine has been creased, coffee beans that have been ground. Jace changed the structure of who I am. What's done has been done, and there's no way to undo it.

Scared to move, I reach out with my still-gloveless hand. Without looking at it, his hand finds mine. The touch is gentle, but I feel the strength behind it. It's not a promise, but it's an acknowledgment. To my delight, his mouth lifts enough to flash a hint of his dimple. I smile in response as he pulls me to skate again, our bodies warming with the movement of skating across the ice.

A few more people have stepped onto the rink, and I've missed all of them until now. They spin or practice their glides, and we skate, hand in hand, sometimes picking up speed. Mostly, we find a rhythm in which his much longer legs move in sync with mine. We don't speak but only skate, the evening passing into night in the comfort of his presence. It's only during the fifteenth or the fiftieth lap that I think I hear him humming the song "Collide."

"So, what are you going to do about your scholarships?" Jace is sitting next to me at the bar at Aesop's Tavern, holding a bottle of handcrafted root beer and looking much too good in his classic, long-sleeved black t-shirt that must be made of some sort of wonder fabric that hugs his muscles impeccably. He's one of the rarest of men who can make athletic wear look like high-end fashion.

Jace told me he doesn't drink anymore, but Aesop's is more than a tavern; it's a place to connect, an increasingly rare anomaly in our modern society. And everyone in town loves Clark, the owner, who happens to be working tonight. Tinsel hangs around the bar and through the rafters, the Christmas lights looking like hanging stars over our heads.

I sigh a bit, trying to rein in my train of thought. "I'm going to pray that the committee will see how valuable they are and allocate some of the funds that would have been used to upgrade our already functional recycling bins to be utilized for my students instead. I know that everything in this town is important, so I'm not trying to say one thing is more beneficial than the others, but I can't say no to children who want to dance. But I also can't keep saying yes. Studio rent in this town is expensive. I consider it worth it, though, if I can get more students to find the outlet of dance that I had."

Jace furrows his brow.

"Don't get me wrong," I continue in his silence, "like I told you so long ago, everyone here is so wonderful. My parents, my brother . . . they've all made it so that I feel their support without ever having to ask for it."

Jace stiffens slightly at the mention of my brother, and the movement gives me pause.

"But?" Jace asks, lightly tapping my shoulder with his own.

Shaking my head, I offer him a crooked smile, meeting his gaze. Pulling my shoulders back, something about the way Jace rubs his thumb over the logo, back and forth as if he could be granted three wishes if it were a lamp, makes me resolute in my decision to open up to him more—or, in this case, again.

I begin again. "But I've always had this feeling of loneliness hovering around me. Never fully consuming but at the edges. The feeling of a void that I've never quite found a way to fill. There was hope once—" My voice almost gives out, my meaning rich and hovering throughout the air. As always, his proximity pulls on the threads of my emotions in a unique way.

Jace nods, head tilted. "For what it's worth, I'm proud of you for working so hard. You don't have to, yet you do."

"I want to. This is my life, Jace. If Grey taught me anything about her love of books, it's that you get to write the story that you want. Be the character that you want to be in your own tale of life."

He hums in acknowledgement. "And what if you don't like the story you're writing?" His eyes are heavy as he looks at the amber bottle of root beer in his hand, nearly a match to the color of his eyes when they hit the light. Then his eyes close completely, a pained expression on his face.

I don't answer his question, sensing that it was more rhetorical than seeking an answer.

His arms flex beneath his shirt as he grips and then releases the bottle over and over, again and again. "I don't know how you're still single, Ivy," he says to the counter instead of me. "And I'm sorry that you've been lonely."

Genuinely, his eyes lift to mine, and I nearly fall off the stool. He's serious.

"I know what it's like to fall asleep alone and question everything." He clears his throat, and I know he's hit a limit on this topic. But the fact that he's been questioning and wondering about my life is clear.

I decide to give him an out. "What about you? I know I

asked if you're planning to still be here for the New Year, but are there any changes to your plans?" The once-hot tea I've been cradling in my hands has grown lukewarm, but I cling to the mug, relying on it as a comfortable way to keep my hands from reaching for him.

"I have Emmy to think about." Jace shifts, peeking down at me from the corner of his eye. "She's been my whole world."

"I know."

"And she'll always need me, especially since I'm the only parent she's had for years—has, actually," he corrects.

"I know that too." At this, I put the cup back on the saucer. It's not Sparrow's Beret, but Clark still has a knack for curating cozy things. Though, I'm convinced there's not an establishment in this town that wouldn't make you feel like you're a part of its family. Centering myself with the comfort of the familiar setting, I try to gather my thoughts, my mind racing with the idea that if Christmas magic were real, there's a future in which I could be graced with the gift of a duo that is Jace and Emmy.

"Starlight . . . this . . . with you"—I hold my breath at his words—"I don't want to lose it. But I also don't know how to move forward. Not sure I'm even good at understanding how to embrace the future." His gaze drops to the bottle, and his jaw clenches. "You know you deserve everything, right?"

At the confidence in his tone, I take a chance and lean my head against his shoulder. I feel the aftermath of the vibration of his breath throughout his chest.

His voice is a murmur. "Sometimes, I feel like my limbs are getting colder. Like my heart just can't keep me from shutting down, preventing warmth from reaching the rest of me. That feeling comes and goes in phases. And I'm scared of never fully feeling again. And I'm scared not to be able to give you what you're worth."

Lifting to my full height on the stool, I wrap an arm around his neck, gently pulling him toward me. I don't typically give this much affection to people who aren't my family or Grey, but Jace unlocks something in me that wants to pour out my tenderness while somehow knowing it wouldn't be wasted. When his face is near mine, I whisper the words that have reverberated through my heart since I saw him again. "I'm scared too. But can't we be scared together?" Forcing myself to be brave, I ask him what I've been wanting to ask all night. "Jace, can I kiss you?"

His eyes widen. "Ivy, I'm not sure that's a good . . . it's just that . . ." He sighs, the tension in his frame enough to break the stool he's sitting on.

"Not on the lips," I clarify. "Just . . ." I reach forward and hover a finger near the place his dimple loves to play hide-and-seek on his cheek.

Jace's shoulders relax. "Yes, please." His voice has become a fragile thing.

He inhales as I tilt my head up and place a gentle kiss on the side of his face. The heat and smoothness of his skin send a rush of warmth through my heart as the clock behind the bar chimes. Jace hums, and a peace moves through my limbs as he leans his head against the top of my own.

"For the record, Starlight," he murmurs, his tone satisfyingly clear, "if I kiss you, I won't want to stop. Just thought you should know."

Chapter Eighteen

Jace

The clock strikes five.

"And a Merry Christmas to you!" says the postal worker behind the counter with a smile stretched so wide it would be creepy if it wasn't so genuine. "Let's. Get. Lit!" he yells as he clicks a button on his atrocious sweater. The tree that's no doubt been hot glued to the front of it lights up, and the customer turns away with an unreadable expression on his face. It would be novel, except I've seen him do the same thing for the ten people who were waiting in line in front of me. The pattern is the same. He clicks it on when he hands over a receipt and then starts the whole process again. Now, it's my turn to be the focus of his attention.

I'm not sure if his level of delusion is due to Birch Borough's genius (or self-sabotaging) choice to defy custom and logic and keep their post office open into the late evening for the month of December. I decide to give him as much grace as I can muster, given the holidays. In the few weeks we've been here, this isn't the first time I've had to deal with the chaos of this town and come out victorious.

I force a grin and walk up to the counter, a package for my parents in my arms. Instead of stowing gifts away on the plane, I've decided to ship them to Florida instead. Edgar and Angie recently bought their tickets to travel with us late on the evening of the twenty-third. It's arguably the worst day to travel, but the timing is necessary due to my siblings' demanding businesses. Weeks ago, we collectively decided to make this holiday as magical as possible for Emmy since I've been essentially hiding from my family for the past few years. With Emmy growing up and the job offer in Florida, it woke me up to the fact that she doesn't have a history with Christmas like I did during my childhood. Emmy doesn't even know what Christmas is like with her mom, so being surrounded by family is going to create memories she'll hold on to for years to come. She needs this; *I* need this. A new path for a better future.

Still, we haven't even left Birch Borough yet, and I already wish I could make it work with Ivy. Canceling my tickets and scrapping my travel plans is sounding more attractive day by day. My resolve is cracking like a pond that hasn't fully frozen over yet.

The postal worker, whose name tag reads *Stewart*, looks up at me from his four-by-four feet of cubic space across the counter. "Say now," he declares, "aren't you the guy that's been seeing our Ivy?"

As pleasant as he sounds, I don't miss the possessive indicator that this town sees her as one of their own. I'm still the outsider, though I believe I've been given a bit of an express pass into the fold, to my great relief. It seems I've been accepted into the Birch Borough social life quicker than Graham or Rafe. It helps that my brother and sister had already built successful businesses here and were members of the community before I arrived. I shudder, thinking of how much grief I would've been given otherwise. Rafe and Graham are friendly; they invite friendship. My demeanor when I first showed up in town was . . . well, not like that.

"I am seeing Ivy . . . in a way . . . yes." The words shoot a spark up my spine as they stumble out. I'm proud of being attached to her in any way, and especially with people thinking that we're together, but the free-for-all prying that everyone around here seems to engage in is still disorienting.

"Excuse me, Mr. December?"

Instantly, I recognize the voice behind me. It's coming from the primary troublemaker in this town, and I feel my shoulders bunching toward my ears, preparing for what's to come. Gladys means well—of that, I'm sure—but she digs deeper than most.

"Stewart!" the older woman yells, appearing beside me and leaning on the counter. She's wearing a festive garland in her hair, and it almost looks like her head is a Christmas tree, her accessories complete with earrings in the shape of light-up ornaments that dangle from her ears. "Are you aware of just who asked you to ship this box?" She looks at the label. "To . . . Florida?" Her mood takes a swift turn. She crosses her arms over her chest and faces me as the line of people behind us sigh with a collective groan. "You'd better not be moving, boy."

I haven't been called a boy since I was . . . well, a boy. "Ma'am?" I reply incredulously.

"Don't you 'ma'am' me, young man."

Caught in the chaos, Stewart simply hums, purposely disregarding what's happening on the other side of his counter.

"I'm going to Florida for Christmas to see my parents." I hasten to clarify, adding in a quiet tone, "But moving there has been the plan."

"*Absoluuuuutely* not."

"That will be twenty dollars and seventy-three cents," Stewart chimes in.

Really, Stewart? Now? My jaw clenches.

"You know that I've been rooting for you. I even put in a good word with Build Me Up, Buttercup Homes for the custom furniture you make . . ." Gladys' voice rises an octave on the last words, and I swallow. "But now, I'm not so sure that was the right choice."

"Gladys, I really need to get going. And these poor people behind us need to ship their packages."

"Again, that will be twenty dollars and seventy-three cents."

"Shut it, Stewart!" Gladys yells as I throw a credit card onto the counter. She leans in, invading my personal space. "Our Ivy needs you. And to be clear, we all could use a strapping guy like you around here. And besides Ivy being happy, Emmy needs this town. *You* need this town. Now, look me in the eye and tell me I'm wrong." Her voice is low.

It would be menacing if I didn't know that this is the woman who left me a chicken noodle soup casserole when she found out that Emmy had a stomachache yesterday. How she found out, I still don't know. I see her eyes narrow in my peripheral vision, unrelenting.

Slowly, Stewart slides a receipt and a pen across the counter so deliberately that I think he's planning to sneak-attack me. However, his humming of the Christmas carols playing across the speaker system is a giveaway that he's listening and only trying to act nonchalant. Quickly, I sign the receipt and then nod toward the door, indicating that Gladys should follow me. She huffs but complies.

As we walk away, "And a Merry Christmas to you!" accompanies us toward the door.

We pause just inside the door leading into the post office. We're not fully out of earshot of everyone in line, but my shoulders relax, and I crack my neck to relieve some tension. "Gladys, you're not wrong. However . . ."

She visibly relaxes but looks at me warily. "What aren't you telling me?"

Word on the cobblestone street is that it's not an option to stretch the truth with Gladys, or she'll call it rubbish, so I answer honestly. "That it could be good for Emmy to move to Florida. My parents live there. It's stable. It's not anywhere my ex has been. And the truth is that our adventure in Birch Borough was always meant to be temporary."

"I see." The wheels in her mind are turning so fast that I should see smoke coming from her ears. "I hear your reasoning, and I raise you just one thing." My nod gives her the permission she doesn't need to keep going. "Ivy."

I nearly groan. She's hitting me where it hurts. "I'm staying in town until December twenty-third, if that helps." My confidence deflates in the wake of her gaze.

"Hardly. Why would you even consider going when you know that the woman who is meant to be yours is here? Help it make sense!"

I sigh. "I can't help it make sense because it doesn't make sense. All I know is that, without meaning to, I lost Ivy once. I don't know if I can survive if I realize . . . if I can't . . ."

"If you're too buff?"

"What? No."

"Too suave?"

"No."

"Too grumpy?"

"I'm not grumpy with *her,* and just, no."

"Too giving? Your sister told me you used to be quite the helpful neighbor."

I run a hand through my hair in frustration, the ends of it now stretching toward the sky. "Ivy should get the best. I could never give her enough."

Gladys ignores me. "Too romantic? Don't think I don't know about your little escapade outside of Town Hall. I may have even seen them myself—well, secondhand through my camera, at least."

"Oh, good Lord, help me." My exhale is enough to get the people walking into the post office to look at me skeptically. Three people have come in, and two have left since Gladys and I stepped away from the counter. I could walk away, but I'm afraid of her. I'm afraid of the ramifications if I even try to move. "No."

"Too . . . what, then? Handsome? Intelligent? Handy?" At the last descriptor, she bounces her brows. I shut my eyes. "Tall? Manly? Punchy?" I sneak a glance to catch her as she mimics a boxer punching a bag and will myself not to laugh. "Too—" she begins.

I cut her off. "I'm not 'too' anything, Gladys. I love my girl, my Emmy, but I made mistakes. I lost hope. I lost my belief in love. Ivy fell in love with a version of me that existed before my sister died. And no, this isn't some condescending sap message. I'm telling it straight. Just like it is. That's all you'll get from me." The last part almost squeaks coming out. I'm not proud of it, but it's honest.

Her eyes widen, but I see she knows that I'm being genuine. "That's the best thing I've heard you say yet."

Out of nervous habit, I scratch the side of my jaw, unsure of how to handle her response.

"Ivy needs love. That's it. And not love from this town, her studio, dancing, or even her family or friends. I've seen the way you two look at each other. She needs love from *you*."

My heart constricts. I'm ready to wrap her up in a hug when she holds up a hand. Suddenly, I notice that Gladys is wearing a pin on the exterior of her coat in the shape of Florida with an "X" over it.

"Where did you get that?" I ask incredulously.

Gladys looks about instead of at the pin that I'm literally pointing at. "I have no idea what you mean." She gives me a wink just as Stewart clears his throat and calls across the space, no doubt hoping to rescue me.

"If you have packages to send, Gladys, then you need to get in line."

Gladys turns on her heels, stepping toward him as he backs up slightly from the counter. "Listen here, Stewart. I'm not here to mail any packages. If I were, I'd be here 'til Christmas!" Her pointer finger extends. "And another thing! If you say, 'Let's get lit,' *one* more time, I'm going to mysteriously cut off your power to this place!"

The whole line claps, and one man lets out a whistle. I'm pretty sure I hear, "Oh, thank God," from a position about eight people deep from the counter.

Stewart swallows and then stands taller. "I have

Christmas spirit, *Gladys*." His shoulders lift, adding about half an inch to his stature.

"Well, good for you," she retorts, "but you're also full of it. Your house looks like the ghost of Jacob Marley himself lives there. You're just doing this whole charade to get more votes when you run for treasurer. Plus, you forget that we went to school together. I've known you since you once confused crayons for pretzel sticks and ate them all. So, mail these good people's packages, and don't mess with me." Crossing her arms, she gives a matter-of-fact nod before turning toward the door again. On her way past me, she winks.

"What a hero," a woman with a baby in her arms whispers loud enough for me to hear.

Stewart looks toward the door and then back to his current customer, his expression clearly torn. Then he takes a pair of scissors and cuts the cord on his sweater. The lights flicker off, making his sweater look reminiscent of a storage container filled with discarded Christmas decorations you'd find in a garage. Poor guy.

I chuckle to myself, thinking that the mystery and weirdness of this small town somehow match my kind of weirdness. I think I might want this for Emmy permanently. If she grows up here and turns out to be half the woman that Ivy is—or even her friends, Sparrow, Grey, and Lily—then I think my girl will be doing just fine in life. There's something special about this place. It produces quality people. Even Gladys' meddling could work in Emmy's favor since her heart is to protect those she cares about. The sentiment of the pin Gladys was wearing looks more attractive to me by the second.

I push the receipt with the package's tracking number into my pocket and step outside. I'm halfway down the front steps when I spot golden-blonde hair wrapped in one of those vintage-style headbands with a knot on top. I know what it is because of Angie's determination to educate me on women's styles, so I'm not clueless when it comes time to help Emmy enter the world of fashion.

She hasn't spotted me yet, but the snowflakes that are starting to fall cast a dreamy effect over her that makes me wish we were alone, hearing nothing but the quiet rustling of snow falling, our focus solely on each other.

"Starlight," I grit out. Instantly, her eyes land on mine, and a smile that I'll feel all the way until morning shines toward me.

"Hi, Bear." Her quiet tone matches the moody weather, though it swirls with warmth despite the cold.

At her gentle greeting, I'm instantly hit with the realization that I can't bring myself to think of anything other than wanting to grow old with Ivy. I don't know why I've convinced myself for so many years that I should be alone. I want to hang up my boxing gloves next to Ivy's pointe shoes every night. I want to wake up every morning and know that, even though I've dreamed of her, holding her in my arms is better than any dream I've ever had. I still need to tell her my deepest fear, but I don't want to be the obstacle that stands in our way of happiness. There are challenges ahead, but if I don't hold out hope for a future love story with Ivy, I may never find my hope again.

I want to be all in.

Trying to overcome the nerves pulsing through my body, I force bravery to the surface as the need to touch her pulses through my body. I draw close, bending over her, drawing strength just from her proximity. The urge to connect is too great to ignore, thawing the fear that's been keeping me frozen. "May I touch your face?" I ask, needing, wanting, hoping for her permission.

The blush on her cheeks matches my own, heat pulsing through my skin. Ivy stares up at me, and her voice is filled with a raw vulnerability. "You can always reach for me, Jace," she whispers.

Without hesitation, I lift my hand to her face, loving the feel of her jaw nestled against my palm. The antique clock in the square rings out, and Ivy laughs, her grin breaking the spell over the two of us.

"I think we're stuck in a Christmas movie, and the clocks are still trying to tell us something," I remark dryly.

"What do you think they're trying to tell us?" Her smoky voice brings a shiver to my spine. Ivy has the best voice I've ever heard. I'd listen to her read construction manuals if it meant being allowed to hear her voice uninterrupted for hours.

"That having the chance to be near you again is better than any Christmas present I've ever received."

The snowbanks are high, and the cold is fierce this December, but I can sense that we're building something here. Sometimes, people give you the blueprints of what's possible. It's a gift. You can build from those blueprints if you find the courage. I don't think I had the courage until this moment.

Ivy and I stare at each other until the cold burns my nose, but I'm too focused on her to mind that we're partially blocking the pathway to the post office. I look deeply into the eyes that have fully arrested my heart, even as my to-do list hums like an annoying Christmas carol on loop. Tonight's responsibilities are plentiful, including teaching a class, picking up Emmy at the pie shop, making dinner, et cetera, et cetera. And if I remember correctly, Ivy is headed to Grey's tonight for their own Christmas celebration.

But neither of us disrupts this moment, even with townspeople milling around us. We're wrapped up in each other's spell until I'm hit in the leg with a bunch of shopping bags from someone passing by on the sidewalk. At my instinctive, "Ow," we seem to startle and draw apart.

Yet, I'm grateful that life gave us a few uninterrupted moments. I want to have more of them with her. The question of how I can accomplish that is on repeat in my mind as we shift back into the rhythm of time moving at its normal speed.

"Okay, Bear," Ivy takes a step back. "I'm running late. Grey and Luke are waiting for me to arrive. This celebration is one of our traditions."

"I'll walk with you." She doesn't hesitate to accept my company. We turn and walk toward Marlee's Books, our hands melded and swinging lightly between us. I don't take it for granted, my gratitude quieting my fears. "And then I'll text you later, since this is our meet-cute for the day."

"How do you know about meet-cutes?" she questions with amusement.

"I watch romantic films." I wink. Ivy's delighted squeal makes me smile. "And what exactly are you two—sorry, three, with Luke—going to be up to this evening?"

"Oh, we put on *White Christmas*, which was Marlee's favorite movie, and then we string popcorn like we could be cast in a film from the eighteen hundreds. Then we watch *Little Women*, the nineteen-ninety-four version, and cry and talk about Laurie while making peppermint brownies. It's a whole thing. We'll be up all night."

"It would be nice for Emmy to have a friend she does something like that with one day." My tone is wistful, thinking of the possibility that Emmy could have a better childhood than I did. I was always a loner, with my siblings as my primary friends. I'd rather have gone to the symphony than high school parties, and it cost me—not that I regret the choice in the least.

"I'm sure she will," Ivy reassures me. "When she's old enough, you know . . ." Her words pause with a shrug, but I know she's suddenly thinking about the future too.

"Yeah, I know, Starlight. I know."

As we walk together, Ivy's arm slides up to wrap around my arm. She initiated the contact, and my pulse beats stronger at the truth that's becoming evidently clear to me. The job opportunity in Florida is going to have to wait, and my parents are just going to have to manage without me . . . at least until the New Year.

Chapter Nineteen

Ivy

"Breathe in through your nose and release a long exhale out of your mouth," Rose says, her perfect posture evident in my peripheral vision.

I'm on a Pilates reformer, stretching out my muscles at the only Pilates studio in the small radius of geography that is usually my life. The studio is on the outskirts of town, past several neighborhoods and nearly in the next town. I close my eyes, my legs in the machine straps, the tension and release of my muscles soothing. I developed a regular Pilates practice early in my dance career, and it's stuck with me. I use it for injury prevention, for strength, and, for tonight, to clear my mind. The emotional waves I've been riding this season have made me feel like it should be summer instead of winter in New England.

Rose speaks again. "The next time your carriage has returned to the starting position, lift your legs to a tabletop." There's a pause as calming music flows throughout the space. "And point and flex your feet. And point. And flex. And point. And flex."

I've worked myself into the rhythm when I hear a whispered, "*Psst*" in my ear. That's odd. No one ever talks during these classes except for the instructor. I attempt to ignore it, crack my eyes open, and then catch a frantic wave to my left.

"Psssssst!" It comes again.

Halting my movements, I disrupt my concentration to find my grandmother on the once-empty machine next to me, the gleeful look on her face a pretense that she didn't somehow stalk me to this location. My carriage crashes with a thump that causes me to wince.

"Gram!" I exclaim in a whisper-shout.

Rose looks my way while my grandmother stretches like she's been doing it for years. Maybe she has, and I've never known?

"What are you doing here?"

A woman on the other side tries to shush me, and I shrug apologetically before flopping back on the reformer. My thoughts are positively scrambled.

Rose's pleasant voice continues, "And carefully release your legs from the straps."

I do as I'm told, trying to rush to get to the part when I can hear what I know will be a wild explanation from my grandmother.

"Hug your knees into your chest, and rock side to side. If that's not available to you, simply keep your knees hugged into your chest." Rose's sweet tones ring throughout the space, and within a few more movements, we're done, and I nearly leap off the machine.

Looking over, my grandmother nonchalantly wipes down her equipment with the provided sanitary wipes and acts as if she hasn't just crashed my class. Hurrying, I wipe my own station, waiting for Gram to be finished. When she has satisfied the basic fundamentals of social hygiene, I—lovingly—grab her hand and pull her toward the lobby as fast as her clearly strong-cored frame can move. How she snuck into the studio within the last few minutes without causing a scene is eluding my understanding.

"Gram!"

"Yes, darling?" she replies serenely. Her outfit is of notably better quality than mine; a little jacket she had stowed in a cubby is now wrapped around her shoulders.

I pinch the space between my eyes with my thumbs. "Gram, what are you doing here? At this studio?"

"Oh, I've been coming here for years."

"You—what?" My mind can't comprehend how the time and space continuum between our lives has merged to this degree.

"Yes, darling. Who did you think you got all your coordination from? It's definitely not from your mom's side of the family, though we love them." With a little laugh, she grabs her purse.

"You've been—and I—" I point to the studio and watch as more students filter in and out.

"I know, dear. Now, let's go get a cup of tea and get down to the business of why I'm really here."

We walk a few doors down from the studio to the national coffee chain on the corner. It's no Sparrow's Beret, but desperate times and all that. Besides, it's the only thing open at this time of night within a thirty-mile radius.

When we're sitting at the table, cups of peppermint tea in front of us, Gram gives me a knowing look. It's the one she's always used when we needed life advice. And it's then I know I'm about to get emotionally pummeled, even though I know she'll be right.

"I have things to say." That's all Gram gives me before taking a bite from her cake pop.

I'm growing more astonished by this woman by the moment. "Okay, Gram."

"My dear, I've watched you accomplish great things, training students, training yourself. You've worked hard. You've traveled the world. You've returned home. And I am immensely proud of you." All the kindness and encouragement disarm me, even though I'm used to her affection. But what isn't she telling me? "Jace is your person," Gram continues.

The sip of tea I took for the sake of doing something with my hands shoots toward the back of my throat and my nose. I cough and take a sip from my water bottle. "Come again?"

"Jace. He's your person. So is Emmy. They're your people. I've seen him around town. I've seen the two of you around town. And I've been trying to work my magic, you know."

"Gram, you can't say things like that."

"I just did."

"Yes, but—Gram, there are feelings involved."

"You love him. Or if you don't fully yet, you will."

"Are you some sort of Christmas fortune cookie reader right now, or what is happening?"

"Your grandfather and I met years before we got married. There was both a misunderstanding and a series of events that kept us apart for a time. I nearly missed out on the most important person to me in my whole life because I couldn't see what was right in front of me."

Tears fill my eyes unintentionally. Even though I've heard this story countless times, I've never heard Gram talk about my grandfather quite like this. Suddenly, it feels like we're sharing in a common experience rather than her relaying it to me as a story.

"It was a magical night. Your grandfather and I met in the winter. It was snowing, and I nearly slipped. He caught me. He's caught me ever since. I realize now it was love at first sight."

"Gram, that's great, but this is different." I swallow.

"What aren't you saying?" Her gentle hand, covered in age spots from her days tanning on the beaches of North Hampton, covers mine.

Taking a sip of tea, I breathe deeply before setting the cup back on the table between us. "That if he leaves my life again"—I shift, pulling the edges of my sleeves over my empty hands—"I'll always be alone." Gram's concerned expression urges me to keep speaking, so I continue, "Sure, I could find someone out there to marry and have a family with. But that man wouldn't be Jace. My heart is so attuned to him that even though he is currently in Birch Borough, he already feels like the one that got away . . ."

"Because he's your person."

I sniffle and wipe my eyes. "Yeah, I think he might be, if he chooses to be. And that's what I'm scared of."

"You're right to be scared. We can't predict someone else's choices. Free will and all that. But hang on, my dear. Have courage and take hope. You're stronger than you know. You always have been." She draws herself up to her full height, the compassion in her tone still present, but on her face is the expression of a woman who's always told me the brutal truth. Gram continues after a moment's pause. "Also, I'm well aware of your innate drive to be perfect. You've always sought to avoid punishment or embarrassment in all things . . . since you were a little girl asking for a middle brownie instead of one on the edge of the pan. And it's holding you back from living the fullness of the life you are meant to have. You're doing better than you were, but you really need to let it go, dear."

"What?" I say incredulously.

Her words come out slowly, as if she's speaking with as much care as I speak to one of my elementary school students. "Perfection isn't going to do you any favors. It steals your joy. It weighs down your heart. It poisons the good things you could think about yourself. If you want Jace, tell him. Because there's no such thing as the perfect way to tell someone you love them. The perfection happens just from loving them."

I sip my tea in silence and shock, and when I'm done, Gram leads us out into the night air.

Pointing her key fob at her car, it beeps as she yells, "Fancy catching you here, darling! See you at the gingerbread competition!"

Her joy releases something within me. Finally, I laugh and slide into my own car, watching as she reverses out of the space, and her headlights light the way back to town.

"What just happened?" I whisper to myself before starting the engine and planning how I'm going to win the upcoming competition on my own this year.

*T*he *clock strikes six.*

"Ready, set, go!" Clark yells from the head table, which is wrapped in Christmas wrapping paper and topped with an outlandish bow. Since he presides over our town meetings, I guess it's fair he's mediating this event as well.

We take Christmas very seriously in Birch Borough, and this gingerbread competition is just even more proof of that fact. I'm set up at my station, all my materials ready to create the sweetest masterpiece of my life to date. Gingerbread sheets, royal icing, chocolates, marshmallows, pretzels, and a cinnamon cereal for the roof shingles surround me. I've prepped for this competition all year. I even have marshmallow fluff waiting in the wings to utilize as a snowscape.

Cheering me on in the corner are Sparrow, Rafe, Lily, and Graham. Since Sparrow and Lily own a bakery, they were banned from participating five years ago because they kept winning. It wasn't a surprise that they would be, since they do make magic in the kitchen after all. My gram is watching me from the sidelines, chewing on a cookie from the table for the attendees.

At the sound of a click, I look up to see Grey peeking out behind her camera with a smile. Sometimes she takes unofficial photos for Birch Borough's social media channels, and it suits her. She always likes being behind the scenes.

I'm used to the stage, but suddenly, I feel lost as to how I can actually win this thing. The prize is a gift card for the local spa, and let's just say, I'm invested. After the holidays, the prize will be a gift to myself to enjoy when my muscles are tight and I've successfully pulled off the after-Christmas performance.

Carefully, I move the pieces of gingerbread together to create a solid foundation, utilizing the icing to act as cement. Several of my students hover nearby, their eyes wide from the hope of a potential sugar rush in about an hour.

When it comes to arts and crafts, or any such thing, I don't usually win competitions. Dance is my art. But Joan from the bank has won for the past three years, and as much as I don't want her to miss out on her annual massage, I think it's about time someone (lovingly) pushed her from her gingerbread throne.

"Okay, think of Christmas, think of Clara, think of the Nutcracker Prince. You've got this."

"Talking to yourself again?" His voice never fails to make me melt.

I turn so fast that one of the walls I was building flops to the side and shatters on the table. "I have got to stop breaking things," I mutter, lifting my eyes to Jace's. His strong arms are holding Emmy. She's perched on her safe space in the way I love to see her, perfectly content to be with her dad. I smile. "Jace, hi. And hi, Emmy. I love your dress."

She's wearing a long-sleeved, green, satin-looking dress with a ribbon around the waist. Jace is wearing his classic athleisure, a mix between runway and business casual, though he could also stop in a gym on the way to his next meeting. Seriously, how does he make the style look so good?

"Starlight," Jace mouths with a wink, "what are you building here?"

I look back at my table and flinch. It's a mess. Emmy stares at my partially constructed house with fascination.

"Miss Ivy, Daddy builds things, remember?" She says it sweetly, but I hear in the hesitation of her tone that she recognizes it's not going so well for me on my own.

"Yes, he does." And Jace is an incredible designer. I've seen his talent in every set he's constructed so far and in every piece of his furniture I've seen displayed at a few shops around town. I now recognize his signature mark on the designs. At this rate, we're ahead of schedule for the performance. There's only one set left to be built and some final painting, and we'll be done. The thought makes me sad. I've loved having him near me in my dance world, even when we're doing different things.

"I'm happy to help," Jace interjects.

"I can't trouble you with this. Besides, it's serious business." I wave toward my collapsing gingerbread house.

"As opposed to what I do on a regular basis, where I actually build real-life things with my hands?" Jace grins and sets Emmy down before crossing his arms, the muscles in his shoulders bulging slightly and causing me to get distracted.

"Five minutes gone!" Clark yells, and I fan my face. *Focus, Ivy.* "Okay, you can help. Maybe." I wave Clark over to my table. He's already eyeing the three of us with interest.

"Yes, Miss Jones?"

I grin at his formal greeting. "Is it okay if I sign these two up to help me finish?"

Clark looks from Jace to Emmy and back to me before looking at the clipboard in his hands that seems to have appeared from nowhere. "Aren't you the one who didn't hold the door open for me after leaving the hardware store?" he asks Jace.

I watch Jace's mouth open and close. "That might have been me." He clears his throat, and Clark raises a brow. His shoulders sink. "It probably was me. I haven't been the best citizen since arriving because I've been lost in my head. I'm sorry, sir."

His hand extends in a gesture of goodwill, and Clark eyes it before clasping it with his own. I grin as Emmy giggles.

"Good job, Daddy," she whisper-yells near his ear, and we all laugh, even Clark.

"Well, I don't mind that you're a team, but there's still only one prize," he says, clearly softening after Jace's apology.

Right. "Well, that's okay."

"What's the prize? I need to know the stakes." Jace's deep voice is clear, even above the Christmas music blaring over the speakers about a grandma getting run over by a reindeer.

"A massage," I answer quietly, suddenly embarrassed

even though I have no reason to be. *I bet Jace could give a great massage.* My charged brain registers the thought that immediately entered my head when he asked, and I realize *that's* why I was embarrassed. I was pre-embarrassed, which seems fitting. I pick up some marshmallows to make a snowman.

"Oh, well, you need that. It goes to you, no question. Besides, whatever it was, I was going to give it to you anyway." The soft grin he gives me is intoxicating. "I mean, they do have couples massages," he starts again and gives me another wink.

The idea of him in a towel or with just a sheet covering his muscles causes my hands to jerk, sending a marshmallow shooting straight for Clark's forehead. Emmy laughs, and I cover my mouth with my hands.

"I'm so sorry. I didn't mean to . . ." I trail off while Clark shakes off the makeshift missile and adds Jace and Emmy to his clipboard.

"No bother. They can be slippery. I've got you all down. Now, get to work." He looks about the space and pivots away while yelling, "Ten minutes gone, people!"

I cringe, turning back to Jace, and see his eyes dancing with amusement. "If I had known the idea would affect you so much, I would've said it sooner."

At this, I laugh and give him the bag of royal icing. "C'mon, Bear, we have a house to build."

For the next fifty minutes, we construct the greatest gingerbread house I've ever seen. We end up with not only a house but a multi-story home. Jace even creates gingerbread furniture off the back patio and a chimney for Santa. Emmy builds the snowman and lays out the snow scene, using gumdrops for Christmas lights. I make a Christmas tree out of candy for the inside. It lights up, because Jace, of course, knows how to wire some lighting with the materials provided—materials that I've never thought to use before. To top it all off, he makes windowpanes with a hot plate and sugar, a tool I wouldn't even begin to know how to use.

In short, when we stand back to admire our work, it's incredible. And if we don't win the competition, it's got to be rigged. This is a gingerbread house for the ages.

"I think we make a good team." Jace's smooth voice is the powdered sugar to my royal icing.

"I'd say so."

"Whoa," Emmy exclaims, awed. I don't blame her. She peeks through the windows, and I look at the clock.

"And hands up! You're done!" Clark yells. A groan comes from the participants around us. Instead of complaining about the shortness of our construction time, I'm counting my blessings that the massage will soon be mine. I can already smell the essential oil and feel the imprint of hot stones on my spine.

"Now, our esteemed judging panel will be coming around to judge. Don't go anywhere, folks."

Jace crouches down to give Emmy a high five. "Good job, Emmy Bear." He stands and holds up his hand for a high five from me as well, but when I smack my palm against his, he holds my hand in place and slowly rubs his thumb against mine. The contact is so minuscule, anyone else would miss it, but it instantly sends heat down my arm. He releases my hand, and I rub the spot that he touched, willing it to hold the sensation.

After five minutes—or ten—the panel of judges that includes Clark, Ronald from the general store, and Annabelle from It's Art huddles in the center. Liam stands in the corner of the room with the speaker and his cat, A-cat-pella—the unofficial mascot of our town—as he lowers the music for dramatic effect. When they whisper to him, Liam lifts his hand for attention.

"The votes are in, Birch Borough. And the winner of this event, for the first time, is Miss Jones!"

"Is that Miss Ivy?" Emmy looks at Jace, who nods. She squeals. I join her, jumping up and down. Jace lets out a whoop and wraps an arm around my waist while scooping up Emmy with his other arm. We're hopping from the excitement, only slowing when Clark hands me an envelope. *Victory is sweet.* I lean back against Jace, my smile enough to power the whole room. I register enthusiastic claps as my friends and their husbands gather around the table. Grey steps back, motioning for us to look at her and smile.

We agree, and she snaps the picture. Even without seeing it, I immediately want to print the photo and frame it. My parents appear beside us. In the pressure of constructing the perfect gingerbread house, I'd missed their arrival, but Gram has already joined them.

"That's how we do it!" Dad yells, and Gram is doing a fist-bump motion into the air.

"I love this for us!" Mom adds as if it's a collective win. "I can add the photo to the inn's gallery wall. What a treat!"

I'm laughing and smiling as I peek up at Jace. He's staring down at me. "Congrats, Starlight." He pulls me a little closer, and I lean into him again, grateful for his strength, thrilled I have him here. His face grows blurry from the emotion stinging my eyes. The scene is so domestic, so very Christmas, that I want to hold on to it forever.

The only thing that could make this moment better is if my brother were here. A man walks toward my table, leaning down to look at our prize-winning gingerbread house. My eyes still blurry, I blink to clear them, thinking sadly that the newcomer resembles my brother in a lot of ways. I freeze as something familiar hits me. *It can't be.*

"Freddie?" I release Jace, leaning forward to confirm that I'm seeing him, dressed in his Marine uniform, a smile on his face as he turns to greet me.

"Hey, sis," he says, and I squeal, nearly knocking over the table to get to him.

I jump into his arms and hold on tight. His sturdy frame is comforting; memories of the nights we used to camp out together in our living room and watch Christmas movies together resurface as I pull him closer. He only gets holiday block leave on occasion. It's been a few months since we've seen each other, and we weren't sure if he'd be able to make it home in time for Christmas.

"You're home!" I yell, tears flowing freely now. I'm so happy I feel like my heart might not be able to contain it. Releasing him, I look at his face, noticing it's slightly more weathered than the last time I saw him. "For how long?" I wipe my eyes.

Freddie gives me his signature grin. "Until just before New Year's."

"Well, I hope you're ready for the rest of the holiday events. Oh, and if Gladys asks you about being on a show, decline immediately." I pull him in for another hug and see my parents behind us, crying from happiness, of course.

Gram is eating gingerbread and shrugs. "I already saw my grandson when he walked in. We're proud of you, boy." She lifts her cookie in a "cheers" motion and then nods toward Jace, her gaze conveying her meaning to me.

I turn with a smile, eager to unite two of my favorite men besides my dad. "Freddie, this is Jace." But my smile instantly falters, alarm entering my heart.

Jace looks like he's seen a ghost, his hands clenched so tight that his knuckles are turning white. I can almost physically feel Freddie stiffen behind me, his amusement gone. When I glance back at him, I realize this is the look he must have when he's on duty. It both frightens and startles me.

"We've met," my brother says sternly, staring at Jace.

"I'm sorry. What's happening here?" I speak from between the men. The noises around us and the mingling of the townspeople through the space fade like background noise in an airport.

"Let's go, Emmy," Jace says to his daughter kindly, though his eyes are suddenly distant, the warmth in them faded. He nods politely to my parents and Freddie, then his gaze turns to linger on me for an extra second. "See you around, Ivy. Congratulations on your win."

Jace smiles sadly and walks away, picking up Emmy after a moment when her shorter strides can't match his. My stomach clenches, wanting to run to him, but I realize I'm being held back by Freddie as he lightly touches my arm.

"Let him go, Ivy," he instructs, and because he's my brother, I listen.

Tonight, I won the gingerbread contest. But as my anxiety deepens and the tension in the room intensifies despite my brother's return home, I watch Jace and Emmy disappear from sight, and suddenly, I'm questioning if I really won anything at all.

Chapter Twenty-One

Jace

So, her brother is back.

Walking swiftly back to Angie's apartment—or at least, as swiftly as Emmy's legs can keep up after she insisted she could walk once we got outside—I cringe. It's been a long day and an emotional trainwreck—the likes of which I haven't been on in a long time. Seeing Ivy so happy about winning the contest made me realize that if I could choose anything I wanted for the future, all I'd want to do for the rest of my life is make sure she smiles as much as she did tonight. We were the type of team that made me believe winning would be found in being together.

Freddie's arrival instantly diminished the momentum I felt as we approached the upcoming holiday. He could easily take my place and cause any contribution of mine to not only vanish but also be unwelcome. He can help her finish the sets. He can walk her home from rehearsals. Understandably, she may not have as much time for Emmy and me this coming week. When I learned Ivy's last name, I was able to familiarize myself with her family tree. Her brother is an actual, national hero. I looked him up and discovered that he was awarded a Silver Star Medal for valor in combat. Once, Freddie warned me to stay away from Ivy, and of course, she's going to listen to her hero-brother over me.

Once we return to Angie's, I put my troubling thoughts aside with a sigh. I boil pasta for a pot of homemade mac and cheese. The hour is later than Emmy usually eats dinner, but I didn't have time to make anything before the gingerbread house contest, and I'm hoping the sugar was able to hold her over until I can feed her a proper meal, although I know that's as likely as me fitting into a size small shirt.

Emmy is practicing her dance in the living room, the song playing from my phone on repeat. My mind is racing. If I could, I would go to In the Ring to get some nervous energy out, but I know how that ended last time. My knuckles still have light-pink marks on their edges.

"Bro, what are you doing?" Angie walks in, a clump of flour stuck to her hairline. Her eyes blink against the overhead kitchen light. I wet a paper towel and stand over her, wiping the white smudge away. "Thanks," she says gratefully. "I was so tired after working on those extra pie orders for the holidays that I came home and crashed."

"Sorry if we woke you up."

"You didn't. I set an alarm so I would eat something, shower, and not wake up at four in the morning."

"Auntie A!" Emmy yells, registering that her aunt has joined us.

"Hey, kiddo." My sister lifts her up and holds her tight.

Emmy immediately relaxes in her arms. "Will you braid

my hair right now?" Her little hands frame my sister's face, and I see the love between them.

Angie has been amazing during this transition. My daughter may not have her mother, and she may not ever have Ivy as more than a dance teacher, but she's deeply loved.

"Of course I will! Get the things!" Angie sets her feet on the floor, and Emmy runs off to grab her hairbrush and what I know will be all kinds of sparkly hair accessories.

"Thanks," I say.

"Okay, we have approximately thirty seconds." Angie ignores my gratitude. I'd tease her, but she's clearly on a mission. "What happened to you? You were fine when you left the apartment this morning." She stares at me. "Never mind Grandma. You look like the one that got run over by a reindeer."

"I hate that song," I grumble.

Angie wears an instigating smile. "I know. That's why I said it."

I grab the pot of pasta and drain it into the colander I had waiting in the sink.

"Twenty seconds."

I turn and release another sigh. "Ivy's brother is back. And why didn't anyone go outside with Grandma in the song? Because Santa would never."

Angie's eyebrows lift. "Oh, no. He's back?"

"Yeah."

My daughter races through the kitchen and into the living room again, spreading out her items on the couch.

"I'm going to take care of this little peanut," Angie says. "Clear your head if you need to. But don't lose hope. Not yet. She's good for you."

I tip my head gratefully and then routinely grab the cheese, milk, butter, flour, and cream. If my anxious heartbeat is any indication, this is going to be the comfort food I need when it's done.

When dinner is ready, the three of us sit at the table and enjoy the meal. I don't always eat what Emmy eats, especially with my training regimen. But tonight, I'm making an exception. Taking my first bite, I realize I was right to choose the road less traveled, and it's delicious.

"Yum!" Angie sighs happily, standing and grabbing Emmy's bowl as well as her own, placing them into the dishwasher quickly.

I'm already on my second helping, crouched over my portion like Beast with his oatmeal. I know this is what I look like because Emmy has giggled no less than three times over the course of dinner.

"Emmy Bear, let's go! You've got your favorite Auntie A tonight on bath duty. Daddy can read your story before bed."

I give my sister another nod, the debt I feel toward her increasing by the moment. I'll gladly welcome her kindness. When they head to the bathroom, I finish my last bite, but my mind is so preoccupied that I miss my mouth, a spoonful of mac and cheese falling onto my t-shirt. I gather most of it with a napkin, frowning at the cheese still streaked across my clothing. Sighing, I pull my shirt over my head and stand to take it to the laundry room. Tossing it into the hamper, I return to retrieve my bowl, walking slowly to the sink. The thought of Ivy withdrawing from my life again weighs on me. My feet feel like they're made of lead. Christmas feels more chaotic than ever.

Earlier today, I convinced Angie and Edgar to change our travel plans so I could stay in town to spend the holiday with Ivy. For a moment, I worried they'd be furious, but they caved like the softies they are. Together, we FaceTimed my parents to tell them we're treating them to a New England Christmas again. I used up my airline miles; it was the least I could do for expecting them to travel unexpectedly over the holidays. And they're bringing back the gifts I shipped. It's a choice I'd make again if I needed to. Except, now I'm not so sure if changing my plans was a risk I needed to take since I'm not even sure where I'll stand with Ivy after tonight.

Just as a sense of despair sets into my heart, there's a light knock on the door. With the slight growl that rumbles in my throat, I confirm that I really can be a bear at times. Turning toward the entry, I call out, "Who's there?" not liking the thought of a stranger knocking at my sister's door late at night. There's no response.

Quickly unlocking it, I fling open the door to see Ivy and Resin standing before it, her hand mid-raise to knock again. Her hand drops, and the arm wraps around her back, her other hand holding the dog's leash as he nestles against her, peering up for further instruction.

"Starlight," I exhale.

Her eyes take in my face, moving over me. They widen noticeably when they land on my chest. I didn't think about the fact that I was shirtless when I opened the door. She's gripping the leash, and I want to flex just to see what her eyes do. I refrain, but I do straighten my shoulders to rise to my full height. It's almost comical the way Ivy swallows before lifting her eyes to mine again. Suddenly, I'm smiling, and I don't even care if that makes me a sap. The girl I care about is visibly attracted to me. And she's never even seen all my tattoos.

"Starlight?" I prompt gently when her eyes venture away and trace across my skin. The ink symbolizes who I am, the story of my life, and the parts of me that stay hidden, and by displaying them, I'm completely exposing my heart.

"There are just so many," Ivy whispers and then clears her throat, shaking her head slightly. "Hi, Bear. Had to see you. Hope that's okay."

I nod and gesture for her to come in.

"Mmm, something smells good in here."

The tentative smile she's wearing is slowly unraveling me. *She came after me.* "I made mac and cheese. You're welcome to some. I made too much."

"I don't honestly know if there is such a thing as too much comfort food."

"My thoughts exactly, even though I don't always allow myself to enjoy it as much as I should." We grin at each other before I realize I haven't taken her coat or put on a shirt. Which do I take care of first?

"May I?" I gesture toward her, and she smiles, removing the coat and allowing me to hang it on the rack by the door. Grabbing a hoodie thrown on top of my gym bag in the entry, I slide it over my head, catching Ivy's stare. Her cheeks hold an adorable blush. I turn toward the living room when my head peeks through.

"Hope it's okay that I brought my guy here." *My guy.*

The thought registers that *I* want to be called that—permanently. But I know she's speaking of Resin. To my disappointment, it appears her dog has clocked more time with her today than I have, which makes sense, but it still feels all sorts of wrong. I look at his sweet face. He's a great dog, one that Emmy would love to grow up with too.

"Of course." I nod my head and gesture for her to follow me. We walk to the sectional couch, and it's cozy because of Angie's superior decorating skills. Thick blankets line the back and sides of the couch. Candles have been lit throughout the space (that was my doing because I'm not sure how people don't love seasonal candles).

Ivy's gaze moves about the apartment I am currently sharing with my sister, drifting back to the entryway, tiny pink shoes and my comparatively massive boots tucked sideways against the baseboards. She peeks into the kitchen and spots the three chairs at the dining table, still slightly pushed out from dinner. When I open the drawer of the coffee table and pull out a package of dog treats, Resin's tail immediately wags. It's possible I bought the treats as soon as I found out that Ivy has a dog . . .

"May he have one?" I ask.

Resin looks to Ivy for permission. She laughs and gives a nod. "Wait, why do you have those?"

"What do you mean?" The dog is already chewing contentedly, flopping on the floor. I smile.

"You don't have a dog."

I look at Ivy. "No, but you do."

Her eyes melt into the deepest version of hot chocolate I've seen yet. "Jace," she says after seconds or minutes. I've lost track of time from being this close to her again. "What does the forest mean?"

It takes me a moment to register that she's talking about my tattoos. I breathe out, knowing she's caught the details of each one. "The trees near home."

"And the book?"

"It's a tribute to my love of reading."

"The North Star compass?"

"For Emmy." My chest tightens with each admission.

"The paintbrush?"

"For Mina." I swallow, knowing what she's saved for last.

"And the ribbon?"

My eyes meet hers. The design in question is a replica of the piece of ribbon she gave me once. "I think you know," I manage.

Her eyes fill with emotion, and a tear slips down her cheek. Ivy wipes it away. "Jace, what happened tonight when you saw my brother? Why did you walk away?"

I hear Emmy and Angie laughing in the other room and know I can keep sharing without little ears hearing. Now that Freddie is back, it's time. "I came to find you," I admit. "After that night, when I couldn't make it to our second date." I round my back in defeat, the gesture more painful than helpful.

"What?" Ivy barely gets out a breath. "What do you mean?"

I shift on the sofa so that I'm completely facing her on a diagonal. "After Mina died. I tried to come back. I asked around town for you."

Ivy covers her mouth with her hand, and Resin perks up, rubbing his face on her knee, clearly sensing her shift in mood. "It's okay, buddy," she says, petting him. He settles back against her feet. It's a comfort to know that although I haven't been here, she's had him looking out for her.

Suddenly, I'm not so jealous of him. I'm grateful. "So, you asked about me," Ivy continues. "What happened then?"

"Everyone here was very protective. People knew your name, of course, but you were back in New York." I rub the back of my neck to try to ease the tension. "I was about to give up when I ran into your brother at Four Leaf Cookies."

"When was this?"

"Four months after we met."

"What did he say?" Ivy's face has turned pale, her eyes widening. I think she already knows how this ends.

"He said I broke your heart. I tried to tell him about Mina and what happened to her, but he wouldn't let me explain. He said to stay away. And normally, I wouldn't have listened. But he made some pretty compelling arguments, and I listened." I let out a self-deprecating laugh.

"Such as?"

"Ivy, we don't have to do this now."

"Such . . . as?" she asks me again, and I cave more quickly than I should.

"Such as the fact that your whole life is—or was—in New York. He said that if I didn't have the decency to show up for our date, then I wasn't worthy to have you as my girl, no matter the reason. He didn't know that I had a life-changing reason for not showing up, but I didn't correct him. He said that you'd been treated like an afterthought by men before and that now you were finally living out your dreams." I struggle to grit out the next words. "And he said that if I cared about you at all, then . . . I would leave you alone."

The reverberation of Ivy's gasp sends a shock through me. "No."

"Ivy—"

"He had no right!" She's standing now, rushing to the door, the rigidness of her turned-out feet alerting me to make a move.

"Ivy, wait." Cold wind hits my chest from the partially opened door. The hair dryer blows loudly in the next room, a contrast of temperatures from where we stand.

Slowly, I lean forward and shut the door, my arm hovering above her head. She turns to face me, her back pressing against the door. Resin looks between us and settles, his excitement fading. He flops on top of our feet, and I give Ivy a tentative smile, hoping it encourages her not to run away.

Her arms are crossed, and she lets out an adorable—I mean, *fierce*—huff. "So, he said all that to you. And you just listened to him?"

I reach out and gently wrap her face in my hands, my hands cradling her delicate jaw. "Is this okay?" She nods, and I sigh in relief, even though my lungs feel heavy. Tears brim along the edges of her hot-chocolate eyes, and my heart picks up speed. "Ivy, please listen to me."

She looks up at me, and a tear slips out.

I stroke her soft skin with my thumb. "You were in New York. You were living your dream. And maybe I shouldn't have listened to him. But I had known you for only one night at that point. A magical night, to be sure, but not nearly as long as I would've liked to disrupt your life like that. He's known about your dreams for your whole life. You must know that I would never want to hold you back."

"But don't you remember what I said? I told you that I wanted someone to really know me. *We* could've known each other, Jace." Deeply, I inhale as she forces her head down, pushing my hands away, a hint of a sob emerging from her heaving chest. "I'll talk to him," Ivy says quietly. "I'm just so . . . Why did we . . . It's so unfair."

"It is. All of it."

"Your sister. My brother. Never seeing each other again. Emmy's mother and whatever lies she told you." Her insight causes my eyes to widen as she continues. "You didn't deserve any of that, Jace." Ivy places her hands on my chest, and I go completely still. "You didn't."

A part of me has always wondered if there's been some sort of cause and effect on my life. Yes, I made some decisions after Mina passed away that I wish I could take back. But I was grieving. And while that's never been an excuse, mourning has a way of altering our reality in ways we don't understand while we're moving through those dark days. And even though I wish it hadn't happened, I understand her brother's motives. I respect him for protecting her.

"Your brother meant well," I reply. "Our timing was just off, Starlight."

Her eyes soften slightly. "Thank you."

"For what?"

"For still using the name you've given only me." She smiles, her eyes red but warmth returning to her face.

"Welcome." My hands lift, and I pass my thumb over the curve of one of her cheekbones as Emmy walks into the living room, rubbing her eyes, with Angie right behind her.

"Oh, hello, Ivy," Angie says with a knowing smile after the initial surprise. She looks at me, making all sorts of gestures I will have future questions about, as Ivy leans down to encourage Emmy's interaction with Resin. I motion for my sister to quit it when Ivy looks at me, and I freeze, my hands still midair.

"Okay, then." Ivy looks between us. "I have a sibling, so I know code when I see it. I'll just get going. I didn't mean to intrude."

"Nope!" Angie yells. "You misread. I was trying to communicate to my gigantic, romance-loving brother here that he shouldn't let you get out the door."

Ivy laughs.

"I can't even repeat what you just called me," I protest. "Why? Just why?"

Angie laughs too, but I catch Emmy's tired swipe of her eyes once more. She reaches for me, and I hold her close, wishing that the days when she lets me hold her like this would never end. My daughter relaxes completely against me, her head facing Ivy, her hair in a braid brushing against my neck. Already, her breathing is steady, her small rib cage pressing against my heart with every breath, and something about having all of us here together makes me try to clear my throat from emotion. I don't let my gaze linger on the fact that the woman I care about is here to observe such a quiet moment. There's no glamour in the four of us standing in the entryway—just the facts. These are the everyday elements that I try to keep moving through, and she's now a witness to them.

"I'll just put her to bed, and I'll be right back," I say as softly as I can, my hand cradling Emmy's shoulders. Ivy clocks the gesture and grins, nodding, as Angie gives a nod and a wave to us both before heading back to her room.

"I'll be here," Ivy whispers.

"G'night, Miss Ivy," Emmy's tired voice breaks through, and Ivy lightly touches her back, rubbing it in a clockwise motion.

Her gaze lands on my left hand, the one with the tattoo of the clock, and I feel the way she's tracing the foliage wrapped around it with her eyes. She searches my face, and I give myself one more moment to cherish having Ivy here in my space, wishing this family scene could go on forever. Then I gather the resolve to walk down the hall to our room. Emmy is too tired for one of the books we've been reading, so I tell her my favorite story: How I felt the night that she was born. She falls asleep easily with her mouth slightly open and her long lashes brushing her cheeks. I tuck her in and make sure there's an extra blanket draped near her feet. For a moment, I stand in the doorway of our temporary shared bedroom and shake out my shoulders before I walk down the hall.

To my relief, Ivy is still waiting in the next room. My brain can't comprehend how we got here, but even after the grace she showed me tonight, I know that if anyone has ever earned the right to know me at my core, it's Ivy. I just hope she's patient enough for us to move through the part of my story that I still haven't wanted to share or relive. Until now.

Chapter Twenty-Two

Ivy

The clock strikes seven.

You know that glorious scene in *While You Were Sleeping*, when the family gathers around the table, eating dinner, and there's so much really great dialogue and banter? Nothing makes sense, and yet, everything is also absolutely perfect. That feels like this moment for me. But instead of Sandra Bullock being the wonderful outsider, the role has been recast to Jace. He's wide-eyed, with a bit of a grin etched continuously in the contours of his face, packing the biggest bite of mashed potatoes I've ever seen onto his fork. Just as he's about to bring the polished silver utensil to his mouth, my grandmother strikes.

"So, Arms McGee . . ." she trails, the heat from my face offset by the chuckles that resonate throughout the dining room.

"Arms McGee," Jace mumbles to me, the mashed potatoes falling onto the plate after the instinctive jerk of his hand at his new title.

"You know, because he's ripped," my grandmother adds

helpfully, looking around the room.

"We get it, Gram," I mutter while my brother chokes on his water, which serves him right. I've been trying to avoid Freddie for the last day or so. Though, we did have a deep chat over coffee this morning. There were tears on my part and an apology from my brother, but here we are. I made him go personally to the boxing gym to ask Jace to join us for dinner this evening. I'm not sure exactly what was said between them, but Jace is now here and surrounded by my family. And it feels like we're on the right track. We're at my parents' inn, nestled together in the dining room. Their amazing chef cooked dinner for us, and we're in the middle of our family tradition of dinner at the inn followed by caroling in the snow.

"And how do you feel about our girl?" Gram launches into her interrogation, interrupting my thoughts. She's clearly not intending to let him eat in peace.

Jace shifts in his chair, the resulting creak the reminder we all need that this giant of a man is sitting on what's practically an antique. It's a sort of Christmas magic that he isn't sitting on a pile of splinters right now. He just took a bite and tries to chew it quickly in preparation to answer.

After Emmy went to bed last night, we held each other, sitting on the couch and drinking candy cane tea. His need for permission every time he wants to touch me is . . . unusual but endearing. We still haven't kissed. After eight years, if he doesn't kiss me soon, I fear I may internally combust from the tension. Regardless of the forces keeping us from showing our affection, I told him he's worth more to me than my brother's opinion. Considering how much Freddie's opinion has meant to my life, the admission says a lot about what I'm hoping for in our future.

"And where's Emmy?" Gram presses, a lifted roll in her hand poised as a potential weapon.

Jace is still swallowing his last bite, so I put my hand on his arm and step in before things get even more unraveled. "Emmy is with Angie and Edgar. They're picking out a Christmas gift for Jace."

"Mom, let him be," my dad says with a smile to Gram and a spark in his eye that tells me he is enjoying another man being in the house. It's probably a shock to everyone that this time . . . gasp! He's here for me.

"I'd let him be, but he seems like the type of guy who enjoys a little banter. A little back and forth? Maybe even some choreography for two?" Gram smiles as my brother chokes on his bite of pot roast.

"Good thing he's with Ivy, then," Freddie banters with a laugh, and my face has already turned pure crimson. I don't need a mirror to know it. "She's an expert at complicated choreography." He winks at me, and I feel the kind of love-filled fury that only siblings can experience.

Jace laughs, his shoulders relaxing. I imagined he's just realized that he's entered a room full of the unhinged types who mean well but also like to disguise themselves as my family. Just when I think he'll try to avoid the question, he lifts his chin, meeting the eyes of every member of my family around the table in turn. The mixture of shock and amusement across their faces is notable. He may be a loyalist, but a part of his charm is being trustworthy. So far, I've noticed that Jace doesn't back down from the things and people he needs to confront. It's one of the things I'm realizing I like most about him.

"Well, everyone," he says with a hint of a grin, "while I do like banter, the truth is that Ivy is unlike any other woman I've ever met in my life." The scent of his pine-infused cologne seems to hover around me, spreading to my shoulders as his arm drapes over the back of my chair.

"And what makes her different?" my brother challenges, an eyebrow raised.

Jace nods as if he were expecting the follow-up question. There's less tension than I expected between him and my brother, but I also sense definite proving-themselves-to-each-other vibes.

"See, I could start with how she treats all her students like they deserve the world, but that's the obvious one," Jace replies to a collective of nods. "If I were only a casual observer, then I'd say her beauty, her kindness, her elegance, or her generosity are her most noticeable qualities."

More nods. Gram may even whisper, "Amen."

Jace speaks more methodically now, his eyes lingering on each of my family members. They're riveted on his speech, as am I. Santa Claus himself could come walking into the room, and I wouldn't be able to tear my eyes from the gorgeous man next to me. And it's not because of his looks. He is beyond handsome; I won't deny that. But it's his spirit that draws me in, the one that focuses intensely on everything he does but is also gentle enough to prompt you to give him your heart and hold his in return. I'll admit, when he first returned to Birch Borough, those qualities were hidden beneath a vibe that was nothing less than crotchety. But after we've been through so much pain and grief, sometimes it's hard to remember who we really are.

Jace continues, "But I'm not casual in how I view Ivy."

His confession causes me to shiver, and I straighten my back, attempting to get more circulation moving through my limbs. His jaw lifts slightly, a twitch on the side of his mouth giving away his nerves. "No, I'm the kind who only had to meet Ivy once before I gave her a nickname that will stick with me—and her—for the rest of my life. I'm the kind who notices the way she relaxes into ballet positions because it's so ingrained in her being that she can't help it. And she hums when she's happy, and she'd rather have the record player she grew up dancing to at her studio, not because she can't afford a new one, but because she'd rather have the memories. I'm the person to whom she gifted her lucky charm because she knew I wouldn't take it for granted."

At this, I inhale sharply. My mother sniffs. Freddie's mouth hangs open.

"I'm the kind of man who, even though I lost myself in grief for a while, I never stopped believing that, besides God and Emmy, Ivy was my reminder there is goodness in this world," Jace concludes, his voice deep and somber.

The only sounds in the room are Resin's breathing underneath the table and the melody of carolers who got a head start outside the windows of the inn. My heart is racing in time to the tune of "Jingle Bells." It's an unhinged thought, but the air is thick with emotion. And I think of how much this moment feels like the Christmas magic I've been hoping for my whole life.

"You'd better hold on to Arms McGee like your life depends on it, Ivy girl," Gram says, staring at me.

I laugh and wipe the side of my face with the edge of my hand while reaching for my water with the other. The warmth of Jace's hand covers my knee through my tights, and I'm electrified. I hope he never stops reaching for me.

"And you, ma'am?" Gram asks then, her eyes directed to me pointedly. I take another drink of water and shift closer to Jace. I need his strength.

"What about me?"

"Don't play coy. How does Arms McGee make you feel?"

I swallow, looking at my parents, who have loved each other since their school days. I glance at my brother, who's a hero in his own right and whose affection for me has never wavered, even if his protection sometimes causes more harm than intended. Finally, I look back at Gram, who meddles because she cares so fiercely.

"Well, uh . . . I'm not sure anyone can make us feel anything, considering that it's our own responses that make the difference. But if I've felt anything, it wasn't because of anything he did. I'm drawn more so to just who he is." I stumble through the words while Jace's hand gently presses into my knee, the tips of his fingers tracing circles around the front of it. I close my eyes, enjoying every moment of contact.

"I guess that's an acceptable answer," Gram says. At last, she seems ready to table the interrogation and focuses on the centerpieces, commenting on their colors being more vibrant than last year. Conversation starts to pick up again around us, and I see Jace resume eating when my gut clenches. I didn't say anything wrong. My words were nice. But it spoke of him more as a person and not who he is to me.

"Wait!" I clink my fork on the glass in front of me and wince. Everyone at the table stops moving. Jace pauses with his mouth open, another forkful of food hovering over his plate.

"That's more like it." Gram's eyebrow lifts, a smirk positively engraved upon her face.

"I need to run it again."

Freddie gives me a nod, and I give him a grateful smile. Jace looks around the table, then his eyes settle on me, concern etched between his brows. I reach up to smooth it out, and he inhales sharply, his eyes widening.

I begin with a rush. "I said he didn't *make* me feel anything, but that's not true. He makes me feel everything." Jace's face is all I see, though my cheeks are hot with the attention I know is directed to me. Why can I dance on a stage in front of thousands of people without shaking, but being seen by Jace leaves me with the sensation of free-falling?

"Jace," I whisper, "you make me feel everything."

His jaw tightens, his chiseled cheekbones shifting with the movement.

"You asked me how he makes me feel." I look at Gram and lift my chin. I'm well aware that this is my own rite of passage with her, owning my emotions and declaring it in front of my family. I can appreciate her intention. And Jace deserves the attention. I shift to look back at him and reach up to touch the side of his face. He leans into my hand with the slightest bit of pressure, and I smile. "You make me feel like everything ever missing or stolen from me has been returned."

Jace closes his eyes. He turns his chest toward me, his hands rising to cradle the sides of my face. The tip of his nose traces from the bridge of my own to my hairline before his warm lips brush against my forehead, and he kisses my skin. I swallow and register the sound of my mother sniffling and Gram clapping. My dad does some sort of grunt in a sound of approval, and my brother is probably taking notes. He should. There's no one like Jace.

"Well, Arms McGee is still a good nickname, despite how mushy the two of you are." Gram takes another bite of pot roast and gives a disinterested shake of her head.

"Don't be offended, Gram. You can call me that instead," Freddie says with a wink, clearly just trying to get a rise out of her.

"Okay!" My mother stands and starts clearing dishes. "I'm just going to go grab the dessert. Ivy girl, can you come and help?"

I nod and stand, moving toward my mom when Jace rises so suddenly that the table shakes.

"I'll help her with the dessert," he says.

Freddie laughs into his hand and tries to cover it with a cough. "Smooth, man," he mutters, and Mom lightly and lovingly pushes him on the shoulder.

Walking away, I feel Jace's strong frame behind me. When we're in the kitchen, he follows me until I'm against the counter. I face him, immediately finding his arms lowering to effectively cage me in. His amber eyes drop to my lips, the pine-infused scent of him engulfing me. Just his proximity is exhilarating. The clock on the stove lets out a little chime, breaking the spell of the moment as Jace smiles.

"What do you think all these clocks are trying to tell us?" I say softly, my breath hitching as Jace leans down slightly.

"That we'd better choose each other before time runs out."

I hum. "Like *The Nutcracker*."

"What?"

"*The Nutcracker*. He comes to life and then returns to the form of a nutcracker—at least, in some versions. It always made me so sad."

"I hate Florida," Jace confesses rapidly.

My brows crinkle in confusion as my eyes search his. "You . . . what?"

"I hate it," he repeats hastily. "Why would I spend Christmas there? You're not there."

"But you said . . ." I begin.

"I changed my tickets. I know what I said, but not being near you for Christmas and thinking that distance from me was what you needed was the excuse I made to keep my heart from galloping away from me."

"Galloping?" I question with a smile.

"Yes, like a noble steed."

"Okay, then." This conversation is so . . . Jace, the Jace I've come to know. I can barely contain my amusement, and I'm about to tease him until I see his eyes swirling like maple syrup pouring from the bottle, their intensity mesmerizing.

His voice rumbles around me with a throaty timbre, consuming me. "Sometimes, I feel like the forces of this world have ripped things from me when I least expect it, the things that I love. It happened with my sister. It happened with you. But I can't be afraid of loss and disappointment. Instead, I have to hold on even tighter and pray that that's enough."

My heart turns over. "What I hear you saying is that you want your Christmas plans to involve me this year. Am I right?"

"That's exactly what I'm saying." His voice is deliciously scratchy, the sound causing me to put more weight against the counter whose job it currently is to hold me up. How he's getting more attractive by the second is captivating.

"That must be inconvenient for your family."

"We missed out on spending Christmas together long ago, Starlight. I don't want to miss out on this one."

"If we wait any longer, I'll be asleep by the time dessert arrives!" I hear Gram yell from the dining room, effectively breaking us from the magical moment we've been sharing.

I shake my head as Jace laughs. As it escapes from him, the movement causes his head to lean forward, the edges of his hair teasing my cheekbone. I want to wrap my arms around him so he can bury his face in my neck, but the thought is postponed when he straightens. He points to a cake that looks like a snow globe and a plate of cookies, and I nod as he grabs them. I grab a chilled chocolate cream pie, a gift from Angie via Jace.

"We have enough dessert to fill the town. Maybe we should invite the carolers to come inside," Jace says with a hint of playfulness. I love seeing glimpses of him when he's more at peace, the real Jace underneath the occasional gruffness.

My mom greets us at the door, her eyes full of love. "I was just about to come after you two!"

"No need," I reassure her as we bring the desserts to the table, finding our seats again while everyone looks at us knowingly.

"Do we need to sanitize anything, or are we good?" Freddie, loving and obnoxious brother that he is, challenges me with a raised brow.

"We're *fine*," I say with emphasis, though "fine" comes out a little more like how Ross would say it from *Friends*.

Freddie laughs and digs into the pie. A cheer erupts from my dad and Gram.

Jace gives me a soft smile. He curves his face toward mine, his deep voice greeting my ear. "Hi, Starlight. Missed you."

I laugh nervously. "We haven't been apart."

He shrugs with a grin. "Still miss you."

Oh my stars, I am so gone on this man.

Gram is busy hacking deeper into the pie and throwing cookies on plates as they pass around the table. Jace grabs his share but passes it to me before taking one for himself. His face lingers so close to mine. I want to feel his warmth, that certain brand of affection I've only felt from him. I want to feel the softness of his lips and the brush of his smooth-shaven jaw. I want to nuzzle into his neck and remember how my heart beats to a rhythm that's only his. As the conversation moves around us, I track it absentmindedly, but my mind is still stuck in the kitchen . . . and the fact that we still haven't kissed.

"Jace, what happens after New Year's?" I ask in a sudden whisper.

His hand flexes around the spoon on the table. His posture is almost comical in the tiny, vintage chair, and I'd tease him if not for the seriousness of this moment. "I want to be with you, Starlight, if that's what you're asking."

I bite my lip and focus on the dessert, finding that I'm not hungry for it at all. The thought of Jace still planning to leave, of Emmy no longer being able to grow up in my dance studio, makes me queasy.

"You know, I think we should go sing!" I stand to my feet, Resin following with a worried wag of his tail, my dog sensing the shift in my mood. Freddie is eating pie like he's in a contest, and my dad is on his fourth cookie. They stare at me, exchanging questioning glances across the table.

"But we haven't even had our tea," Gram chides.

I sit back down, feeling like my tights are now too warm and my fingers are too cold. Jace extends his hand, a pained expression on his face, until I thread my fingers through his. I hold him tightly, unsure if I should find his touch comforting or commit it to anxious memory. He's here. He's in a place so familiar to me, yet somehow, tonight, I feel the call of loneliness in my soul. Maybe it is possible to miss someone while they're still next to you. If it was hard to try to move on without him the first time, I can't imagine what it would be like to lose him and Emmy now.

Chapter Twenty-Three

Jace

The clock strike eight.

"Do you mind if I just . . . sit here for a moment?" I hover the majority of my weight just above the bench placed against the wall in Ivy's dance studio. It's sitting close to the dance floor but just off to the side.

"As long as you don't mind the sound of my shoes on the floor while I practice." She lifts her shoulder a bit, but I see her uncertainty. I feel it across the room. She isn't sure if she wants me to watch her dance.

Ever since the dinner at her parents' inn, the look in Ivy's eyes has been hesitant. I wish that wasn't the truth of it, but here we are. And I created this because I panicked. After Mina passed and Jenna left, I haven't seemed to be able to make long-term plans. I thought I was finally making progress by choosing to move to Florida months ago, but those plans are now precariously in danger of being destroyed. And it scares me. I'm scared to give my heart to another woman. I'm not sure it could handle Ivy finding me to be less than what she's hoped for all these years.

"I don't mind." I want to say so much more, but I force myself to settle for the simple words. Because I want to tell her that her presence feels like a balm upon the pain that sticks to my joints and settles in my bones, though I know the source of it is really all coming from my heart.

Music begins to play from the antiquated speaker in the corner. The lights are off in the studio, apart from the twinkle lights she has strung all throughout the space. Multiple strands are lighting the ceiling and walls. There's a stack of records and compact discs stacked together in the corner under a record player. Immediately, I want to build her a new one, etching my signature into the piece so a part of me could live here too. Ivy presses something on the remote in her hands and slides it across the floor until it's under a barre.

Taking a long drink from her steel water bottle, I notice the stiffness in her shoulders and the way her lungs expand and contract rapidly through the thin material of her leotard. It's long-sleeved and white, the color a contrast to the dark-colored practice tutu she's wearing. I'd expect her to be wearing her red lipstick, as usual, but tonight, only a gloss paints her mouth, her natural beauty radiating even though I see the tension in her limbs.

Gracefully, she moves her feet while facing the barre, the rhythmic and steady quality of her movements in harmony with her rich hair that looks as if it's spun with dark gold. The waves are loosely pulled back with a bow resting near the crown of her head. I want to reach for her, but I don't want to hurt her.

I never want you to touch me again.

The words that seem permanently stuck to my soul after

Jenna said them cause me to groan inadvertently. "Can I confess something?" I ask, hesitating.

Ivy nods while she continues to dance.

"I'm sorry about last night. I feel like I didn't make it clear that I still wanted to hold you after the holidays."

"That's the thing, though, Jace." She stops and bites her lip before releasing it. "I don't think I'm capable of being held. Not truly."

My eyes widen. My brows furrow. "You can't mean that," I grit out.

"Oh, I've been touched all over," she says lightly, like the information is nothing.

I hear a slight growl escape my throat as I rise from the bench, the room nearly blurring in my peripheral vision.

Ivy jumps back as one of her eyebrows lifts. "Oh. *Oh.*" Her words come out in a rush. "No, it sounds far worse than I meant it."

My shoulders lower, no longer hovering near my ears, ready to take names, and . . . I don't know what exactly. The idea of other men touching Ivy makes my head spin. I never put together the mental picture of the number of dance partners she's probably had. It hurts that I'm not able to fulfill that role for her. I sit down again and grip the bench, aware that my feelings are shimmering too close to my skin, ready to be unleashed.

"Sorry, no. I mean, yes," Ivy continues. "I have been touched quite a bit. I've been held. You don't become a ballerina and dance with men not to have them lift you and spin you and carry you time and time again. It's not romantic in any sense of the word, I can assure you. It's messy and sometimes uncomfortable, even when the guys don't mean it to be. And there are lifts where their hands are just . . ." She motions in the general vicinity of her lower body, and I shut my eyes.

Crack. I look down to see a piece of the bench in my hands. I broke it. Embarrassment creeps through my spine as I close my eyes and rush through my thoughts, trying to pick one—any *one*—that will help make this situation any better. I've never broken anything from emotion. I'm not a violent man, except to my heavy bag at the gym. Though, at times, I just don't know my strength. I'd never want Ivy to be afraid of me.

"Oh, my goodness, are you okay?" The pitter-patter of her shoes on the floor grows louder as she approaches. It's the only thing I can focus on until I open my eyes to find her kneeling before me, her knees barely grazing the ground.

"I'm not dangerous," I mutter.

"I know that."

"I . . . I'm sorry. I'll fix it."

"I know you will."

My eyes shift to hers. "How do you know that?" My breathing is heavy now, but the possibility that she's still seeing me in a clearer light than I realized does strange things to my system. Somehow, she knows I'm not talking about fixing the bench.

"Because you're someone worth trusting. You bristle at affection from others sometimes, and yet, you're anxious to give it. You protect the ones that you love, especially Emmy. You love her so fiercely. It's incredible."

I'm silent as emotion begins to creep up my frame.

"Thank you for saying that," I reply softly, letting my words ring clearly.

Ivy looks at me as a blush starts to form on her cheeks, like it's being magically painted in the air between us. Her eyes dart down to the piece of bench still in my hands, and she releases a laugh from somewhere deep in her soul. "You really broke it."

"Yep." There's no point in denying it or adding sparkle to my words.

"And now it's clear that you really don't like the idea of me being touched." Her eyebrow lifts in a teasing dare until she catches my expression.

I will myself to remain neutral, but what I'm really thinking is *not unless it's by me.*

Somehow, she catches the duality between my expression and the intensity of what I'm not saying, and she clears her throat. "C'mon, Bear," she adds with a playful lilt to her voice.

"You're still calling me that?"

"Mmm," she hums. "It's a bit obvious, but it seems to fit you well." I refrain from permitting the growl wanting to escape my throat when she peeks over her shoulder. "Besides, I like bears." And with that, she winks. She actually winks.

And I know that the only hibernating I'm doing this winter is continuing to fight to keep my heart in one piece. "So, you were saying?" I ask, desperate to get back on track. I motion with my arm for her to keep practicing. It's no good if I distract her from what she needs to be doing. I wanted to find some peace while she practiced, not keep her from doing what she loves.

"Oh, right." She catches my eye over her shoulder before placing a foot on the highest level of the bar and leaning forward. Her arms flow about her as she stretches, folding over her leg in a way that looks like a flower closing up in the rain. She takes a deep breath. I assume she's not going to answer me until she's stacked her spine back to standing, her leg still stretched in front of her, and her fingers stretched over her head, arching toward the ground. I'm mesmerized by the sight of her graceful rhythm until her rocky voice crackles through the air.

"I can't be held because I just slip through." Ivy shrugs and switches legs, and I notice the way one of her leg warmers seems to slide down with the movement, revealing a bit more of her calf wrapped in those pink tights. She stares at the wall ahead of her.

Those pink tights are starting to invade my thoughts more and more. I tell myself it's the color of them, not quite pink, not quite white. Through the haze of my fascination with her, I realize she's telling me how she feels. And it hits me that this is how I feel too. I'm slipping through the cracks of my own life. The truth is that it wasn't until Ivy entered my life again that I started to understand what it might feel like to be present once more.

"What do you mean?" I ask her, wanting to be certain that my stony heart isn't making up stories.

"It's like I'm made of smooth stone," she begins, still staring at the wall and moving up and down on the balls of her feet. I think I've heard Emmy call the movement a *relevé*. "I'm the marble statue that men seem to want to look at or touch, but then they let it slide through their fingertips until the next, better piece comes along. And I've hated it."

If I were a different man, if I had made other choices that hadn't led me to a point in my life where my daughter was the only force over the past five years keeping me from staying in bed all day, I might try to prove her wrong. Because if she wants to be held as she deserves to be held, I'm afraid my grip is loose. Just the image of wrapping her up makes me wish that my hands could work again. Just for her, I'd pray for them to work again.

Ivy looks toward me, her eyes slightly wide, unmeasured emotion in them, while she scans my face. One of her legs has regained the highest level of the barre. Her body is still facing the barre, but when her arms rise and trail over her head toward her extended leg, she peeks at me from beneath the arch of her arms, eyebrows lifted. I sigh and nod, wishing I could tell her just to ignore me, but I can't seem to get the words out. I probably shouldn't even be here, but I can't bring myself to leave her alone tonight. We're in a sort of magic land with the fairy lights woven throughout the space, the music drifting through the air, and the warmth after the chill of the outdoors wrapping around us.

I lean back against the wall, allowing my eyes to close and the memories of our first moments to float through my mind. I've tried to hold them back, afraid that the resurgence of them would drown me rather than free me. But it's time to honor the moments—even through the fear, the disappointment, and the decisions I made following our ill-fated acquaintance. Running from those memories all this time has been exhausting, and if anyone is going to help me through to the other side, it's Ivy.

The light patters of her slippered feet brushing and lifting off the floor soothe and calm my nerves. My courage lifts with every beat she moves to, so I open my eyes to take it in. Her body flows to a song featuring a cello, the music uniting with her in a way that's magnificent to behold. Her whole body moves and flows with the soul of the sound, and I'm captivated. Once, she told me she'd been injured in New York, but the way she moves speaks of her determination to do what she loves without apologizing for it.

Before I can overthink it, I rise to my feet, slowly removing one shoe and then the other. I don't want to startle her, so I stand at the edge of the studio floor with socked feet, waiting to make sure she even wants me in her space. After pirouetting a few times, she stops, and her eyes catch mine. Gracefully, she glides to the center of the room, her short tutu hugging the top of her waist. Her gaze shifts to my feet, and she smiles. To my surprise, her eyes brim instantly with unshed tears. I hope my gaze conveys my request.

Then Ivy nods, and I walk toward her, the sensation of my feet on the spongy floor bending beneath my weight a contrast to the feeling of my heart pounding within my ribs. When we're only inches apart, I go still, unsure what to do next. We're in the middle of the studio, but we might as well be in the middle of the ocean. I want to hold her, touch her. And I want what I've believed about myself to be rewritten.

"Dance with me?" Ivy asks, and the music stops, making the last word louder than the first. She looks at the remote under the barre and moves toward it, holding up a hand to temporarily pause what was between us. Soon enough, she's back in the center of the space, and I smell the vanilla radiating off her with a hint of amber, the scent reminding me that this isn't a dream. I can never smell her when I dream.

"I will dance with you. I *want* to dance with you," I add

as our eyes connect. "But I want to do your kind of dance."

"My kind of dance?" Ivy asks breathlessly, searching my face. I let her search, knowing that she'll find the truth.

"How would someone . . .?" I clear my throat as the thought of how many times other men have danced with her clenches my heart. I want it to be my turn. "How would a man hold you to support you while you dance? I don't want to hurt you."

"Jace, they've had years of training. And it's an act, a show. It doesn't mean anything."

"Well, then you shouldn't have a problem teaching me."

"No!" she says firmly, and I feel my spine stiffen. "No, that's just it . . . if you danced with me, it would mean everything."

A tear escapes from her right eye, and I reach up to wipe it with the pad of my thumb. More tears fall, and my hands act like windshield wipers to gently clear them. Her hot-chocolate irises are hazy, the warmth in them increasing and steaming with emotion.

"I want to hold you, Ivy. I want to support you while you do what you love. And I promise you that I'm doing everything I can to fight what's in my mind. I don't want to leave you alone in the cold this time."

In response, Ivy turns to the barre, using her fingers to lightly brush any remaining tears from her face. Her face is flushed, her eyes are glassy, and her lips are slightly open as she takes a deep breath.

"Okay, then," she says, twirling toward the front of the room, her eyes now facing forward. I follow the direction of her line of sight until our gaze clashes in the mirror. To my delight, a slight grin lifts one side of her pouty mouth. The urge to kiss her just to make sure this is real overwhelms my senses. She motions with her head to encourage me to move, and I stand behind her, waiting for my next instructions.

"I wanted to kiss you." I let out an exhale. "I feel . . . almost desperate to kiss you again." With a tentative chuckle, I shake my head. "But that's me, ever the romantic."

Ivy turns to face me, her eyes wide as she watches me silently.

"I know we said we've changed, and it's true. But right now, it's like . . ." Once again, my words get caught.

"Is it like you've never wanted anything more?" Ivy asks me.

"Like I've never been so hungry for something in my entire life."

"Jace," Ivy says into the space between us, the lights that shimmer like stars surrounding us. "Don't go hungry. Not when I'm right here."

She rises on her toes, and I focus on the smoothness of her skin, the flush in her cheeks, and her eyes trained on my lips expectantly. I don't want to keep waiting. I'm tired of waiting. For the first time in a long time, my desire to show affection silences the lies I've believed. So, I close the distance between us, and suddenly, her soft, warm lips are pressed against mine. And my heart thinks: *This, I remember.*

She hums. A sigh escapes from the back of my throat, the controlled humming in my palms the only indication that I haven't actually left my body. It feels too good to be real. Ivy's mouth moves over mine, as gracefully and elegantly as she moved earlier, dancing over the doubts I've carried with me since we last saw each other. All I know is that I haven't felt this level of peace since we last kissed.

The calming sensation pulsing through my system brings emotions to the surface that I've never before felt. It's all the tears I never allowed myself to shed. It's the understanding that all the heartbreak was worth it if Ivy is the one to mend it. The anger and the disappointment melt in the electrical shock of her desire for me. It's like being near the fire while a storm rattles the windows. It's the exquisite quietness of freshly fallen snow. It's the miracle of recognizing that we're so small in this world, and yet, somehow, we each matter deeply.

I reach up to nestle my hands in her hair, the softness of her skin and the silkiness of the wispy bits of her ribbon-tied hair twirling around my fingers. Ivy shifts in my arms, and I let her take the lead, losing myself in the release of the tension that's been building since we reconnected. The feeling of wanting to be even closer to her is overwhelming. I have an urge to immortalize the moment and forget the cold that hovers on the edges of my consciousness and the sadness that's been weighing on my heart for ages. I feel her hands move into my hair too, and I hum in response, enjoying the pressure of her touch now cradling my jaw. Those soft hands move to my neck, her slight but strong frame complementing my sturdy one, both of us steady in our own strengths. Her kisses flow like the beloved river in this town, dancing rapidly on the surface but running smoothly as it's pulled by the current. I'm filled to the brim with peace, and yet, I feel as though I already miss her. We're only brought back to reality by the sound of a clock chiming at Town Hall.

I break the kiss, my lungs heaving. I'm nearly out of breath, but my eyes diligently scan every detail of her face, searching for answers. "Did you—Was that . . .?" I start to ask, barely getting the words out.

The furrow in her brow and the uncertainty in her expression cause a slight shiver to run down my spine. This woman. If she needs reassurance, I'm happy to give it to her. Not only because she should have it, but also because I respect her. And I make a vow in that moment, no matter what happens, no matter her response to our kiss, that I'll never be the one to leave her wondering about her worth.

"Was that even better than I ever could've imagined? Do I already wish we were still kissing?" She grins, and in the soft golden glow of the twinkle lights, I see when she feels the way my hands are shaking, still wrapped around the curve of her waist. She covers my hands with her own. "You'd better believe it." Relief overwhelms me as I lean down to gently tap my forehead against hers.

"Was it everything *you've* dreamed?" she asks quietly.

"Ivy," I plead, releasing my hands from her waist to cradle her face. I begin leaving a soft trail of kisses—one on her forehead, one near the height of her cheekbone, and one at the corner of her mouth—before placing a searing kiss on her lips. Like we've done this a thousand times before, but with a change of choreography and location, it all feels new again.

Ivy holds me close and then turns back to face the mirror. Her lips are slightly swollen, the lip gloss she had on now slightly blended along the edges. She reaches back toward me, focused on our reflection, and I extend my hand to reach hers. With that, she reaches for my other hand and then slowly, almost painfully, places them on the sides of her waist. My fingers are on fire as I swallow. I'm water with a current. I'm a radio that found a frequency. I'm a lost ship that's sighted a lighthouse.

"Do you still want to learn my kind of dance?" she says softly, her voice taking on a dreamlike quality, hazy at the edges.

I nod and am riveted as Ivy's smile softens and widens slightly. Her hands cover my own before she drops them, her arms smoothly moving to a position arched above her head.

"Okay, Jace, I'll teach you."

Chapter Twenty-Four

Ivy

The clock strikes nine.

"C'mon, Starlight," Jace rasps out, the embers of his tone like a flint striker catching a spark in the crisp night air. "Let's find you a Christmas tree."

The grin on his face alone is enough to make me follow him through the snow in the forested Christmas tree lot, the warmth of the expression overriding the numbness in my feet and the tingling in my hands. Essentially, Jace's presence could persuade me to disregard frostbite, as would the memory of our kiss. I won't be able to look in the mirror again without recalling the image of his hands wrapped around my waist in the studio.

"You know that it's way past my bedtime, right?" I tease. "I think you're single-handedly changing my circadian rhythm."

Jace chuckles, the sound catching on my ribs. I want to breathe more of it into my lungs. Due to the busyness of the holiday season and the wild chaos of daily rehearsals on top of teaching my regular classes, plus investing my time and energy into the holiday performance, I haven't had a chance to get my own tree. My parents offered to help me, knowing how much I love the tradition, but I wanted to be the one to pick it. But the weeks passed, and now we're less than a week from Christmas, and I still don't have a tree. I would just forget it, but it's what I do every year.

Jace extends a gloved hand behind his back, clearly an open invitation to connect more deeply with him, and I take it. It strikes me just how many times I've been offered a hand like *this*. In every *pas de deux*, in every partnering exercise, a man's hand was extended, and I took it. But the gesture never meant anything more than a move to get to the next part of the choreography. The extended hands represented safety, a promise that the other person wouldn't let me fall. But off the stage, the offer means even more. It's more than a routine. It's an act of trust, an act of surrender, and I hope it's also a chance for us to move on and move forward . . . which is what I need to focus on if I'm going to move through this snow.

The drifts of snow are high and require effort to trudge through, but this is the weather in which I feel most at home. Whenever I've considered leaving Birch Borough—apart from my time in The SoHo Ballet—I can't bring myself to imagine being anywhere that doesn't have snow. Each year, I long for the moment when the iconic birch trees framing our town stand out even more prominently against the winter white and when the tall fir trees are coated in a layer of ice, glistening in the winter sun.

During a Birch Borough winter, everything looks like it sparkles, no holiday required, no special occasion necessary. It's just the world showing us that even after the coldest night, there are stunning possibilities. And I'm so glad I live in a world where there's snow.

"Jace," I speak into the quiet landscape surrounding us, "where are you taking us?" As we've wandered together this evening, talking and laughing, we passed the usual spot where my family has found our tree for the past thirty years. But his steps don't slow, and there's a steadiness in their rhythm that doesn't frighten me in the least.

The scent of pine wraps around us, and it melds so perfectly with Jace's natural scent that I hope it will stay in my lungs for a bit so I can hold on to this feeling a little longer. A subtle glow flickers between the trees, and we see a clearing overhead. Wicked Good Farms hosts seasonal activities throughout the year, and I remember they put on one on the outskirts of their property around Christmastime that I've never been to. But it's renowned in our area for being one of the most romantic events in this region. Of course, there was no one in my life to ever bother to take me to it, even though I've always wanted to go. The sound of a horse neighing confirms what I've dreamed. We're going on a sleigh ride.

In the excitement, I switch places, taking the lead and directing us toward the clearing. Now, it's my hand extended behind me, never losing hold of Jace. When I step fully into the glow of the lights, the sight of two horses strapped to a sleigh with flannel jackets bright against their white coats sends a thrill up and down my limbs. A giggle escapes me, and then a laugh follows before I feel Jace step behind me, wrapping his arms around my waist. He doesn't once let go of my hand.

Instead, he leans down, and I feel his warmth seep through my own jacket. The man is a furnace, even in these temperatures. I lean my head back, feeling the softness of his lips brush against my temple, causing both a shiver and a hum to escape.

"Do you wanna take a sleigh ride?" he says against my skin.

I nod, content to savor the weight of his words near my ear. But then I leap into action. "Let's go, love," I sing, a smile escaping as I head toward the edge of the tree line, the sleigh ahead. Before I can take two steps, I'm pulled back and spun around in the snow. The immovable statue behind me draws me into his chest. "Oof!" I say ungracefully, looking into his face. His eyes have grown as dark as the night sky, and I search them, looking intently for something I don't know if I have the right to say.

"Love."

I didn't mean to use the term of endearment with him, but I won't confess I'm sorry about it. Because I'm not. "What is it?" I tug on his hand, suddenly a bit afraid of his frozen posture.

"You said 'love.'" His voice is soft but clear.

I laugh nervously but then steady my voice. "I did."

He nods, the movement so slight I'd miss it if I weren't so close to his beautiful face. I register his furrowed brows, clenched jaw, and glassy eyes. He's wrestling with something, and the heat of his stare burns into the blush on my face. But I won't relent. Jace needs to know I'm a dancer, not a runner. And when he's ready, I'll willingly convince him that he's my love for the rest of my life, if he'll have me.

I lift my chin and press closer, watching as his eyes track my every move, the truth in my expression my only defense. Taking a deep breath, I wrap my arms around his waist and lean my chin on his chest to stare up at his handsome face.

I'm convinced there's nothing like the feeling of him being near me in the whole world. I keep my voice soft and measured.

"Jace, my gut is telling me that there are a whole lot of lies spinning around your head right now. Untruths that I know make you doubt what we can be. Perhaps hindrances that weren't between us before but now are because of time or something else. Maybe it's the wonder of winter or just the magic of being near each other again, but I'd like to tear down those lies together, if we can."

I watch a twitch of his mouth, a few blinks, and an exhale before the stiffness in his shoulders lifts, and I can almost see him being relieved of a weight I think he's been carrying since we met for the second time. Capturing me with his gaze, he pulls me in again. I lean toward him willingly, waiting until Jace's lips meet my forehead. There's a gentle kiss, and then he places his forehead against my own. The soft nickers of nearby horses mimic the gentle galloping in my heart, and the truth burrows deep into my chest.

I love him.

I've wanted to love Jace for years. And now I have the opportunity to try. This will be my Christmas wish for the rest of my life.

"Ivy," he confesses my name like a prayer, confidently and drenched with affection. He clears his throat. "Starlight, I'm sorry I didn't go to New York for you." It's the first time he's said the words out loud. "Can you ever forgive me?"

I think of Emmy and the fact that Jace was the understudy of his own life when he first returned to Birch Borough, a feeling I know all too well. I think of him with my students and the way he gives everything of himself, every time, even in the unseen moments. I think of myself, combatting both loneliness and the vapor of a future stolen from me for eight long years. So, when I speak, the words pour from my heart.

"You have nothing to apologize for. You didn't have a choice."

"We always have a choice."

"That sentiment may be true, but Jace, I do feel like I need to know. Emmy's mom . . . is she . . .? Will she . . .?" I don't know how to finish the sentence, but I see his jaw clench.

"She released custody of Emmy entirely." At the grit in his voice, my eyes widen, the revelation devastating. "It's just Emmy and me. And I know our situation is different from what you may have originally wanted, but I'm confident we can work through it if you are willing. There was a time when I made choices that I'm not proud of. Yet, I believe they reflect the man I once was and not the man I want to be. The man I am now."

It hurts me to think of what he's gone through, the regrets that he has. "We all make mistakes," I murmur. "But Emmy is a gift. And I know you know that. Sometimes, the things in which we find the most pain also have a way of giving us the most joy. It's grace we don't deserve, but it's real and true." I cling to him a little tighter. "Jace, what's been weighing on you the last few days?"

His gloved hands tug on the pockets of my coat. I've realized he refuses to stop touching me in some way for any period of time tonight, ensuring that his hands are placed gently upon me at all times. It's actually adorable—not that I'd tell him that.

With a fluid movement, he reaches into his coat pocket and pulls out something shiny and small. I lean toward it, my mind unable to process what I'm seeing, but it looks like a snipped piece of ribbon from a pointe shoe. It hits me. Not just any pointe shoe—my pointe shoe. I recognize the method I used to melt the edges to keep them from unraveling. I always crack the center part once melted because I've always joked that I like to live on the edge. It's become a habit, and it also makes the pattern distinctly mine.

"Jace," I marvel.

"I think this belongs to you."

Tears sting my eyes. "How do you still have this? Have you carried this with you this whole time?"

He shakes his head slowly. "No, I didn't always. For about a year after we met, I did. And then I put it in a book on my shelf. Later, after Emmy was born, I tried to move on." He gives a slight shrug. "Once Jenna was gone, though, I'll admit, I've carried it ever since."

"How long?"

"What?" His voice cracks.

"How long has it been with you?"

Jace's eyes close slowly before they open again and look off into the distance. "A long time."

Sharply, I inhale, my fingers wrapping around his, still holding the evidence of the history between us. Life has moved and shaped us, but somehow, it's also molded us back together. I stare at the ribbon, studying it. There's a spot that's nearly see-through, as if his strong fingers have rubbed the fabric like a man trying to make a wish against a magic lamp.

"What happened here?" I murmur.

He mimics exactly what I expected, his thumbs rubbing a pattern into the worn ribbon. "It was a way to remember that I once wished to see you." He clears his throat. "If it happened once, it could've happened again, right?"

"You've nearly rubbed a hole through it."

"I really wanted my wish to come true." His voice is quiet and soft, like the folds of a blanket.

The words spark my emotions, and a tear trails down the side of my face. I feel the coolness of the satin against my cheek as his strong hand wipes the tear away, his voice hesitant.

"Maybe we decide to enjoy this Christmas season and stop trying to talk ourselves out of the good things because we're so scared of what could happen if we do." I know he's speaking to my fears and his own. The unanswered questions we have. The messiness of life that still needs to be worked through.

At a sudden gust of wind, we grip each other, and I notice flakes of snow circling above us. All at once, we're in a snow globe, and the town I've called home most of my life becomes a winter wonderland. There's something, though . . . a gentle hum beneath the surface that's kept me from feeling relaxed.

When I first met Jace, I caught a glimpse of the life I didn't want to miss. But thinking it was long gone, I've destructively sought out other ways to fill the void: failed dating experiments, tolerating toxic almost-relationships, and losing myself in work when no one ever seemed to stick. But it was no use. The void remained. Jace was always meant to be in my arms. And with hope finally spoken between us, I let myself bend. I allow myself to stretch into the feeling of being grounded.

Maybe a home isn't really a physical place. Maybe home has always been how we feel instead of where we are. And maybe home is actually a person.

As if confirming my thoughts, one of the horses attached to the sleigh nickers, and I laugh.

"I think they're waiting for us." Jace offers me an enchanting smile, bringing memories of mugs of peppermint hot chocolate and ice skates.

"Let's not keep them waiting, then!" I hop toward the sleigh with Jace right behind me. He offers a hand to help me step up, and I tilt as his weight shifts the carriage beside me.

"Hello, Moses," I greet the man dressed in Dickens-era fashion. He works at Wicked Good Farm and Orchards, bouncing between the two, depending on the season.

"Evening, Miss Jones. Nice to see you again."

"You as well. How's Lucy?" His daughter works at the Train Car Diner that we've been going to for years.

"Oh, just fine and dandy. Now, where are you two headed?"

I look from Jace to the back of Moses' top hat. "Surprise us."

Moses laughs and sets the horse in motion when I get an idea.

"Say, Moses"—I glance slyly at the man sitting next to me—"do you think the horses are okay with Jace being in this thing with me? He is quite large after all."

Jace's mouth drops open.

"I wouldn't worry, miss. They're used to hauling large loads."

I stifle a laugh.

"Hey, now." Jace lifts a faux stern eyebrow. "I'm not *that* big. If horses could once transport Vikings, they can transport me."

"Just make yourselves comfortable and enjoy the snow. It's romantic, isn't it?" Moses quips.

"It sure is," I whisper, turning to Jace, knowing exactly how I'd like to spend the rest of the ride. "To be safe and for the sake of these gorgeous horses, I think it might be better for them if we combine efforts to distribute our weight. Perhaps we should have you sit in the middle."

"And where would you go?" he says.

I'm pretending to look around the sleigh when Jace catches on. Within seconds, his hands find my waist, and I'm sitting on his lap, his arms wrapped around me. The sound of my laughter rings through the night air as I nuzzle into Jace's neck. When the steady *clop* of the horses' hooves, muted by the snow, becomes the soundtrack of our experience, I turn to Jace and find him grinning at me.

"Hello," he says sweetly.

"Hi, love," I answer, using the term again, and he closes his eyes briefly. I'm choosing to care for him even if he's still learning to believe he's worth it. There's a part of me that needs to know what happened, but I must learn to wait.

Jace reaches into his pocket and pulls out a bunch of greenery. It takes me a second to realize it's mistletoe. He doesn't break eye contact as he holds it over our heads. I look up at it, delighted as it swishes through the air with the movement of the sleigh.

Reaching up for his hand, I grab the sprig and toss it into the snow. Before he has a chance to register my action, I press my lips to his. The pure bliss of the sensation causes a laugh to escape me. I lean back and give him my brightest smile, noting the wonder etched across his face.

"As much as I'm glad for the result, do you want to tell me why the mistletoe I brought is now buried in the snow?" His grin tells me he's not upset in the least, just curious.

"I'm sorry," I laugh, the happiness radiating out of me too much to contain. "But honestly, Jace . . ." I bring my mouth closer to his, our lips barely brushing as I confess, "We don't need it."

His mouth captures mine before I register what's happening, and the joy of it immediately settles into my bones and heart. Even with the mistletoe long abandoned, that's how we spend our sleigh ride in the snow, holding each other and sneaking delightful kisses, the fluffy falling snow catching on our hair, blanket, and coats. The scent of pine trees and crisp winter air surrounds us as Jace holds onto both me and the worn ribbon that really has been my lucky charm.

Chapter Twenty-Five

Jace

The clock strikes ten.

The world is covered in winter white. Ivy paces the stage, causing my nerves to tingle. When you grow up in New England, you expect there to be storms. You anticipate things getting canceled due to snow, though most of us are usually prepared to drive in it. We rarely lose power in this area, and the community has learned to adapt.

But over the course of this afternoon, as I've been painting the last details on the sets and Ivy's been arranging the wings and the makeshift dressing rooms for her students, the inches of snow have fallen higher than predicted. I had my phone on silent for most of the time, only allowing notifications from my brother and sister in case Emmy had an emergency. As of five minutes ago, I received a text from Angie, asking if I am going to make it home tonight. Seeing as her apartment is only a few miles away, the question seemed concerning, so Ivy and I stepped to the windows.

Now, we're staring through the glass at the snowstorm happening outside the high school, the streetlights in the parking lot illuminating the scene and creating an untouched canvas to clearly see the amount of snow blocking us in. My Jeep has several inches stacked around the tires. We could make it out if we leave now, but it's not going to be pretty.

My phone lights up again with a text from Edgar.

Edgar: Wait to drive. The plows haven't come through yet.

I sigh, knowing that we could be waiting an hour or more until the plow comes by with the rate that the white flakes are coming down.

"Jace . . ." Ivy says my name with a hint of fear, the word laden with meaning.

"I know, Starlight." I tilt my chin down, noting the intensity with which her hot-chocolate eyes focus on the blanket of falling flakes. Their speed is impossible to track. If we stepped outside, I think we could disappear in a few steps.

"My kids. The scholarships. We had one more practice, and . . . I'm so tired." Her bottom lip quivers, and I want to wrap her in my arms to hide her from the storm. I'd be her own personal igloo . . . except the warm kind. The analogy doesn't work, but I want to be her shelter right now. I have nothing else to offer her except a distraction. And we'll continue to make sure everything is perfect for her last rehearsal tomorrow.

Reaching for her hand, I give her a gentle tug, and her footsteps are barely audible as she glides across the tile floor. She's a small woman to begin with, but I'm not sure I'll ever get used to being unable to hear her walk due to her ballet training.

I open the large wooden doors to the auditorium and

release her hand to walk through, but Ivy stops and turns toward me. She grabs my hand and pulls me into the room with her, looking around as if she's forgotten something.

"Did you finish everything in here you needed?" I ask her, surprised by her urgency.

Ivy gives a tentative nod.

"I just want to finish some of the ornaments on the Christmas tree for the party scene. And then we'll be good to go."

"Can I help?" she asks.

"For now, I think you should sit and relax. Keep your feet warm. Find us some amazing music, and if it's from a musical, even better."

Ivy's laughter lets me know I'm on the right track as I give her a wink and walk back to the sets. Picking up a paintbrush, I focus on the task at hand, knowing that, despite her laughter, Ivy's heart is heavy. I know my daughter is safe at home, and I know that we'll be safe, especially in this school, but Ivy has given everything for her kids to succeed during this performance season. She's banked on donations coming in and on her studio being given what it needs to thrive for another year. But that's who she is—selfless, giving, and, as is becoming abundantly clear, the woman I want to spend the rest of my life with.

Distracted, I drop the paintbrush and kneel to pick it up. Rather than rising, I stay down, closing my eyes for a moment, suddenly unable to picture anything but Ivy in a white dress, looking at me in the way that only she does. In the vision, I'm declaring that I'll take care of her, honor her, and hold her until my last breath. It's the image I've tried to push down since we met, yet somehow knowing this is what my heart wanted all along.

A chair in the audience seats creaks.

"Jace? Are you okay?" Her worried voice approaches me, the scent of her vanilla perfume and the warmth of her small hand on my back bringing me back to the moment. My mind returns to the present, but my soul knows it's never left my heart's confession.

"I'm okay, Starlight. I'm okay." I stand, and Ivy follows.

"You worried me there, Bear." When my eyes well with tears, her fingertips press into my forearm. "You're crying."

I wipe my eyes with the heel of my hand and sniff. I take a moment to regard her fully, the wisps of hair I've grown so fond of wrapping around her angel face. I appreciate the strength in her frame and the grace in her limbs. And then a chime on the back wall of the auditorium rings throughout the space.

"That's odd," Ivy muses. "I've never heard that chime before."

Neither have I when I've been here setting up for the performance. But I've realized that when it comes to Ivy and me, time and space seem to move both for and with us. It's as if Christmas magic influences each of our interactions.

Holding out my hand, I choose to use this moment— snowed in as we currently are—as a chance for me to get another piece of my life back. "Will you teach me more of how to dance with you? Your style of dance." I nod toward the stage.

Ivy lifts her chin to study me. I dip my head and motion toward the center of the stage. She follows, pausing when we reach the taped marker on the old wooden floor.

"Do you have your music?" My hand grips hers as she

pulls her phone from her pocket.

"I do." A breathy laugh escapes her. Gracefully, she sits on the stage and slides on her pointe shoes, lacing up the ribbons nimbly. I watch her, realizing it's a mesmerizing process. "I can't believe we're really going to dance again right now."

I grin, my nervous system catching up with what's about to happen. This isn't going to be a waltz or a middle school dance where we sway and awkwardly place our hands at odd angles. I'm about to lift her, hold her, and ask her to jump so I can catch her.

"We'll go slow," she says, the music now flowing from her phone as she stretches and begins to warm up her feet.

What Ivy doesn't know is that I've memorized the piece since I've seen and heard her dancing to it over the past couple of weeks. I may even have added it to my own playlist, but I'll pretend to faint before I admit that. Good thing Emmy isn't here to reveal that fact in her excitement.

She pulls her wrap sweater tighter and then extends her right leg and moves to her toes, her left leg brushing past my arm. I place my hands on her waist gently, careful to hold her steady.

"Guide me up and hold on," she instructs.

I do as she says, and she peeks up at me, the length of her midsection almost fully resting against me. She's significantly taller in her pointe shoes, and it gives me a better angle of her hot-chocolate stare. I want to get lost in that gaze for a while, but not when I'm responsible for keeping her steady.

"You can grip me tighter. You won't hurt me."

I swallow and do as she says, my fingers connecting with

her lower ribs. The softness of the leotard and the warmth of her skin underneath feel as if they are creating a current of energy through my hands. My hands are magnets, stuck to her, refusing to let go.

"Now, walk with me," she guides. "Hold out your left hand." She uses my hand as leverage, her body moving through what I now know are arabesques and extensions, her gracefully poised hands swaying through the air.

"Okay, next, you'll gently wrap your hands around my waist. And when I spin, use your left hand to rotate me—I'll spin faster."

"Umm . . ." I don't want to hurt her, but my hands hover near her waist. To my shock, Ivy goes up en pointe and starts to turn. In the sudden blur, I'm able to find her hip and help guide her forward. I've watched her favorite version of *The Nutcracker*, so the technique isn't completely foreign. But with my assistance, she's spinning faster than I've ever seen her, and it's giving me a thrill to catch the flashes of a smile on her face.

"I'm coming out of it," she says between us, and I let her stop. Our transition isn't the most graceful, but we're doing it. It feels akin to when someone starts training with me at the studio. There's a rhythm to it that makes it look effortless. In the past, Ivy has been accustomed to dancing with men who are trained, and I'm used to choreography being the pattern by which I attack a punching bag. When we danced at her studio together, we only practiced a basic spin, my arm extended for her to use to balance. What we're doing tonight is much more intricate.

"You're doing good, Jace." Her words warm my lungs, pushing me to be a little more daring.

"Should we try a lift?" I take a risk and suggest.

Turning to face me, her hands land on her hips, her feet pointing away from me on either side. Glancing down, I think of how much I love the way her feet never seem to want to face forward. With her eyebrows raised, she holds the back of her neck with one hand, regarding me curiously.

"You want to . . . lift me?" A flush creeps up the sides of her neck, and a delighted expression crosses her face as she peeks up at me.

"Unless you're uncomfortable with that," I hasten to adjust my suggestion. "I just thought I could try." Suddenly, I backtrack, wanting to rewind my words. I wasn't trying to get too cocky with her.

"No, it's . . . no. You never make me uncomfortable. I mean, actually, you do . . ." she trails off, and I stiffen. "But only because I care about you so much. It's like the good kind of being on edge, you know?" Her hands paint the air between us.

I grab them, bringing them close to my chest so she can feel the way my heart is pounding just for her. "I do know."

Ivy's grin is worth the honesty. "So, I trust you." Her voice fades as she turns mid-sentence to face the empty auditorium, her delicate yet muscular back now facing me. "I'm going to jump up . . ." She spins back, her face coming into view again. "Actually, wait, do you want to lift me over your head or dip me?"

I can't imagine either of these scenarios happening in the way she is probably thinking, and I'm racking my brain to try to remember an instance in the YouTube videos I've watched in which I've seen a man lift his female partner in ballet. "Um . . ."

"You know what?" She scrunches her nose in concentration, and I'm struck by how much the expression resembles one I've seen Emmy make. "Let's try the dip. So, I'm going to jump up, your right arm will wrap around my waist, and your left hand will reach underneath my thigh, and then you'll dip me forward. Got it?"

"Um . . ." Once again, words fail me as I imagine all the ways this could go terribly wrong. "I can try."

Ivy nods. "On the count of three: one, two, three!"

She jumps up, and I move my right arm to wrap around her waist, but I forget to catch her left leg when it extends. Instead, I grab near her knee. Thankfully, I don't drop her, but our choreography is less than graceful. The effect sends us off balance. Ivy's body lands at an odd angle, like a beautiful fairy trapped midair. I see her wince when her right foot hits the floor, and she lets out a hiss.

Instantly, my adrenaline spikes. I spin her midair until she's fully facing me. She's wrapped in my arms with my left arm under her knees, and my right arm is around her back and waist, holding her close to my chest. With a dazed expression, she looks around as if she's trying to figure out how she got in this position.

"How did you . . . ?" Her eyes are wide, her mouth slightly open as her gaze meets mine.

"Did I hurt you?" The tension in my voice causes her to lean in quickly, a hand moving to rest on the side of my face.

"What? No? It was just an awkward transition, and I shouldn't have put my foot down . . ."

My chest heaves, the adrenaline starting to move out of my system now that I know she's okay. But the grimace on my face betrays me.

"Hey, Jace, it's okay," she reassures me. "You've never done this before. But you're doing amazing. You *are* amazing. I can't even believe you'd want to do this with me." The genuine awe in her smoky voice sticks to the edges of my brain.

"But I could've hurt you."

"However, you didn't."

The adrenaline feels as if it's ramping up. "What if, because of my lack of experience, you couldn't dance anymore? I don't know how I'd keep moving through life if I hurt you again, Ivy."

When I grit out her name instead of using her usual nickname, her eyes narrow, searching me deeply.

"Put me down, please." A fierceness enters her words, a rare glimpse of her determination rising to the surface of her skin.

I set her down as softly as possible and straighten to my full height. It's quickly becoming clear that this was a terrible idea. She's angry, and I feel the weight of her frustration crushing me. Closing my eyes, I turn toward the backdrop, deciding how I'm going to pack up the paint as quickly as possible and silently praying the roads are now plowed so we can put this night behind us.

"Where are you going?" Her voice stops me in my tracks.

Slowly, I close my eyes and count to three before opening them again. "Just headed to pack up."

"You don't want to dance with me anymore?"

The doubt in her voice makes me turn so quickly that I nearly get whiplash. "What?"

Her chin lifts slightly. "You don't have to dance with me

if you don't want to."

"That's what you think this is? That I don't want to dance with you?" I motion between us, the tension in my frame building. The pressure of it stacks against the vertebrae of my spine, threatening to collapse from the weight of the lies that have been crushing me.

"Well, you were just walking away."

"I'm not walking away; I'm protecting you."

"How are you protecting me?" She throws her hands out to the side. "To do that, I think you need to stay near me, no?"

I clench my jaw, my brain inconveniently reminding me of the tension in her shoulders when she thought I almost dropped her. While I would never intentionally do so, it's clear she's not convinced of that yet. "Ivy," I begin.

"Jace," she retorts. "What's going on? If you don't want to dance with me, it's fine."

"I already said that's not it." My teeth are nearly grinding together from my anger over her ever believing that I wouldn't want to hold her.

"Why are we fighting right now?" Her arms are now crossed, her head shaking.

"Because."

"Because . . . Why?" Her eyes are on fire, their intensity staggering.

In three steps, I'm back in front of her, but she doesn't flinch, even though my frame towers over her. "Because you don't know how beautiful you are." My voice becomes low and lethal against the fears that I realize are lacing themselves within her mind. "Not want to dance with you? I never want to dance with anyone else for as long as I live."

Her eyes widen. Her hands drop to her sides, and she looks like the air just left her lungs. But I know I have to get my truth out.

"You're so mesmerizing that you're impossible to forget. You make me believe that maybe there is some sort of magic in the world, if only because I've seen your face. Ivy, you look at me, and I want to freeze time. But I can't because it just slips through my hands."

Tears now stream down her face, dripping along the curves of her leotard at the delicate line of her collarbone. But she doesn't speak. And because I'm nothing if not intense, I keep going. This woman is going to hear me loud and clear, if only to shine the brightest of lights on why she should believe she's the most stunning woman in the world.

"When we met," I continue, "in those life-changing hours, you made me believe that there could be a love just for me. And when I couldn't get to you . . ." My breathing is heavy, and my ribs feel like they could crack from the pressure of all I'm holding back, but I don't relent. "A piece of me died, Ivy . . . a piece of me that wanted to believe. So, I tried everything and anything to get over you, never thinking I'd see you again. And I hate that I made the choices that simply took me farther from you. I own my mistakes."

Ivy wipes the tears from her face with the back of her hand and inhales twice. Just that alone is enough to make me want to reach for her, but I convince my body to wait.

"And then I saw you again. We're back in the same place. My daughter is learning to dance from you. We've reconnected. We're kissing. I'm able to touch you. And suddenly, I'm seeing possibilities again. It's like you reminded me why I believed in dreams in the first place."

"Then why do you keep drawing close and then pushing me away?" Ivy's words are knives, slicing away the protective layers I've forged around my heart.

"Because I don't know if I'm really what you need. But I also don't want to let you go."

"Impossible," Ivy whispers, and the hint of possibility in her tone makes me both frustrated and unnerved.

"No, Ivy, you don't know," I say, hearing the pain caught in my throat.

"What don't I know?" she demands.

Dread settles in my stomach, the realization hitting me that it's finally time to give her what I haven't been able to give her before now. "Jenna—" Just the name makes Ivy's jaw clench, and it's enough vindication for me to keep going. "She told me . . ."

This is the part that is the hardest to reveal because even recalling the words makes me feel emasculated. I know my ex's cruelty shouldn't affect me, but it does. The words have lingered for years.

I clench my fists. "She didn't want me to touch her anymore. Near the end of our relationship, she said she hated how it felt when I held her," my voice cracks. "After she had Emmy, she told me that she regretted ever being with me. It disgusted her to have me touch her. She also added that anyone who told me differently would be lying."

Ivy gasps. I extend my palms to make a point, looking at my callused fingers, willing them to become more than I've regarded them as for the past few years.

"I believed her. Because of that, if you ever . . . if you didn't want me to . . ." And that's all I can get out. I'm emotionally exhausted, the weight of what I've shared enough to sap my strength.

"Hear me loud and clear," Ivy says, her voice startling me. Without warning, she jumps into my arms.

Immediately, I wrap my arms around her and hold her as her legs wrap around my waist. Her warm, elegant hands curve around the bottom of my jaw, her thumbs extending toward my cheekbones.

"Here's the truth of it, Jace." Her breath hitches. "Whatever happens between us, I never want another man to touch me again. I never want to dance with another man. Do you hear me? It's only you. It *has* to be you."

A tear leaks from my eye, but I don't wipe it away. I'd rather it fall than to put her down. I won't let her go. I'll always hold her if she wants me to. Even so, I can hardly believe her words.

"Ivy . . ." A second tear leaks out.

She wipes it before motioning for me to put her on the stage. Holding my gaze as she stands, she reaches for my hands, turning them until my palms are facing up, her fingers tracing each one as if she's memorizing both my fingers and my calluses. Her eyes close as she explores, and the flush in her cheeks is enough to undo me. And then I am undone when she pulls my hands around her waist once more.

"Hold me, Jace," she says softly.

Tentatively, I pull her close to me, and it strikes me anew that just one of my hands is large enough to cover most of her back and shoulders. She reaches up, pushing her fingers into the hair behind my neck and pulling me down toward her. When our mouths are merely inches apart, she traces each of my features with her eyes before they trail up to mine. In their depths, I see a warmth I've never seen from her before and a fire of determination that I already knew burned within. It's now aimed fully at me.

"Your hands only. Do you hear me?"

For a moment, I let her words sink in, willing them to be true. Her statement burrows into my heart, and I wonder: Maybe what's most important to our lives isn't the people who leave us or scar us but the ones who heal us. Maybe we should focus on the ones who find as much magic in being near us as we do in being near them. For the truth is that it wasn't that I couldn't hold someone well. For so long, I was just holding the wrong things, the wrong people.

All along, Ivy is the woman meant to be in my arms. And if she wants me to stay near her, then nothing else matters. Without another word, I eliminate those final inches between us and kiss her like she's the one I've been waiting for my whole life. I kiss her like there's a piece of heaven that can be found on earth within her love. I kiss her as if, in doing so, I'm conveying how much I missed her and how much I never wanted to give up. I kiss her like I believe her.

And with my hands wrapped around her delicate form and my heart securely in her grasp, she kisses me back the same way.

Chapter Twenty-Six

Ivy

"Good morning, my darling friend! Merry Christmas Eve!" Grey says as she enters my apartment, her hands full of gifts and snow stuck to her cat-eye glasses.

Resin rushes over to his second favorite woman. (I'm his favorite, of course.)

"Hello, sweetheart," she says to him after putting down the gifts over the back of the couch and pulling a treat from her coat pocket. The treats are one of the many reasons she's secured a top spot in my dog's affection, though Jace is intent on earning the same distinction.

Crunching on his treat, Resin goes to the living room, waiting for us to join him. I hand Grey a mug of coffee as we settle in. I'm still in my Christmas pajamas, and Grey looks like a vintage dream, per usual. We often shop at the same vintage and thrift stores, but she's the queen of exceptional finds. She could easily fit in another era, looking like the unassumingly gorgeous person that she is.

"Merry Christmas Eve." I hold out my mug in a "cheers" gesture and take a sip of the comforting, creamy coffee.

"Oh! Sparrow sent this over!" Grey rises to grab one of the boxes on top of the pile. "I hope I haven't ruined it. I got so distracted by Resin's cuteness when I came in."

Gingerly, she places the box on the coffee table between us and unties the ribbon wrapped around it. I can see now that it's a pastry box, and the smell of chocolate and sugar brings an instant smile to my face. Sure enough, when Grey opens the box, I see the most gorgeous Bûche de Noël, a traditional chocolate cake rolled with whipped cream throughout and topped with chocolate ganache. It looks like a winter masterpiece, the chocolate shavings perfect—no doubt Lily's handiwork—and the detail work makes it look like an actual piece of wintery tree bark. The smell is absolutely heavenly.

"I'll grab some plates!" Grey squeals before taking off for my kitchen.

I laugh, but honestly, this is the best Christmas Eve breakfast I could've asked for.

"So, where's Jace?" With a knife and spoons in one hand and napkins and plates in the other, Grey sets to work hacking into the French Christmas dessert.

"He's with his family this morning. We'll be meeting at the Christmas Eve service tonight at church." The gathering is a tradition. As a community, we meet at the old stone church, the very one in which Sparrow and Rafe were married. We light candles and sing Christmas carols. It's one of my favorite events of the holiday season.

Last night, when we got home from the high school, it was after midnight, but the roads had finally been plowed, and my heart was full. I suspect Emmy didn't let her dad sleep in this morning, so we'll both need to enhance our energy in the form of sugar and caffeine. I wonder if I can save him and Emmy a slice of the cake.

"Excellent. And you're feeling good about how things are going between you two?" Grey hands me a spoon and sets two alarmingly large slices of cake in front of us both. She settles into the couch, taking one of the biggest bites I've ever seen before she even leans back. We make eye contact and laugh, her mouth full as her eyes roll back with delight. "This is criminally good!"

I take a bite and echo her sentiment. The cake is incredible. Grabbing my phone, I text Sparrow and Lily a note of thanks and then excitedly return to eating their work of art.

"I'm feeling good. We're feeling good." Thoughts of Jace's hands wrapped around me and the way he kissed me after I told him I wanted only him send a flush creeping up my neck. Already, I can't wait to hold him again.

"Did you ask if he's staying past New Year's?" Grey lifts an eyebrow as she takes another bite.

"We haven't talked about it. But I have hope." I glance at her slyly. "Speaking of people being here for the holidays, will Boston be here for Christmas?"

Grey shuffles a bite of cake around on her fork before it settles on the plate with a clunk. "Not for the actual day, but he'll be in town for the gift exchange."

The day after Christmas, the four of us girls—Sparrow, Grey, Lily, and me—gather to exchange gifts and celebrate. It's our way of extending the family time over the holidays, even if we're technically chosen family. While the four of us may not always get together during the year as much as when we were teenagers, especially now that a couple of husbands have been added to the mix, we haven't stopped this Christmas tradition. Now, we just include the men.

"I'm glad you'll get to see him." I'm careful not to push too much when it comes to the man I know she loves but can't admit to loving for some reason. "I'll be bringing Jace this year," I reveal shyly.

"Oh, that's excellent! I can't wait for him to meet Boston." Her smile is genuine, even though I see the tightness in her forehead whenever her friend is brought up.

My phone startles us by ringing with a number I don't recognize. "Hello?" I say hesitantly when I answer it.

"Miss Jones?" an older man's voice resonates through the line.

"That's me." I shrug to Grey, who's paused mid-bite to listen to this mystery call.

"It's Arthur from the Music & Arts Committee," says the voice.

Immediately, I stiffen, setting my half-finished piece of cake on the table. His tone gives nothing away. It would be weird and decidedly Scrooge-esque to call with bad news on Christmas Eve, but okay. "Hello, Arthur. Merry Christmas Eve."

"Yes, same to you." There's a shuffling of papers on his end and what sounds like a briefcase clicking closed. I didn't even know people still used briefcases anymore.

"Thank you." Rising, I start to pace. Resin lifts his head to check on me.

"I won't keep you," says Arthur, "but I wanted you to know that we received an anonymous donation this morning, specifically addressed to your studio."

"What?" I whisper, choosing to sit on the edge of the

coffee table before I fall over. Resin is already up and at my side, his face resting near my knee.

"Quite a generous one. I think it should meet your goals for the next year and possibly even exceed them."

When he gives me the number, my hand flies to my mouth in disbelief. My students will receive another year of dance. I can purchase more portable barres so we can add more students to my classes. There's also enough for me to take on at least five more scholarship students. I laugh disbelievingly.

"This is so appreciated. Thank you, sir."

"No need to thank me. I'm just the messenger. But I wanted you to know so you could just enjoy the performance. Anything that comes in that night will just be more lights on the tree—or whatever analogy you want to use for this season."

"I can hardly believe it." My breath catches as I think of how hard I've fought over the past few years to keep my dream alive and to make dance more accessible in this town. If I hadn't received this donation, I would have had to take on another job to keep moving forward with my studio.

"Now, now," Arthur protests. "From everything I've heard about you in this town, I think you've earned it."

Something in his tone makes me realize he's been my guardian angel all along. I'm strengthened by his encouragement. "Arthur, I recognize that this goes against the meaning of the word, but would you happen to be the anonymous donor?"

The movement on his line stops, and I know that I've stumbled across the truth. Grey mouths "donor" with wide eyes as I wait for Arthur's response.

"I can't confirm anything," he finally speaks. "As I said, Miss Jones, it's anonymous. But my wife and I are looking forward to your show. She has a soft spot for dancers, having been one herself once."

"Thank you. Thank you so much. This means the world to me and to my students and their families." I wipe my eyes. The relief of not having to worry about funding as we go into our performance is one of the best gifts I could've received.

"Great. From what I've observed, your methods may be unorthodox, Miss Jones, but I know leaders when I see them. And my granddaughter loves your class."

My mind races. "Wait, is Nova your granddaughter?" I think of my second-level student who started with me just this year and lives to dance. I'd never put together the pieces that she could be related to Arthur.

"The very one," he says with a softened voice. "And we love to see her and her friends happy. Again, Merry Christmas, Miss Jones. Enjoy your holiday."

"I will, sir. Thank you so much."

He hangs up, and I rise to do a series of turns across my living room floor. Resin barks happily, and I jump about.

Grey follows, joining in the fun even though she still doesn't have all the details. "You got your Christmas miracle?" Grey opens her arms, and I step into them, hugging her tight.

My thoughts go to my students. My studio. The upcoming performance. My family. My best friend, whom I'm holding close. This town and its belief in me. Emmy. Jace.

"I think I got more than one miracle this year," I confess,

already anxious to tell the man I love the good news.

"Well, I'm off. We'll open gifts later. I just wanted to drop them off and share this delicious cake with you. I'm so glad I got to be here for the good news."

"Thanks so much, Grey. For everything."

"Of course," Grey says, reaching for her purse that she left on the floor near the door.

"No, Grey, I mean it." I hold her by the shoulders and make her really look at me. It's understood that we're more family than friends, but she needs to understand how much she means to me. We never know how much time we have remaining with someone. I've learned that lesson because of Jace. "You need to know that you make my life better. There have been so many times I wanted to quit or just give up, and you've always found a way to make me feel important. You make me feel brave by the way that you've always supported me and acted like my dreams are never out of reach. Your words have always meant something special to me. I know you have your own heartache, but I hope my friendship has made your life easier just as you've done with mine."

Grey wraps me up in a hug so tight I'm nearly unable to breathe. "Thank you, Ivy—for being my friend and showing me what true friendship really means. You know I'll never forget it. Never could."

We release each other just as her phone goes off. "That would be my dad. I need to get back to the shop. We're opening for a few hours for last-minute gifts, and I need to deliver my books! But I love you! I'll see you tonight!"

She leaves, and it's just Resin and me. Reaching for my phone, I text Jace that I have good news and get a series of emojis back that make me laugh. Collapsing onto the couch, I breathe out a heartfelt thanks when I feel Resin's cold nose on my hand.

"Hi, my love bucket." His trusting eyes stare into my soul, searching me out. I pat the couch and stretch myself out so he can lie on it facing me. He settles in, a position we've snuggled in so many times before when I've been heartbroken or moving through disappointment. "I love you, Resin."

He shifts closer as if in response, and I could cry at his innocence. This dog has loved me when I needed him to with no questions asked. He's been there with me through so many tears over the past years. I wish I could keep him close to my side forever, but even if I can't, he'll always be a part of my story, and I'll have been most of his.

"Thank you, love bucket." I alternate between petting his face and wiping my tears. His loving eyes regard me wisely, as if he knows he's been everything I've needed. "You've been there for me through every moment. And I can't thank you enough." I hold on to his front paw as he settles deeper into the cushion.

"Now, I know you already love Jace." His ears perk up at the mention of the name. "And Emmy." Another flick of his ear. "Yes, well, I just need you to know that even though there may be another man in my life, you've been the steadiest one I've ever had. Just like I told Grey, I'll never forget it."

He makes a little sound of comfort, the one he uses when he's happy, a mix between a moan and a contented sigh. And while our lives may be changing, and we're adding more love to our duo, there's nothing like a pet who becomes part of your heart and your life. So, for Christmas Eve morning, we fall asleep together on the couch for old time's sake.

"Truly He taught us to love one another; His law is love and His gospel is peace."

The words of the famous carol echo off the walls of the stone church on Christmas Eve, the wooden pew I'm standing within packed with my family, Jace, and Emmy. His family couldn't fit, so they're in the row in front of us, including his parents, whom I've met for the first time tonight. For the second time this season, I think of *While You Were Sleeping* and the scene in the church, except we're not talking about neighbors or furniture. Although, funnily enough, Jace is in the furniture business.

He stands beside me, his singing voice strong and deep, my heart full as I listen to him honor the sacred reason for which we've all gathered here tonight. His face is lit by the candles we're holding, the glow highlighting his features as he closes his eyes. What a transformation from the Beast of a man he was when I saw him again a few weeks ago. We may have aged since we first met, but I see more and more glimpses of the man he was. Now, he's even better. Because the spark we shared has not only rekindled, but it's also turned into a flame, and I can only be grateful.

We'll be heading to the theater soon for another tradition of watching a movie on Christmas Eve night. For now, as I peek at Jace with Emmy at his side, I choose to focus on the hymns and give a prayer of thanks that, sometimes, the things we fear are gone forever have a way of coming back to us. And sometimes, they are far better than we could've hoped.

When we're filing through the church door back into the chilly night, my brother stops us. "Listen, Jace," he says in his stoic way. I'm not sure if that's a good sign or not.

"Should I leave for this?" My arm wraps through Jace's arm, hoping my brother isn't going to say something he'll regret.

"I'd like you to stay, Ivy." Freddie shuffles on his feet, the only hint that nervousness or emotions are warring within him. He gets right to the point. "I'm sorry for how I treated you all those years ago. I'm sorry I didn't give you the chance to tell me what happened to your family. And I'm sorry about your sister. I can't imagine . . ." He looks at me and clears his throat. "You didn't need my anger. And I feel like I stood in the way of you two when it wasn't my business."

Jace nods, his shoulders softening slightly. We're on the steps of the church now, with Freddie a few steps below us. He's still taller than me, but Jace towers over him.

Slowly, Jace extends a hand, and my brother exhales, taking it and clasping it in both of his own. "We both care for Ivy," Jace says. "Like I told you when we spoke, I respect that you were trying to protect her. Don't hold on to what you can't change."

Freddie nods, his eyes glassy, and releases Jace's hand. "You'll be at the theater?" He looks between the two of us, and I nod gratefully. "See you then."

It's only when my brother is halfway into the parking lot that I look at Jace in disbelief. "Wow, all kinds of Christmas miracles are unfolding for us. I mean, think about it. Freddie apologizing. Gladys' decision to remove you from the calendar next year. Your family and mine are getting along, not that I doubted it. The anonymous donor whom I know in my bones was Arthur." Snowflakes start to fall from the sky, and I give an incredulous laugh. "And now, snow!"

"Don't forget the best part of all." He draws me close, his words meant only for us, the timbre of his voice bringing warmth to my bones.

"And what would that be?" Even though I know the answer, I want to hear him say it.

Jace bends down to kiss my cheek before moving his lips to the shell of my ear. I can already feel the tingles down my spine as he takes a breath and, on an exhale, simply says, "The hope of us."

Chapter Twenty-Seven

Ivy

We're going to be late, love," Jace says to Emmy, pulling bobby pins from his pocket, a pink practice tutu hanging from his left wrist. Leisurely, he places it on the bench behind him and rummages through his jacket pocket. And then, without a word, his large hands are somehow gently arranging and gathering Emmy's hair into a tiny ponytail, the wisps surrounding her face smoothing under the movement of his palm. It's methodical and precise, just like him, and yet, it works. He grins sheepishly at me when he uses one hand and his teeth to pry open the bobby pin before it disappears into the bun forming from Emmy's hair.

My mother was the one who always helped to pin my hairstyles for dance, and I'd stare at her hands moving in the mirror's reflection while we played music on an old-fashioned boom box. She'd hum along while I sang, and we'd fall into an easy rhythm. When I got too tall for her to reach the top of my head, I sat backward on the toilet with the seat down. It wasn't that I couldn't do my own hair—it's that she wanted to spend the time with me. And now I realize how much that small gesture meant to me. To this day, I can still feel her hands in my long hair, her mother's love pouring through every movement. The fact that Emmy will think of dance classes and remember Jace's hands in her hair as an act of love makes me ache.

"I know, but I needed to get my things so I can practice with Eddie." Emmy's voice is already tired, slower than usual as she lets out a giant yawn.

I hold one back myself. It's been a long day; we've just arrived at Angie's apartment after the Christmas Eve church service, and as much as I'm ready to see Jimmy Stewart in all his glory on the big screen, I'm more ready to lean my head on Jace's shoulder while we watch one of the most iconic Christmas movies of all time.

"Okay, let's go, Emmy Bear," Jace says while bending to scoop her up.

"No. Miss Ivy," she counters softly, looking to me instead of hopping into his arms.

"What?" I ask. Jace rises to his full height.

Emmy continues to look at me, a hint of hesitation in her expression. "You, Miss Ivy. Will you carry me? I'm too tired." It makes sense that she's used to being carried since her father can hold her without breaking a sweat, but I'm not built like him. I don't see how I could be as comforting as Jace. Looking into her sweet eyes that are so much like her dad's, there's nothing I would deny her if she asked.

"Of course I will."

Emmy's tiny arms lift like she's going to do a dance move, and she holds the pose, waiting for me to bend and lift her into my arms. When I do, she nuzzles into my neck like I've seen her do with Jace a few times before. My heart sighs. I've always wanted a family, and it's felt so out of reach. Now, between the two of them, a hazy dream is unfurling.

Jace grabs Emmy's backpack containing her stuff for the night, but I don't miss him rubbing his own eyes with the heel of his hand. He's such a handsome softie. Angie's been keeping such long hours at the bakery that Jace's parents are going to watch her tonight at Edgar's house while we're at the movie. Edgar will bring Emmy back in the morning, so they'll all be together on Christmas morning. I appreciate all the steps he's taking to be a part of our town's Christmas tradition.

Despite her excitement to show her grandparents her part in the choreography for the upcoming performance, Emmy falls asleep on the way over. Jace tucks her into bed when we arrive. He leaves me with her for a moment to make sure he has the tickets, and I stare at her little face, her features so like her father's. There's a hint of someone else, of course—someone she will always share a history with— but I'm finding that the affection building within me for the little girl is terrifying. Yet, it also silences the fears I've felt over Emmy wanting me to be close to her. Maybe someday, I'll even be a mother figure to her.

"Sleep well, Emmy Bear," I whisper, wiping a rogue curl from her forehead, yet another reminder of Jace that makes me smile.

The clock strikes eleven.

The lights are dim in Nostalgia, Birch Borough's old

theater. The space holds so much history, including the fact that our friend Rafe has played here a few times over the past couple of years, his first gig booked right after he met Sparrow. While it's mainly a performance venue these days, when a movie showing is scheduled, the staff pulls out portable theater seats with cupholders. They transform the hall into a makeshift cinema that holds some of my favorite holiday memories, and they all seem to hover around the common theme of the movie *It's a Wonderful Life*.

Jimmy Stewart will forever be my incomparable hero in all his black-and-white film glory. There's such an innocence in the time period, not to mention the magic of the music and the feeling of wanting to both change your life and hold on to what's familiar. When Jace agreed to go to the showing with me, somehow, my parents bartered a deal out of the owner for two tickets seated together. The event is usually packed on Christmas Eve, so my family is seated a few rows ahead of us, and Jace and I will be cozied up near the top section of the seats. It's the perfect spot for sneaking kisses or for a general sense of privacy from the town's inquisitive eyes. Of course, I'm not thinking of the next moment when I can capture his mouth with mine (I totally am).

I'm slowly shuffling my way up the steps to the top section, allowing attendees to find their seats while Jace is at the concession stand getting us snacks. An animated popcorn bucket is dancing on the screen, but with Jace so near, I can't bring myself to enjoy it as I usually would. There are more exciting things to think about. Just as I lower myself into my seat, I hear shuffling and a hint of a grunt. Gladys is at the end of our row. Jace, who has just stepped up to it, is uncomfortably pushed in front of her. On her face is a wicked grin as she resumes whatever mission she's given herself tonight.

"That right there is your seat," she says authoritatively, pointing to the seat next to mine, her countenance all seriousness, if it wasn't for the giveaway of the sparkle in her eyes.

"I know it's my seat, Gladys." Jace looks exasperated, and I hide my laugh behind my hand. "I already have a ticket and planned to sit there . . . with her." He nods toward the seat since his hands are occupied with popcorn and a box of M&Ms.

"I thought there wasn't assigned seating tonight?" I ask, looking around and under the tops of the chairs, searching for any sign of a number or row.

"It was on your ticket," Gladys says sternly. "So, I hope that you are intending to honor your assigned seating and keep this young lady company tonight, young man."

With a furrowed brow, I pull out my ticket stub because, of course, we still use paper tickets in Birch Borough. I find there's nothing written on it.

Jace, God bless him, looks as though he couldn't be more uncomfortable. Although so much has happened between us and the air is laced with uncertainty as to how we should act in public, I can't decipher if he's more unsettled by the idea of all the attention suddenly turned on him or the fact that Gladys has gripped his sherpa-lined jacket in a death grip. It's as if she's almost daring him to retreat or argue with her.

"Please, let's just . . ." I motion to the seat next to the one I've chosen, pulling together just enough courage to look into his dark-amber eyes. I've felt their intense depths focused on me throughout this entire exchange.

Gladys wipes her hands on her coat as Jace sinks into the seat beside me. In an act of audacity that only our resident fairy godmother could pull off, she winks and hurries away.

Jace shifts, trying to fit his very large frame into the small, vintage-inspired movie theater seats. I lean away to avoid his knee that's taking up most of our collective space, hoping to give him more room. Once I'm settled, I turn back to find him staring ahead at the screen, the glow casting shadows on his face. They make his already devastating features look as though they're cut from granite. It's captivating. It's heartbreaking.

"Are you ready for this?" I say quietly as the lights dim. My words could have another meaning, and I'm not sure if he'll pick up on my subtlety or not.

"Always," he says with a grin.

My heart flutters at his reply. Most men I've met found it odd that I like classic movies and that some of my favorite stories are displayed in black and white or in other certain hues that give away the fact that the movie was filmed decades before I was born.

As I anticipate sharing this experience with Jace, I watch him reach into his pocket and pull out an eyeglass case. I've barely registered what's happening before he opens it, and a pair of glasses settles on his face. My attraction to him intensifies. "Uh—uh," I manage to stutter out.

Jace looks toward me, an incredulous look crossing his face. "Oh, this is what's doing it for you, huh?" he rumbles cheekily. "Just wait until I eat a candy cane while wearing them." My insides are on fire as he bites his bottom lip, looking away from me toward the blank screen, knowing fully what he just did.

"You have good taste," I finally say with a grin, and his body melts deeper into the seat next to me.

"I do, especially when it comes to the people with whom I share M&Ms." He smiles.

I settle in as well, allowing our legs to touch and melt together like they were meant to. Jace lifts the end of the yellow candy box, and a memory resurfaces. "Your sister. Those were her favorites."

A soft quiet settles between us, but I remember his sweet nickname for Mina. It stuck out, but I hadn't recalled it until now.

"They were," he replies. "Now, I always eat them during the holidays. It helps me remember her. Odd, I know."

"Not odd at all."

Jace pops a few more of the hard-shelled candies into his mouth. Then he extends his hand toward me, palm face up. Glorious sparks flood my skin as I slide my own palm across his and interlace our fingers.

The lights in the space go completely dark, and I'm riveted by the screen as it begins to play the classical Christmas tale. It's a heady feeling to watch one of your favorite movies with someone you care about. We've shared so much this holiday season, and now this—being here, watching this film together—feels more intimate than most things.

It's when Jimmy is busy talking to Donna (aka Mary) and telling her that he'd lasso the moon for her that Jace shifts again. He hasn't touched his popcorn yet, intent on catching every word on the screen. But now he turns to me, and Jace and I make eye contact, finding each other in the darkness.

"Ivy," he whispers into the staticky space, his breath moving the tiny particles of dust dancing from the light of the machine, finding my ear over the humming of the projector just above us. He reaches inside his jacket and pulls out a piece of paper, handing it to me and nodding encouragement for me to open it.

When I do, I find the words, lit by the white glow of the screen: *I'd lasso the moon for you—J.*

He planned this. His nervous energy and the way he hasn't been snacking make sense. And in the iconic words that bear repeating, I lean close to whisper in his ear. "I'll take it."

The flash of his grin causes moonbeams to shoot through my skin, and I finally understand this scene of *It's a Wonderful Life*, especially when Jace's muscular arm lifts to wrap around my shoulders and pull me closer to him. There's an old wooden divider between us, part of the charm of this place, but it gives me leverage, my elbow resting on it as I lean my head closer to his chest.

Near the end, when Clarence gets his wings and the entire theater is wiping away tears, I catch Jace digging the heel of his hand into one of his eyes. He's such a glorious gentleman. Green flags are waving all over by the fact that this movie still gets to him, even though he mentioned that he watches it every year.

Just as slowly as they arrived, people shuffle out of the theater, filling the aisles. We wait, blessed to have people in our row go their separate ways quickly, giving us more time together in the quiet space. It's nearly midnight now, almost officially Christmas Day.

"Merry Christmas, Jace."

"Merry Christmas, Starlight." He leans his forehead down to meet mine.

I smile. "I'm so glad you were here for this," I confess. "Do you think . . . if you could do it over, you would?"

He leans back to look at me then focuses again on the still-humming screen. It's not playing anything, but it hasn't been turned off either. People are still filtering out, and I wave to my parents and Gram as they point to the lobby. I nod. Considering I'm walking home with them tonight—since I always stay over with them on Christmas Eve—they're my figurative ride home. Jace turns his attention back to me.

"I wish we could have had all of it, the chance back then to create a future together. But I could never imagine a life without Emmy. So, I think I'm grateful for everything that's happened this time around." I nod as he continues. "Ivy, we've confessed a lot to each other over the past few weeks. You've somehow been mending my heart like it's your superpower." He pauses and ruffles a hand through his hair before letting it drop back on his thigh. "I just want you to know that even if it didn't seem like it, you've always held a part of me. But now, I want you to hold all of me. Are you . . . are you ready for that?"

I'm almost expecting it this time. A chime carries into the theater from the lobby, and I smile again, his words warming me from the inside. Reaching up, I turn his face toward me, wanting him to hear and see my response fully. "Bear, I'm more than ready. And I want you to have all of me too."

He sniffs, tears brimming on the edges of his whiskey-colored eyes, their radiance dim in the sconces surrounding us. "And Emmy?" he asks.

"Will never have to worry if she's loved."

He nods once, his arms completely enveloping me, his dark curls caressing my skin, his face buried in the curve of my neck. I feel his tears and the relief in his very bones. The urge to feel his hair between my hands comes over me. I need him to understand the sensory experience of being fully held, the thought consuming me. Shifting and sliding my hands along his limbs, I embrace him. A sigh escapes Jace as he cries quietly, a deep inhale echoing through his lungs as his emotions release, my fingers meeting his scalp.

He leans down and places a tentative kiss on my lips. His large hand presses into the space between my shoulder blades. I feel his smile before his kiss moves from the familiar patterns I've grown accustomed to, the feeling and taste of his lips something long ago imprinted upon my soul. His touch shifts to the fiery, a level of gentle care shifting the energy from what's been to what could be. His hand feels like a hot stone pressed against my skin, warming my neck and tethering me to him, his five o'clock shadow now brushing tiny sparks around my mouth. Our breath mingles until I can hardly take a full breath. We pull apart just enough to look into each other's eyes.

"Starlight, once you asked me what I wanted to be known for," Jace murmurs. The theater has gone quiet, most of the moviegoers having departed, some lingering in the lobby before they wander home. A few workers have started to clean up, and while the moment could be anything but romantic, the fact that he isn't rushing through it only makes him even more attractive to me.

"And?" I encourage softly.

Jace's voice is steady. "I want to be known for loving you. I think I always have."

The clock strikes twelve.

"Santa!" Emmy's happy yell stirs me from sleep, and I open my eyes on the couch to find my daughter flinging herself on the ground next to the still-lit Christmas tree in the corner.

Last night, I returned so late that I spent almost all night wrapping gifts. Then I fell asleep with tape stuck to my face and wrapping paper on my pants in my sister's living room. Thankfully, Emmy doesn't even notice as I stuff the incriminating evidence under the couch and sit up. Angie appears in front of me and laughs, her hand waving near my forehead. I reach up and feel another sting of adhesive as I pull it from my skin.

Emmy is busy assessing the gifts under the tree. The half-drunk glass of milk and cookie crumbs from Santa's cookies that we left out before bed last night are still evident around my mouth. I swipe a hand across my face and sigh with gratitude that I remembered to break off the carrots too, so Emmy would know that Rudolph also enjoyed visiting her on Christmas Eve.

"Good job, Jay," Angie whispers as she settles beside me and leans her head on my shoulder. I hear stirring in the kitchen, and the scent of coffee brewing tells me that Edgar is already preparing the fuel we need to stay awake this morning.

"Daddy! Santa came, and it's just the best, isn't it? So many presents! And look, he even left me tape!" Emmy's hands are tucked under her chin, and she's twirling around the tree.

I feel Angie's suppressed laughter against my arm, and I hold back my own laugh.

"It's the best." My brother walks in with a full mug of coffee and hands it to me. I give him a grateful nod. "I texted Mom and Dad that you're all up. They'll be here in ten minutes."

Our parents are staying at Ivy's parents' inn in Birch Borough and have spent the last couple of nights with them, playing cards and eating charcuterie boards. To our shock, it turns out that Mom and Dad went to high school in the area at the same time as Ivy's parents and already knew them. They were on rival teams, but it seems they've created their own team as simply our parents now. They're having the time of their lives, and I'm loving that we're all in one place for a while.

"Sounds good," Angie says. "Jay, there's some of the quiche in the fridge if you need some protein to start off your day."

My stomach rumbles, and I rise, walking toward the kitchen. A knock on the door halts my steps. I change directions and head to the door. Opening it wide, the instant blast of cold wakes me up and blows my curls around. It's a sea of winter white everywhere I look, but there's no one there at the door. Instead, I look around and find a tiny, wrapped box on the steps with my name on it.

"Who is it?" Angie asks. Something in her tone sounds far less surprised than I would have expected.

"Maybe it's an extra present from Santa," Edgar adds.

I cast a glance over my shoulder in their direction. Something is definitely up with these two. I know because the two of them never could keep secrets very well. Keeping them in my line of vision, I unwrap the diminutive box. Inside, I find a keychain with a tiny boxing glove hanging from it. Holding it up, I notice a scrap of paper still inside the box.

You may lasso the moon, but I'll bring the stars. Meet me at In the Ring at twelve, the note reads. A smile breaks out on my face: Ivy. I already expected to see her tonight, but this just gave me an extra reason to enjoy the day.

When I'm back on the couch a few minutes later, my mouth full of quiche and my sister sitting beside me, I hear her sniff.

"You two are so cute," Angie says, and I look over to see her smiling.

"Oh, goodness, don't start," Edgar laughs.

"Stop!" she yells at him, wiping her eyes and laughing at herself. "I know I look ridiculous, but he's happy. Did you think he'd ever really be happy again?"

Edgar's smile drops as he looks between Angie and me, and I know we're all thinking of Mina and the heartache we've collectively experienced together since. "I love you, bro." Edgar's eyes mist over as he looks at me. "I'm just happy you have someone like Ivy now. She's good for you, and she's good for Emmy."

I swallow and reach for the half-empty mug on the coffee table. "She's always been good for me."

"True. But you have to admit that this is a Christmas miracle if ever I've seen one."

Seeing my sister and brother being this emotional about the transition my life is going through makes it all the more real. As we reflect silently with a knowing look at each other, a knock sounds at the door. Emmy runs to answer it. She struggles with the lock for a moment, but once it's open, she squeals and jumps into my dad's waiting arms.

"Merry Christmas, everyone!" my mom practically sings as she walks in and systematically wraps each of us in a warm hug one by one. "And you . . ." She pauses when she gets to me, her hands framing my face and her eyes bright. "I'm so proud of you. I'm proud of all my kids, but I've seen you work so hard to give Emmy such a wonderful life. You've got heart, and you've got character. And it's so good to see you looking more like the boy I raised this Christmas." She hugs me again, and I hold my breath to prevent my emotions from pouring out.

"Love you, Mom," I murmur into her greying hair, trying to absorb her gentle words as she pats my head like she did when I was a kid.

"Oh, and by the way," she announces, pulling away from me suddenly. "You're not moving to Florida, even after New Year's."

The shock silences me. I seem to be the only one who has heard her instructions. Angie and Edgar have found their way to the tree. They are coaching Emmy—my daughter sitting on Dad's lap on the floor—instructing her on which present she should open first.

"What do you mean?" I lean in, turning my ear toward her to make sure I heard correctly.

"You know what I said," Mom replies. "You need to be here. Your siblings need you. This town needs you. Emmy loves it here. And Ivy is here. As much as I would love to have you closer, nothing is worth letting all that goodness go." She pats my hand and turns toward the living room, stopping to look up at me with a mischievous expression. "Besides, you never know; we're having such a good time here that we might have to come back more frequently—or just come back."

I give her a grateful smile, realizing that all I feel is relief. I was dreading having to tell my parents that I've changed my mind about moving. Now, I don't have to. It's another Christmas miracle. Every day, I feel more like the kid who once believed in miracles. "Thanks, Mom," I say sincerely, feeling the weight of the words.

"Do you love her, Jay?"

"I do." There's no hesitation. No mulling it over. It's as true as anything I've ever known.

"Great," Mom replies. "Then know that, if she's the one for you, even when you think you're lost, you'll be found."

I wrap her in another hug, and we spend the rest of the morning drinking coffee, eating the special secret recipe Christmas pie Angie baked for us and doesn't sell at her shop, laughing, and unwrapping presents. For a few minutes, I sneak away to shower and get ready to meet Ivy. When it's time for me to leave, Emmy is asleep on the couch next to my dad, with *Elf* playing in the background.

"We've got her," Mom reassures me with a steaming

mug of tea in her hand. "Now, go get your girl." With a wink, she turns back to her latest needlepoint project that travels with her everywhere.

I've stepped through the door and onto the street when I see Gladys walking briskly toward the middle of town.

"Oh, you fine specimen!" she calls. "Merry Christmas!"

I'm mortified and weirdly flattered. "Thanks, Gladys. Merry Christmas to you!"

She waves and then disappears . . . I don't even know where. There aren't many people out and about, considering the holiday, but I wave to the people I see on the street, some I recognize and some unfamiliar. But if they live here, I'll learn who they are. I'm determined to make this the place where I can grow and thrive. After the New Year, I'll talk to a few businesses about the custom furniture I can make. I have five clients wanting to sign on for private training sessions at the boxing studio. And Emmy can continue in her class at school with the teacher she enjoys.

When I approach In the Ring, I pause, noticing that the strands of Christmas lights are turned on inside. As I move toward the door, it flings open, and I watch Grey pop out.

"Oh, hello!" She draws her coat tighter around herself. "Merry Christmas!"

I step back to give her more space, surprised to see Ivy's best friend at the studio. "Merry Christmas, Grey. Were you boxing?" I know she wasn't, but it is an odd sight to see her leaving the place.

Grey laughs. "Not today. But Lily told me I should try it sometime. She said something about pretending that the heavy bags were the villains in my favorite books to get in a great workout."

I chuckle. "That could work."

"Well, I'm on my way to pick up some books. For Christmas. Or rather, for other people's Christmas. I've got deliveries. Oh my goodness, I just was here because—well, oh, I don't know how to say anything without ruining this whole thing." Her arms wave about, and then she brings them to a prayer position, pointing them toward me. "I'm going to stop there. But Jace, it was lovely to see you. I can't wait for you to step inside and for me to hear about . . . nope, enough, Grey." She's talking to herself now, looking at her shoes. "I'm going to stop there about that."

With a full smile, she looks up at me then turns to walk away. She pivots back within a few steps. "I just want to tell you, Jace, that I'm really grateful you've made Ivy so happy. She hasn't been the same since she met you—or rather, since she thought she lost a chance with you. I'm just really glad you two can try now. Love isn't always guaranteed, and it requires bravery." She pauses, and her face brightens. "Ivy's my *best* friend. So, I just want you to know, while I know you have your own friends and family, you can stop by my bookshop anytime to see my dad and me. You'll always be welcome."

I clear my throat, knowing it had cost the shy woman something to say these things to me. But I'm grateful. "Thank you, Grey. And thanks for looking out for her all these years. I promise I won't ever let her slip through my hands again."

Grey tilts her head and smiles even wider. "Go get her, then." Her thumb hitches toward the studio, and I roll my shoulders back.

"Merry Christmas, Grey," I say to her, my hand already

on the doorknob and twisting it open.

She walks away toward her bookstore, her arms swinging, humming a Christmas carol as flurries start to fill the air.

Taking a deep breath, I slowly push open the door and then forget to exhale. The studio is covered in what looks like snow. Dark fabric has even been draped along the back, covering the practice areas and the office. The studio looks like a winter wonderland under the night sky.

Even the boxing ring has been covered with Christmas lights, each strand wrapped around the ring ropes, with LED candles lining the canvas. And then I see Ivy, standing uncharacteristically barefoot in the middle of the ring, clothed in a dress that hugs her curves, her hair tied back with a ribbon. She holds out her hand as I walk toward her. I dodge paper snowflakes hanging from the ceiling, reminding myself to keep inhaling and exhaling so I don't pass out.

Ducking, I slide off my wet boots, weave through the ropes, and step onto the mat in my socked feet. My breathless voice breaks the silence first. "Ivy, if you told me that you're an actual angel, I'd believe you, wholeheartedly." When I finally grasp her hand, I don't drop it. Instead, I lift her fingers still clasped in mine and wrap my hands around her gorgeous face, leaning over her and pressing a kiss to her lips. In response, Ivy hums and leans back, placing one of her hands over my heart and sliding the other around the back of my neck.

"It's beating for you," I confess, knowing she can feel my heartbeat pulsing rapidly in the place she's making contact.

She responds with a smile. "Are you liking your Christmas surprise so far?"

I look about the space again and let out a disbelieving laugh. "It looks like something out of a movie or a book."

"That checks out since Grey helped me," Ivy practically sings. "Did you have a good morning?"

"I did."

"Emmy was excited?"

"She was." Ivy's knowing grin pulls me in. Closing the distance between us, my eyes rove over her angelic face. "And now I'm happy to be here with you."

With another smile, she releases her hold to step away to grab a blanket from a basket sitting in the corner. She spreads it across the canvas floor.

"Does this mean you're taking up boxing?" I ask with a teasing lilt to my voice, crossing my arms over my chest to restrain my affection.

She just laughs and shakes her head with a smile. "Not yet," she replies with a laugh and a shake of her head. When she bites the edge of her lip, I find it irresistible. Something about watching Ivy move around the ring where I train students to box pulls on my emotions. I'm a boxer, and she's a ballerina. I dance around the ring; she dances across the stage. And if we can find a way to dance together for the rest of our days, I'll be happy.

"Stay with me?" The assurance and peace in her smoky voice cling to me.

"Always." Her eyes widen as she smiles, not realizing yet that I am completely serious.

Ivy shuffles around, leaning over the edge to pull things from behind and around the ring, and then we settle in next to each other on the blanket. I watch her in amusement as she reaches for things around us, clearly having a plan in motion.

"Not that I don't love everything that's happening right now, but what are we doing here exactly?"

"You'll see!"

I lie back on the blanket, stuffing a second blanket that's been thrown this way beneath my head. Christmas music fills the air, the arrangement featuring the deep, moving tones of a cello. I close my eyes and take it all in. I have so much to appreciate in this moment: Ivy's signature scent, the way she's made the studio space cozier than a blanket fort, not to mention the way Ivy is not only showing me how much she cares but also making memories we'll get to hold on to for many years to come.

Because I believe we'll have many years ahead of us, I'll do my best to make sure that happens.

"Nearly done!" More blankets and what I think is a pillow land near my legs. "Okay," I hear her say to herself. "I think we're ready."

I open my eyes slightly and catch the way she's pulling a sweatshirt over her head. Not just any sweatshirt. *My* sweatshirt. Something primal in me unlocks at the sight of her wearing something that has also touched my skin. "Where did you get that, Starlight?"

She doesn't reply at first. Instead, she leans back and snuggles against me, her head on my chest and her hair brushing my face. Her shoulders shake with silent laughter. "I may have stolen it?"

"How in the world?" I can't even remember a time I've left Ivy alone or given her an opportunity to snatch an item of my clothing. But now I not only have Ivy in my arms again, but she's in my arms while wearing my clothes? This moment is vying for the best Christmas gift ever.

"I've been working on things not having to be perfect, but I think this actually is perfect," she breathes contentedly.

It's my turn to give her a gift. "I'm not going to Florida," I say quickly. Of course that's the first thing that rushes out when I see her in my clothes.

Sharply, the woman in my arms inhales, lifting to lock those hot-chocolate eyes with mine before she settles back onto my chest. I glance down and catch her smile nestled against my shirt. "Good. You belong with me, Jace."

"Good. Because you belong with me." I kiss her forehead, the hum she gives slightly vibrating against my own mouth. I can feel her smile. "I fully believe that."

"And you're really staying?" she asks softly, and I let out a relieved laugh. Her excitement reflects mine.

"Yes."

She squeals. "This really is my kind of perfect. Maybe only one thing could add to this moment . . . are you ready?" Happiness vibrates through her voice.

I look around us, trying to figure out what Ivy is planning, but my response is quick. "With you? Absolutely."

A tiny remote control appears in her hands, and within seconds, the ceiling has transformed into the night sky. Stars flicker, so tiny and microscopic it's like we're looking at a perfect image of the sky outside on a clear night. Millions of them sparkle throughout the space.

"Starlight," I say reverently, overcome by both her and the magic recreated through the lights surrounding us.

"'Give me the gentle, steady light from the stars any

night to remind me that the world still holds beauty,'" she murmurs.

My chest burns with emotion. "You remember that?"

I look down and see her golden hair splayed over us in the dimness. Her hand lifts to wipe a tear from her face, but I feel the others soaking into my shirt.

"There's a chance I may have written your words down. That moment felt like the first time a man ever really saw me. Didn't want to forget it."

My fingers settle near the curve of her neck, my thumb at the base of her head, cradling it. Pulling her closer, I kiss the soft wisps of hair near her forehead. "And I never want to forget you."

"Then don't," she quips. Ivy pushes herself up, one hand resting on my chest and the other draped over the side of my ribs.

I wipe the remnants of her tears with my thumb, and she leans into my hand. With a gentle nudge, I signal for her to come closer. Immediately, she lifts herself to drape over my chest again, moving closer to my face. Her chest rises and falls against mine. She's close enough that she nearly goes out of focus.

"I love you, Jace."

The words cause tingles to move through my mouth and travel through my face as the edges of her lips brush mine. "Starlight," I rasp, a deep need shimmering through my veins. "I love you with all that I am."

She answers with a kiss that I feel beyond time and space. My only thought is to will myself to memorize the sensation of her lips as they move over mine, the taste of her when she pulls on my bottom lip, placing soft kisses along the edges of my mouth, the scent of her as she traces my jaw with her nose, and the relief when she returns to kiss me and I feel her sigh.

Bells from the stone church in the distance chime, and I smile against her mouth. Sometimes, even a missed connection can turn into a miracle.

Chapter Twenty-Nine

Ivy

"We're here!" I yell into the house as Jace and I step through the front door of the charming historical home, gifts piled in his arms and his presence a steady protection behind me.

As we step into the entryway, yells and sounds of cheers and a "Get in here, you Christmas ornaments!" greet our ears. There's no doubt the last is from Lily. We're here for our annual Birch Borough "crew meetup," also known as the "four-friends celebration." Sparrow, Lily, Grey, and I get together the day after Christmas every year to exchange gifts. Now, that celebration (thankfully) includes all the men in our lives.

The foyer we're standing in is beautiful. We just walked into Lily's childhood home. Graham bought it for her as a surprise last year. I remember visiting this place when we were kids; the old place had character, like most of the homes here, and a creaky floor. Some of the original elements have been updated or changed, and it's now a home that could be featured in a New England magazine.

As we take off our shoes and boots near the hallway bench, piling the gifts temporarily on top of it, my eyes catch sight of a framed picture hanging on the wall. It's a sort of collage with a picture of Lily and Graham taking a selfie and laughing on what must be their elopement day, given the attire. Included in the collage is a page from *Pride and Prejudice*, with a quote highlighted on the page, which says, *"I am the happiest creature in the world. Perhaps other people have said so before, but not one with such justice."*

I smile as Grey comes to greet us in the entryway. Her cheeks are flushed, and she looks the happiest I've seen her in months. Wrapping her arms around me, I laugh.

"Well, don't you look radiant," I tease her. She leans back and bites her lip as I see the reason for her happiness walking toward us with a smile. "Ahh, I see," I whisper to Grey with a grin before turning my attention to her closest friend as he approaches.

"Boston!" I yell, noting his signature glasses in place and his disheveled hair whipping in all directions like it couldn't decide which way to land. He looks like a literary type, and standing beside Grey, the two of them look like they could be trapped in a library together for the rest of their lives and be happy about it.

"Hi, Ivy," he says, giving me a warm hug. "Merry Christmas."

"Same to you! Oh, this is Jace." I step aside slightly to let Jace and Boston do the whole handshake thing. To my delight, even though they are complete opposites and yet still wildly attractive in their own right, they're quickly caught up in a discussion on something. Jace smiles broadly. I smile too, shaking my head and turning back to Grey, knowing we only have a few moments before we're wrapped up in the festivities that carry out to us from the other room.

"How long is he here?" I whisper.

Grey's eyes dim slightly as she turns her attention to Boston. I take note of how open her posture is to him. It's the same as she's always looked when he's around. Near Boston, my friend is the most comfortable version of herself.

"Just a week," she murmurs. "But he might be back next summer."

I give a nod, but my smile dims. It's hard to see her wilt whenever he goes back to New York City, but seeing her so happy, I can hardly be mad at Boston. If I've learned anything from my experience with Jace, I have to believe that when it's time for them to be more than friends, they'll be ready.

"Where are all my people?" Lily calls from the direction of the main living area, though it sounds more like a yell. We stand at attention.

With a rush, Graham appears in the front hallway with a grin on his face and a shrug of his shoulders. "My love would enjoy it if you'd come into the other room."

"Well, then, lead the way," I say with a laugh. Rafe and Lily are bantering like siblings, and their voices only get louder and louder as we round the corner into their open-concept kitchen and dining area. Lily is sitting in a plush loveseat across the way in the living room with her hands on her stomach when we enter. Her bump looks like it's grown exponentially larger since I saw her just last week. A chocolate wrapper shimmers on top of it like a star on a tree.

My eyes widen at the spread of pastries piled high on the

dining room table. It's been so fully covered that I have to question if there used to be a table under there. I catalog croissants with a cranberry swirl, plus tartlets, macarons, sugar cookies, madeleines, a variety of cream puffs, and an actual bowl full of decorated gingerbread men. And in the kitchen, the counter space has a small feast of mashed potatoes, some sort of casserole, a ham, and a charcuterie board. We can all clearly see where the priorities lie.

Jace lets out a low whistle and places a hand on my lower back to guide me toward the living room, where Sparrow is nestled in with Rafe. The couple is sitting on the couch, tucked together like two birds in a nest, which is not surprising. Graham resumes his seat next to Lily, who shifts so she can lean against him on the small loveseat. There's another couch, but given Jace's size, I don't see all of us fitting on it. As if reading my mind, Grey grabs a few floor pillows from a basket in the corner, setting them near each other but not touching before she plops down, Boston following suit.

Jace and I move toward the remaining couch, but instead of sitting as close as the married couples in the room, we sit with the sides of our legs touching. He extends one arm across the back of the couch, and I lean my head back, using it as a pillow. I look up at him and grin, a dopey smile on my face, and he smiles down at me.

"Well, you two are adorable," Sparrow says softly from her perch near Rafe, who gives Jace an enthusiastic head nod.

"My man," he says with a grin, and it makes me laugh. "*Joyeux Noël,* you two!"

He's so French and yet so American. I'm not sure how

he carries both off so well, but he does. He's allowed more of his French side to emerge since he's been with Sparrow. Occasionally, his words hold more of an accent, but he still says modern American phrases like the boys I went to high school with.

"Merry Christmas, Rafe," I say back, not even attempting the French. I don't need to see his brow furrow like it does when he hears his native tongue being mispronounced. It's ingrained in him to be appalled, no matter how authentic the attempt, so we don't hold it against him.

Lily holds up her hand and moves her pointer finger between Jace and me, her eyes narrowed. "I called this. Don't forget that."

"Yes, Lily, you did." I shake my head playfully. "And so did Gladys, so try not to say that too loudly if she's in the vicinity, or you'll never hear the end of it."

Lily scoffs. "We already never hear the end of it. But wait, does this mean you're truly done with the apps? This calls for more chocolate!"

I laugh again, something I think will be the theme of the evening. Graham is already halfway to the kitchen, returning with a towering chocolate cake with marshmallow creme and what looks like a peanut butter drizzle over the top.

"Fluffernutter and chocolate?" Grey asks almost reverently.

Lily grins. "It's an upgrade from Graham's favorite sandwiches and our story. Plus, it's Christmastime, so clearly, we had to have it tonight."

"No arguments here, even though my training regimen has been shot to pieces this season," Jace adds beside me with a laugh. Lily nods approvingly.

"Where's George?" Grey asks, and Graham looks up, even though Lily hasn't used that nickname for him in a while. Instead, she named their dog George to keep the memory alive.

"Oh, he's already asleep on our bed. I think he's nesting."

"Lils, that's not a thing," Sparrow says with a laugh.

"Well, tell him that Resin says hello," I interject with a nod.

"Absolutely. Okay, enough with the pleasantries. Honey," she says, looking at Graham, "will you please grab the gifts and bring them in?"

"I'll help!" Rafe says, jumping to his feet and heading toward the door leading to the entryway. Sparrow looks at him like he's all the gift she'll ever need.

Jace's arm moves from behind the couch so he can sit up straighter, his hand drifting to my leg. His fingers wrap around my entire knee and a few inches above it, causing warmth to spread through my whole leg. As if to completely melt me, the tips of his fingers begin making his signature move of aimless circles, the feeling of them through my tights enough to cause me both insomnia and the desire to want to curl up in his arms.

I move the arm closest to him behind his back and place it between his shoulder blades, rubbing the middle of his spine slowly and smoothly. His eyes flutter closed, and he makes a low hum that I feel through my own frame.

"Okay, you two are clearly having a moment," Lily's voice breaks through, "which I support, by the way. And you remind me of an episode I just saw of *The Man is a Rake*. I loved that one! Anyway, my party people, we need to give out gifts. This baby has me craving my bed more than Rafe craves maple croissants."

At this, Rafe gasps. *"C'est impossible!"* His quiet affront has us all laughing.

"Then let's get this moving before Lily passes out on the couch with a pyramid of chocolates around her," Graham instructs.

"It's happened before," Lily confirms.

Piles of presents are brought to the living room and arranged between us, their tags addressed to each other. Jace shifts slightly in his seat next to me.

"Doing okay?" I whisper in his ear, the scent of him, all pine and sandalwood, like a dreamy walk in the woods.

"I'm good, Starlight," he says with a grin, that dimple peeking out. "I was just thinking again of how much I want Emmy to have this when she's older. A group of friends who are close like this."

I clear my throat of sudden emotion as I look about the room. The people gathered here are some of the most important people in my life, and I love each of their quirks and idiosyncrasies. Graham and Lily are at war as she tries to peel off the tape to take a peek at the gift in front of her. Gently, Graham brushes her hand away. Sparrow looks at Rafe instead of the gift in her hand as he speaks rapid French with a smile, his hands waving about. Grey and Boston are huddled with their heads close together, whispering about something that has made her laugh.

There's so much love in the room, and with Jace beside me, I realize that this is what life is about. Having people nearby who support you and love you but who are also allowed to be themselves, move through their fears, and choose love.

"Yeah, she would be one lucky girl if that were the case." I push off the couch slightly to press a kiss on his cheek where his dimple likes to hide. His skin is smooth against my lips. I shift to press my forehead into his neck. And then we're nuzzling, and it's the holidays, and we're spending the evening together, and it's glorious.

"*Allez!*" Rafe's voice nearly sings. "Let's get the Santa's secret—"

"Secret Santa," Sparrow whispers.

"*Quoi?*"

"It's secret Santa, not Santa's secret."

"Why would it—I don't understand this phrase," he says with obvious confusion but then moves on. "Okay, we'll accept it. Let's get this 'secret Santa' gift exchange going. We'll start with Ivy."

I lean back in surprise and accept the gift box handed to me.

"*C'est parti!*" Rafe yells with a whoop, and then we begin our gift-giving tradition.

Christmas music plays on a record player in the corner. Cradling the gift on my lap, I take a minute to glance around the welcoming space again, realizing that this is only the second year the other couples are married (the Durands and the Winnings). Lily and Graham have done so much to this place. They've restored the old house into a cozy nook that makes you want to stay awhile and raise a family.

At the thought of Jace and me having a family one day, potentially giving Emmy a sibling, my heart lifts.

"Well, open it!" Lily interrupts my daydream with a yell,

and I focus on the gift in front of me. Tearing open the paper, I find a snow globe with a scene from *The Nutcracker*, a tiny Clara dancing with the nutcracker doll in front of the Christmas tree. Behind her is a tiny mockup of a house, with a night sky and speckled stars visible through the window.

Sharply, I inhale and feel Jace stiffen next to me. With a glance at him, I turn the snow globe over to find a handwritten message on the bottom, which reads: *Starlight, our magic will never run out. I loved you then. I love you now. I'll love you for all time.*

And loosely taped to the wind-up mechanism is the piece of ribbon that used to be mine. My lucky charm has returned. My eyes are cloudy through my tears, and I let them fall.

"Don't lose that now," Jace whispers. "I hear it's good luck."

Without releasing the snow globe, I wrap my arm as far around his shoulders as possible and pull him to me, kissing him with all the emotion I can muster. Our love story may have unfolded quickly, but it's also unfolded over a lifetime. Gently, his mouth moves over mine, and I can't bring myself to care about the six pairs of eyes probably watching us, my sense of perfectionism taking a back seat to my love. Because love may be messy at times, but it's also the most freeing feeling I've ever known. His kiss tells me of the way he wants to hold me. It reassures me that he's always going to protect me. And it's a promise that he'll never let me doubt his love.

Another whoop from Rafe breaks us apart. I laugh, trying to hold it together. Yes, I just kissed my handsome hunk of a man, whose heart I want to deeply shelter—even in front of my friends—and I love it.

"I won't apologize," snarks Jace, now wearing a hint of my lipstick on his upper lip.

"Clearly, Jace pulled Ivy's name. Hmm, I wonder how that happened . . ." Lily tries to move to the edge of her seat to reach for another gift but loses her balance and falls back with an exhale. "C'mon, Cruffin! It's gift time!"

Collectively, a laugh echoes around the room.

"Graham, does it bother you that your wife refers to your unborn child as a baked good?" Grey asks with a smile.

"I'm just glad she's carrying my child." It's the most Graham thing to say, and that's why we love him.

Boston clears his throat and reaches for a gift, reading the tag and passing it to Sparrow. That's when the real fun begins.

Tonight, it turns out, the rest of the gifts are somewhat hilarious and scarily specific items that we all picked for each other. Sparrow receives an oversized sweater with a whimsical croissant pattern from Grey (it's adorable, and I love it). Rafe is pleasantly overwhelmed by a journal and a bag of guitar picks with French sayings on them from Lily, which is great, considering Sparrow still hides them from him as a nod to a game she started when they were fake dating. Written on the journal cover are the words *The only pain I want while writing music is a pain au chocolat,* which feels perfectly appropriate, considering the giver.

Grey receives a personalized library set from Graham. Lily is given an actual, miniature vending machine that dispenses wrapped chocolates from Rafe. Graham holds a leather-bound edition of *Pride and Prejudice* from Boston (he has access to rare books and clearly takes advantage of it).

Jace is gifted a new sweatshirt with the Wicked Good Farms branding from Sparrow, which I know I'll eventually steal. Finally, Boston is given a laptop cover that looks like an old paper checkout card from the library, the gift chosen by me.

With wrapping paper thrown about the living room and our hearts full, we chat for a few minutes. Then Lily yells, "Let's eat!" while popping another chocolate in her mouth. The woman's ability to consume chocolate is untouchable.

Collectively, we rise and fill our plates with delicious holiday food and desserts. Soon, we're settling back in the living room in the casual and comfortable way that feels like a holiday with friends. Over the years, we've long abandoned the idea of trying to sit at the dining room table, which is still covered in enough dessert to feed the entire town at Sparrow's Beret tomorrow. We settle into our respective places, *White Christmas* playing on the TV in the background, and I'm laughing so much my stomach hurts. The night is beautiful, full of everything I love about the holiday season. I'm with people I love, everything has a special glow to it, and our New England snow is the perfect excuse to curl up with a blanket.

It's only later, when we're walking home, my hand in Jace's as he walks me back to my apartment, that I feel the truth of who we are together sinking in. Jace is my person. And I'm his. I don't know how life works—if we missed our original connection or if it has all gone exactly according to plan—but I know now we were always meant to be something special to each other.

"Jace," I say when we cross the bridge, the lights and garland wrapped around the antique streetlights casting a warm glow on the edges of his hair, which is flipped in all directions. He turns toward me.

"Starlight." His voice is gritty and low in the cold, the timbre of it like a drink being poured over ice.

I let the nickname carry me home, the assurance of his presence enough to calm any fear. When we stand outside my apartment door, he lingers, and I bring him inside to make some candy cane tea. We haven't spoken a word since we entered my home, and I find that we don't need to. It's a comfortable silence, the kind that can take years to cultivate, but when you find it, you sense its presence.

Instead, we fall into a rhythm, boiling water, getting mugs, preparing the tea bags, adding some honey, and soon the vanilla-scented candy cane fragrance rises around us from the counter, the delicate scent steaming between us. As the tea brews, I stare up at him, my chin tilted at the angle that's just perfectly keyed to be able to study every detail of his face. During my life, movements have often been associated with ballet positions, but the feeling of standing close to him and lifting my face toward his just so will always be associated with only Jace.

"Your message on the snow globe . . ." I break the silence but let the words trail off.

He inhales, and the sound catches. I only register the swish of the bag holding our gifts before I'm wrapped in his arms, his cold nose buried in my neck, but the warmth of him makes up for the chill.

"I love you so much," he confesses, outlining a constellation of kisses from my jaw to my cheekbone and then repeating it on the other side. He's mapping the night sky with his love. "It's always been you, Starlight." Jace's large hands frame my face, his palms moving from my cheeks to my neck and back again.

I lean back to study his face. His eyes are glistening, and his heart is open. The vulnerability in his gaze undoes me. He's no longer the alternate version of the man I met once on a night long ago. He's back. I pull him closer, my arms wrapping around his neck, my lips near the shell of his ear.

"And I already love Emmy, Jace . . . deeply." My breath hitches. "I can't wait to watch her grow up." I choke the last words out with a smile, my emotions surging at the thought of the precious little girl who will be a permanent part of my life.

His shoulders relax. He lets out a soft sound, nuzzling back into my neck. Tears stream down my face, his hair brushing my skin as his shoulders shake silently.

"You've done a good job with her, Jace. She's okay." My hands play with the ends of his hair, my fingers caressing the nape of his neck. And then in a quick motion, I'm lifted into his arms and carried to the couch, where he sits with me on his lap, my chest turned into him. Emotion still plays across his face.

"I'm here now, Jace. Wrap your arms around me. I'm here."

He holds me, my hands tucked with one placed over his heart, the sound of our breathing and the feeling of his heartbeat the only measure of passing time. At some point, I feel his warm tears against the side of my neck and patiently wait until his breathing evens out.

Eventually, he leans back and lifts my chin, the amber eyes I love so much staring back at me with a level of clarity that I haven't seen from them since he returned.

"Thank you, Ivy," he murmurs.

"For what, love?"

"For being you." Before we can get emotional again, Jace continues with a smirk, "Speaking of honey, I think our tea is cold . . ." he trails off, a brow lifting toward the kitchen. His eyes are still reddened and his cheeks a bit swollen, but he looks at peace.

I realize I couldn't love this man any more than I do now. And yet, somehow, I know I will. "We'll reheat it. We've got time."

Jace's handsome face turns to mine once more. "Yeah, we do. We've got time, Starlight."

Chapter Thirty

Jace

The night of the performance has finally arrived. My hands and legs are tingling because this is it. This is my moment to make sure both of my girls shine.

Emmy is dancing her heart out on the stage, her tiny ballerina movements making my fatherly heart proud.

Ivy is going to take the stage, and I'm going to join her. I've been practicing for a couple of weeks now. I don't know what took over my mind to think I could do this in front of other people, but here we are.

I'm a boxer and a father. I make furniture, and I teach others a sport I've loved my whole life. Still, I'm questioning if I have the ability to not fall on my face during a ballet performance. Only time will tell. But I'm in love with a dancer, and I'll do anything to make sure she feels safe. She told me that she only wants me to hold her for the rest of her life. And I'm going to do just that.

Besides, male dancers in Birch Borough are limited. While there's Liam, whom I've met a few times and can confirm that he's a good guy with musical ability, there's still no way I'm letting him or some other dancer from a nearby town get near her.

Am I delusional enough to think I'll be graceful? Not really. But will I embarrass her is the real question.

I'm waiting in the right wing of the high school auditorium stage, wearing an outfit that Shirley from All Sewn Up made for me. It had to be a rush special order because I don't fit in any of the dance wear options at the local shop and would have had no idea what to order online. Also, I wasn't about to wear tights. Instead, I'm wearing a shirt that shimmers and pants that aren't too tight. The loose fabric comes in at my ankle and is tucked into leather boots that are slippers but look way cooler, in my opinion.

Liam appears beside me, wearing a headset and carrying a clipboard. The man has been a willing participant in this surprise, and I'm grateful. He greets me with a grin. "Okay, Jace. So, the next number is about to start, and then it's you and her. Are you sure you're ready?"

"I'm honestly not sure. But I will be ready for Ivy."

The truth is, I snuck backstage after I slipped out from the audience ten minutes ago so Ivy wouldn't suspect anything. She's been on stage for the last few numbers with her students. I waited until I could sneak out unseen and wait in the wings, watching the end of Emmy's performance from my hiding spot.

"She's gonna love this," Liam says with a grin and a shake of his head. He reaches up to clap me on the shoulder and then walks off, telling someone in the microphone attached to his headset that "the bear is in place."

I shake out my limbs and try to stretch. I'm not doing much movement out there. My only hope is that I at least complement Ivy to some degree. My goal is to channel less of the "I could punch anyone in the face like I do a boxing bag" energy and more of an "I'm a gentle tower in the middle of this art scene" vibe. I'm also hoping that showcasing Ivy in this way will be another reason for the Music and Arts Committee to see the importance of dance. And if Ivy can fly because I can lift her a little higher, so be it.

I'm caught between pacing a little and continuing to stretch when I hear the music winding down. My heart rate accelerates with such speed I hear it pumping through my ears. Grabbing a water bottle from a small table placed nearby for the dancers when they leave the stage, I consume half of it in one gulp and then put it down against the wall.

It's time.

A troop of little dancers flutters past me, their role in tonight's production complete. Ivy will close out this year's performance for the town with a dance routine that shows the skills their children are on the way to learning. Emmy's eyes catch mine as she runs up, her face lighting up with delighted surprise. Swiftly, she throws her arms around my legs for a hug before dashing off with her friends.

The music for our song begins, and I see Ivy from my position. She takes center stage, lifting her arms and moving to her toes. Gracefully, she dances through steps I recognize from seeing her practice for the last few weeks.

"Okay, Jace. You can do this." Yes, I'm talking to myself, and yes, it feels necessary.

When it's my cue, I think of Ivy's selflessness, of her ability to care for others so well, and of how I want to do the same for her. It's that driving force that pushes me from the wing and onto the stage. I walk forward, immediately hearing the crowd murmur in surprise, and extend my arm, just like I've seen on YouTube. My eyes fall on Ivy, my heart overwhelmed with the feeling of loving her. There's not going to be much acting on my part tonight, and I hope it shows.

Ivy's head is turned toward the audience, her toes positioned and dancing through her complex steps, so she doesn't notice my presence right away. Instead, I have a few seconds to get across the stage before she spins. As she turns downstage, her gaze lands on me. I register her look of wonder as her eyes scan me from head to toe before a smile breaks out.

My arrival causes her to miss some steps, but she makes up for it by swaying her arms above her head and acting like it's a surprise to see me appear before resuming her original choreography.

Softly, I grin as she waltzes toward me, an energy in her steps I haven't seen before. She looks like an angel, her dress having a shimmery layer sewn over it so she can move freely. It catches the light. Sequins have been attached over the bodice and across the sheer long sleeves, and she wears a clip in her hair that catches the spotlights. I prepare my stance, assuming one I've watched the great male ballet dancers use. Since my arm is already extended, when she's close enough to reach me, Ivy only slows for a moment before she places her hand on my arm and balances in an arabesque. She dips toward the ground in a fluid motion, my strength lending itself to her grace.

When Ivy rises, I move behind her, positioning my arms and feet carefully, waiting for her to spin, ready to move her like she taught me. And then she spins, and it's the most graceful move I've seen her make yet. After completing seven of them, she turns to me, her back to the audience, her arms lifted, and she winks before she bends backward, completely trusting my hands to securely grab her hips so she doesn't fall, her elegantly athletic body showing off her incredible flexibility. When she rises and is facing me again, she nods and turns once more to the audience as my arms extend so she can dance and balance while holding on to me. Together, we walk from one side of the stage to the other. I continue to support her when I can, as Ivy seamlessly adjusts her performance to include my presence.

"Almost ready," she murmurs as the music builds to a crescendo. When it peaks, I know it's time to try our lift.

"Okay, Starlight, I've got you," I reply softly on our slow walk to the back wall of the stage. She presses gently into my hand as a sign that she heard me, and then we're off. I grasp her waist and lift her off the floor. Ivy splits her legs in the air for a few seconds and leans forward to land. Then she spins. We repeat the movement twice before we're at the front edge of the stage, and she faces the audience once again. I hold her hips and add pressure so she knows she can jump. And then she's over my head. We've only tried this once, but I know her arms are extended and her legs pointed down while her back arches elegantly over my head. I pictured a candy cane when she showed me the picture, but now that I'm participating in it, it's so much more than that. I feel what she brings to the stage and what she brings to my life.

Ivy is exquisite. Her energy pours from her limbs when she moves. It's elegant, and it's sharp. It's clear, and it's expressive.

When I lower her gently back to the stage and her feet land, the swell of the music in its final notes causes the audience to stand on their feet. Ivy holds the final pose for a few beats, and then she breaks character to cover her hands with her face and turn to me. I smile and give a nod, motioning for her to turn back and bow. And then I do what YouTube showed me to do. Stepping back, I extend my arm so more of the attention is directed to her, because I wouldn't have it any other way.

Liam pops onto the stage with a bouquet and hands it to Ivy. With her face all smiles and blushes, she looks like the queen of all things beautiful. She should be able to enjoy every bit of this.

When the applause finally dies down after a full minute of yelling and cheers, Ivy grabs my hand and pulls me backstage. My eyesight has barely adjusted from the change in lighting before her arms are around my neck, and she's hopping up to wrap her legs around my waist. I grab her to steady her and grin. The troop of tiny dancers returns to shuffle out of the wings amid squeals and excited chatter. I wink at Emmy as she runs past.

"You just danced with me! On stage!" Ivy proclaims with excitement, trying to contain herself, knowing there's still one more number for her students to perform. We have about two minutes.

"I did."

"And your outfit!" She looks down, trying to look at it, when I know the most she can see are my shoulders from the way I'm holding her. "Who made this?"

"Shirley."

"Shirley! She did good. I mean . . . you look *good*."

I laugh, the pleasure of hearing her approval of how I look in this outfit giving me a little too much confidence. "So, this is also what does it for ya, huh?" I tease. "If I had known, I would've worn it from the start."

Ivy's laugh is like music, and her smile is free-spirited. "You did this for me?"

"Yes."

"I'll never forget it." Ivy glances toward the stage, checking on her students as I wrap my arms tighter around her.

"They're doing fine. You taught them well," I assure her, solely focusing on her angelic face, my gaze lingering on the curve of her nose and the red of her lips.

With that, she turns back, leaning in so close that I feel her breath on my skin. Ivy kisses me so softly and sweetly that it's like she's savoring the moment and doesn't want it to pass too quickly.

When our lips part, I murmur against them. "I'll always show up for you, Ivy. I know I didn't—or couldn't—the first time. But it won't ever happen again if I can help it."

The music swells, indicating that the pocket of time we've had to celebrate while most of her students are on stage is about to end, and the class is ready to take a bow.

"Even when you weren't with me . . . in my heart, I think I left a light on just for you," she whispers back.

Our foreheads meld together. If I were a sentimental guy (which I absolutely am), it would be giving romantic-movie vibes where the light comes through the profile shot of their faces. And if I've somehow landed in the equivalent of a romance movie with Ivy, then I think I've done pretty well with my life.

Most of us need a person in life who is our shelter. And knowing they've chosen you to move through life with them is a gift. That's my dream to have with Ivy.

Hearing the marker for the final steps on stage, I slide Ivy down slowly, not missing the glow that radiates from her hot-chocolate eyes. I didn't believe that anyone would want me to hold them again. And she defies that lie every time I feel her reach for me.

From my place in the wings, I spy Emmy on stage, a smile overtaking my face as I see how happy she is. Ivy did more than bring me back to life. She gave the gift of dance back to my girl, and that will inform the rest of her life. She's made more dreams come true than I expected, and I'm never letting this woman go.

As the audience claps and the students take their bows, Ivy stretches her feet and neck before hopping back up on her toes and giving me a sweet kiss. "C'mon, Bear," she urges.

"I'm going with you?"

"You're always going with me. We're in this together."

The smile on my face carries me from the wings to the stage, my pace matching Ivy's all the way. In the end, I'm surrounded by Ivy, Emmy, and dozens of students of various ages in their tutus and slippers or pointe shoes. The Andrews boy, who still has a way to go before he hits puberty, is the only other guy out here. This holiday season, I'm the giant in the middle of a sea of tulle, taking a bow in front of the town I now call home. And I don't mind it one bit.

Chapter Thirty-One

Ivy

O kay, it's just Emmy." Jace looks as if he is about to be sick. "We can do this." His mood has taken a sharp turn from how it was at Sparrow's Beret just a bit ago, where we told our overjoyed friends the news that Jace is staying for good, and he drank two more coffees.

"Jace . . ." I laugh. "Are you seriously concerned that Emmy isn't going to be happy about this?" I motion between us. We're on our way to Angie's apartment to officially tell Emmy about our relationship, and Jace's nerves have fully set in.

My words seem to reset his frame of mind. Instantly, he relaxes with a sigh, reaching up to tug on his hair. I want to touch it, but he's too tall for me to reach the top when standing, so I wait, turning my attention back to the task at hand.

"No, of course not. I know she'll be thrilled. I just . . ." He lets out a breath like he's blowing out imaginary candles. "It took everything in me to care for Emmy after Jenna. I don't know what I'd do if—"

"Bear, look at me." He does, and the boyish way he grins at my term of endearment radiates warmth. "We can't control the future, but I'm yours. You're mine. We have to choose not to let fear or regret lead us. We must keep choosing love."

Jace nods. "You're right. All right, let's get my little bear cub and tell her." Kicking off his shoes at the entryway, he steps into the hallway. "Emmy Bear!"

"Daddy!" her little voice chimes through the air with happiness.

"I've got Miss Ivy with me!"

"Yes! Yes! Yes!" She's already jumping up and down when she appears. Her Christmas performance outfit has been put on again, and makeup leftover from dress-up lingers on her face. Angie appears after her with an affectionate smile and a shake of her head.

"She won't take it off." She looks at me with a laugh.

"I remember those days."

Emmy has already jumped into Jace's arms, and he holds her close then sets her back on the floor a moment later. She turns to me next, running toward me and nearly knocking me over. She's used to throwing herself into her dad's arms, but I'm clearly not built like that mountain of a man. We topple over, my shock and her laughter causing me to start laughing too.

"Oof! You got me."

She giggles and attempts to help me up, but it's really Jace who pulls us both up together with one tug.

"Angie, you can join us for this too," he says to his sister. "We have something to share." Jace wraps his hand around mine before kneeling on the floor to get to Emmy's level.

"Emmy," he says with a smile, using his free hand to hold hers.

Her fingers are so tiny in his and bring up memories of my own dad's kindness, guiding me through life and encouraging me to follow my dreams. Jace is so different from my dad, yet he has so many of his good qualities that I know I've found the best sort of man to give my trust and love.

"Ivy—*Miss Ivy*—and I care about each other very much. And I really want her to be a part of our lives as more than your dance teacher." He pauses to let her process his words.

Emmy's brow furrows, and my heart rate escalates. "Would you two get married?" Her voice is only curious.

"I would like to marry her one day." He steals a glance at me, and I know my smile is radiant.

Emmy hums and nods, and her tulle skirt swishes. "And would you two kiss and stuff like that?"

I hold back a laugh, but Jace's mouth just hitches up in a maddeningly attractive way. "We would. And stuff like that." At the last words, he looks my way with a wink.

Oh. My. Stars. Thankfully, he faces Emmy again and misses my face turning the same shade as my red lipstick.

"And would she live here?"

"Well, not here." Jace glances up at his sister, who has tears in her eyes as she watches us silently. "But, one day, we'll plan to live together. When we don't live with Auntie A anymore."

Emmy looks from Angie and back to Jace, and then her eyes slide to mine, her brow still furrowed. "And you'd want me too, Miss Ivy?"

"Of course I'd want you," I whisper as my voice catches.

"Not just my dad. You want me to live with you?" She points to herself, and I nod quickly, the fact that she feels the need to ask breaking my heart.

"I'd want you, Emmy girl."

"Like a mommy?"

Sharply, Jace inhales, looking at the floor, his throat working to swallow.

I nod again. "If your dad and I get married, and if you ever want me to be your mommy, I'd love to be."

Emmy's eyes fill just before she launches herself at me again, and this time, I'm ready for it. I wrap my arms around her and let her sniffles match mine. Jace is wiping the edges of his eyes, and Angie is a blubbering mess in the kitchen.

Leaning back to hold my face in her hands, Emmy closes the distance between us as only kids without concern for personal space can do. I can see her freckles, the glitter of her eyeshadow, and the cheek stain she put on. She smells like sugar cookies, which I happen to love.

"Do I still have to call you Miss Ivy?" At this, our laughs mingle throughout the room.

"Just in class."

"Okay, I guess I can do that." Her arms wrap around me once more, and I hold on tight until Jace joins in. I knew he couldn't stay away for long.

"My girls." His strong arms wrap around us both, and I snuggle in, resting my head against his chest.

"Will I get a brother or sister now?" Emmy squeals, and Jace coughs.

"One thing at a time, Emmy Bear. One thing at a time."

I bury my face in his chest once more to hide my laughter, but the feeling of his hand wrapping around my hip and the gentle pressure he adds to it tells me there's more to our future if we want it. Because just when we thought time could be running out, it turned out it was just catching up. Emmy is the added bonus—a gift that's better than I could've imagined.

My smile stretches wide, letting the joy of the moment and the fact that we've finally made our way back to each other sink in. A part of my soul recognized his soul from the beginning. Somehow—someway—we're each other's. In the changing of seasons, in the heartache and the disappointment, in the missed connections and the choices, and in the strangers and the loved ones, we've passed each other, and we've been brought back together.

Emmy rushes off to her aunt to grab another cookie from Four Leaf Cookies in the kitchen. I think we'll be revisiting that tradition during the holidays from now on—cookies and hot chocolate—though, of course, coffee for Jace.

I turn to look back at the man I love, the ease in his expression and the openness of his smile warming me from the inside. When I reach for him, he pulls me close, nuzzling into my neck.

"You're so swoony," I admit. I feel Jace's chuckle through my rib cage. He straightens to his full height, one eyebrow perfectly arched.

"I'm not sure a boxer is the type they write love stories about."

I rise up on my toes, steadying myself by anchoring my hands around his neck. "Jace, you're my love story. And that's all that matters to me."

At my confession, his hands are in my hair, and he's

kissing me, his passion enough to warm me up until next Christmas. We match each other in every way, and our story is one for the ages. From a fateful night at an ice rink, to losing touch with each other, then somehow finding our way back, the magic of the season couldn't be clearer. There's enough love between us to build a life we'll be proud of. We'll build a family to hold and a home to grow old in. As we treasure each other and enjoy what it means to be fully and purely ourselves, all the nights I spent alone were simply the fuel for me to hold on tightly to love if that means they've led me here. After all, it's because of the chill of winter that we appreciate the warmth from the light.

I've been searching but never found. I've been lonely, though not alone. I've been dancing while on my own. I've wandered in an attempt at finding peace in the dark. But now, in the winter wonder that is the Christmas season, a light in my heart turns on, and my whole soul knows that I love him like home.

Epilogue

Jace

SPRING

"D addy!" Emmy yells, standing between the open front doors of Birch Borough Elementary, acting as if she hadn't just seen me this morning over the homemade waffles I made for her last day of school before spring break.

Resin sits patiently beside me, but at the sound of Emmy's voice, he perks up, tail immediately wagging. My daughter rushes toward me, and I prepare to catch her when she launches herself, waiting for the moment when her tiny hands—getting bigger by the day as she grows—wrap around my neck.

"Emmy Bear," I say affectionately. When she wiggles out of my arms, I set her down gently so she can hug Resin, who's now groaning and impatient for Emmy's attention. "How was your day?"

"Fantastic!" she yells again with her hand raised to the sky. Emmy has clearly been spending more time with Grey if her vocabulary is any indication. And she's thriving in class as well. The love she has for her teacher and classmates is a testament to this town and the way it really emphasizes community.

"That's excellent." I nod to the staff member on duty for pickup, reaching for Emmy's hand so we can walk together toward the house that we moved into a few weeks ago. It took a few months before I finally moved out of Angie's apartment and put down permanent roots. The house contains a few extra bedrooms, because I have plans. My heart warms at the thought.

Now, the leaves are starting to return, colors appearing where there once was only winter white. There's a balminess in the air that wasn't there until recently. The thought of getting ready for a new season and seeing both of my girls continue to thrive and grow is intoxicating. Christmas, once again, is my favorite holiday, but I'm looking forward to the rest of the year. I've already got fresh flowers waiting in the garage, ready to plant in the garden as soon as the weather is warm enough. But, for now, I'm ready to move through another year, and a lifetime, with Ivy by our side.

"Okay, Emmy Bear, you've got to get ready for dance class. And I'm keeping Resin for our surprise."

"Yes, can't be late for Miss Ivy. Let's *goooo!*" she shouts happily once more.

I assess her hair, knowing I'm going to have to spend extra time getting it smooth and in place before we can leave the house, given the amount of fun she clearly had while at school. I would pin it back in the morning, but nothing seems to tame her curls. She definitely got those from me.

The three of us walk back to my house, and when we enter, the gift I have for Ivy catches my eye in the entryway. I've spent months working to get it just right, knowing the whole time that this was my plan. I'm hoping to surprise Ivy in a way that, hopefully, she'd never expect but will be delighted by.

When we finally get out the door again, we run toward the dance studio. Our house is only a few streets away, which was intentional. I know how much Ivy loves this town, and I wanted her to be able to get to her studio no matter the weather.

While I didn't take the position in Florida, an opportunity opened shortly thereafter for me to work with a company in Connecticut. Now, I work remotely and provide pieces of furniture that are soon to be manufactured throughout New England. They even let me keep my signature mark on each creation. I also have pieces displayed in shops throughout town, and In the Ring is close enough to walk to on days I teach classes or one-on-ones as well. It works.

We pass Sparrow's Beret, the smell of the maple croissants enough to beckon me to pause. Rafe was right; they are the best things on the menu. Although, I think the bakery's cinnamon rolls are a close second, for reasons Lily has banned us from mentioning in the presence of young children. Apparently, kissing a certain way in public is not encouraged by people who just want a latte.

"Daddy, can you get us croissants for later?" Emmy runs next to me, and the sight of her little legs in tights but the rest of her frame covered by a hoodie makes me laugh. Resin keeps pace beside us, clearly wanting to see Ivy as much as we do.

Arriving at the studio, I open the door and let Resin walk in first, taking in the sight of dance moms and little ones fixing their hair, getting slippers on, and more as they wait for class to start. It's a tight space, and I do my best not to make too much of a disruption with my entrance.

"Ladies," I say to the women, knowing that the only lady I'm interested in seeing is on the other side of the wall.

"That's it for today. Take a bow!" Ivy's muffled voice rings through.

I hear the clapping of hands before the studio door swings open, and the exchange of this class leaving for the next takes place. Harlow gives me a knowing look from the front desk as Emmy bounces excitedly beside me. Resin sighs, impatient.

"I know, buddy," I encourage him, petting his head.

The new group of students heads inside, their pace slower than the time it takes to wait for the train at the railroad crossing. Nerves are hitting my system by the time Emmy rushes forward, wrapping herself around Ivy's tights-clad legs. I'll never get tired of seeing her in dance wear. I swallow, awaiting my turn. Emmy rushes ahead to the studio after her hug, and Resin flops his tail, greeting his mom happily.

"Hello, love bucket," Ivy says to him, leaning down to pet the dog. I've learned by now that she likes to wait until last to greet me because she can give me her full attention and a smile that I've learned is just for me. "Hi, Bear," her smoky voice rings out, and I want to kiss her so much it's painful.

"Starlight," I nearly sigh, knowing I'm so fully gone on this woman that I can't imagine ever thinking of life or love without her.

"What are your plans this evening?" she asks.

"Oh, they involve you," I reply with a wink, and the blush on her cheeks is enough for me to think: *Worth it.*

Ivy looks me up and down appreciatively, the way she always does, but even more so today because I'm wearing a fitted long-sleeved t-shirt, which seems to be another of those things that just does it for her.

"You'd better keep moving, or I'm not going to have the strength to teach my next class."

The thought of her being too distracted to teach makes me clear my throat. Yes, I definitely need to get out of here before we make a scene. "I've got Resin. You teach your class. And I'll cook us dinner. Sound good?"

Ivy's shoulders relax, and her eyes close sweetly. "That sounds like a dream."

She leans in to kiss me. I hear snickers and giggles before I look over to see her entire class crowding in the doorway, Emmy included.

"They always do this," Emmy says with a smile.

Ivy lets out a defeated sigh and mouths, "Later."

It's a promise I'm greatly looking forward to.

"Honey, I'm home!" Ivy yells as she walks into my house with Emmy.

I'm sure my daughter has already kicked off her shoes and is running toward Resin, who gave a playful bark at their arrival. Classical music plays throughout my home, featuring one of my favorite composers to calm my nerves.

"Daddy, can I take Resin upstairs to play?" Emmy's excitement is contagious.

"Yes, of course. Don't try to put makeup on him this time."

"Okay!" Their footsteps echo up the stairs, and I let out a contented sigh at the sight of Ivy appearing in the doorway of my kitchen.

She's still in her dance wear but has added a wrap sweater and joggers, the waistband rolled down in a maddening way, revealing a hint of her light-blue leotard. "It got chillier out there."

I stir the stew on the stove just for something to do with my hands, but I can't resist her words. "Come here and let me warm you up."

Ivy's blush is my answer as she glides over to me, letting me wrap her in my arms. It's my favorite moment of any day.

"I have a surprise for you," I mumble against her hair.

"You do?" Ivy says into my chest, not moving at all. I've learned enough about her to know that she's most content with her nose pressed into my collarbone. And from experience, I've learned that she'll fall asleep standing up if I hold her like this for too long.

"Yes. But we'll wait until after dinner. So, I need you to stay awake." I pull back and wink down at her.

She whimpers, her hair adorably mussed on one side. "But you're so comfy."

I laugh. "I want to be more than comfy." Standing a little taller, I give her my best stance.

Ivy shakes her head sweetly. "You're trouble, is what you are."

"The good kind?" I say with a wink.

"The best kind." She sighs happily, turning to take a

spoon from the drawer and dipping it into the massive pot of beef stew and doughboys—Ivy's favorite meal. Her grandmother gave me the recipe, and it's still cold enough for it to be comforting.

"Delicious." She waves the spoon in the air. "Now, what's this about a surprise?"

Emmy's giggle and another playful bark from Resin upstairs make more nerves settle in my stomach. There is a surprise tonight, and both of those two are in on it. I just need to keep it a secret for a little longer, and then we're in the clear.

"After dinner." My tone is soft but also promising as I reach out to wrap an arm around her waist again. The little sigh she gives snaps something inside me. A moment later, I abandon all attempts to stir the stew, reaching for her waist and lifting her up on the counter instead. I step between her legs, my hands now resting on the counter and framing the sides of her hips.

"Did you make dessert?" Ivy asks, and I honestly can't form the proper words to answer her, given her proximity.

"I . . . uh . . . yes. In the fridge." It's a pie from Angie's, but it's also her favorite. There's also a small box I made with carvings of stars now hiding beside it.

"How about something sweet now?"

I've barely opened my mouth to answer her when Ivy's lips are pressed to mine. She's devastatingly sweet, the taste of her enough to satisfy me for the rest of our lives. I give in to the kiss, moving my hands to wrap around her waist as her fingers find the spot she loves at the back of my head, pulling me closer to her. It's been far too long since I've kissed her like this—as long ago as last night, to be precise.

It's a good thing that I'm hoping our living arrangements will be changing soon. I'm not sure how much more I can take of this irresistible woman without crossing lines we're not ready to demolish.

"Ivy . . ." I exhale, bending down to kiss the spot on her neck that never fails to make her lean deeper into me. As predicted, she does so now. I smile against her skin before resuming what I feel to be my duties as her boyfriend. To make her happy and never resist how attractive I find her. Or how connected I want to be to her.

"Jace . . ." she whispers, and I move to her mouth once more, capturing her surprised inhale. She returns my affection and adds a hand clenched in my shirt to pull me even closer to her.

I'm thriving in her orbit as sure as new life will grow outside the windows as the season changes.

The pot of stew boiling is the sound that buoys me back to the present. Once I step away and turn down the heat, stirring the delicious-smelling pot of beef and vegetables, I look back at her, still perched on the counter. I lose all sense of time and space with her. My heart is racing; our breathing is heavy between us.

"Starlight, you are *everything*, you know that?" I wrap my hand around the back of her neck in the way I know she finds comforting and kiss her forehead. Her swollen lips are like sirens calling me back to them, but I drop the hand on her neck and hold it out for her to take while I stir the stew on the stove with my free hand.

"What's this doing out?" her smoky voice answers.

My stomach drops as I turn toward her. She's now holding the piece of ribbon she gave me so long ago, having discovered it on the counter near her. She never did get it back, as I stole it off the snow globe right after last Christmas, like she did my sweatshirt. Turns out, I'm still attached. But tonight, I have it out for a very special reason.

Just as I'm about to act impulsively, the alarm goes off on the stove for the stew, my phone buzzes with another alarm I don't remember setting, and Ivy's phone chimes with some sort of alert. It's a symphony of noise, and above it all, I hear the antique clock I got for the kitchen chiming the hour. Everything seems to go still, and then I know, without a doubt, that this is the moment I've been waiting for. There's no need to wait any longer.

"Ivy, I—I have a question for you." I step forward and wrap my hands around her waist, lifting her gently and setting her feet on the kitchen floor. The setting is not fancy or elegant, but it's such a domestic scene that I know I couldn't have planned this better if I tried. The scent of the stew on the stove and the lemon-meringue-scented candle on the table set the mood. The alarms and clocks have now gone quiet, and only the classical music remains. The glow of the light over the stove and the way Ivy is looking at me strengthen my heart. This is the scene I've hoped for all my life. I just didn't know until I was in it.

I begin with a husky tone, lifting the tattered piece of ribbon between us. "Starlight, I know that you deserve the world. It may be soon, but I know you're my person with everything that I am. I promise I will spend the rest of our lives showing you how much you mean to me. But here, in this moment, it feels like the perfect time to ask if you'd like to spend your life with me. Not just as we are now, but as partners. Sharing this house. Sharing my bed. Raising

Emmy. And maybe, one day, we can bring more children into our home."

Ivy's eyes fill with tears as I speak. I'm not even sure she can see through them until one tear falls down the side of her face. Moving slowly, I get down on one knee, holding her hands and willing the depth of what I feel for her to be tangible in this moment.

"Ivy, you're my light in this world. You're my Starlight, to be exact."

She lets out a laugh despite the tears that are freely flowing down her cheeks.

I clear my throat but feel the emotion pulsing behind my eyes. The wisps of hair framing her face become blurrier the longer I look at her. I wipe my face on my sleeve, not willing to let her go. "Will you be my wife, Ivy? No matter your answer, without fail, I'm yours. But I would love for you to be mine in every way."

Ivy's smile is radiant, her eyes full of love.

Quickly, I add, "And I do have a ring. It's in a box I made in the fridge. I was trying to hide it, but in hindsight, that probably wasn't the best place. I'm sorry if I messed this up, but seeing you look so beautiful, the feeling of you being here, I couldn't wait another second to ask."

Instead of answering, Ivy perches on my bent knee, wrapping her arms around my neck until we're so close I can smell the warm vanilla on her skin again. "You didn't mess this up," she says as her voice cracks. Her hands play with my hair while her eyes scan every inch of my face. She studies me like she loves me, and it's one of the things I appreciate the most about her. Since we've been together, she's always reaching for me, touching me, wanting me close to her. "I belong with you. Jace, you loved me to life. And I'll forever be grateful."

I kiss her softly, taking my time.

"Yes," she answers, not waiting for me to ask her again.

I stand, lifting her into my arms, one wrapped around her legs and the other around her waist. She laughs and then drops back dramatically, her neck arching elegantly, her laughter ringing through the kitchen.

At the sound of descending footsteps and paws, we swing to see Emmy and Resin just as they enter the kitchen.

"Did she say yes?" Emmy squeals, and I nod. "Yes! Yes! Yes!" Emmy rushes in with her signature chant of three affirming words. She hugs us, and I set Ivy's feet on the floor so she can lift our daughter up.

"Does this mean I get to call you my mom now?" Emmy asks with so much hope I feel my heart crack.

I nod to my future bride, who can't contain her smile or her tears.

"Yes, darling. I would be honored to be that for you."

Cue the waterworks. I'm reaching for a paper towel to wipe my eyes when I feel both of my girls bring me into a hug. Even Resin leans against my legs. And I think that nothing in my life will ever be better than this.

Later, when we've settled in and finally eaten dinner, Ivy's parents, Gram, Angie, and Edgar all rush in for dessert and a celebration. We FaceTime Freddie to tell him the news, and there's so much laughter and love in my house that I almost can't believe this is my life. To go from where I was to where I am now, to lose both the woman I love and my sister, but to get a second chance with the love of my life is a blessing I can't comprehend. It's more than fate. It's hope.

Before we say goodnight, we set in motion wedding plans to take place before Christmas—because when you know, why wait? As we plan, more kisses and words of love pass between us. And with Emmy passed out on one side of the couch and Resin softly snoring beside her, I hold Ivy close.

"I love you, Ivy. Thank you for loving me. It's the best thing I've ever believed in."

She kisses me softly. "And thank you for truly knowing me, Jace. I love you deeply. My heart was always searching for you, because your heart is my home."

Acknowledgments

Dear Reader, thank you for trusting me enough to read my third book (can't believe I'm writing that!) and for wandering to this page. This past year has been one of the hardest of my life, both personally and throughout the writing process. Through a series of events, both life-altering and seasonal, I've moved through grief and needed to rediscover the magic and wonder of Christmas myself. It's a holiday season I've always loved, and writing this book was more than the next one in the series. It was a promise I made to a friend who passed and a promise to myself to not quit on the dreams I have to be an author. My prayer is that you've found, somewhere within these pages, a glimpse of what it means to hold on to hope, even in and through the darkest of nights. Even when light returns. And even when it's challenging to remember that loneliness isn't who you are. Like I've written in my books by these characters I've come to love, if you do happen to find your heart broken or in need of some comfort, you're always welcome in Birch Borough. It may be fictional, but I've personally found it to be a good place to remember the goodness of love, healing, laughter, and belief again.

Hailey, I couldn't have imagined writing this book without you. And, in many ways, I haven't. Thank you for giving me the name for Jace, and for all of the thousands of things you did, both big and small, to forever remind me of what a gift it was to call you my friend. You were the rarest sort of brilliance in a person, and I'm forever marked by your words. Love you so.

Britt, cheers to book three! Thank you for your patience, for pushing me to find the words that were challenging to carve out of my heart and for caring about my stories and my characters in a way that truly blesses me. I not only found the best editor for these books, I found a dear friend. I will always be grateful.

Jenn, thank you for being a part of this process as an author. I hope to keep sending you more books for years to come.

Erica, I'm so happy that we've connected and that you are the one who transforms my books into a chaos of spacing and indentations and makes it ready for readers. I'm so grateful!

Karyssa, you have been such a dream to work with! Thank you for taking a chance on being the artist for not only this book but all of the gorgeous things you created for it. It felt so serendipitous to connect, and I've been consistently in awe of how you've brought this book to life. I appreciate you so very much.

Tay, thank you for helping to get my books out in the world. You're the early morning and late night (and last minute) text, the one I know I can reach out to and always find kindness, support, and the skills I desperately need to ensure that I don't make a mess of things online. You've been my friend for so many years, and it's a comfort (and a joy) to have you with me through this process. May so many blessings be yours for all that you've done over the years. Thank you!

Amanda, thank you for always cheering me on and for your support, kindness, and love. You encourage me to keep moving forward on this writing journey. I'm so grateful that we've connected and that, in her own way, Hailey brought us together as only she could do. Your insights were so appreciated, and I'm grateful to be on this journey with you!

Rebecca, your constant support and care have meant so much. Thank you for believing in me and for always giving of your time to encourage me! You provided such thoughtful feedback on this book. I'm grateful to call you my friend.

Kara and Ally, my heart is full! Thank you for trusting me enough to give this book a first read and to allow me to be vulnerable in that way, and for all of the value you added in the early reader experience. If I had to do this process for the first time, how lucky am I that you were a part of it with me? Pinching myself that I get to have some of the most encouraging and loveliest of readers through you. The comments you gave had me smiling, and I'll forever be grateful for your valuable words and the heart and care you added to the process. You remind me of why I'm determined to keep writing.

Jen Grisanti, you have been a North Star of wisdom, of encouragement, and a measure of growth in and through my writing. I will always love learning from you. It may take a few years for everything to sink in from your brilliance and your process, but what you've invested will stay with me.

Mama, thanks for giving me so many books and for believing that the worlds I create are valuable.

Thank you to the glorious community of readers I've found. Your messages have given me strength, made me laugh, brought me to tears, and reminded me of why I've always wanted to create stories. I couldn't do this without you, and I am deeply grateful. I hope that this book bridges the gap between the love I share and the love you feel on the page. I'll do my best to keep following this dream.

Finally, but most importantly, a heartfelt thank you to Emmanuel, God with us. The One who has given peace, whose presence has eased the heartache and has brought healing, and through whom nothing is ever wasted. This book exists only because of who You are.

ABOUT SARA NORTH

Sara North is a New England native who often dreams of Paris. While books held her heart first, Sara's training included writing and story development for both film and television scripts and fueled her desire to create with heart.

With a passion to cheer on creatives and writers across art forms and industries, Sara recognizes the power of stories to bring healing, hope, and happiness. When she's not writing books to build a dream on, her loves include 90s rom-coms, Old Hollywood films, Hallmark Christmas movies, beloved sitcoms, music to match her mood, café hopping, baking, enjoying peppermint hot chocolate, and celebrating all things fall.

AuthorSaraNorth.com | @AuthorSaraNorth